D1110674

RENDER SAFE

RENDER SAFE

A Novel

PASCAL MARCO

SHEXi,
I can't
Thank you
enough for all
you've done for me!

(signature)

SAN TAN PRESS

Mesa, Arizona

Library of Congress Control Number: 2016911279
ISBN: 978-0692750308

Published in the United States of America by
San Tan Press
Mesa, Arizona

www.pascalmarco.com

To any of you who have ever doubted you can do

something special, or ever wanted to give up and quit

and

To John and Isabell

I dedicate this book to you.

THE FLOOD

It happened quickly, as if a diviner's staff had struck the ground. Water flashed onto the dry earth. Its dark and wringing hands plunged over cactus and sage, welling around the trunks of sparse cottonwood trees. The desert groaned as its thousand parched mouths opened to an empty summer sky.

—Craig Childs, *House of Rain: Tracking a Vanished Civilization Across the American Southwest*

Unexploded ordnance (UXO). Military munitions that:

(a) have been primed, fuzed, armed, or otherwise prepared for action;

(b) have been fired, dropped, launched, projected, or placed in such a manner as to constitute a hazard to operations, installations, personnel, or material; and

(c) remain unexploded whether by malfunction, design, or any other cause.

—*Military Munitions and Explosives of Concern: A Handbook for Federal Land Managers With Emphasis on Unexploded Ordnance*

"The Mk-82 General Purpose High Explosive Bomb is one of the main offensive weapons systems in the U.S. military's air arsenal. This quarter-ton bomb is designed to provide maximum blast and explosive effects to its target. The 192-pounds of special high explosive filling its metal encasement produces a fragmentation range of around 750 meters, dangerous blast radius of 60 meters, and will leave an impact crater that is 4 meters in size. As a current Explosives Ordinance Disposal Technician for the United States military there is a phrase that embodies the EOD community: Initial Success or Total Failure.

'Going down on' an unexploded Mk-82 is one of our most dangerous missions. On the day you go face-to-face with this five-hundred-pound monster during a render safe engagement the true meaning of initial success or total failure becomes all too real."

--Sean R. Kemp, Major, Military Intelligence, Army National Guard; Former Commander, Arizona Army National Guard, 363rd Explosives Ordinance Disposal (EOD) Unit; Special Agent, Bureau of Alcohol Tobacco Firearms and Explosives

CHAPTER 1

Phoenix, Arizona
2001

S tan Kobe's personal cell rang just before noon on Tuesday, April 10. He was sitting at his office desk, prepping for an upcoming trial. But this wasn't just any trial. Stan hadn't slept a full night's sleep since his boss had assigned the undefeated prosecutor the unprecedented job of getting a guilty verdict against the highest ranking Roman Catholic clergyman to ever enter a Maricopa County courtroom. To say Stan was stressed over the high-profile, deadly DUI case would have been the biggest of understatements.

"I'm only answering because it's you." He recognized Detective Brian Hanley's cellphone number. "You know, I can't believe I'm saying this but I could really use one of your lame jokes right now."

"I wish I had something funny to say," Brian replied.

"What's up?"

"Scottsdale PD . . . it has a big one on its hands. Their commander phoned . . . asked me to come out to their scene. But I'm in court. Can . . . can you get over there, Stan? Pronto?"

Best friends, Stan was closer to Brian than anyone. His buddy's staccato response was way out of line with the cop's always-the-jokester character.

"Well, if they want you on the case, it must be something special. What is it, Bri?"

"The short of it . . . is . . . see . . . a house went up in flames." Brian took a longer than usual pause. "A mom and her two kids were inside."

Stan was certain Brian was holding something back. "What aren't you telling me?"

"Stan . . . pardner . . . it's on the block where you live."

What? Did he just say 'where I live'?

Stan felt a sharp pain in his chest. He struggled to breathe. He couldn't speak.

"Stan? Did you hear what I just said?"

Stan bolted up, pulling loose the knot in his tie, gasping for air. He fought to get the words "I'm on my way" out of his mouth before hanging up on his friend. As he double-timed it down the hall to the elevator, Stan speed-dialed his home number from his cell.

No answer.

He tried his wife Maxine's cellphone.

Right to voicemail.

Panicking, he tried her office but the department secretary said she hadn't seen Professor Kobe all morning. An uncontrollable rush of adrenaline shot through his veins. The feeling of fire in his blood made him feel like his whole body would incinerate.

Had he and his family been found?

His imagination ran wild with the terrifying thought that not only may have someone finally discovered his whereabouts after nearly three decades in hiding, but, worse yet, may have gotten to his wife and two children.

*   *   *

Sweating profusely, Stan drove the ten miles distance to his home in a South Scottsdale neighborhood not even thinking of how fast he was going. By the time he got there, terror engulfed his entire being. As he whirled his car around the final corner to his street he hardly recognized his tidy neighborhood. Emergency vehicles packed the intersection closest to his house. From that point to the scene, police had done a thorough job of cordoning off the area from onlookers.

Flashing his credentials allowed him to maneuver his car around a barricade and wind his way down the street. Mid-way to his house, a cluster of first responder vehicles stopped further progress. He abandoned his auto and sprinted the final half-block.

Please, God. Please tell me they haven't found out where I live. Please tell me everything's okay and they haven't hurt my family.

When he reached the scene, he stared at what little was left standing of a stucco and wood-framed structure destroyed by fire only a few doors from his own.

That's the Stewart house!

Relieved to see his own home untouched by flames, he breathed a sigh of relief. But moments later his heart sank when realized what may have happened inside his neighbor's home. A plainclothes cop stepped in front of Stan.

"You must be from the County Attorney's Office. Detective Hanley said you were on your way."

"Yeah, uh, Stan Kobe." Stan pumped the man's hand, not looking at him, unable to take his eyes off the scorched scene, but more so distracted over still wondering if his wife and children were okay.

"I'm Detective Kemp, lead investigator for Scottsdale PD. There's something I need you to see right away." Kemp narrowed his eyes and grimaced. "I hope you haven't had your lunch."

*   *   *

On The Mogollon Rim
Near Payson, Arizona
Ten Days Later

Located only one-hundred miles north of Phoenix's Valley of the Sun, the Mogollon Rim is nothing less than an eight-thousand-foot-high, two-hundred-mile-long escarpment of pure, volcanic rock. This geological rarity forms an impregnable barrier between the southern end of the Colorado Plateau and the arid Sonoran desert, the latter of which stretches for hundreds of miles south, all the way into Mexico.

Gila County Sheriff Micah Lund stood with his hands on his hips, scanning the area

where he stood. His deputy, Kirby Ferrin, clung close to his side, looking more like an errant orphan. The scrawny Ferrin looked up at his boss. "Do you think this guy Stewart shot his own dog? What kind'a man does that, Sheriff?"

The man Ferrin referred to was Paul Henry Stewart. Stewart had become a "person of interest," law enforcement's politically correct way of saying he was steps away from being charged in committing one of the most heinous crimes in Arizona's history ten days prior in Scottsdale.

Ferrin's two questions seemed simple yet his boss glowered over the deputy's naïveté. Lund punctuated his anger with a scowling answer, "Kirby, this guy supposedly killed his wife and kids down in that hell-hole valley. So my guess is, son, he'd have no problem putting one to the head of an animal, even his own pooch. Anyways, the Lab would'a followed his master, made him easier to track. It was a smart move to kill the hound. Very smart move."

A black Labrador, shot once in the head, laid at the two men's feet. The Lab's skull had swelled to twice its size, most likely a result from the close range of the gunshot's entry point. A leash needlessly tethered the dead animal to the rusting chrome bumper of an abandoned pickup truck.

The barrel-chested Lund barked an order at his deputy. "Get back to your patrol car and pull me the topo maps of this area. And get me an exact GPS reading of where we are right now. We'll lay out a hundred square mile grid."

His squirrelly-looking underling stood motionless, working his gums with a toothpick, mouth agape.

"Move, Kirby!" Lund growled.

Ferrin snapped an about-face and scampered back toward his police cruiser parked on the nearby Forest Road H-1. Lund reached inside his vest pocket and pulled out a pouch of Redman. Digging two fingers into the pack, he pulled out a wad of chewing tobacco and stuffed it deep inside his cheek. He put a hand on the butt of his side-holstered .38 Colt Special and cupped the other around his mouth, like a bullhorn. "Better get Coconino and Navajo counties on the radio," the sheriff shouted at Ferrin, careful not to let any chaw spit down his chin. "I reckon we might be doing some deep tracking in their backyards, too."

*   *   *

Later That Same Day

Hours after the news a hiker had stumbled upon the 1974 pickup registered in Paul Stewart's name, Scottsdale PD Homicide Division presented enough circumstantial evidence to the Maricopa County Attorney's Office to bring formal charges. Not only multiple first-degree murder but felony arson of an occupied structure would comprise the four count indictment leveled against the utility company worker. That latter charge was added when initial evidence showed the missing man, a former military explosives expert, may have also purposely set his ranch-style home ablaze in the once tranquil neighborhood in an attempt to cover up the monstrous act.

Mentally distressed over the unprecedented crime just yards from his own home—and unnerved the attack could have very easily been against his family—Stan Kobe made the request to his boss, County Attorney Rick Romley, to personally work the case. Without hesitation, Romley approved handing off the investigation to his office's top prosecutor. With that, Stan immediately began his research, delving deep into the life of Paul Henry Stewart.

*   *   *

The drive from Phoenix to the location where Stewart's truck had been found on the Mogollon Rim, or "The Rim," as locals called it, would take Stan and Detective Kemp a little more than two hours. Along with them was City of Chandler Homicide Detective, Brian Hanley.

"Thanks for agreeing to let Brian come in on this, M.C." Stan shot a supportive look over at Kemp, driving one of his department's Crime Scene Unit SUVs.

Kemp sat rigid behind the wheel, hands at ten and two, eyes glued to the ever-winding Beeline Highway, the only major road from Phoenix to Payson. "No problem. I'm glad to have him along for his expertise. Plus, my chief told me you and Hanley go as a pair. From what I've been told, having you two guys on my first case makes me feel a whole lot better."

Stan smiled at the rookie detective.

Kemp spoke again. "Stan, I got a kick out of what the other detectives said everyone calls you. What was it again?"

"Maricopa County's most ruthless prosecutor," Brian teased from the back seat.

"That's it!" M.C. cried.

"Am I never gonna get rid of that handle?" Stan's plea belied his pride with his media-given nickname. In all his years of handling some of the biggest headline prosecutions for the largest populated county in the state, he'd never lost a case.

"Not while you're still the heavyweight champ, pardner," Brian teased.

M.C.'s tone turned serious. "You must have been shocked when you found out this fire was practically right next door to your house. How well did you know this guy Stewart?"

Stan wasn't sure how to answer the inquisitive detective. He didn't want to admit he wasn't really close to any of his neighbors. That he kept to himself and rarely interacted with people outside his job. As a matter of fact, Stan wasn't close to anyone, except his wife and children, and his best friend sitting behind him.

"Stewart was a loner. He didn't mix with the neighbors. I really didn't know him at all."

Stan hoped M.C. wouldn't prod him further with any more personal questions.

"I still don't get it," M.C. said. "What could drive a man to kill his wife *and* his kids? Then torch his home. It just doesn't register with me. I'll never understand it. Never."

Stan wondered if M.C. was just like him—a man who wouldn't give up until he got a satisfactory answer. The distress in M.C.'s voice mirrored Stan's own ugly thoughts from the sordid crime scene, images so incomprehensible he couldn't stop visualizing them in his mind.

Did my own neighbor slaughter his entire family?

Stan struggled to grasp the possibility. As a doting father and devoted husband, he knew personally how the loss of something so precious could never be understood—or replaced.

M.C. went on, shaking his head. "I'll never forget the sight of those charred bodies, especially those kids, huddled in the corner of that bedroom, next to each other."

Reliving Kemp's description, Stan fought emotions that might have caused him to choke-up—something he never did. Still having his own family's safety at the forefront of his mind, he responded in a slow, deliberate voice. "Don't worry. We'll get this guy . . . and when we go to trial . . . well, let's just say, I'll keep my record intact."

A respectful hush fell over the interior of the car for the remainder of the trip. Stan's silence was an outcome of not wanting any more questions thrown at him about his personal life, coupled with dwelling upon what horror the victims must have endured. He presumed the silence from Brian and M.C. was for the latter reason.

When the trio reached their destination—a clearing four miles in off State Road 260 near Christopher Creek—an army of law enforcers stood under a group of tents providing shade from a cloudless sky. The serenity of the location, amidst the area's iconic Ponderosa pines and their carpet of fallen needles, made it seem more like a setting for a church picnic. But the assembled entourage rather had turned the pastoral place into a bustling quasi-military encampment; a noisy staging ground for thirsty man-hunters. They had formed into a classic Arizona posse, standing ready, waiting for their orders to be unleashed upon the daunting Rim on foot, horseback, and ATV in search of their prey.

"Detective Kemp?" A fast-walking, thin man had his hand stretched out. He approached the three new arrivals as soon as they stepped from their SUV. "Gila County Sheriff's Deputy Kirby Ferrin at your service, sir. We've been expecting you."

M.C. obliged him a handshake.

Ferrin looked to his left. "Sheriff Lund's in the command center over yonder. He's been waiting for you so he can get his search underway. I better warn you, he's not feeling very chipper this morning."

"Thank you for letting us know," a cordial Kemp said. "By the way, this is Detective Hanley, assisting from Chandler Homicide." M.C. tipped his chin toward Brian. Ferrin nodded a hello. "And this is Maricopa County Prosecutor Stan Kobe."

Ferrin diverted his attention to his feet rather than look Stan in the eye. The quirky deputy's voice quavered. "Oh boy. Sheriff's gonna be surprised."

"Surprised?" M.C. asked.

"Yeah. You know," Ferrin murmured, peeking up at M.C. "Surprised he'll be working with a . . ."

The pallid-faced deputy unsuccessfully tried to whisper his slur into Kemp's ear. The spineless man then darted toward the tents. He left so quickly he surely didn't see the embarrassed frown that had washed over Kemp's face at the utterance of the deputy's archaic comment.

Stan remained unperturbed but Brian's face turned red with anger. He leaned in toward Stan and whispered to his buddy, "Did that little turd really just say what I think he said?"

"Hey. We're in Rim country," Stan said. "Some of them are stuck in the dark ages up here. No pun intended."

Brian chuckled. "Good one."

The threesome followed Deputy Ferrin and made their way over to Sheriff Lund's command center tent. Once there, the deputy introduced the detectives to Lund. When he came to Stan, he hiccupped his words.

"And this, Sheriff . . . this is . . . Attorney Kobe . . . from Maricopa County."

Micah Lund puffed out his huge chest. "*The* Stan Kobe? Heard a lot about you, boy. Big time prosecutor who's never lost a case. Right?"

Stan gave him a quick nod of his head, then cracked a knuckle.

"Not even *once*?" Lund asked.

"Not once."

"Good. I like that." He slapped Stan on top of his shoulder. "Never judge a book by its cover. That's what my daddy always says."

"Is that right?" Stan snuck a look at Brian who rolled his eyes.

"Sure as I'm standing here," the sheriff said.

Knowing he was being patronized, Stan paused a moment, then decided to turn the tables on his guest. "Well, sounds like your daddy is a very smart man, Sheriff."

"He better be. He was a prosecutor in your office for many years. I'm sure you must know of Jacob Jeffrey Lund."

Jacob Lund! I should've made the connection!

"Yes, forgive me. I do know your father. That is, I should say, I've heard stories of him and his reputation. He had left the office right after I was hired, then served on the Superior Court bench. Unfortunately, he retired before I had the pleasure to have one of my cases tried by him."

"Well as much as I'd like to take a trip down memory lane with you about my father's career in that hell-hole of yours down in that valley, we've got ourselves a man to catch. Don't we, boy?"

Stan already didn't like the man. He gave Lund a weak nod and a terse reply. "That we do."

Deputy Ferrin jumped upon a tree stump and shouted out to the group. "Gather 'round, everyone. Sheriff Lund's gonna brief y'all now."

"We are after *this* man." Lund yelled through a battery-powered bullhorn, pointing to a blow up of the fugitive's DMV headshot his deputy held overhead. Printed sheets of the picture were passed around. "Judging by the remaining warmth of his campfire and the dog not being in complete *rigor mortis*, my guess is Stewart hasn't been gone from here very long. Twelve-to-twenty-four hours tops. He probably hasn't gotten far, either, especially up here on my Rim. Over yonder, near Promontory Butte, the drop off is nearly a quarter mile. Without knowing this country, no man can survive out here in this wilderness for more than a few days. Especially alone."

"Excuse me, Sheriff, but I think it's important to point out to the posse that Stewart is a survivalist," Stan countered. "He was trained by the Air Force."

Lund pulled the bullhorn away from his mouth. "Is that so?"

Stan heard the cynicism in Lund's voice loud and clear, even without the bullhorn. "Yes, it is." Stan's reply was pleasant yet he still made his point.

Lund leaned in toward Stan and spoke to him in a voice only he could hear. "Do you mind taking a little walk with me?"

Lund motioned his head toward a large tent a few feet away. He and Stan walked over to it and stepped inside. Lund closed the flap behind them. They were now alone.

"Are you trying to make me look like a fool in front of my men, Kobe?"

"That wasn't my intent. I was just stating the facts."

"Oh? The facts, you say. And what are these facts I don't seem to know?"

"Stewart's ex-military, hardened to stay alive in any environment, under all types of conditions. If he planned this in advance, like he may have, then he's probably got water buried out there along with other provisions. No telling how long he can last and evade us."

"And you know all this because . . ."

Stan suppressed his nervous tick to crack a knuckle that would overcome him when challenged. "Because I did my homework, Sheriff."

Lund fumed. "My family has lived up here for nearly eight generations. A man on the run in this part of the forest couldn't do it solely on foot. He'd need a horse and a pack mule filled with supplies to last any decent amount of time. Your theory is preposterous!"

Stan didn't flinch at the sheriff's bravado but admitted to himself the guy knew more about this land and tracking someone through it than he did. The Mogollon Rim remained as untouched today as when Francisco Coronado—on his famous quest for the magical seven cities of gold—got lost for weeks in its hidden canyons and arroyos over 500 years earlier. This primal wilderness had an unforgiving topography. Stan fought an urge to second-guess himself and question whether even someone like Paul Stewart, trained at one of the country's most elite survival schools, could subsist in such a desolate landscape.

"Stewart's no gringo," Stan countered back. "Our investigation so far has discovered he's frequented these woods a lot. Camped probably right near here many times. His Air Force survival school training would take him a long way."

Lund scowled. "If the elements or his ignorance don't get him, you fool, a bear or mountain lion will. Our Lord Yahweh's magnificent creatures would relish the unwelcomed human intrusion."

Stan took a deep breath. His long pause allowed him to regain his composure and keep himself from telling the backwoods lawman exactly what he really thought about him. "I think we may have gotten off on the wrong foot, Sheriff. Let's just both agree to disagree on this, move forward, and get on with our search. Sound like a good plan?"

Lund spit his chaw on the ground, barely missing Stan's shoes. Stan held off the desire to punch the uncouth asshole in the face but stood his ground and didn't move as the rotund man shouldered by him, storming out of the tent.

*   *   *

After his private pissing match with the sheriff ended, Stan didn't rejoin the posse briefing. Rather, he grabbed Brian and went to check out the nearby precipice Lund had referred to: Promontory Butte. Now mid-April, the snow season was over— at least in terms of normalcy for Rim country. Stan had read where the latest official snowfall ever recorded in the region had occurred six years earlier exactly to the day—April 20, 1995. Even though snow here typically stopped by March, nighttime temperatures on The Rim still plunged well into the low thirties and, at times, below. It was, like many parts of Arizona, a region of surprising and relentless extremes. *El Despoblado.* Coronado had so correctly named the region, Stan thought.

From their protruding vantage point, Stan gazed out on the vast forest before him, beginning to show signs of bloom from the benefit of the deep winter snows. Ancient pine trees blanketed this part of northern Arizona for thousands of square miles, literally as far as the eye could see. This virtual sea of timber was growing thicker every day now and would make their search for Stewart even more challenging.

Brian stood at Stan's side. "Where would Stewart go, pardner? I mean, if he made it through all that." He pointed out to the distance.

Stan's buddy was a no-nonsense cop. Brian had a knack for being able to look at complex situations and break them down into their simplest terms. It was one of the qualities Stan liked most about him. Contrary to Stan's own thinking pattern as a prosecuting lawyer—always looking at the motive behind the crime—he thought of Brian as a "meat and potatoes" thinker. He knew his style probably came about as an outcome of the detective's Chicago Irish roots.

"I don't know. I'm wondering the same thing. Why go through all those woods? And what direction would he head?" Stan stared out across the treetops. He was baffled. Perhaps, more so, he was perturbed. He didn't want to admit Lund knew the Rim better than him, better than any man there. He couldn't deny the gruff man's expertise as a seasoned lawman, either. A man who had probably participated in more posses than Stan had even read about.

Stan looked out across the vast expanse of uninhabited wilderness, deflated but not defeated. He vowed to himself he'd find the killer and bring him to justice.

Brian interrupted his thoughts. "And I got another question. Why would Stewart start running from here?"

"That's a very good question, Bri," Stan replied. "I really don't know."

*   *   *

Scottsdale, Arizona
Later That Week

After several days of participating in an unsuccessful search with Sheriff Lund's immense posse, Stan decided to return to the Valley, Brian and Detective Kemp in tow. Dejected over failing to pick up Stewart's trail, he was nevertheless glad to be home. When he walked in the door, he received a warm hug from Maxine and cherished the smiles on the faces of his twins.

Even though he was thankful for all he had, he couldn't relieve himself of the stress he felt over not finding Paul Stewart. On his first night back, he struggled to fall asleep. When he finally did, a recurring boyhood nightmare roused him—and Maxine.

"What is it?" Maxine asked, eyes closed, head still on the pillow. "That same dream again?"

Not wanting to confirm what she suspected, he lied.

"No. It's the case. This Stewart guy. How could a man do what he did?"

Maxine rolled over to him and wrapped an arm around his chest.

"Some men are evil, honey. You of all people know that. You've seen them do all kinds of terrible things."

"But not like this," he replied. "If you only knew . . ."

His voice trailed off. He sat up in bed, propping his back against the headboard. Maxine did the same.

"And then, the guy acts like Houdini and vanishes into thin air."

"That is a bit strange. But didn't I read in the papers where this guy was trained in military survival school?"

Stan nodded. "Yes. But still. I can't figure out how he pulled this off. And why would he drive all the way to the Mogollon Rim to lose himself. It's just not making any sense."

What Stan didn't want to admit was what troubled him most was his terrible dream and the reminder of how change could come so sudden, as it had happened to Stanford James Kobe. Once, long ago and without warning, he was forced to perform his own disappearing act, leaving his former life behind and no trace of who he had once been. Stan knew the feeling first-hand of sudden and unexpected loss. Loss forced upon him against his will, totally out of his control. As a grown man he still struggled to bury that pain-filled childhood memory, the end result of a judge's unexpected verdict. A decision that thrust him into a secret life, forcing him to hide his real identity and keep secrets from everyone he loved or who loved him.

Stan struggled now as he recalled those still aching memories, knowing how hard it was to let go and bury his own lost identity.

Maybe Stewart is no different than me. Maybe he's trying to hide his past. Trying to hide his true identity. But, would he need to hide it so badly that it would force him to slaughter his entire family?

He snapped back to reality and stopped dwelling on his own clandestine life. As an officer of the court, he had a job to do: stay focused on the disturbing, headline-making killings of three citizens in his county, savagely murdered only a short distance from his home. He had no idea whether the presumed actions of Stewart were random acts of violence or if the fugitive had more intended victims. What was imperative to focus on right now was finding this killer, and finding him fast in case he might strike again.

CHAPTER 2

Outskirts of Chandler, Arizona
Ten Years Later, April 14, 2011
2:00 a.m.

Covering his mouth and nose with a crumpled white kerchief, Stan Kobe tiptoed around three human heads, every one gruesomely separated from their respective torso. They oddly reminded Stan like the wayward melons he'd often seen in this rural part of the valley fallen from shabby produce trucks coming up from Mexico, haplessly left along the desert roadside to petrify. A fresh, decapitation killing was something he had not experienced before and the forty-nine-year-old Maricopa County prosecutor struggled to comprehend the sight at his feet.

Inside the dilapidated, wood-framed house located in the last remnants of undeveloped Chandler, Brian Hanley had already been on the scene half-an-hour. Stan looked at his partner cop, his eyes begging for an answer to the abysmal crime scene. Even as a veteran, the amount of blood rattled Stan.

"Tell me what you're thinking." What Stan really wanted to hear back from Brian was something different than what his gut told him.

"I'm at a loss for words," Brian said from underneath a handkerchief he also held against his mouth and nose.

If there were incriminating clues to be found in this morass of ripped skin and congealed human fluids, Stan knew

Hanley would find them. His crime scene investigative skills were above reproach.

"But I do think this has Sinaloan cartel written all over it," Brian added. "So we need to figure out how we spin something like that fucking possibility for the media."

"We don't."

Stan's curt answer brought a puzzled look to Brian's stone face. Though Stan knew Brian couldn't possibly understand why he was so abrupt with his answer, he wasn't prepared to share what churned inside his stomach. Something dark troubled Stan, besides the macabre scene splayed before them, and Brian couldn't possibly know.

"Stan, Chandler PD is going to have to tell the media something."

Snapping back from his troubling thoughts, Stan shot back an answer. "Just tell them the deaths are under investigation. If they continue to ask questions, defer them to my office for answers."

Brian shrugged off Stan's reply and circled the crime scene. While he scanned and rescanned the room, Stan struggled to deal with the disquieting remembrance thrust back into his mind. He pulled out his notepad and drew a quick sketch of the scene: two corpses—more like slaughtered carcasses—lay on a badly-worn carpet; one remained on the couch, sitting but slumped forward as if the loss of his head skewed the body's ability to keep itself upright.

He watched as Brian walked behind the decrepit sofa, its matted, brown velour fabric swathed in crimson, still moist from the horrendous bloodletting. The seasoned cop grimaced as he looked down at the lifeless body. The stench was overwhelming.

"This is some nasty shit. Reminds me of that murder at that frat house. Kappa Dappa Dew or whatever the hell those college dudes called themselves."

Stan appreciated Brian's dark sense of humor, especially at the most grisly crime scenes. Most cops used it as a shield, keeping them sane on a job filled dealing with the sordid aftermath of depraved behavior. He noticed a quizzical look on Brian's face after his quip.

"You wondering, too, why this body isn't on the floor like the two other victims?"

"Yep," Brian said. "Crossed my mind. What's your take?"

Stan lifted his pen from the pad where he had scribbled his sketch and pointed at the body in front of Brian on the blood-drenched piece of furniture. "I think they made your guy on the couch there watch it all."

"Possibly." Brian sounded open-minded to Stan's idea but looked unconvinced.

"Think they got out of him what they were looking for?"

Brian shrugged. "Dunno. But my guess is if I'm watching two guys get their heads lopped off right in front of me if the first one doesn't get what they want from me I'm definitely singing like a bird or doing whatever they tell me to do when the second head rolls."

"Yeah, but I think they killed your guy there on the couch before they chopped off his *cabeza*," Stan contended.

"What makes you think that?"

"Come back around this side and you'll see what I mean." Stan crept up to the couch victim, Brian behind him. Getting more acclimated to the horrific smell, Stan tucked his handkerchief back into his pocket. "Look. See? Right here. This looks like a stab wound." Using the tip of his pen, he pointed at the victim's shirt, careful to avoid touching the spot. "Must have entered right under the fifth rib. It had to pierce right through the aortic arch then sliced through his aorta. I'm guessing that's why no blood spew from this victim when they severed the artery in his neck."

"That's a military move," Brian said. "That's one of the quickest ways to kill a man when—"

"When you're sure you're done with him?"

"Maybe . . . so . . . maybe the last beheading was a message? If that's the case, the question is, to whom?" Gloves on since he entered, Brian made a quick check of the soles of the shoes on all three victims. He turned to a uniformed officer, one of several on the scene. "Make sure the crime analysis unit bags all their shoes."

"That's your hunch?" Stan asked. "Three crossers and their coyote turns on them?"

"Not sure," Brian shrugged. "Coyotes usually abandon their victim right at the border, or in the middle of the crossing, deep in the desert. Lately, though, I've been involved with cases where they've been extorting them once they reach their destination, holding them hostage until their families back in Mexico promise to send more money. That bust . . . the one I did with Sheriff Joe . . ." He paused for a moment, then swallowed, regaining his composure. "They tortured those poor bastards for days."

Stan knew how painful it was for Brian to recall an ill-fated bust he had made with Maricopa County's Human Smuggling Unit, the only one of its kind in the country. HSU had been formed by the county's controversial sheriff, Joe Arpaio, following his efforts to stem the tide of illegal human entry into the U.S. In the assault, not only had Brian been seriously wounded but he fired his weapon, killing one of the assailants. Physically, he came out of the altercation with just a few scars, but he was still seeing a shrink from the resulting post-traumatic stress.

"I agree. But why kill them?" Stan paused, looking around the room. "Maybe—"

"They're not crossers? Maybe they're mules?"

Stan never questioned Brian's opinion when it came to deaths incurred from illegal human smuggling activity between Mexico and the United States. Hanley had been loaned to more local police departments and federal law enforcement agencies for his expertise than any other cop in Arizona.

Stan nodded a "could be" look. "You can't deny where they look like they came from."

"Hey. SB ten-seventy says we can't profile like that."

Stan caught Brian's sarcasm about the contentious legislation. "These guys are already dead. We can't be violating *their* civil rights." He scanned the scene for a few moments, then looked back at Brian. "Seriously, what's your take on this?"

Brian shrugged. "My local PD's had no reports anywhere in this area of drop house activity. No calls about constant movement of vehicles, no unusual comings and goings during the middle of the night. Not one neighbor phoning in about suspicious activity, domestic disputes or noise complaints. This is Chandler. You sneeze in this town and someone's calling nine-one-one. Even way out here." The detective raised his eyebrows high and continued. "Then again . . . maybe this place has been missed by everyone."

Stan thought Brian's assessment of the situation had merit. Although Chandler had its share of homicides, it was way off the beaten path to hold way stations for illegals coming up from Mexico. That dubious honor of hosting the most drop houses went to sections of south and central Phoenix.

"Have your forensic team go over this scene with an extra fine-toothed comb," Stan said. "See if your hunch is right. If it is, I'm guessing something will show up to support your theory." He paused then stuck his pen back into his shirt pocket. "If it is cartel-related and your team needs any help from my fed pals, just let me know."

Brian smiled while shaking his head. "How'd you ever get along before without having those guys in your life?"

"Very funny," Stan replied. "If I'm not mistaken, I've got you and my wife to thank for developing the beautiful relationship I have now with them."

"Hey, what are friends for?" Brian quipped. "But you do owe me."

"Haven't I thanked you enough for turning my life around, saving my marriage, making me a better person? I stay longer at parties now, too, don't I?" Stan wisecracked.

Brian nodded and smiled.

Stan went on. "Well, anyway, all the DOJ departments are available to you. FBI, DEA, ATF, and U.S. Marshals, of course."

Brian grinned. "Oh. Of course."

"And you already know they're real good about keeping stuff on the QT, too."

"Yeah, yeah, I get it." Brian said.

"Detective Hanley?" Brian turned to the uniformed officer interrupting their banter. "That forensic gal has something she thinks you need to see."

The three men walked over to an area in the far corner of the living room. There, a young woman scoured the floor, holding a small, high intensity flashlight. A long-lensed digital camera hung from her neck. She, as well as everyone else on the scene, wore surgical boots over her shoes and plastic gloves on her hands. Along with another technician, she wore a white, Tyvek jump suit with the letters CSRU stenciled across the back.

"I found this," the female tech said through a surgical mask. She held up a piece of metal pinched between the tips of a long pair of tweezers.

Stan concentrated, trying to focus on the object in the dim light. She pointed her flashlight on the item while everyone stared at the shard.

"What is it?" Stan asked.

"I'm not one hundred percent sure since it's such a small piece," said the Crime Scene Response Unit technician, "but it looks like a part of something I used during my EOD deployment in Afghanistan."

"EOD?" Stan asked.

Brian jumped in. "Explosive Ordnance Disposal. The bomb guys."

"Girls, too," the thirty-something CSRU tech said, correcting him.

Brian chortled. "Bomb girls? You gotta' be kidding, Burnett."

"No, sir, Detective." Mary Ann Burnett pulled her mask from her mouth, looking as if she wanted to make sure she was being heard. "As a matter of fact, I'm the *only* woman in the *only* EOD company in Arizona. I'm National Guard. CSRU's my day job. This is simple stuff compared to EOD. Never had to render safe a crime scene."

"Render safe?" Stan asked.

"Yes, sir. That's EOD speak for disarming a bomb—making it safe."

"So tell me again what you think this thing is you've found."

"I'm not one-hundred percent sure, but this looks like part of the receiver for a Mark one-fifty-two remote control firing device transmitter. Navy trained us on how to use these babies at Eglin Air Force Base. Only place that's got 'em. Their use is classified. Restricted to EOD training or active military operations exclusively." Mary Ann shrugged. "Until now it seems."

"Headless Mexican illegals and a classified U.S. military part," Brian said. "That's one very odd combination. Don't ya' think?"

"If you're asking me for my opinion, sir," Mary Ann offered, "maybe you have a rogue EOD soldier on your hands."

Stan's eyes widened. He had an instant flashback. *This all sounds so familiar to me . . . wait . . . shit! Can it be?*

He mumbled to himself. "My ten-year-old cold case may have just warmed up a bit."

CHAPTER 3

Stan's mind wandered far from the scene. He recollected how just a few weeks ago he had accessed the National Crime Information Center files, made available to him courtesy of his friends at the FBI. At that time, nearly one-hundred thousand people were listed as missing in the bureau's NCIC database. Paul Henry Stewart was still one of them.

Ten years ago, on April 10, 2001, the former electric utility worker had disappeared after his wife and two children were incinerated inside their house. The case had not only shocked the city but garnered section one space in national newspapers. The triple homicide had never been solved, and had never stopped haunting Stan. To this day, he struggled to forget the crime. Now the ten-year anniversary had arrived and yet Stewart remained on the list, missing and still considered by law enforcement as "at large."

When the case had occurred, it had a profound effect upon the then thirty-nine-year-old Maricopa County prosecutor. For months, Stan and then rookie Scottsdale homicide detective, M. C. Kemp, had worked the investigation but failed to find any irrefutable evidence as to who had committed the monstrous act. More importantly, they had failed to find out how and why the husband and father, eventually charged with murder in absentia, had taken flight and disappeared off the face of the earth.

The last sighting of Stewart, still on the FBI's Ten Most Wanted list, had occurred the same day as the fire-homicide. A security camera encased in a bank's walk-up ATM, less than one-mile from Stewart's house, had snapped his photo as he made the maximum cash withdrawal. The picture's date and time stamp generated during the transaction confirmed it had taken place precisely at the same time firefighters fought to extinguish the raging inferno at his home.

A copy of the low-resolution thermal paper photo, which Stan had placed in a protective plastic sleeve, had stayed pinned to his office wall for years after the murders, a constant reminder of a killer on the loose. He had asked himself hundreds of times: what would send a man to such depths that he would kill his loved ones and in such a horrific manner?

"Stan?" Brian's voice snapped Stan back from his thoughts.

"Yeah. What?"

"Did you just say something about a 'cold case'?" Brian asked.

"Yes. The Paul Stewart case."

"The Stewart case?"

"Yes. The Stewart case." Stan took a deep breath, wondering if he should share his secret with his buddy. He knew letting Hanley know now hidden details about the case he hadn't shared with him back then could backfire on him. Then he recalled how he had once tried to keep an even deeper, darker secret from Brian, nearly causing the end of their friendship. Worse than that, Stan's lies almost ended up getting them killed on the south side of Chicago.

Stan motioned with his head for Brian to step into another room of the house. They were now alone. He kept his voice low. "I never told you this when we were investigating the case but the heads of Stewart's wife and kids were cut off, too. Like these three tonight."

Brian stuttered his words. "What–did–you–just–say?"

"The heads of Stewart's two children were cut off. Same as the wife."

"Wait a second," Brian said, an incredulous look still on his face. "I don't remember that being part of the crime scene report I got. The case sheets Scottsdale PD shared with me only stated the kids' and wife's COD was undetermined due to the charred condition of their remains."

Stan's eyes were devoid of emotion and un-apologetic. "We knew the cause of death. The killer decapitated the two children while, we think, he made the tied-up mother watch before decapitating her. Detective Kemp chose not to release those facts to anyone. We even sealed the lips of the firemen on the scene. Then we made sure to cordon-off everyone else from the immediate area . . . and the case."

Brian's voice rose in anger. "You kept those details from *me*?"

"Yes. Even from you. We didn't want *anybody* to know what truly happened. At the time we shared what we wanted only with those we thought absolutely needed to know. We sure as hell couldn't risk the media frenzy if those macabre facts had been disclosed."

"I went to the Rim with you two. Kemp used me for my expertise. We were all on the same team, for crissake."

"This was something completely new for me, Bri, investigating a beheading, let alone three of them. It was a crime no one had ever committed before in our county. It was completely out of our league. *None* of us had seen anything like it. That's why we brought in the FBI and asked for help from their profilers."

Stan took pause but then went on, his voice rising now. "Look. The whole thing made my skin crawl, too. That's why the Arabs had such a devastating effect on Americans when they videotaped and broadcasted those beheadings after we retaliated for nine-eleven. They scared the living shit out of people. When you see something like that it makes you want to run as fast and as far away as you can. We just couldn't risk letting people know some psycho had beheaded an entire family. Especially in Scottsdale."

Brian kept shaking his head, the look of disbelief over Stan withholding facts from him still frozen on his face.

Feeling like he had just put a chink in the armor of their friendship, Stan attempted to soften the blow. "I know you're upset but the FBI profilers believed the type of deviant who did this, contrary to foreign terrorists, internalizes the event and would never boast about what he had done. The feds told us that beheading a person gives the perp some form of gratification, either sexual or ego-based. After getting those insights, we wondered if we'd ever nab the lunatic. The bureau advised us keeping the facts secret might help us down the road in solving the case. We discussed the decision for hours, even argued about whether to share the facts with the other police departments. Kemp and the FBI believed it was the right move to not share this detail outside of a very small group of people. I disagreed, but in the end, it wasn't my call. Even though it was the first time M.C. was the lead detective on a murder case, his chief backed him up one-hundred percent."

Brian put his hands on his hips, looking disgusted at hearing Stan's decade-late confession. "How hard did you really fight it?"

Stan knew Brian fully understood it was against protocol to contest a lead detective's and his superior's decision to withhold information, especially in high profile crimes. He had hoped Brian would accept his explanation. But the tone of his accusing voice rattled Stan. "Just what the hell are you implying?"

Brian jabbed a finger in the air toward his friend. "What's really going on here is you still can't let go of that case."

Stan fumed over Brian's accusation. "*Let go?* How the hell do you *let go* of something like that? Nobody wanted to find Stewart more than I did. *Nobody!* I wasn't worried about egos getting bruised. I wanted to find this guy and find out why he cut off their heads. I mean, it's tragic enough that he killed his own family. But . . . *to cut off their heads?*" Stan shook his head. "That, I will never 'let go' of."

Brian's tone softened. "Look, Stan, it's been ten years. It's one for the cold case squad at Scottsdale PD to work, not you."

Stan stared him in the eye. "I'll never stop working that case." He spun away and walked back into the room with the corpses. Brian followed. Stan glowered at the carnage, arms folded tight across his chest. "That was the only decapitation murder we had ever had in the state until—" He paused, halting his speech. "There's . . . just . . . something . . ." The prosecutor squatted down then cocked his head as he took a closer look at what was left of the neck of one of the victims. "These markings—"

"Whoa, whoa," Brian interrupted him. "Where you goin' there?"

"I'm not *going* anywhere," Stan said without looking up. "I just thought there may be something familiar here to me, that's all."

"Familiar? What looks familiar?"

Feeling he owed it to Brian and knowing he had already broken protocol about the Stewart case, he went on and shared with Brian what he was thinking. "After the murders, I studied the cause of death reports on Stewart's wife and kids for weeks, actually months. Although the bodies were burned beyond recognition, when the medical examiner did the autopsy he examined multiple cross-sections of each of the victim's wounds. On all of them, he identified a distinct pattern from the blade the killer used to slash his victims' throats and then used to cut their heads off. We haven't had a murder by decapitation in Maricopa County before or since. Now another beheading, another *triple* decapitation pops up. I'm just saying it's worth taking a look. Seeing if there are any similarities. Anything that matches the Stewart victims. That's all."

"That's *all?* Okay. Look. I get how much that case meant to you, Stewart being your neighbor and all. And I know how much you still want to find the bastard. But these two cases are *not* connected. They have nothing in common. Trust me, I've seen this same scenario across the border when I worked on a task force down there and this shit here has Sinaloan cartel written all over it. They've been beheading their enemies for quite some time now, even dumping a few heads and headless corpses over on our side of the fence. That possibility alone is bad enough. Now, on top of that, it looks like they've come into my backyard."

Stan couldn't deny Brian's assessment of the situation. He

was the state's top homicide cop, clearing more cases in
Chandler alone than anyone had in the history of the nearly
century old city. Based upon Brian's solve-rate, the detective
worked a homicide better than any other dick in the county.

"Well, that may be, but just humor me and have your
crime unit check and re-check everything. If Stewart was here, I
want to know."

"Stewart here? C'mon. If he isn't dead, Paul Stewart is
long gone, probably living somewhere in Mex—"

Stan finished his partner's sentence. "Mexico. Yep. Just
like these three once were."

CHAPTER 4

Maricopa County Attorney's Office Building
Phoenix, Arizona
9:00 a.m.

Stan arrived at his office bleary eyed. The return of a childhood nightmare, which he hadn't experienced in almost half-a-dozen years, interrupted his too few hours of sleep. Braced with a cup of coffee, he pulled from his office closet a worn file box labeled—STEWART, PAUL HENRY: OPEN—APRIL 2001. Having studied the case file daily from the time it broke a decade earlier, he had packed away its reams of documents long ago, shoving the box deep into a corner of the closet.

Wanting, though, to keep the files close in case something should develop, he had refused to let clerks transfer it to off-site archives. In actuality, he had kept the cold case stored in a deeper—and darker—corner of his own mind.

He couldn't exactly remember the last time he had looked at the case files. But after what he saw last night he wanted to again leaf through the local police and FBI reports on Stewart's life. He re-read the details of the native Floridian's childhood, growing up a military brat in the Sunshine State. His father, Karl, an Air Force JAG as well as a decorated fighter pilot, had often taken his only child to Hurlburt Field, the special operations airfield near Eglin Air Force Base. Located in nearby Ft. Walton Beach, Florida, it was the elder Stewart's base station. Strictly forbidden to bring non-cleared personnel onto the restricted base, Karl had received formal reprimands for breaking the rule multiple times.

Inspired by these visits, a week after his eighteenth birthday—April 20, 1979— son walked into a local recruitment office in Destin, Florida and enlisted in his father's Air Force. On Paul's application, a copy of which Stan now re-read, Stewart stated he wanted to be a Special Ops soldier. After completing his basic training at Texas's Lackland Air Force Base, he was shipped back home to Florida to complete technical school preparation at Eglin. Graduating at the top of his class enabled Stewart to qualify for an elite assignment. Eglin was the nation's sole training facility for personnel like him who wanted to join an exclusive group known as Explosive Ordnance Disposal or EOD.

EOD. I knew that acronym sounded familiar last night.

Stan Googled the job description of an Air Force EOD soldier and just as the Chandler CSRU tech Mary Ann had said their main role was to defuse or detonate unexploded bombs, known by their acronym, UXO. The focus of every successful EOD mission: render safe the ordnance to avoid unintentional loss of property or life, commonly referred to in the military as "collateral damage."

Stewart's service record showed he had successfully finished his technical training at EOD School at Eglin, exclusively run there by the Navy. When completed, he earned the rank of 3E831 EOD Technician. Two years later, he climbed the ladder to 3E851. His promotion was followed by six months of clandestine training in Air Force Special Operations Command, or AFSOC, back at Hurlburt. At the end of that school, Stewart's clearance level zoomed and the soldier went "full black," another euphemistic military term, this one coined by the counter-intelligence community for personnel off the normal tracking grid. In other words, his deployments would be top-secret.

It seemed, according to notes FBI agents had hand-written in the margins of the original reports, Stewart had gotten his wish and became a Black Ops soldier, meaning he was taken completely off the regular military's radar. His missions, the agents had told Stan back then, were so closely guarded and so sensitive that only one-tenth of one-percent of the military community were privy to his whereabouts. That meant only those with top-secret SAP, or Special Access Program, clearance would have known details of Paul Stewart's assignments. Stan also recollected how an FBI agent had also confidentially shared with him at the time that the federal agency kept its own secret list on the whereabouts of every current and past EOD soldier.

As he re-read the fugitive's official military record, Stewart's military discharge papers caught Stan's eye. Form DD214 had been checked with an honorable discharge. The form also showed the date and his last known address: 1 APR 1999, 525 WEST MOGOLLON RIM DRIVE, RED ROCK, ARIZONA, 85245. In the margin of the form, Stan saw the FBI agent's scribbled note: MOTHER DECEASED, FATHER REMARRIED FORMER HOUSEKEEPER.

Stan closed the over-stuffed manila folder and ran his fingers across its worn, tattered tab. During the initial investigation and for several years that followed, he had scoured the contents of all of the folders dozens of times. Re-reading about Stewart's past brought forth the memory of the sight of the charred bodies of Stewart's wife and children and what had been done to each of the victims. Stan felt nauseous all over again.

To settle his stomach, and clear his head, he stood up and went to the window of his eighth floor office. He stared out, looking in the direction of where Stewart's house had once stood, only a few doors from his own so long ago. He envisioned the empty lot after the structure had been torn down. That sight had etched a haunting image in his mind of the horror incurred inside the home which once stood so near his own. A neighbor in name only, like most people in The Valley, he and Stewart had stayed hidden from one another, each for their own reasons, only seeing glimpses of the other as they pulled in and out of the garages of their stucco-walled homes. Even though they had lived so close they both had chosen to cloister themselves behind seven-foot-high cinderblock walls, never knowing much about each other's lives until a house burned down with a family inside.

Stan's gaze remained transfixed on the distance, recollecting on his own one-time secret past life. His gut grumbled, telling him somehow the ex-secret military operative Paul Henry Stewart might be connected to the two triple-homicides, each ten years apart, almost to the day.

Maybe he's the EOD guy gone rogue like Mary Ann the tech surmised? If he is and he's still out there, is he getting ready to strike again?

Stan struggled to connect any dots between the Chandler case and the Scottsdale cold case. His intuition sensed the decapitation murders were linked. He went back to his desk and read the reports—again—looking for any kind of pattern or for facts that seemed more than coincidence. He tried to find similarities but the commonalties were circumstantial at best. His mind ran through several different theories but he knew he needed more information before he could pin down one that made sense. All he had to go on now was to do what those in law enforcement people know best—follow your gut—and his was a roiling chamber churning to the point of eruption.

As for the current case and the three victims in the Chandler drop house, he wondered if the Maricopa County Medical Examiner's report would give him more details about the deaths besides the obvious fact that the victims' heads had been chopped off. He couldn't wait to get the coroner's report but knew it might take days or even weeks before he'd see an official cause of death report. That overworked department of the county had an extraordinary caseload, its stainless steel autopsy tables clogged with five or more homicides a week. Bucolic Chandler, on the other hand, experienced a mere modicum of that number with only five homicides a year.

Stan wanted his beheadings case pushed to the top of the pile and would do everything he could do within his power to make that happen. You could expect that perk as the top prosecutor in the county and he'd be a squeaky wheel until his got oiled.

He sat and reflected upon revisiting the Stewart murders case files and refreshing his memory of the homicides. As he did, something he had read gnawed at him. It was about Stewart's time stationed at Davis-Monthan Air Force Base in Tucson as a ground crew member of an A-10 Thunderbolt wing. The detail had triggered Stan into recollecting an unusual military incident tied to that same base. That unique event, too, had its own set of still unanswered questions. He Googled the incident about a rookie A-10 pilot who mysteriously went off course, eventually crashing his multi-million dollar aircraft into the Colorado wilderness.

Hmmm. Stewart and this guy were stationed there at the same time.

Stan stood up and walked back to the office window. He gazed at the vastness and immensity spread out before him of one of the largest cities in the country. The Davis-Monthan incident got pushed out of his head by chilling thoughts he learned from a workshop he had recently attended dealing with threats to the state's power and water infrastructure. He spun away from the window and went back again to the storage box on top of his desk. He dug through it and pulled out a different collection of papers. He sat down and flipped through the pages to find what he was looking for. When he did, he skimmed them and made some notes on a pad sitting on his desk. He paused for a long moment when he got to a section with details of Paul Stewart's work history after his discharge from the Air Force until the time of his disappearance.

This could be a connection.

Stan's mind raced. He picked up his desk phone and dialed a number. On the other end, a female voice answered. "Arizona Division of Emergency Management. May I help you?"

CHAPTER 5

Red Rock, Arizona
Fourteen Years Earlier, November 1997

Sergeant Paul Stewart quickly came to know his fellow rednecks serving at Davis-Monthan Air Force Base, his new assignment south of Tucson, Arizona. Upon his first weekend leave, some fellows from Georgia introduced the just transferred Stewart to their favorite bar, Wilma's Red Rock Tap House, twenty-miles north of the base on Sasco Road off Interstate 10.

For the past fifty years, Wilma's, an offbeat dive, had served as a local watering hole for area miners and farm workers as well as day travelers to the nearby Ironwood Forest. Stewart soon found out the real attraction these "ridge-runners"—as he liked to call these backwoods Southern hicks—had for Wilma's. Once-a-month, the bar's owner hosted a "Klan rally." That's what the good old boys called the Friday night gatherings where patrons walked up to an open microphone and ranted about whatever pain the burr in their saddle was causing.

At his first rally, Stewart sat at the bar, closed-lipped, listening to the night's first speaker—a tall man, sporting ratted hair and matching goatee. His greasy, denim motorcycle vest proclaimed on its back his affiliation with the Desert Outkasts. The biker brought the boisterous crowd of about a hundred people to attention as soon as he opened his mouth.

"The white man is the descendant of the one and only true pure race. Our duty is to protect the purity of our whiteness along with our mother tongue. That means we need to stop this fucking invasion of garbage flowing into our country from the south. So I say, how about we shoot every Mexican man, woman, and child as they illegally cross the border?"

Did he just say what I think he said?

The crowd clapped and screamed their approval. The extremist's words and the enthusiastic response of the crowd shocked, yet thrilled, Stewart. He snapped to attention. He had never heard such bravado spoken so openly before, especially not in the military. Words like those he had just heard spewed had only been used behind closed doors, amongst like-minded comrades. Not in public. Not like this. Being a career military man, Stewart had been witness to hidden bigotry within the ranks—from all sides. His father had often lectured him about the importance of keeping the races separated, drilling into him biases that remained ingrained in him today. He sat up and listened closer. The thin-as-a-rail biker, sidearm strapped to his hip, went on.

"What going on down there at the border is fucking illegal. Period. But our government refuses to protect us. So I say we shoot every dirty, filthy wetback sneaking illegally into our country." He pulled his firearm from its holster and popped off a round into the ceiling. The crowed went nuts.

You ain't shittin', man. You tell 'em. Let me up at that microphone. I'll give 'em an earful.

As the crowd settled down, a big man waddled up to the bar and sat next to Stewart. "I'll drink to that," the man bellowed. He took his beer bottle and held it up, looking for a clink of approval.

The sergeant obliged the stranger. Stewart smiled wide and gave a big nod of approval to the hulk. They swigged in unison.

"I know first-hand what that guy up there's talking about," the big man offered as he placed his bottle on the bar. "I see these fucking Mexicans running like rats through the desert, day and night. Actually, they're more like cockroaches. *La* fucking *cucarachas.* If we don't stop them they'll take over this country someday. You mark my words. Once there's enough of them here, they'll breed out of control. Their wetback kids'll become fucking U.S. citizens. Not a good thing for this country or for white guys like you and me."

Stewart, dressed in civilian clothes, nodded, agreeing with the burly man with the full, thick beard. The brute's immense frame took up nearly two bar stools.

"You ain't from around here. Are you?" the big man asked.

Stewart shook his head.

"Davis-Monthan?"

Stewart affirmed the titan's guess with a dip of his chin.

The big lout smiled. "I knew it. I can tell a square GI when I see one. In uniform or not. Can see it by the way they carry themselves. And by what they're packin'." He winked down at Stewart's side while patting himself under the arm. "We need more like you in the service. Fucking military today is filled with too many niggers, too many Mexicans, and too many fucking faggots, especially here in Arizona."

"You can say that again."

The stranger pressed on for a conversation. "What do you do down there?"

"I'm a specialist," Stewart said.

"Oh yeah? What you specialize in?"

"Munitions." Stewart took a swig from his bottle, looking around the smoke-filled room.

"Interesting. Very Interesting. A guy who knows a lot about bombs and stuff, huh? You're a lucky man. If I could, I'd be blasting every fucking Mexican back into Mexico right as they're sneakin' their goddam wetback asses over the border. What I wouldn't do to get my hands on some good old, military-grade, high-octane explosives. The good shit. Like we had in 'Nam."

"Well, as much as I'd like to help, pal, that'll never happen. At least not from our base," Stewart answered. "Things are locked up ass tight down there. They've actually got a detail that counts every bomb before we go to bed each night. Nobody ever wants to have to go explaining missing explosives to a superior officer. Air Force is just a little bit anal about keeping track of their explosives." He motioned to the bartender for another beer.

"Let me get the next round." Stewart's new friend ordered them two more. They tapped their current bottles before swigging them dry. "Well, you just let me know if there's any chance of gettin' you to talk one of your fly boys down there into havin' some of his bombs go missing one day. Maybe they could just disappear on one of those practice flights they're always doin' around here. Sorta' drop 'em in the wrong place. Used to happen all the time over in 'Nam. Me and my crew would be happy to just kind'a *stumble* upon them out there in the desert, if you catch my drift." He belly laughed at his suggestion.

"Hey, I'd like nothing more than to help you blow up a few rats coming across the border, but you must be dreaming." Stewart scoffed at the idea with a chuckle, shaking his head. His mind wondered for a moment. What would make this guy think that after meeting him for the very first time he'd be willing to commit such a treasonous act? He dismissed his concern and merely answered, "Anyhow, fighter pilots are all pretty straight arrows."

"Yeah, well that may be so. But don't tell me they like these illegals comin' across any more than me and you do."

"I didn't say that. There's plenty who think like us and who know there's a huge problem. I'm just saying, I'm pretty sure none of those guys would be willing to risk a career and doing time in federal prison for something as far off the charts as what you just suggested."

The big man stayed silent. Stewart took a deep swig of his beer, then continued. "Look, all I can say is there are a lot of guys like me who hate to hell what's going on in this country and in the military with its political correctness and all that bullshit. And we especially don't like what's going on at the border, since our job is to fight and protect the country."

While they sat there, the scrawny biker at the microphone

was replaced by another speaker, this one bleating even louder and looking more crazed than the first. Stewart inched back and propped his elbows on the bar.

Stewart went on. "Look. I don't have the answer on how to solve this goddam invasion. Everyone in power, though, seems afraid to stop it, especially the feds. But all this fucking posturing going on in Washington is hurting and effecting good folks. It'll have to take one of these asshole politicians getting held up by some goddamn illegal or have his house broken break into and his daughter raped. Then they'll sit up and listen. But by then, it'll be too fucking late."

The bearded man looked as if he was taking time to digest Stewart's mini-tirade. He looked Paul square in the eye. "You know. You sound like an awfully smart fella."

Not certain what the man was getting at, Stewart pulled himself forward and leaned in toward him. "Yeah. So."

The big man smiled, looking as if he had just speared his food for the night, salivating for the feast ahead. He spoke softly. "We're puttin' big plans in place to make a statement about this invasion goin' on—'cause, like you just said, that's exactly what it is, pure and simple." The man took a deep swig of beer, swallowed hard, then went on. "We need to quit givin' all these lowlifes in our country a free ride. It's bad enough we got the niggers on the dole. Now the wetbacks are robbin' this country fucking blind." He lowered his voice. "We whites got to unite together and let the government know we won't stand for it anymore. And the only way they'll listen is when we strike back at 'em."

"Strike back?"

"Yep, that's what I said. That's what I like about a special little crew I belong to. We got the balls to stand up against all this illegal immigration shit. Fuck, we're even gettin' backing from people you'd never guess would be on our side."

Stewart paused at the bearded man's last statement. "Like who?"

"Can't tell you that, bro. But there's a *lot* of money in store for someone willin' to help us. If you want to know more, we meet privately, right back here, night after next. You seem like you'd fit right in. But you gotta be serious about dealin' with the problem. What we're proposing ain't for the fuckin' weak of heart."

Hmmm. Some head-knocking. Music to my ears.

Stewart took another sip of his beer, then stared back at the huge man. His piercing blue eyes looked as if he was looking right into Stewart's soul. Paul Stewart had met many evil men in his nearly twenty years in the military, many of them conducting Tier One Black Ops for agencies the U.S. government officially denied. But this man's eyes were different. Hate seethed in them.

"I might be interested," Stewart said, coldly.

"What's your name?"

"Stewart. Paul Stewart."

"Stewart, huh? I'll make sure to run your name when I get back to my office tonight. Check you out to see if you can be trusted."

"Run my name? You a cop?"

"What do you think?" The big man roared out loud, laughing uncontrollably. Then he abruptly stopped. "Look, I like you. You're all right. Here. You'll need this." He grabbed a bar napkin, took a pen from his pocket, and wrote on the small, white paper square. "You come back when I told you. At midnight. The place will look all closed up. Just go 'round back, knock on the center door four times, and mention the name on here." He folded the paper in half and placed it under Stewart's beer bottle sitting on the bar.

Stewart grabbed the bar nap, unfolded it, and read the single scribbled word—TARSHISH.

CHAPTER 6

When Paul Stewart returned to Wilma's Red Rock Tap House, it was just past midnight. Just like the big man had told him, the place looked deserted. A dim bulb over the door, covered by a rusted metal shade, struggled to light the entrance. The MR. FUN IS HERE bright neon sign in the front window—which had flickered off and on in alternating colors of red, white, and blue the other evening—stood eerily idle.

Stewart pulled his green Ford pickup around the back of the wooden building. A line of six SUVs and three trucks were parked there. He parked across from them and cautiously walked up to a door at the back of the building, looking around several times to make sure he was alone in the dirt lot. He felt like he was being watched and turned his head, scanning his perimeter. He reached the sun-dried portal and gave it four short knocks. Stewart waited a moment but no one answered.

Is this a setup?

Following instinct from his time in covert ops, he reached inside his jacket, hand going to the warm handle of his .45. The only discernible sound was made by the cool desert wind rustling through the needles of a giant saguaro cactus, cutting the ebony silence with its soft shrill. He rapped his knuckles harder this time with four more knocks. Seconds after the last knock, a bolt slid back on the other side of the door, then creaked open.

A man stood in the shadows of light emanating from a yellow-hued bulb in the ceiling, backlighting his lean figure. From what Stewart could tell in the dim light, he surmised the person was in his late teens or early twenties. He also noticed the guy wore a holstered Glock on his right hip. A gun preferred by many cops, this gringo didn't have the look of police since the punk looked scared, standing there, frozen like a statue. Stewart hoped the youngster's inexperience wouldn't cause him to make a mistake and reach for his firearm, forcing the airman to shoot him.

"Yeah? Whadya want?" the man asked. He rolled a toothpick between his teeth.

Stewart emitted no emotion when he answered the question with only one word. "Tarshish."

"Oh," the kid answered. "Come in. Come in."

Stewart relaxed his grip on his .45 and stepped through the doorway. He followed the scrawny guy down the poorly lit hall covered with ratty carpeting. The stench of stale beer and smoke hung thick in the air as they walked by several closed doors. When his escort got to the end of the corridor, he turned the handle on the last door.

A well-lit room opened before them, empty except for about a dozen men who sat on folding chairs forming a semi-circle. At the top of the arc an elderly man with long gray hair sat on a wooden captain's chair, the only one of its kind in the windowless space. To his immediate right was the bearded man Stewart had met the other night. He didn't recognize any of the others.

"This is the man I told you about, Brother Jacob," the bearded man said.

"Ah! Enter, friend. Please. Come. Join our prayer group." Jacob Jeffrey Lund's voice bellowed as his words reverberated off the empty walls and the bare, concrete floor. The dank room looked more like a large prison cell rather than a place of worship. "Brother Kirby, please seat our newcomer."

The skinny door attendant snapped to attention. He scurried to grab a chair from against the wall, then placed it at one end of the semi-circle.

"Sit, brother. Sit and be welcome," Jacob urged. "The Lord Yahweh has sent you to us, this I know."

A powerful magnetism seemed to emanate from the old man who dressed and spoke like a preacher. His essence made Stewart's earlier feeling of uneasiness dissipate. Jacob began to preach to the assembled men and related story after story of illegal immigrants sneaking across the border, many of them, he told them, "ending up in my courtroom." He used words like, "heathens," "vermin," "plague," and "Satan-like," while sharing his views on the current state of what he called "the unabated invasion of the United States by illegal Mexican Nationals."

In between his flowing, yet at times rambling rhetoric, Stewart listened as the gathered shouted an "Amen" in unison, affirming Jacob's statements. They grew particularly loud when he referenced the Lord Yahweh or the Lord Melchizedek, which he did often. An hour passed as Stewart sat transfixed, listening to the man lecture about the problems he claimed faced the people of Arizona. Finally, the elderly man ended the evening's gathering by giving an emotional tirade, emphasizing in particular his stance on what he called, "The current situation in this country with the Negro problem."

Stewart watched and listened, eyes focused firm, unwavering from the charismatic man.

"I tell you, my brothers, the Lord Yahweh has spoken to me. He has come to me in a vision. To me, his Lord Melchizedek. I, in turn, have asked him to direct his fiery angel to me here on earth, to help us strike down the people who allow these heathens to come to our fair country and ruin it for our pure, beautiful white children. To strike the politicians and government bureaucrats who do nothing to halt this tide of filth. Crush them like the animals they are. Keep them from encouraging and fostering this mingling with our pure white race."

When the old man finished his rant of intolerance, the group stood and clapped, each yelling "Amen" over and over. They patted each other on the back, clasping and shaking hands, nodding in agreement and telling one another something had to be done to solve their problem. With enthusiasm, Stewart joined in on the threatening chatter.

* * *

While Paul Stewart had listened to the impassioned words of Jacob Lund during his first visit to Wilma's backroom, a mesmerizing feeling had come over him. Lund's speech had catapulted him into a dreamlike state, captivating him. His mind drifted back in time, awakening unresolved issues with his own father, his one-time hero, who had irrevocably damaged his son's heart. A burning desire had overtaken him: he longed for a new father-figure. The allure of Lund's aura had been so profound it was as if a hand had been thrust into Stewart's chest and grabbed his heart. The old man had taken control of the organ's rhythmic beat, answering the muscle's aching desire for a deeper connection.

Stewart's yearning for this renewed spirit drew him back again and again to the secret gatherings of the Aryan Sons of Arizona, the group's real name. But Lund preferred to call the evil cabal his "Church of the High Country." He addressed his followers as "Brother" and during his sermons referred to himself as "The Lord Melchizedek," a Biblical character who, he had told them, was "the king of righteousness" during the time of Abraham.

One night, several meetings after Stewart's inaugural visit to the bitter room of hatred, Lund delivered an especially vitriolic racist diatribe. When it was over, Stewart turned to his now friend with the beard and asked, "Those explosives you mentioned wanting when we first met. Just how much are you looking for, Brother Logan?"

CHAPTER 7

Phoenix, Arizona
Present Day, April 15, 2011

The majority of the construction of today's Western power grid was put in place after World War II. As the burgeoning geographic area took shape, it became apparent two key resources would be minimally required to push the rampant expansion of the country's most arid region: water and electricity. One historic project, aimed at the reclamation of water, came prior to the Second World War with the completion of Boulder Dam. Now known as Hoover Dam, besides diverting water from the Colorado River, the six-and-one-half-million ton dam began generating electricity the same year of its completion, 1935.

Stan Kobe learned these facts from Kelli Begay, agency director at the Arizona Division of Emergency Management, ADEM for short. Kelli had become the state's first Native American to hold the top position when appointed by the out-going governor in late 2008. Stan sat across from Kelli inside her drab, government office housed in a one-story non-descript building on the Papago Park Military Reservation off Scottsdale's McDowell Road. The site—named after two, huge, red-rock buttes in the center of the complex—had been there since the beginning of The Depression.

"So, Kelli, is it really true there's a secret bunker built underneath those two buttes out there?"

She laughed at his question about the persistent rumor.

"Yes, and under one of them we have Bigfoot."

Stan chuckled back. "Touché." He liked the fact that she had chosen to lighten the conversation with a little levity, easing his anxiety over the visit.

"Stan, I know you're not here looking for Bigfoot. Those were some very thought provoking questions you asked when you phoned. I sense you've done some additional reading since our workshop about our Valley's struggle with its fragile infrastructure."

Kelli and her staff had made a presentation to Stan's office last month on what they called "what-if scenarios" revolving around large-scale terrorist attacks within Arizona. During his phone call, Stan had told her he wanted to talk about some thoughts he had as a follow-up. What he hadn't told her was that he was not only trying to allay his personal fears regarding the future for him and his family living in the Valley, but was chasing angles in trying to solve his murder cases.

"Yes, quite a bit of reading, Kelli. I've got to tell you, after what I learned in your seminar and doing my own research, I'm really worried. When you shared that our water supply is on the brink of being in grave danger . . . well, as a family man that really hit me hard."

The sustainability of life in a desert environment was a subject of great importance to Stan. He had read where Phoenix was only as strong as its weakest link. It was a city, according to some scientists, that could literally collapse should the flow of its water and electricity be compromised.

Kelli was straight forward with her response. "It *is* a real concern. Although we are technically the wettest desert in the world, we still get less than nine inches of rainfall per year. Statewide, we've been in and out of various degrees of severe drought since nineteen-ninety-four. Couple that with the ongoing lack of snowfall up north due to global-warming. It's taken its toll on our water supply."

Stan shook his head. "Right. When you talked about how crucial our water reservoirs are, especially in the Salt River corridor, and what the ramifications would be if these dams were struck by terrorists . . . well . . . that really got my attention."

"As a grad student back in two-thousand-three, I helped do some of the original research conducted by the Nuclear Regulatory Commission for the House Homeland Security Committee. We informed them that foreign terror groups were known to have considered targeting U.S. energy and water facilities. Here at ADEM, we're training constantly to respond to an attack on one or multiple key pieces of infrastructure to our electric grid or water supply. It's no secret that either resource could be a key target. If we had a breach or stoppage in one or, God forbid, both, it would be a calamity. The result could be mass panic."

"Sounds eerily like the past and what happened to the Anasazi and Hohokam Indians."

"That's not as far-fetched as it sounds. There are some who believe Phoenix could literally disappear if its water or electric supply were gravely damaged."

"I need to know, Kelli. What exactly would be the ramifications of a direct hit here?"

"Take for example our state's power grid or, for that matter, the entire network west of the Mississippi. This grid is like a complicated jig saw puzzle. Maybe more accurately like the proverbial house of cards. Pull one card out from the pile and the rest could tumble down. Now if that card happens to be Palo Verde, well the house not only comes crumbling down but maybe even melts down."

As a father, Stan didn't like hearing the scenario Kelli had just painted. He knew Palo Verde Nuclear Power Station, a mere fifty-five miles west of the Phoenix metropolitan area, had been opposed by detractors from ever being built, let alone placed upwind of one of the nation's largest populated cities. Commissioning the facility's three uranium generators meant the possibility of a catastrophe in the making should anything ever happen to the reactors at the largest nuke plant in the United States.

"The *entire* western grid is fragile. There are many

sections a step away from crisis in the southwest, and especially in Arizona. We've taxed it so much with our unbridled population growth. And now we've got these Internet server farms and big data centers popping up right here in Phoenix. An unexpected glitch could trip the whole system. Plunge huge portions of not only our state but southern California and Las Vegas into blackouts. It could even reach down into Mexico."

"Mexico? Our power grid is tied into Mexico? Where have I been? When did that happen?"

"Americans keep demanding more and more power. We can't bring new plants online either because they don't burn clean or their construction, like nuclear, has been halted by environmental groups. Mexico has no EPA, so there's no regulation on plants down there generating electricity. Their energy generation wreaks havoc on the global carbon footprint but the upside is that it's very, very cheap. We've been buying power from them for a while now."

"Unbelievable. I never knew that."

"Nor do most Americans. What politician do you know in Washington, or here in Arizona, would want to admit to that little fact? No one running for office would want to go on record that they don't want Mexico's illegal border crossers but we'll buy their dirty energy for a dime on the dollar from unregulated plants causing harm to the world environment."

"So what about our grid? What exactly is being done to protect it?"

"The utilities have been working to put safeguards in place, mostly by adding relays that, if tripped, will affect limited geographic areas. But, frankly, that's not foolproof. But our biggest worry is over the exposure of our transmission lines. The grid's so big. There's just no practical way to put security along the network routes that tie it all together."

Stan shook his head in dismay. Kelli went on.

"It's a huge and frankly impossible task to protect these lines. Phoenix gets over two-thirds of its power in the summer from SRP's Navajo Generating Station up in Page. *Two-thirds*. The transmission lines bringing us all that power stretch for almost three hundred miles, most of it through desolate wilderness, totally unprotected. If those lines were attacked and damaged, we'd literally be crippled. Can you imagine what a catastrophic situation we'd have when the thermometer reaches one-hundred seventeen degrees with only one-third of our power available?"

Stan shook his head again while he tapped some notes into his smartphone, not looking up. A hopeless feeling befell him, similar to the painful memories of his broken childhood. He didn't conceal the distress in his voice. "There's more bad stuff you're going to tell me, isn't there?"

"I wish you didn't know my job so well. What I tell you next you may not want to hear."

Stan's gave her his full attention, looking up from his note taking.

"That loss of electric power isn't the only thing we're worried about from an emergency management prospective," Kelli explained. "One of the cripplers we least like to think about would be a hit at any of our state's major dams. Of particular concern, of course, is Theodore Roosevelt Dam and Reservoir. Besides losing the source for the majority of our drinking and agricultural water supply, as well as a huge component of our electrical generation, models we've been working on show that if the dam was breached the flooding caused in the Valley along the Salt River would reach five miles north and south of the shoreline."

Stan's eyes bulged. "*Five miles?*" he shrieked. His nervous tick took over and he cracked a couple of knuckles.

Kelli stood up and approached a huge state map on the wall behind her desk. She grabbed a pointer. "Not only would our military base flood here where we're sitting now but the waters would also engulf buildings occupied by many of these high-tech companies we've done such a good job of luring here the last few years. A number of them, located along Tempe Town Lake, are housing big data server farms. We've been told—confidentially, I might add—by our federal sister agency, FEMA, that some extremely critical and highly sensitive data is being stored at these farms. Much of it is corporate data but a lot of it is governmental. Even if that data is stored redundantly, a hit there could still be a national catastrophe."

She turned back to Stan and looked him straight in the eye. "I can tell you one thing we're almost one-hundred percent sure of, and that is, companies who do business in the desert rarely, if ever, think of flooding as a risk. No one is truly prepared for it."

"I hope they got a wake-up call when the Tempe Town Lake dam burst last year," Stan said.

Kelli sat back in her chair and leaned her head across the desk toward Stan. She lowered her voice a notch. "Speaking of that mishap, investigators still haven't been able to determine with certainty why only a single bladder of that rubber dam burst. Every theory Tempe Police detectives chased down suspected a fatigue failure, thinking it was a forced-age issue, the elastic material drying out earlier than anyone anticipated. But actually, Alcohol, Tobacco and Firearms agents told us the event could have just as easily been caused by a small pipe bomb on a timer."

She leaned back and tapped her finger on the top of her metal desk, then continued.

"A bicyclist reported hearing a loud explosion, then the sound of water and the ground rumbling. When ADEM discussed a possible terrorist attack with the feds, they said there would be no way to tell for certain, since if it was a bomb that caused the rupture then any remaining parts of an explosive device would have been washed downstream, never to be found."

"I never heard this theory," Stan said.

"We've kept it on the QT, figuring if it was a rogue bomber then he'd someday want to take credit for it. But so far, ten months later, there's been no statement made to the media or to the authorities from any person or group."

Stan jotted some more notes, then questioned her. "So, tell me more about this 'big data' thing you referred to a minute ago."

"Big data is just what its name implies. We've got Fortune 500 companies relocating or expanding to the Valley every week, enticed by cheap real estate and cheap power, especially compared to California where they most often seem to be coming from. Like I said, a few are building new structures but most are buying up huge amounts of existing, vacant space, capitalizing on the fallout from the economic downturn. They're filling up these buildings with thousands of computers, all storing unbelievably huge amounts of data—and using gobs of electricity."

"You said the data is mostly corporate?"

"Yes, most, but like I said, there's also been a recent influx and acquisition by certain departments within the federal government. As you can imagine, security is key but so is the need for reliable power. Many of these server farms that have been put in are redundant systems for the D.C. area. But some are sole storage sites. That last tidbit is off the record, by the way."

"Seriously? They're storing one-of-a-kind, non-redundant, confidential information here."

"They're in a transition. Data was being hosted off-shore, but with some world economies on the brink of collapse and security overseas always being suspect, the government is willing to forego the cost savings and store this data in the States. You probably drive by half-a-dozen of these buildings every day and are none the wiser."

Stan pondered her last statement. "How many of these facilities does the government have here now?"

"I'm really not at liberty to say. But if they were to be breached or, God forbid, go down due to a loss of power or by flooding, it would cripple us, particularly communications for first-responders."

"I remember this from your talk. You called it 'IFI'."

Kelli jumped in. "Infrastructure failure interdependencies."

"That's the domino effect you were talking about at your presentation."

"You're a good listener. And, to make matters worse, we had an eye-opening situation at Palo Verde Nuclear Plant that was extremely disturbing."

"When?"

"Just the other night there was a security breach there. News media doesn't have it yet as the NRC and the FBI have sealed this one off from them until they do a thorough internal investigation. No telling how long they will keep a tight lid on this, though."

"What the hell happened?"

"Security staff at the plant discovered and detained a Mexican worker. Turned out he's an undocumented construction laborer who got past three levels of security."

"What? How did something like *that* happen?"

"Nobody seems to know. The company he was brought in by had security clearance from the utility, meaning all of its employees would have been required to have had background checks. Somehow, though, they managed to bring in a day laborer they had picked-up at the Home Depot in Avondale. A diligent junior security officer discovered him."

"Please tell me this was the illegal's first day on the job."

Kelli shook her head. "I wish I could. Looks like he'd been a hire there for four straight days. They actually caught him on an exit search of the construction outfit's panel van on the midnight shift."

"That's incredible!"

"That's putting it mildly. The FBI, of course, had to report this to the Department of Homeland Security. Director Napolitano called me personally. I guess she was going down the line giving ass-chewings. If and when this does come to light, there's gonna' be a lot of fallout over this. No pun intended."

"But it's one random occurrence. A slip in judgment."

"I wish I could say that for sure. The harbinger of all this started even before I came on board when, within hours after nine-eleven, this department here started doing 'what if' scenarios revolving around an attack on Palo Verde. They focused on an external attack. Jets, small planes, cars, trucks, what have you, profiling involvement by Al-Qaida-looking terrorists. Top brass certainly never envisioned a scenario where an unauthorized intruder might be a Mexican National, and an illegal one at that."

"But no one can dream up every possible picture, Kelli."

"No, you're right, but an internal attack from a non-Al Qaida terrorist wasn't a high priority on the list. That's now changed."

Stan scratched his chin. "Besides worrying about illegals being in the mix now, what else is your biggest concern?"

"We're still concerned about an attack from a lone wolf, Stan. A McVeigh-type. We know there are still people out there like him. Actually, we're told by the FBI there is more risk of this type of attack than ever before."

Stan once again tapped notes on his cell as Kelli continued painting him the dark picture.

"Anti-government groups have increased exponentially all over the country since Obama was elected, and especially here in Arizona. All the intelligence we've been getting from either the Joint Terrorism Task Force or our own sister agency, ACTIC, says it's not an 'if' situation but a 'when.' Both agencies predict there's a high probability it will be some kind of cyber-attack or an attack on our physical infrastructure in some manner by a domestic terrorist, by one of our own, although I hate to call them that."

Stan chimed in. "The dam burst in Tempe could certainly have been perpetrated in this manner."

"Right," Kelli said. "But the scariest part is with the scenario from last night at PV. We've never drilled for an unauthorized intruder there to be an illegal border crosser, one who we have no security data on, which in essence is exactly what happened. That's quite disturbing."

Stan's skin felt cold and his stomach turned queasy. Memories flooded back of when as a boy, gang members chased him on Chicago's South Side, running in fear for his life with no place to hide except out on the dangerous rocks along the lake shore.

"Stan?" Kelli's voice roused him from his fright-filled childhood memory.

"Sorry," he said, snapping back from his daydream. Still trying to push aside the painful feelings from his past, he really wasn't sure he wanted to know more. He asked anyway, "Anything else you want to share with me, Kelli?"

"Yes, there is one more thing FBI profilers have told us. They've said that in order to make a concerted strike on our Arizona infrastructure, to pull something off of this magnitude, that it would take someone with a highly trained military background. In our extreme climate it would also require someone who knows and understands the desert. Someone educated about how to survive out there for long periods of time. Someone extremely patient and willing to wait, perhaps even for years, for just the right moment to strike. He'd also need to know about explosives and perhaps the knowledge of how to breach extremely thick, reinforced concrete walls. And, someone who knows or who has learned all about our state's power and water grids and how they work and inter-relate."

Stan cracked his knuckles in rapid succession as thoughts came rushing into his mind of everything he had read and knew about the missing Paul Stewart—his military explosives training, his Black Ops stints with top-secret status, his civilian work experience with a utility company, and his lengthy, solo sojourns into the Arizona wilderness. Stewart fit the description of Kelli's lone wolf.

She paused before going on, looking to Stan very much like she was already regretting what she was about to say.

"And, lastly, someone who has the belief he's got absolutely nothing to lose."

CHAPTER 8

Later That Same Day

Stan drove south from Phoenix on I-10, Brian riding shotgun. Lefty Frizzell's dulcet voice crooned low on the radio as he sang his heart out about Saginaw, Michigan. Stan wondered if his trip back to the area where Paul Stewart once lived was as foolish as the woeful man digging for gold in the lyrics of Frizzell's country classic.

The investigators were heading to Red Rock, Arizona, a remote, dusty hamlet northwest of Tucson, to meet the town's Chief of Police, Logan Athem. Athem's family had lived in the area since the mid-1800s, one of the region's original white settlers. Stan figured not only would Athem have insight regarding past and present goings on in the sleepy farming community but the chief's extended family, which ran most of the few remaining businesses in town not devastated by the recent economy, might also provide some leads. Stan hoped if anyone had more details about Stewart's life there two decades ago, someone in the Athem clan surely would.

"You really think this is going to get us anything more than we already have, talking to these people again?" Brian asked, staring out the window at the blooming Sonoran desert hugging the roadway's corridor. An earlier rain had brought forth the smell of the creosote bush, saturating the air with its sweet aroma.

"The Athems know everything about anyone who's ever lived in the area. I'll bet they even knew some of the Hohokam before they went extinct."

Brian chuckled. "That's probably not far from the truth. You know, they're kind of funny folks down here. Might get a bit testy, you bringing Stewart's name back up and all."

"What you really mean is they aren't going to like that uppity nigger lawyer from Phoenix coming back and asking more questions again."

"Hey, I didn't say *that*. I'm just saying these people are set in their ways, that's all. You remember the reception you got up there on the Rim all those years ago from Sheriff Lund and his posse when they found Stewart's truck in their backyard."

"How can I forget that? I know the Lunds and the Athems are related and that they're as thick as thieves. They hate me because I'm black and because that's all they know."

"I'm not saying they're right, Stan. I'm just saying these folks are in their own little world. You're rattling the hornet's nest, coming back down here and trying to get info from these yokels. I just don't wanna' see you get stung."

"I appreciate your concern. I do. But I've been fighting prejudice my whole life. I can't let that stand in the way of me doing my job." Stan spoke while keeping his eyes fixed on the unbending ribbon of concrete stretching for miles, the sun's brightness creating a mirage on the road's surface ahead. The visual phenomenon looked like an inland sea, shimmering in the distance.

"How do you do it?"

"Do what?" Stan asked.

"You know. How do you do put up with all the shit? Deal with all the hate and prejudice and still turn the other cheek?" Brian stared over at Stan. "I've never quite figured that out about you. Why you don't hate people more? Why you don't give it right back to them and tell them to stick it where the sun don't shine?"

Stan loved the fact his buddy thought so much about his well-being. Brian cared about him more than his own brothers did, he thought, both of whom Stan hadn't seen since the Kobe family's break up not long after their arrival in Arizona. The brothers hadn't spoken to Stan in decades.

He knew his best friend, the loyal cop, felt pain every time someone called him a nigger behind his back, or for that matter, right to his face. There were too many times to recall when the pair had been involved in an arrest or more often an interrogation when the person in handcuffs called Stan every vulgar epithet imaginable about the blackness of his skin or the nappy texture of his hair. But Brian had never expressed quite so vocally how he felt about all that until now.

"Don't worry about me, buddy," Stan said. "I can handle them."

Brian changed the subject. "Before we left, I ran one of the names you gave me over at the local FBI office for anything unusual going on down here. I spoke to an Agent Schwartz."

"Malori Schwartz? She's good people. One of the top field agents down here."

"Yeah, she said she knew you, too. Said to tell you to be especially careful where we're going. She and her team have Athem and his cronies on their radar. They suspect them of being involved in white supremacist activities in the area."

Stan acknowledged Brian's news with a nod as Frizzell's voice wailed on the radio about looking for something he'd never find. After hearing Brian's warning from Schwartz it made Stan wonder if coming back here again after all these years was just as crazy an idea as Lefty sang about in his sad song. Was Stan looking for a link, searching for clues, where none existed?

After the ninety-minute drive, Stan and Brian arrived at their destination. Stan pulled his Tahoe in front of the police station on Crested Butte Drive. When they entered the first floor of the modern-looking building, the lobby area smelled of burnt coffee. A stodgy, middle-aged woman sat behind a Plexiglas window. She didn't bother to look up when she spoke.

"Who you hear to see?"

If this lady's job responsibility was to make a good first impression, Stan didn't get that from the sound of her curt voice. "Maricopa County Attorney Kobe and Chandler

Detective Hanley for Chief Athem."

"Do you have an appointment?" she droned, looking at them now over the glasses on her nose. She didn't attempt to hide the perturbed look on her face.

"Yes, we do, ma'am." He bit his lip and looked over at Brian, who raised his eyebrows back at him.

The surly woman furled her brow and buzzed them in through the door to her left. "Over there," she said, jerking her thumb back over her shoulder toward the corner behind her.

The two men ambled to an office in the farthest corner. Stan knocked on the open door.

"Detective Hanley. Mister Kobe. Please come in and have a seat."

Logan Athem was a monstrous hulk of a man. Sitting behind his desk, he stood to greet his visitors but his huge frame struggled to release itself from the grip of his undersized chair. Stan guessed he weighed over three-hundred pounds, far too much weight for his five-foot-five height. With the full gray beard and an office isolated in the middle of the desert, he looked like a displaced Viking, sans the horned helmet.

Stan and Brian took a seat in front of the chief's massive oak desk as Athem closed the door behind them. "I hope you don't mind."

In unison, the guests shook their heads.

"I'd really like our conversation to go no further than this room." Athem squeezed himself back into his chair, which emitted a loud creak as if aching in pain. "I don't need to tell you how shocked I was when you told me the reason for your visit, Mister Kobe. People around here have moved on with their lives. We've put the memory of this whole Paul Stewart thing behind us."

"I understand that, Chief Athem."

"Do you, Kobe?" Athem snapped. "Paul Stewart hasn't lived in this area for over a dozen years. Your original investigation didn't turn up a thing on him and his *very* brief time living here. I don't have to tell you how it made people feel in our nice little town when the FBI stayed for weeks, interviewing just about everyone that breathed. Do I?"

"The Stewart family homicides are still officially open cases in our county, Chief. I'm sure I don't need to remind you of that."

"No, you don't, but my job is to protect and serve. That's not just to protect and serve my residents from the bad guys but to also protect them from government harassment. It's one of the main reasons the Tea Party's become so strong in our state. There's no need to be resurrecting Paul Stewart's name around here when we've got much bigger worries, like illegals crossing our border every day, ruining this beautiful country of ours, let alone our precious desert."

Athem swiveled in his chair and waved his hand behind him, across the wall of windows. The plate glass framed a picturesque view of the Ironwood Forest National Monument in the distance. He completed his motion, coming full circle back to the men sitting across from him and slammed his enormous hand on the desk.

"And when you get back to that hell hole of yours up there in Phoenix—and I hope that's sooner than later—tell that FBI agent, Schwartz, the same thing. Quit poking that Jew-bitch nose of hers down here where it don't belong."

Stan straightened up in his chair and leaned on Athem's desk. "Chief, as a professional courtesy this one time, I'll pretend I didn't hear what you just said about Special Agent Schwartz. I didn't come here to open old wounds. We've had a recent homicide in our county that looks suspiciously familiar to the Stewart family deaths ten years ago. It's our duty to investigate. As a brother in law enforcement—"

Athem scoffed at his words, puffing out his chest. "I'm not your *brother*, Kobe. Now, Detective Hanley, I consider him a brother but—"

"But *what?*" Brian demanded.

"Brian." Stan jumped up and halted any further words from his buddy with an open hand. "Thank you for your time, Chief Athem."

Brian remained seated, staring a hole through the bearded

cretin.

"Let's go, Bri," Stan said again, this time urging him with a tap on the shoulder.

Looking reluctant, Brian got up and began to walk out of the office behind Stan. As Stan opened the door, Brian turned back to Athem and said, "You fat, fucking prick. Who the fuck do you think you're talking to? Nobody talks to my friend like that. *Nobody*. Matter of fact, you couldn't be a pimple on my buddy's ass."

*   *   *

Stan spoke first when they got back into the car. "Well, that went well. Shit. I thought he was gonna burst a blood vessel in his neck when you said that he . . ." Stan tried to talk through his laugh. "'Couldn't be a pimple on my buddy's ass?' That's the best you could come up with?"

"Well, the moron really pissed me off . . . I guess that was pretty lame, though. Huh?"

"You're a piece of work, you big dumb Irishman."

"Hey, you weren't saying anything to that bigoted son-of-a-bitch. Somebody had to."

"I don't give a rat's ass about Athem and his beliefs. I do admit, though, any chance of getting something valuable out of him or anyone else around here I'm sure is pretty much shot. What I want is to find Stewart. I came down here to pick up his trail."

Brian shook his head. "I know you've read that case report a hundred times. But I guess Arizona geography is not one of your strengths. You do remember the little detail, don't you, that his trail ended up on the edge of the Mogollon Rim? They found his abandoned truck about three-hundred miles northeast of here. So, what are we doing down here?"

"I know you don't agree but my gut's been telling me the decapitations in Chandler and the Stewart case are connected. I'm not exactly sure how yet, though. I think re-visiting details about the first case can help us solve the new one. I just need a

way to figure out how I'm going to explain to my boss why I'm
re-opening the Stewart cold case."

"I'll go along and presume for a moment they are related.
So? What exactly are we looking for here?"

Stan turned the radio volume all the way down. "When
Stewart was in the military, after he married, he rented a house
nearby in Marana Estates on the east side of I-10. The place
was on a street named West Mogollon Rim Drive." Stan waited
for the "so what" look on Brian's face to wear off, then went
on. "You think that's a coincidence?"

Brian shook him off. "My guess is, yes, very much so."

"Well, yes, most likely it is," Stan smirked. "But you won't
think it's a coincidence when I tell you the property is still
rented in Stewart's name." He didn't wait for Brian to wipe the
look off his face. "So? Where's one of your smart-aleck
comments about that little tidbit of information I just shared?"

"Don't have one. Still in *Stewart's* name, you say?"

"Yep."

"Okay. I give up. What's the catch?"

Stan beamed a wide grin. "The house is rented by *Karl*
Stewart, Paul Stewart's father."

CHAPTER 9

Stan drove into Marana Estates, a trailer park of quaint manufactured homes. The community looked similar to any one of scores dotting the remote desert encircling the greater Tucson area. In front of most of the homes vintage vehicles were parked in carports and Old Glory flew in front of every other double-wide. The whole place reeked of being filled with either patriotic retirees or ex-military personnel.

He pulled up to a home with a wooden placard hung over the carport etched with the name STEWART in a script font.

"How did you find the father?" Brian asked.

"I reached out to one of my pals in D.C. He got me his current address and phone number. I called and Stewart senior said he'd be happy to talk to us."

As Stan and Brian got out of the car, the screen-door inside the carport opened. An elderly man, wearing a blue and white baseball cap, stepped out onto the concrete driveway to greet them. He looked trim and fit but walked with a distinct limp.

"Mister Stewart?" Stan asked.

"Mister Stewart was my father," the man retorted. A cane assisted his slow but steady gait. "Call me Karl."

Stan identified himself and introduced Brian. They all shook hands. Stan noticed the front of Stewart's cap was embroidered in gold stitching with the words VIETNAM VET above the war's green, yellow and red campaign ribbon.

"You fellas want a beer?"

"No thank you, sir. We're on the job. Water would be fine," Brian replied. "But please, go ahead if you want."

"Nope. Not me. Haven't had a drink in ten years. You know, since . . ." The man's voice trailed off as he lowered his head, avoiding eye contact. "Please sit down."

A picnic table, draped with a plastic checkered tablecloth, sat against the back wall of the carport. The day was perfect as the sun gently warmed the white fiberglass roof above them. A cool desert breeze spun through the air. Karl pulled bottles of water from the outside fridge and set them on the table.

"So, I'm curious to know. How'dja' find me?"

"I've got some friends in Washington. They know where every living vet resides."

"Even the ones living on the street?" Stewart's voice dripped with sarcasm. "I'm not surprised by anything our government knows nowadays."

The elderly Stewart sat across from Stan and Brian. He pursed his lips and put a bottle of water to his mouth, taking a small sip. The guests opened their bottles and joined him.

"You said on the phone you wanted to come see me to talk about Paul. Have you found my boy?"

"No, sir," Stan said. "He's still missing. Frankly, he's presumed dead in the eyes of authorities."

Karl looked down at the table. "Still missing after ten years. Presumed dead, you say." He shook his head while looking off in the distance. "Just don't sound like my Paul."

"Why is that?" Stan asked.

"Oh, I don't know. Just my gut." Karl looked back and forth between them. "See, Paul, well, he's always been a survivor."

Stan gave him a respectful nod. "I know that, sir. I'm familiar with his military record."

"Oh heck, man. I'm not talkin' about what those military bastards trained him for with all that damn survival school stuff. Paul survived *me*."

Stan's puzzled look begged for an explanation to Karl's statement.

"You see, I was in bad shape when I got back from 'Nam. When I went in-country, I was a hotshot flyboy. Flew the F-100

Super Sabre. Fastest plane around. We all thought we were invincible. Then the unthinkable happened. I got shot down. Spent four years . . . hellacious years . . . at the wonderful Hanoi Hilton. If I told you the details of what my captors did to me, you'd never believe me."

Karl took his hat off. Scars riddled his scalp from his forehead to the back of his bald head. Stan and Brian winced.

"Yeah, it still sometimes feels as bad as it looks. Besides the limp, this gift up here is a little something the Viet Cong left me with as a remembrance. They poured boiling oil over my head as they held me over a snake pit, trying to make me talk, to break me. They succeeded. But that pain was nothing compared to what I suffered after hearing about the loss of my grandchildren and daughter-in-law and how it happened."

Stan shook his head. "I can't imagine your pain."

"I eventually escaped 'Nam, but came home a broken man. Looking the way I did, I didn't believe my wife could ever love me anymore. Didn't realize until after she left me she could handle the physical scars but the emotional shit I piled on her was too much. Within six months of being home I started taking it out on her and Paul. Years later, after they both were gone, I wish I'd never escaped. That I woulda' just died there, a hero, rather than come back the way I did."

"Didn't the Air Force help you?" Brian asked.

"Fuck the military and fuck the VA." He slammed his fist on the table, almost knocking over their open bottles of water. "I saw too many ex-soldiers go to those bastards for help and all they did was make them wait. Then, when the doctors finally do get to you, it's too late. All they can do then is fill you with dope and lock you in a room. I wasn't gonna' be wrapped-up in no strait-jacket the rest of my life. Lookin' back, though, maybe I shoulda' done it. Might have saved my kid. And . . . I would have had two grandchildren to visit me rather than me visiting their graves."

Stan and Brian remained silent as Karl went on with his story. The old man struggled to hold back tears.

"If . . . I could just see my boy one more time . . . talk to him and tell him how sorry I am for what I did to him and his moth . . ."

Stan pulled his handkerchief from his pocket and offered it to the man.

Karl took it and rubbed the corners of his eyes. A car pulled up to the curb and an elderly African-American woman stepped out. "Excuse me a minute, will you?" Karl handed the handkerchief back to Stan, composed himself, and went down the driveway to her. The lady handed him some grocery bags. They exchanged a few unheard words before joining Stan and Brian.

"Gentlemen, this is my wife, Charisse."

Stan and Brian stood to greet her. She waved her hand at them. "Please, gentlemen, sit, sit. My honey bunny here told me you were coming so I went to the store to pick up a few things. I didn't expect you so soon." She turned to Karl and took the bag of groceries back from him. "Talk to your guests, dear. I'll be inside making some lemonade and sandwiches."

After the door closed behind her, Karl spoke in a hushed voice. "She's what saved me, ya' know. Hadn't been for that woman's love, no tellin' where I'd have ended up. She got me on the straight and narrow. Supported me while I got back on my feet. But that wasn't justification enough for my Paul. He never understood how an old ridge-runner like me could end up with a black woman after all my years of preaching bigotry to him, telling him to hate nig . . . oh, sorry, my apologies. Old habits are hard to break. I vowed to not use that word ever again."

"No apology necessary," Stan replied, sensing the man had led a life full of contradictions. Stan nodded for Karl to continue.

"I filled Paul with all that misguided animosity. Couple that with the way I treated him and his mother. Well, it's no wonder he snapped. All Paul ever wanted was to be like his old man. Be just like me. But when he found out after coming back from Bosnia that I was with Charisse, he thought I deceived him. That I was a hypocrite. 'How could you?' he asked me over and over."

He paused, grief wrinkling his face more than age. He took a sip of water. Then he continued with his emotion-filled soliloquy.

"Unfortunately, when he was young and impressionable I had focused on preaching hate and bigotry to him and not compassion and tolerance. He called me a fraud. Said how he regretted all the time he had wasted, staying with me, helping his drunken old man. He was devastated. It was if I'd hit him in the chest with a sledgehammer, that's how hard he felt my betrayal. His rage made him insane. Everything he believed in, trusted in his life, came crumbling down in one fell swoop. How could his father be *in love* with people I had taught him to despise?"

The elderly man stopped, punctuating his pain with a low moan. He took another sip of water before going on.

"Paul came back state-side after doing all of those missions, all of that Air Force bomb stuff, doing things I know he could never share with me or anyone. When I told him I loved Charisse and wanted to marry her, he was livid. He lost his mind."

Karl stopped and caught his breath. Stan could feel his pain but hoped his cathartic story was helping to cleanse the father of his guilt. Karl struggled but went on.

"Paul didn't know what to do, how to react. He was filled with so much rage. But rather than deal with that hate and let it go, he sank deeper. Dug his heels in. He yelled at me as he left the house that day down in Florida, *'I'll show you! I'll show you what hate really is!'* I'll never forget those words. I found out later he ended up at the Air Force base near here. My guess is he wanted to get as far away from me as he could. Later, he forbid me to see my grandchildren."

The elder Stewart wiped the corner of his eyes with the palm of his hand.

"That's about the same time he got involved with that group. Bad people. Folks who'd rather hate and fill each other with poisonous thoughts more than anything else. One day, the

Air Force cleared me to come on the base. I went to see him but he'd have no part of me. Wouldn't allow his hatred to leave him. Thank God his wife, Stacey, never felt like he did. When he left the Air Force and went up to Phoenix she would meet me half-way in Casa Grande just so I could see my grandkids. Several times, when he'd go away on his camping trips alone with his dog, I'd drive up to Scottsdale and see the three of them and stay there for a few days. Stacey was wonderful. I miss her so. She loved my son with all her heart. He was a lucky man."

As Stan listened to Karl's sorrowful tale, he knew all too well the deep emotional pain brought on by family disintegration. He wished he could offer the man more than a dry handkerchief. Yet, Stan sensed that by merely being there—listening, letting the old guy pour out his grief—he was giving him some small measure of help toward healing and coping with the loss of his first marriage and the deaths of his daughter-in-law and grandkids. And, as everyone presumed, the death of his only son.

"When Paul and his family moved up to Scottsdale, I moved into this place. It's their old house. But I'm sure you know that," Karl said. "It's the one they lived in while he was stationed at Davis-Monthan. I guess in some small way it was my way of staying linked with him, coming here to live."

He paused and stared out at the empty street for a moment. Then he returned his attention just to Stan, looking him right in the eye.

"When you find my boy . . . my Paul . . . when you find him . . . I need you to let me know right away. Won't you, Mister Kobe?

Stan stared back and nodded.

Then Karl dropped a bomb of his own on him. "I'm a lawyer. I've passed the Arizona bar and am licensed to practice law in the state. I plan to represent my son when he's found. A man, even one reviled as much as him, is presumed innocent until proven guilty. Everyone seems to have forgotten that tenet, though. But I sense you haven't and that you'll honor that."

As a father, Stan understood the man's loyalty but did question his sanity of appointing himself legal counsel for the missing felon.

Karl Stewart returned his gaze to the street. "You know . . . he's out there somewhere . . . I can *feel* it . . . a father knows that sort of thing."

Stan agreed with the man's intuition, feeling the tug grow in his own gut that Paul Stewart was still alive, too. If that was true, then Stan vowed to be the first one to find him.

CHAPTER 10

Outskirts of Red Rock, Arizona
Near The Ironwood Forest National Monument

When Stan and Brian pulled away from Karl Stewart's manufactured home in Marana Estates, neither spoke. Just before leaving, Stan had promised the anguished Stewart that he'd find his son and, when he did, Karl would be the first call he made.

Minutes went by before Brian broke the silence inside the SUV. "They teach us from day one at the academy not to make promises to families we know we can't keep."

"I couldn't help myself. The man not only lost his son but his grandkids and his daughter-in-law. When he said the pain of losing them all on the same day was worse than all the time he spent as a POW . . . well, I nearly lost it myself."

While he drove, Stan flashed back to what he had lost and how he had suffered after witnessing the murder of his close friend. A man who had befriended and mentored him, an elderly man not much different in age at the time than Karl Stewart was now. The pain and all the bad memories of what had transpired came rushing back.

He pushed aside his ugly feelings from the past and worked to stay focused on what he had just heard from the father, especially the unusual request to act as legal counsel for his own son. For now, he placed that potentially controversial situation into the back of his mind and shared with Brian a bigger issue bugging him.

"After talking to his dad . . . I don't know . . . I keep

thinking we missed something basic all those years ago when Stewart disappeared off the Rim."

"What are you feeling, buddy?"

"I'm not sure. But after what we heard from his father, well, something just doesn't add up."

Stan drove west on Avra Valley Road, heading toward the Ironwood Forest National Monument. "What his old man said about the whole survivor thing is still ringing in my ears. Paul Stewart trained in one of the military's elite programs, Explosive Ordnance Disposal, as well as trained as a para-jumper. His record also said he was schooled as a combat control technician."

"That's a pretty heavy resume. What my crime scene technician Mary Ann said about that piece she found makes his EOD training intriguing, and I know what a para-jumper is. But what's this combat control technician thing?"

"They're called CCT's. Guys who go in early, often by parachute, behind enemy lines. They call in the air strikes and shoot the laser for pilots to their target. I was thinking how maybe all of his highly specialized training might have once been an instrument for good but later might have been turned into an instrument for evil. Hearing what his father had to say about his son's inability to accept his old man's change of heart about hating African-Americans . . . then his father marries a black person . . . that obviously devastated Stewart. It may have very well been the thing that pushed him over the edge."

Brian shrugged. "So, how do you think it all ties in?"

"Our County Attorney's Office got a briefing earlier this month. The state's been doing some first responder training scenarios with Homeland Security in a remote area not far from here, revolving around an attack on Palo Verde."

"That's one scary thought. If terrorists hit our nuclear power plant that would *not* be good."

"That's an understatement," Stan replied. "Palo Verde is the largest nuclear plant in the country. Striking it could have a ripple effect on the electric grid from Washington State to Texas, even into Mexico. And a potential radiation leak could contaminate not only the air but ground water, too. I researched where Arizona is part of the Great Basin and Range Aquifer, which stretches from Mexico to Oregon. *Over two-hundred-thousand square miles* could be affected."

"Well, I take back now what I said earlier about you being a geography neophyte."

Stan chuckled at Brian's wisecrack as the SUV cruised along a deserted stretch of Pinal County back road. Ahead of them was the heart of the pristine Ironwood Forest National Monument, stretching across the endless horizon before them. The federal land was home to the densest growth of saguaro cacti in the world. This beautiful yet formidable part of the Sonoran desert didn't stop the area from becoming one of the most active routes for illegals making their unlawful passage from Mexico to the Phoenix. Stan noticed Bureau of Land Management placards on posts along the shoulder, advising drivers not to pick-up hitchhikers. The twisted arms of the giant saguaros, which dwarfed the warning signs, looked as if they were signaling motorists with a cautionary wave, telling them to be wary of doing such a thing.

"I've got an odd feeling we're not out here sight-seeing," Brian said.

"Like I was telling you, Stewart had cross-trained in more than one exclusive EOD Air Force units. Two were para-jumper and combat control technician. He also spent time training in a group named Red Horse. It's a division of the civil engineering command and supports demo ops."

Brian's voice rose in concern. "Demolition operations?"

"Yep. Teams trained to breach walls and take down bridges."

"That's intriguing."

"That isn't the half of it. My friend Kelli Begay is running the Arizona Department of Emergency Management now. I went over and had a talk with her, following up on some thoughts I had after a presentation she made to our office. She told me that ever since nine-eleven they've been worried about a terrorist breach at Palo Verde or at one of our state's dams.

Everything would be effected—telecommunications, Internet, the whole western U.S. electric grid. There'd be no way for first responders to communicate with each other if any of this happened."

"Shit. That ain't good," Brian said. "And Stewart figures into this how?"

"It would take someone like Stewart with expert knowledge in how to detonate explosives *and* a special ops background to coordinate an attack like that. A highly-trained soldier."

"Stan, we're all familiar with ex-military guys going whacko but what you're talking about would take a whole team of people to pull-off something that elaborate. Where would Stewart find people like this?"

"Out here." Stan waved his hand over the steering wheel, across the width of the windshield of his over-sized vehicle. "Where else can you find people, desperate to survive, willing to do anything to make their way to freedom?"

"You're not serious, are you?"

Stan rebuffed his friend's remark. "Believe me, my theory's not so far-fetched."

"Let me get this straight. First, your theory has Paul Stewart alive, reappearing after being on the lam for ten years. Next, he somehow intercepts illegal Mexican Nationals travelling north through the desert. Then he recruits them and convinces them to help him blow up highly secure targets. Do I have that about right?" He waited for Stan's reply. None came. "And you're saying that's not far-fetched?"

Stan shrugged, feeling a bit deflated by Brian's frank assessment of his wild theory.

"And anyway, since nine-eleven, where do you imagine he'd put his hands on the amount of explosives he'd need to do all this?" Brian asked. "The FBI keeps a close track on that kind of stuff now. If he farted while trying to score some, they'd sniff him out."

Stan wasn't sure if he should lay out the next part of his way-out-on-a-ledge theory. If Brian thought the Paul Henry

Stewart-illegal Mexicans connection was already a bit over-the-top, the second part might make Brian think he had lost all his marbles.

Stan sat up straight behind the wheel, stretching out a longer than usual pause. Finally, he answered. "Now hear me out all the way on this, okay?"

Brian raised his eyebrows but nodded.

"Do you remember back in late nineties when that Air Force pilot, flying an A-10 Thunderbolt out of Davis-Monthan, went off course during flight?"

"Sounds familiar."

"Captain Benjamin Forster was participating in a training exercise. His A-10 was loaded with live ammunition and bombs and took off with some other A-10s, headed north, northwest. Minutes into the flight, he peeled off formation, leaving the other pilots in his dust. The guy started flying all over the northern half of the state, completely on his own."

"Yeah. Now I remember this. They guy even went off NORAD radar for a short period, right?"

"Right. Right. Good, you remember it. Well listen up. There's more. So, like I said, he flew in this erratic, nonsensical pattern for almost an hour, covering almost a thousand miles. The last two points the Air Force had him on radar was just east and north of the Mogollon Rim. The other just south and east of the Great Sand Dunes National Monument in Colorado. Then he completely disappeared off the radar screen. *Poof! Gone!* It took the Air Force weeks to figure out exactly where he ended up by triangulating the final bits of data they had recorded when radar operators out of Peterson Air Force Base in Colorado Springs last painted a signal on him. Then they made an educated guess as to where they think his plane went down."

Stan took a deep breath before rattling on, excitement building in his voice with each detail he revealed.

"They focused on the Sangre de Cristo Wilderness just west of Pueblo and east of Alamosa, Colorado. When they eventually found the plane, a select team of recovery specialists from the Air Force went in. They recovered Forster's remains and completed an exhaustive search for the war bird's armaments. All of the ammunition from his 30mm Gatling cannon was found intact. Scattered, but all there on the ground surrounding the wreckage. That fighter plane carried over a thousand rounds. But every single one was accounted for. Not one round was missing."

Brian jumped in. "Is all this leading somewhere?"

"Oh yeah. Now get this." Stan's voice ramped up another notch. "Like I said, they found all the rounds of live munitions, but the recovery team never found the four, live Mk82 bombs he had under his wings."

"Really?"

"Yep, really. No sign of the bombs. Not a one. And no reports on the ground from military or civilian personnel of them being detonated anywhere along his recorded flight path. The Air Force even checked with the National Geological Survey for any unusual readings from their Advanced National Seismic Survey. That group has sensors scattered throughout the Four Corners area. Nothing reported from any of them. Not a blip. Each of those bombs weighed over five-hundred pounds. If Forster had dropped them and they exploded, these sensors would have definitely picked them up. Yet those bombs were nowhere to be found and haven't been found since."

"The Air Force believed this pilot committed suicide, right?"

"That was the Air Force's official ruling. They supposedly found a suicide note but they never released it."

Another long pause occurred between the two men as if each was waiting for the other to speak first. Brian broke the silence.

"I have a feeling you haven't told me the real hook of this story yet, have you?"

Stan smiled, knowing he had reeled Brian in with his tale.

"Spit it out, Stan."

"On that Air Force recovery team that went in after they

found the A-10, there was just one lone EOD technician. Paul Henry Stewart."

"*Stewart* was on the recovery team?"

Stan nodded, grinning ear-to-ear.

"So? What about these never found bombs?" Brian asked.

A loud boom outside their car was followed by the sound of shattering glass from the Tahoe's windshield. Shards from a thousand pieces of cut glass fell upon the two occupants. Stan squeezed his eyes closed and grabbed the wheel hard with both hands as he slammed on the brakes. The vehicle swerved off the road, tearing up the gravel of the soft shoulder. Then it careened down the embankment before coming to an abrupt halt, nose-down in a ditch.

CHAPTER 11

Red Rock, Arizona
Thirteen Years Earlier, April 1998

During Paul Stewart's time stationed at Davis-Monthan Air Base, he attended many more meetings of the Aryan Sons of Arizona at Wilma's Red Rock Tap House. But talk had been floating around, especially among ASA regulars, that the FBI had put the fifty-year-old establishment under surveillance. After the Oklahoma City bombing, a heightened awareness by federal authorities to expose homegrown extremists fueled suspicion of groups like theirs who harbored extreme ideologies of hate. This new consciousness prompted the feds to put a bull's-eye target on the back of the tavern and place the ASA squarely in its crosshairs.

When Stewart got wind of the rumors, he began limiting his attendance, but not before becoming an officer in Jacob Jeffrey Lund's Church of the High Country army. Then, one night, the tavern mysteriously imploded and burned to the ground. The local proprietor had conspicuously left town several days prior to the fire, making the whole event stink of arson.

Even though Wilma's was under federal surveillance, a formal investigation—the responsibility of Pinal County authorities—never materialized. County fire inspectors did term the fire "suspicious" but never determined the exact cause. In the end, lack of substantive evidence precluded the local county's prosecutor from getting an arson case off the ground.

* * *

In the Baca Grande Region of Colorado

A few months prior to the fire at Wilma's, Stewart had received a personal invitation, extended to him personally by Jacob Lund, to come to his secretive commune, Tarshish. Even though from all outward appearances Stewart looked the epitome of bravery and strength. But underneath the self-assured exterior lay a hurting man, one buried in gambling debt. Desperate, he needed help. Still saddled with the feeling of abandonment from own father's betrayal, he yearned for a mentor. A fatherly figure he could turn to and fill his emotional void.

During that first stay in southeastern Colorado, where Tarshish was located, Jacob Lund filled that emptiness and Stewart fully succumbed to the spell and influence of the bigoted Lund. The old man's rants on the importance of white supremacy and the mad man's plans for stopping the feared destruction of the Aryan race mesmerized the airman.

"I created Tarshish as a place to come to reenergize myself. The Lord Yahweh speaks to me here," Lund said to Stewart during one of his many subsequent visits to the remote sanctuary, a virtual island set against the base of the Rocky Mountains.

Stewart and Lund walked along a stone path Jacob had created with the help from members of his Church of the High Country, the cover name he used for his religious sect when he had first registered the entity as a non-profit corporation. Aided by a cane, Lund meandered through the maze of rocks left over from the days prior to his owning the land when hippies had camped in the area. The societal drop-outs had used small boulders to create a healing footpath. Contrary to the real purpose of a labyrinth—to meditate upon peace and harmony in the world—the radical zealot circled through the stones thinking of ways to manifest violence and hatred against those he despised.

"How so?" Stewart asked.

"He communicates with me here in so many different ways, Brother Paul. Sometimes he sends me messengers. Like you. I knew the Lord Yahweh had sent you to me the first time I saw you that night in Red Rock. To be one of my finest disciples."

The other oddity about the elderly man was that his speech many times sounded stilted when he spoke, as if he measured every syllable for each word that sprung from his mouth.

"And . . . like the time he sent me . . . Brother David."

"Brother David?" Stewart asked. "Will I get to meet him?"

"Oh no, no. I'm afraid not. The Brother David I speak of came here long ago, when I first created Tarshish. He inspired me greatly during his one and only visit. Brother David had promised he would come back and we would finish the plans we had made here. But, the heathens struck him down along with his family at Waco."

Stunned by the story, Stewart stuttered his reply. "This Brother . . . David . . . you speak of . . . was David Koresh? He came *here?* To *Tarshish?*"

"Yes. It is so. We walked right along this same path, which I later enlarged in tribute to his memory, using only the most beautiful and brightest red stones I could find from these very mountains." Lund pointed to the nearby Sangre de Cristo range, towering to the east, high above them. These mountains rose over 14,000 feet against an exquisite, deep blue Colorado sky, the massifs of its peaks shimmering in the bright sunlight. "He loved the Sangre de Cristos so very much from the first, and sadly, only time he saw them."

"I haven't heard this story from Brother Logan or Brother Micah."

"Although they knew of Brother David's visit they would not have told you. I have commanded those who have heard of

Brother David's visit to keep this silent within their hearts. If any of them were to break their vow, they would suffer the gravest of consequences."

The threat-filled talk didn't surprise Stewart. He had already heard several stories of Jacob's trigger temper, along with rumors of his having commanded holes dug in the desert for anyone who opposed him or threatened to escape his inner sanctum.

"I am the only one who can choose with whom this story is shared," Jacob said, "and I have only shared it with those two, one other believer, and now with you. Only those closest to me. Those within my circle of trust, of which, I'm happy to say, I have now invited you to enter."

"I don't know what to say. I'm humbled."

"'Many are called, but few are chosen,' sayeth the Lord."

"Matthew twenty-two, fourteen," Stewart said.

"That's correct. But probably the most important message in Matthew twenty-two comes in verse twelve, when the king casts out the wedding guest for not wearing his wedding clothes. Cast out into the darkness."

"I know the passage well. 'Tie him hand and foot, and throw him outside, into the darkness, where there will be the weeping and gnashing of teeth.' But forgive me, Jacob. I'm not sure why you quote this passage."

Lund took pause in their conversation. As he continued his slow walk, he looked again to the mountain range only a few miles away. He stopped on the stone-lined path and turned his piercing eyes to his student. "Listen closely, Brother Paul, to what I tell you here and now. 'Then he said to his servants, *The wedding banquet is ready, but those I invited did not deserve to come. So go to the street corners and invite to the banquet anyone you find.* So the servants went out into the streets and gathered all the people they could find, the bad as well as the good, and the wedding hall was filled with guests.'"

Stewart stood at his side, looking at him, uncertain what Lund's words meant. He still reeled from the surprise of being invited inside his circle. His teacher's stare back at him seemed to reach all the way down into the deepest part of his soul. A part of himself he had lost.

"I know of your pain. Pain caused by your birth father co-mingling with African blood," Lund said. "I also know of your gambling addiction and your whoring down in Nogales."

Stewart was stunned, wondering how Lund knew not only his troubles with his father but secrets about his personal life.

Lund went on. "There will come a day where I will ask you to do your duty, just as you so dutifully served your sick and drunken father. A father, I might add, who abandoned you. I, your new father, will never abandon you."

Lund turned away and began to walk again, staying silent for another fifty yards. He moved outside the labyrinth. His disciple followed him. When they reached a ridge of sand, they climbed its soft ten-foot slope. At the top, the old man stopped again, this time pointing to the horizon. The wide base of a much higher sand dune rose hundreds of feet in the air ahead of them. Lund pointed to the dune and the crystal-clear, blue sky above the drift.

"It was here where I received my inspiration. When Brother David visited and stood right on this very place with me. The exact spot where you stand now."

Stewart looked down to the ground and stared at his military boots. He paid close attention to Lund's next words.

"It is here where it came to me how we shall strike at the multi-headed serpent. It is here where the Lord Yahweh revealed what task there was ahead for me and my followers. For my chosen ones. And it shall be you, Brother Paul Stewart, who will be at the very tip of the Lord Yahweh's spear. It is you who will deliver the tools to complete our calling. Deliver unto me one of his fiery angels!"

CHAPTER 12

Stewart kept repeating Jacob Lund's last words in his head as he stood next to his leader.

And it shall be you, Brother Paul Stewart, who will be at the very tip of the Lord

Yahweh's spear. It is you who will deliver the tools to complete our calling. Deliver unto

me one of his fiery angels!

He had no idea what the man was talking about. The elder Lund often spoke in this manner, regularly quoting obscure passages of Scripture, an ostensible challenge for his followers to know their Bible verses backward and forward.

"I'm not sure what you're referring to," Stewart sheepishly replied to his Aryan mentor.

Lund's fatherly tone and calm manner of speech changed. "It's quite simple. Don't think too much into it. I will tell you, though, that I have quite a sphere of influence with many powerful friends in very high places. Places you'd never think someone like me could reach to get the information I need. As you are now aware, I know all about your personal background. Besides your debt and your cheating, I've been briefed on your entire military career. Even your secret assignments for the Air Force in Bosnia, helping the CIA. I also am aware of what you do now at Davis-Monthan and why you transferred there. Most importantly, I know your role with the A-10 Warthogs, working on the ground crew and having access to all the various munitions. I wondered when I read about you, why that role? Then I found out about what happened with the psychologist when you left Bosnia for the last time. He deserved the beating you gave him because he was a coward just like the coward fighter pilot who left your father's wing in Vietnam. Left it unprotected, letting your father be shot down and tortured for all those years."

Stewart was speechless. He was overwhelmed by all the details the man new about his life.

"You and I both know, don't we, Paul, that it's no coincidence that both of those cowards were black men."

Stewart nodded an affirmation, his face still showing shock.

"Don't be surprised by my gift of knowing all things, my son. Because I know, too, how weak your own father was to you as a boy and the especially sickening act he's perpetrated against you by making that negress his new wife."

Stewart was unnerved. The elderly man's controlling presence actually made him feel helpless, something he hadn't really experienced since his last failed assignment in Bosnia. Lund's charisma overpowered him.

"Bring me the fiery angel, Brother Paul. The A-10 that breathes smoke from its mouth. Bring the beast to my doorstep here. Bring me its spears—its bombs—so that we may use them against the heathen invaders of our land; against a government who has no concern, no belief in the importance of protecting its white citizens, its chosen ones, like you and me. Bring the beast to me so we can use it explosives and strike down men like your father who exchange their bodily fluids with non-whites."

Stewart was dumbstruck by the magnitude of the request. If he complied and was caught, he'd certainly be court martialed and most likely imprisoned. But Lund's power over him was too strong. The old man was right on about all the points he made about his father. He still harbored hatred for what his father had done to him and for the hypocrite he had become. Still, he wasn't sure he could be part of such a nefarious act, an act with high probability of being considered treason by the U.S. government.

Not wanting to show his leader his shock over his request, yet alone his complete fear now of the man, he tried to stay calm when he gave his innocent sounding reply. "I'm not sure what you're asking me, sir."

Lund's tone was short and to the point, void of hyperbole. "As I said, it's a very modest request. I want you to divert one of your A-10 Thunderbolts, fully-armed, here, to these very sands before us." Lund extended his arm and waved it across the dunes. "Bring one right here. Have the pilot drop his unexploded bombs so we can retrieve them and use them to strike against the Goliath." He placed his open palm on Stewart's back.

The shiver of fear Stewart felt down his spine was like nothing he'd ever felt before, not even when he had performed some of his most dangerous missions. Lund's cold hand sent a chill directly into Stewart's bones, racing through him as if he'd been touched by the devil himself. The feeling scared him more than he'd ever been frightened before.

Stewart stuttered his answer, "What? That's . . . that's . . . an . . . impossibility!"

"You're a highly skilled explosive ordnance disposal technician. Trained by the most deceptive and secretive organization in the world, the U.S. military. You'll think of something. Plus, you'll be compensated extremely well." He stepped a few feet away from Stewart and surveyed the landscape. Some of the dunes rose hundreds of feet into the sky. He lifted both arms above his head and pointed his hands skyward, shouting, "Bring me the fiery angel in from the east, the one who breathes fire from its belly. Bring the beast and his bombs to these sands of my Tarshish so we can use them to strike back against our enemies."

Still overcome at the sheer immensity and improbability of completing such a task, Stewart gasped for air before replying to Lund. "I wouldn't know how to accomplish such a task. What you're asking for is impossible. To have an A-10 pilot knowingly drop his bombs here in the sand for us to use against the country he's vowed to serve and defend . . ."

As Stewart's voice trailed off, Lund turned around and approached Stewart. The old man put his weathered yet still strong hands on the shoulders of the younger man. Lund squeezed hard with his open palms. A sinister smile came over his face.

Stewart held back a grimace from the pain. As he stared back at Lund, he wondered what

this maniacal extremist might do or say next.

"Such a look, Paul. Why? Where is your imagination, son? Your record shows that you're an extremely resourceful man."

The man's compliment gave Stewart a small boost of encouragement. His anxiety momentarily subsided.

"Perhaps you may have misunderstood me," Lund said. "Who in the world ever suggested that I'm asking this pilot to *knowingly* do such a thing? I'm sure you'll figure out how to do what I have asked."

Lund released his grip on Stewart's shoulders and clasped him in a bear hug embrace. As Lund squeezed the air from Stewart's lungs, Paul closed his eyes and made a silent prayer.

CHAPTER 13

Paul Stewart had been placed in a most uncomfortable position—physically and emotionally. He knew Lund would never take no for an answer. Aside from the rumors, in his brief time knowing him, he had seen Jacob, as well as his son, Micah, and nephew, Logan Athem, mete out punishment on members of the group who didn't toe the line. If Stewart didn't cooperate, he fully believed that putting out the word to dig a hole for his body somewhere in the desert was something that would readily be carried out.

Stewart, however, didn't plan on becoming a missing person. That's because, down deep, he was not totally adverse to Jacob Lund's idea. In fact, the more he thought of it, the more it intrigued him, especially if there was cash in doing it. The crazy man's money would certainly help with his mounting Indian casino gambling debts. Give him a chance to double-down and score big.

Since first meeting Logan, when he had been asked by the big man to consider smuggling out explosives from Davis-Monthan, Stewart had given the group a sympathetic ear. He had already made a few items go "missing," as he had later stated in his official munitions control reports. And the money Logan had given him for doing that was well worth the effort. He wondered how much Jacob would offer him for more than one-hundred times the high explosives he'd given the ASA so far.

He never imagined in his wildest dreams he'd someday get a request to supply Lund's ASA with four, five-hundred-pound Mk82 bombs. That type of high profile ordnance couldn't just end-up mysteriously lost—at least not easily as the C-4 and a handful of blasting caps Stewart had already supplied to Logan and his ASA operatives to derail a train south of Phoenix.

Stewart was maddened by Lund's arrogance in presuming a highly trained and strictly regimented A-10 pilot would just fly his plane—one he cherished and loved sometimes more than his wife or girlfriend—off course and drop four bombs at Lund's doorstep. His request was either the epitome of the bigot's own conceit or just sheer lunacy.

Yet, as wild as it seemed to him, during his return drive to Tucson from Tarshish, Stewart began running scenarios through his mind of possible ways to send an A-10 Thunderbolt off course. Perhaps he could divert one during a training exercise. As a ground crew member and chief munitions officer, Stewart was mindful all flights were closely monitored by instructional pilots. But he also knew many times things went awry, especially with rookie drivers.

But Stewart would need a very sophisticated plan. More than merely attempting to send a newbie pilot erroneously off course. There would need to be a very good reason why a multi-million dollar aircraft, with a highly intelligent officer behind the rudder, would pull off formation, fly hundreds of miles to the Baca Grande in Colorado, and drop their bombs into the sand near Jacob Lund's Tarshish compound at the base of the Sangre de Cristo Mountains.

Stewart would need to create an extraordinary ruse, one that wouldn't be questioned—at least not as it happened—in order to give him enough time to pull off such an elaborate deception.

He did say the pilot didn't have to knowingly agree to do it.

Stewart's challenge—and not a niggling one—presented by Jacob was clear: figure out exactly how to pull off a seemingly insurmountable assignment. All Stewart had to do was create a way to get one of the military's most dedicated and intelligent personnel—an Air Force fighter pilot—to unwittingly supply bombs to fellow Americans who wanted to kill people in the pilot's own country, one which he had sworn with an unbreakable vow to defend.

Could I possibly pull this off?

Several Black Ops mission popped into his mind, which he had successfully executed, each more elaborate and involved than this. Behind enemy lines, no less. Although Lund truly scared him, Stewart had performed missions where much more significant danger had threatened him than just a fanatical old man bent on destruction.

You know, if there's anybody who could do this, it's me.

CHAPTER 14

In The Ironwood Forest National Monument
Present Day, April 15, 2011

Its windshield missing, Stan's Tahoe sat ass-end up in a shallow retention ditch in the middle of one of the most desolate regions of the Sonoran desert. When the windshield imploded, it seemed to Stan as though a million tiny shards of glass had showered down upon him and Brian.

The moment the car had come to a throbbing halt Brian leapt out, his Glock drawn from its shoulder holster under his windbreaker. He crouched now behind the open door.

"You okay?" he shouted to Stan, who remained strapped in the vehicle.

Stan nodded. He felt dazed but didn't think he was injured.

"Get out of that seat-belt and crawl over here," Brian instructed, looking around and out into the surrounding desert landscape. Teddy bear cholla, twenty-deep and as many wide, stood at attention, like soldiers guarding the horizon. The cacti shimmered gold in the mid-day sun as the ever-present wind honed needles hypodermic-sharp inside paper-thin sheaths.

Stan obeyed Brian's order. He crawled along the front seat and inched himself out of the vehicle. He squatted against the side of the car. "What hit us?" he asked.

"Don't know." Brian checked him over. "No blood. You look okay on the outside. Anything hurt on the inside?"

Stan rubbed the left side of his scalp. "I think I hit my head."

"Nothin' up there. No loss," Brian quipped. "Stay here. I'm going to take a look around."

Stan watched Brian creep hunched over military-style around the propped-open door, gun pointed out in front of him.

Brian stopped at the front of the car and peered around the fender, looking toward where they had been heading. Stan surmised, too, that whatever hit them must have come from in front of them.

He watched Brian scan the horizon, then called out in a hushed voice, "Do you see anything?" While waiting for Brian's answer, he took out a pen and small pad from his coat pocket, glanced at his watch, and jotted a note. When he looked up from his notepad, he no longer saw his partner. "Brian?"

No answer.

He raised his voice a bit higher. "Bri? What's up? You see anything out there?"

Stan rose up from his crouched position, pen in one hand and pad in the other.

"Don't move, *Señor!*"

The voice from behind Stan startled him. He spun around.

Hispanic male, five-foot-seven, thin-build, wisps of black hair dotting his chin and upper lip.

Stan memorized his mental note.

A man stood at the back of the Tahoe pointing an AK47 assault rifle right at Stan's head. The gunman wore a baseball cap with an Arizona Diamondbacks logo. A quite pronounced sweat stain ringed the hat above the brim.

Not waiting to be asked, Stan raised his hands above his head, his writing tools still clasped in them. As he did, Brian came around the front of the Tahoe. Stan turned and saw Brian followed by a tall, muscular, white male dressed in Army fatigues. This man, too, sported an assault rifle but this one was clearly stenciled with U.S. GOVERNMENT. The barrel had a PEQ-15 night vision laser targeting unit mounted on top.

Blond-hair tucked under a camouflage hat, he wore sunglasses and a blue bandana, curled around his neck, covering the lower part of his face. The outfit made him look like a Hollywood-inspired version of an albino-looking Mexican *bandito.*

He spoke in Spanish to the Mexican-looking man holding the gun on Stan. *"Amigos, Jaime! Son los amigos!"*

CHAPTER 15

A short time ago, Stan had decided to take beginner's Spanish lessons at the Scottsdale Library. He didn't think the first time he'd need to formally speak the language would be while a rifle was pointed squarely at him, and another at his partner's back.

"*Son los amigos?* We're your friends?" Stan shouted his next words at them. "My friends don't point guns at my head!"

You can lower your hands, sir," the blond-haired man said. "Detective Hanley here told me who you are. We're on your side."

The man spoke perfect English with a Midwestern accent. He pulled down the bandana covering his mouth. For a split-second, Stan thought he had stumbled upon the fugitive Paul Stewart and that the felon on the run had fallen right into his lap. He wondered if the bump on his head was responsible for making him think that or if the thought was brought about as a result of wanting so desperately to find the man after just meeting his father.

"We saw you guys fly off the road after your windshield blew out. We were in our Humvee, sitting behind a stand of mesquite. Over there." The man motioned with his head toward the vehicle down the road. "Do you know what hit you?"

Stan and Brian shook their heads.

Perplexed, Stan asked, "Who are you guys?"

"UC Border Patrol." The man barely moved his lips.

Brian raised his eyebrows. "Undercover Border Patrol?"

"Yep. Special operations group, intelligence unit. I'm

Sergeant Caleb Tancos."

"Thanks for not shooting us," Stan said.

Tancos motioned his head at Stan's SUV. "Nobody but tourists come driving through here at this time of day in a vehicle *that* color. We knew you were friendlies."

"I told you to leave the wife's car at home when we're conducting important business," Brian deadpanned.

Tancos smiled. "That there is my partner, Jaime Ramos." He motioned again with his head toward the man standing behind Stan. "He's on loan to our fed team I'm deployed with down here courtesy of CISEN, Mexico's version of the Department of Homeland Security. They sent Jaime to help me out, especially with the language."

"*Buenos días, Señores.*" Jaime tipped his dirty baseball cap, switched the safety on his AK47, and swung the iconic Russian-made firearm around his back.

"Well, it was a good day," Stan said as he began an inspection, walking around his vehicle. Jaime followed Stan, circling around the SUV with him.

"No look so good, *Señor.*"

Stan nodded then looked down the road ahead. "I wonder what hit us."

"*Coyotes.*" Jaime's terse assessment sounded quite definitive. The quick reply caught Stan off-guard.

"Why do you say that?"

"This is the main route from Mexico to Phoenix, *Señor.* The area is crawlin' with *coyotes,* bringin' their cargo through here. Illegals. Drugs. They don' wan' no one interferin', stoppin' their mules. They'll kill to protect the mules, *Señor.*"

Stan knew the *coyotes* the Mexican agent referred to were Mexican National thugs in charge of coordinating illegal border crossings. The greediest *coyotes* moonlighted for drug cartels. At the point of departure they would surprise desperate crossers, forcing them to carry bundles of contraband—cocaine, methamphetamines, heroin, marijuana, or many times, all four—strapped to their backs. Hence, the well-described "mule" moniker to which Jaime referred.

"We thin' *coyotes* have passed through here twice already today, *Señor*," Jaime offered. "We're on their trail and they're very jittery. I thin' maybe one of them sent a message by smashin' your windshield there."

"Just who do you guys work for again?" Stan asked.

"I work for Special Agent Tancos, *Señor*."

"And Tancos is Border Patrol?"

"*Si.*"

"*Undercover* Border Patrol? Just what the heck does that mean?"

Jaime shrugged his shoulders.

The Mexican agent's talkativeness ended when Brian pulled his muscular frame out from the back seat of the car. In his hand, he held a three-inch-long slug of heavy metal. Brian raised it above his head and said, "I think I found what broke our windshield."

CHAPTER 16

Stan stared at the dull metal object Brian held between his thumb and index finger. About three inches in length, the projectile looked like a small bolt but with no threads. The thing had an angular-shaped end.

"This might have been what broke the windshield," Brian declared. He held the piece of metal on one end with a piece of tissue he had grabbed from the SUV's glove box.

"What is it?" Stan asked.

"Dunno."

Stan looked toward Tancos and Jaime. They both shrugged their shoulders. Brian lifted-up the pewter-colored slug and held it against the low, mid-day sun. The whole group examined the half-inch-in-diameter object.

"Maybe it was already in the car," Tancos offered. "You got kids? Something one of them dropped?"

Disagreeing, Stan shook his head. "Brian, do you see any markings on it?"

"Nope," Brian replied, "but it's definitely precision-milled, that's for sure."

Jaime tapped on his AK47. "Maybe it's a gun part."

Brian turned the piece, scrutinizing it from every angle. "Not from any gun I've ever seen."

"Let me have that." Tancos grabbed the foreign object along with the tissue right out of Brian's fingertips. "I'll take it into our crime lab when we get back to civilization."

Stan held out his hand to Tancos. "I think we'll take care of that." The agent hesitated but complied, placing the mysterious object and tissue into Stan's hand. "Snap a couple of shots with your phone, Bri."

Brian took the pics, then looked at his screen. "No service out here. I'll email these to my Chandler lab when we pick up a cell tower on the way back."

"I can radio the Red Rock PD. You're going to need a tow," Tancos said.

"No, don't do that. We'll contact someone in Tucson." Stan looked at Brian and broke a smile. "My buddy here doesn't get along too well with the local *gendarmes.*"

"Cute," Brian smirked.

"*You* don't get along with Logan Athem?" Tancos asked, looking at Brian. "Now it wouldn't surprise me if you told me he didn't like Stan here."

"That Athem guy. He doesn't much like people of color like you and me, *Señor.*"

Stan nodded at Jaime's statement. "I'd say Athem's not the most open-minded law enforcement officer I've ever met."

Tancos took an apple from his pocket and cut the fruit with a very large knife he had pulled from a sheath on the side of his boot. Stan looked over at Tancos's huge knife. Tancos lifted his chin, offering Stan a piece of the fruit he'd cut and stuck on the knife's tip. After Tancos was so quick to grab the metal slug, Stan eyed him with care. One side of the knife's blade, which looked almost a foot long, had a highly honed-edge. The other side was serrated. He took the apple bit, making sure his fingers avoided the sharp side of the blade.

"Thanks," Stan said. "That's quite an interesting *cochillo* you've got there."

"Coo-chillo," a smiling Jaime said to Stan, correcting his Spanish. The Mexican pushed back his sweat-stained cap and wiped his brow.

Brian brought the conversation back to Athem. "Word is that gorilla is a card-carrying member of the ASA."

"The Aryan Sons of Arizona." Tancos said. He sliced more of the apple and stuffed a piece in his mouth. "White nationalists. Bad motherfuckers, too."

Brian snuck a look at Stan. "So . . . you've heard of

them?"

"They're on our radar."

"You're radar?" Stan asked, sounding surprised.

"Everyone is on our radar," Tancos replied. "Our state's a hot bed for skin heads, biker gangs, and ex-cons. We're even keeping track of some former Iraq and Afghan war vets."

Brian jumped in. "What do you mean, 'we'?"

"We're working with the Defense Intelligence Agency, the DIA. They've got a presence down here, tracking certain ex-members of the military. Most are dishonorable discharges, but not all. The DIA wants to know where they end up, what kind of life they lead after their tour. In most cases, tours."

"The DIA *tracks* former soldiers?" Brian asked.

"Oh, yeah. Even though most of their work is international, they have a small but little known footprint in CONUS."

"In—?" Stan said.

"Inside the continental United States. Their spooks pull intel on our guys who were involved with covert ops during their tour and keep tabs on them after they've returned, especially if they've been diagnosed with post-traumatic stress. They keep an eye on what they're doing now that they're back in civilian clothes. Kind'a like a domestic version of the CIA."

"Earlier you said 'down here'. Where exactly?" Brian asked, his voice rising a bit.

"Their detachment office is in Phoenix but they've got a covert facility in Tucson."

Brian's voice rose even higher. "Where in Tucson?"

"I'm not one-hundred percent sure but word is they're set up in an office at the University Medical Center there. Some egghead gal is running it. She sees these guys who are diagnosed with post-traumatic stress disorder but she's really DIA. I hear she's pretty hot, too."

"How do you know all this?" Brian's voice sounded even more suspicious.

"I told you. I'm Border Patrol. We're part of everything that goes on down here. We protect the border in a lot of different ways and we don't distinguish who to protect it from. There's just as much of a threat from people within our own country legally than from those coming into it illegally. You know the oath, 'all enemies foreign *and* domestic'?"

"Tell us more." Stan's interruption in their conversation pre-empted Brian's chance to continue his line of questions at Tancos.

"We're being told in our classified bulletins the biggest threat to our country right now is from our own people. Americans like the three of us here. No offense, Jaime."

"*Yo conozco. No problema, amigo.*"

Tancos continued, "We have everyone suspicious under our microscope. *Everyone.* What we're doing down here . . . well, let's just say we're an equal opportunity group. We don't fucking trust nobody."

Stan's interest rose. "Who are you focusing on though?"

"Like I said, neo-Nazi groups like the ASA are on our list. Many of them are a haven for ex-military. FBI tells us some have recently posted on their Web sites they want to see our border closed to every Spanish-speaking person between here and Tierra del Fuego. But this Reconquista movement is especially concerning to us right now. Much more so than a few crazy skinheads."

"Reconquista?" Stan asked, sounding even more intrigued.

"*Si, Señor. Reconquista.*" Jaime's perfect Spanish inflection gave additional mystery to the word, much more than that derived from Tancos's nasal-drone voice.

"The Mexica Movement," Tancos said. Finished with cutting his last piece of apple, he wiped his knife and put it back inside its sheath. "C'mon. We'll tell you all about it while we drive you two back to civilization."

Stan and Brian piled into the back seat of a camouflage-painted Humvee. Jaime got behind the wheel and headed northeast, Tancos riding shotgun. The Mexican drove using back roads, avoiding Silverbell Road, the main paved access and egress roadway to the Ironwood Forest National Monument, a three-hundred square mile sanctuary protected for all time.

Although humans had inhabited the area for over 5,000 years, the most common travelers through the pristine wilderness in modern times consisted of workers from the grandfathered mines dotted throughout the region. Recently, however, the region had become an active passage for illegals coming up from Mexico.

"Looks like you two know these back roads pretty well," Stan said as he was tossed to and fro on the uncomfortable back seat.

"There's nearly six hundred miles of roads traversing this area, marked and unmarked. For our job, you gotta' know every inch. It's even more exciting at night. Right, Jaime?"

"*Si, si. En la noche.* That's when the real fun starts, *Señor.*"

Tancos pointed a finger out his side window. "Take a Ralph down that wash, Jaime."

"*Si, compañero. A la derecha.*"

"So tell us more about this Reconquista Movement," Stan said, keeping an eye on the road ahead.

"You really have to understand the Mexica Movement before you can understand Reconquista," Tancos began. "The Mexicas, as they're called, are a group of ideologists who reject the notion that the North American continent should be divided at all. In their estimation, borders are artificial divisions that only came about after what they believe was the illegal invasion of their land by Europeans. They consider white people to have no inalienable rights or endowments to be here, like us white people think we do."

"They call themselves *Nican Tlaca.* The indigenous people," Jaime added. He down-shifted into a low gear, jostling the vehicle's occupants.

Tancos braced himself, placing a hand on the dashboard. "They reject what they believe has been a white supremacist fueled takeover of their native lands. They claim it all started when Columbus landed here in 1492 and, at least in their minds, continues today."

"Is this group a serious threat to the U.S.?" Brian asked.

"Like I said, everyone who promotes overthrowing our government—which, by the way, is documented in their literature and on their Web sites—we take as a serious threat."

"You must admit, they do have a point," Stan offered. "They didn't invite the white man to come to this land. Just like black people didn't ask to be brought here from Africa."

"Hey, no black folks in America means I got no best friend . . . and no Motown music," Brian joked, elbowing Stan in the side.

Tancos ratcheted his head toward the occupants in the back seat. "So you're saying we should just throw out everything our forefathers did to create the country we live in today and what, erase all the borders between here and, what, Colombia?"

"No, I'm just saying they have a point," Stan replied as he continued to watch where Jaime drove.

Tancos turned his head back to the front. "Well, the Reconquistas have another *point* you just might want to hear. They openly promote, in essence, a Trojan horse attack against the U.S., but one even more sublime than the one that surprised the Spartans."

"How so?" Stan asked.

"The Reconquistas are actively *invading*, if you will, our great nation by taking advantage of the generous nature of our democracy while at the same time undermining us. Their plan, which again they openly describe on their Web site, is to legally take-over the country by gaining voting rights for illegal aliens and their children. Then, once they have a significant enough constituency, they'll vote in candidates who back their platform of returning portions of the United States back to Mexico. These *cabrones* actually believe the Mexican-American War is still being fought."

"Have they made any real progress in this?" Brian chimed in.

"It's hard to measure. Voter registration of people of Hispanic descent is higher than it's ever been. But the real fear is what's being proposed in Washington of giving amnesty to illegal aliens and in many cases a quick path to citizenship."

Stan quickly realized that Tancos's words sounded more like those of a nativist than a sworn federal agent hired to protect the border. "That's fear mongering."

"I call it telling it like it is," Tancos rebutted.

"You know," Stan retorted, "there's only one letter that separates vigilant from vigilante."

Tancos didn't reply to Stan's sarcastic statement.

"You can't possibly agree with your partner. Can you, Jaime?" Stan asked.

"I got no opinion, *Señor*. I am a dual citizen. So, to me, *no es importante*. But I do thin' that if you're goin' to come to this country you should do it legally. My ancestors lived on this land well before the *gringos* came. We had land granted to us by King Ferdinand of Spain in Colorado in the Baca Grande."

"Right, Jaime. Even though *La Mexicas* believe the king had no right to give land away that wasn't his in the first place." Tancos's voice reeked of sarcasm.

"There are no easy answers, *Señor*," Jaime said as he expertly maneuvered around a large boulder. Dense salt brush hugged the sandy wash he was using as his thoroughfare.

They came to a clearing where a paved road stretched out before them.

"This is Sasco Road. It will take us to I-10," Tancos said. "There's a post office right near the Interstate. You'll be able to pick up a cell tower there."

When the dust-caked Humvee pulled in front of the postal building minutes later, Tancos and Jaime got out of their vehicle and said farewell to Stan and Brian.

"You guys take care of yourself now," Tancos said.

The four men shook hands in vigorous up-and-down motions.

"We owe you guys," Brian said. "You ever get up our way, look us up. Maybe we can catch a ballgame."

"Love those Dbacks!" Jaime pointed to the emblem on his cap. "Miguel Montero. He's a monster."

Tancos retorted. "If you were only a Cubs fan, Jaime, you'd be a perfect partner." Tancos turned to Brian. "Hey, Hanley. Let me know what your lab says about that metal piece. Will ya'?"

Brian dug out a business card from his wallet. "My cell number's on there. Give me a call in a few days. I'd also like to know more about that DIA operation in Tucson. Send me all you know on it. Okay?"

"No problem," Tancos replied. "Will do."

CHAPTER 17

Kobe Residence
Scottsdale, Arizona
April 16, 2011

Maxine Kobe had taught American history at Arizona State University ever since graduating from the same school with a PhD in 1988. Her academic forte for her first seventeen years at ASU was teaching lost history of the Civil War, writing several highly recognized books on the subject. Facts she discovered doing research for one of those books turned out to be critical in helping her husband, Stan, solve one of his most puzzling cases back in 2005.

Not long after that case, she chose to refocus her teaching specialty. At that time, she had decided to change her emphasis to the study of the Mexican-American War. She immersed herself so deeply into the subject matter that today she had become one of the country's top scholars on the subject. She often spoke in public decrying the validity of the Treaty of Guadalupe Hidalgo. In a few days, she would deliver her biggest speech as the opening speaker at a huge immigration rally scheduled for downtown Phoenix.

"Maxine, have you ever heard of something called *La Mexica?*"

Stan asked his question as the two sat on the patio of their North Scottsdale home, reading the weekend papers.

She stopped sipping her cup of tea and looked at him with concern. "Where on earth did that subject come up? Not in one of your cases, I hope."

"No. It's not about a case. This border agent me and Brian met when we went down to Red Rock mentioned it to us. He called it 'The Mexica Movement.' I was intrigued by what he told us. And, after reading more about it, I figured I'd ask the expert."

She smiled at her husband's compliment. "Well, it's really not that simple to explain. At the core of the group there's a faction comprised of both Mexican Nationals and Mexican Americans who believe the 1848 Treaty of Guadalupe Hidalgo, which officially ended the war, is an illegal document. That the land Mexico was forced to give up after the war was, in essence, stolen from the people of Mexico and rightfully still belongs to them."

"Do you believe that?"

"Actually, I have a tendency to agree."

"Why?"

"I think you can guess why. Since I discovered so much about my unique Mexican-Irish heritage, being a descendant of a member of the San Patricio Battalion, I lean toward that position now. Anyway, it's a cold, hard fact that the war between the two countries was instigated by President Polk. I've written and lectured about the subject enough to be certain of that. Actually, that's the topic of my speech for the immigration rally." She paused, wondering exactly where Stan was going with his questions and what information he was looking to find. "So, what is this all about anyway?"

"The agent told us there's a Hispanic faction in the U.S. actively working on re-conquering the lands they believe, like you said, were stolen from Mexico after the war."

"Yes. I know of it. It's referred to as *Reconquista*."

"Yes, that's the term." Stan had brought his legal pad and a pen to the table. He began taking notes.

"It's a grassroots effort that revolves around the belief that if the group can get legal or even illegal immigrants registered to vote in the U.S. then once registered in large enough numbers they believe they'll have the power to seize control. They would accomplish this by taking over small local governments at first, then moving on to larger and larger municipalities. Once they gain a toe-hold, they believe there's no stopping them . . . even from entering the White House."

"So that explains why so many conservative politicians are against an easy path to citizenship for illegals. Especially here in Arizona. It's all making sense."

"That's definitely part of it but not all of it," Maxine said. "They believe if they can elect enough candidates of Hispanic heritage to law-making positions, then they'll be able to rescind some of the most egregious past actions perpetrated against their people. The most significant, of course, would be to return land to Mexico the United States stole when they illegally attacked Mexico to start the war."

"Do you believe that's possible?"

Maxine shot back a shrug and raised her eyebrows. "You have to admit, it's a Trojan horse with intriguing possibilities." She poured herself another cup of tea.

"C'mon. You can't possibly believe that right-wing factions in our country would ever allow that to happen. Most of the fear-mongering hurled at *Reconquista* and *La Mexica* I've read so far on the Internet comes from these ultra-conservative groups."

"I'm not saying I promote the ideology, I'm just saying anything's possible. Political strategists are already predicting the Latino vote will determine the outcome of the 2012 presidential election. If that happens then why wouldn't these same people be able to gather an even deeper and bigger coalition to slate their own candidates in other, especially local, political arenas?"

Stan jotted in his pad while he spoke. "I guess it is the best way to achieve equality. Through the democratic process."

"It worked in Selma." She winked at him as he looked up from the tablet, then brought the cup to her lips.

"But this Mexica movement is a bit different. The feds consider them a hate group and their Web site is blocked from public access points," Stan said.

She placed her cup down and took pause before

addressing his concern. "Yes. La Mexica is on the fringe and they do preach separation. They believe there is no concept for such a thing as a border, let alone one that is forcibly closed to them. They believe there was an illegal invasion of North America by Europeans in 1492, forcing them to stop their natural desire and inalienable right to move freely across lands, uninhibited, without the need to claim any sort of allegiance to a nation or a nationality. They call themselves, Nican Tlaca, the indigenous people."

Stan flipped through his notepad. "Yes. That's what I have here. The agent's Mexican partner called them that name, too. This is probably why the feds consider them a threat. It's because *La Mexica* doesn't recognize the United States."

"I think more precisely our government considers them a threat because they refuse to acknowledge being referred to or labeled by others as Latino or Hispanic or immigrant or illegal. It's a very complex subject that really relates to our country's whole concept of itself and the outcome from its early manifest destiny policy."

He stayed silent and watched her take another sip of tea before she continued.

"Look, Stan. It all boils down to this. Why do Americans think, that is, the United States and its citizens think, we can run this country any better than it would be run by giving it back to the people we stole it from?" She leaned in close to make her next point. "As a lawyer, you can argue with the legality. But as a man of color you have to sympathize with one of the most tragic results from the invasion by whites of the land of the native peoples of North, Central and South America—the annihilation of entire cultures. You being in America versus Africa is a direct result of the conquering sword."

She sat back, looking at the blank stare on her husband's face. She knew the look and understood he was digesting her words. "Put the shoe on the other foot," she continued. "What if tomorrow China calls in our government's debt? And what if the good old U. S. of A. can't repay it? Then what? Would

China have the right to take over our land? To start repossession procedures? Would they have a right to throw people from their homes and make slaves of us because of our country's inability to pay its obligations? Think about it. You know what would happen?"

"War?" Stan replied.

"Not just war, honey, but the annihilation of an entire society."

CHAPTER 18

The Tee Pee Mexican Café
Phoenix, Arizona
The Next Day

Pauline Dorrey had been practicing psychology for nearly fifteen years and, although the temptation presented itself to her numerous times, she had always refrained from fraternizing in any manner with a patient. She'd always chosen to take the higher, professional ground versus succumbing to her carnal desires.

That all changed when she met Brian Hanley.

She thought back to the first time the detective had entered her office. It was eighteen months earlier, shortly after he had recovered physically from a gunshot wound. His mental recovery had been another matter. One of about three dozen patients Dorrey treated as part of her post-traumatic stress disorder clinic at The University of Arizona Medical Center, he was still under her care.

"Thanks for coming," Pauline said.

Brian sat in the seat across from her at the small Mexican restaurant in Phoenix. The two had never met outside of their private therapy sessions in Tucson, one hundred miles south. The rendezvous today, so close to where Brian lived in the Valley, certainly posed a risk.

She tapped her foot against the floor, nervous about meeting and possibly being seen together in public. She felt ashamed and put a hand over her eyes, unable to look at him. "I didn't plan for this to happen between you and me." She dropped her hand and looked right at Brian. "I know it's wrong."

Brian looked around the room. "This took both of us to let it happen. Besides, Claire knows it's not just me that's changed since the shooting. But she blames me for being a cop, for staying a cop, and making her live on the edge of her emotions every day."

She ached inside when he mentioned his wife's name. "I feel for . . . both of you."

"Look, I'm sure you didn't call me here to listen to me talk about what you already know about my marriage. So, what's so important that couldn't wait until I saw you again at our next session?"

A waiter came by and interrupted their conversation. Brian ordered an iced tea while Pauline opted for a margarita. She waited for the server to leave, then leaned in closer to Brian, keeping her voice low. "I had to come. I needed to tell you this in person. You know that Border Patrol agent you told me you met in the desert?"

"Yeah. What about him?"

Now it was Pauline's turn to look around the room. She felt as though she was being watched. She bit on a nail and leaned in a few more inches. "Well, a new patient, a soldier who just got back from Afghanistan, mentioned that agent's name."

She looked at the people nearby to make sure they weren't listening. Her paranoia was hard to hide, but she went on.

"This kid was off the charts. Worse case of PTSD I've ever seen. He goes on and on and then says that he, along with a lot of other soldiers, firmly believe the illegals coming across the border are not just Mexican Nationals but Afghans dressed to look like Mexicans. He tells me someone's got to be told about this. That we can't let this happen to our country. That someone has got to stop them."

Their drinks came and Brian stirred a packet of sugar into his tea. "It's probably just the PTSD talking. Right?"

"I considered that but he's not showing any signs or symptoms of being delusional. He expressed everything coherently and was quite vocal about wanting to send a message to Washington about what the government's *not* doing to protect our borders." Pauline took a deep swig of her drink. Then she took a breath and went on, keeping her voice low. "He rambled on about why we have to keep our own borders safe versus fighting on borders in the Middle East. I asked him what he thought he could do about this 'invasion.' He told me that if he wanted to get involved in stopping it, some fellow soldiers had told him when he got back to the States there was a guy in Arizona to hook up with."

"And?"

"And . . ." She paused and took another sip of her drink, relishing the relief she was getting from the libation. ". . . that's when your border agent's name came up."

"The guy to get in touch with is Tancos? You're sure?"

"Yes." Feeling a catharsis, she took yet another long sip of her drink, then looked to Brian for his reaction.

"So, what do you expect me to do with this information? It may be incriminating but it's certainly not anything Tancos could be arrested for. It's hearsay."

"You're not going to look into it?"

He shook his head. "If you think it's important, maybe you should phone in an anonymous tip."

"But what about doctor-patient confidentiality?"

"Pauline, I think you've already broken that code by telling me."

"I know, I know." Her head was spinning from downing the margarita so fast, but she ordered another anyway when the waiter came back. She regained her thoughts. "But . . . the problem is . . . the soldier never told me he *knew* what Tancos did. He just knew his name. The only way I could possibly have known about Tancos and what he does is through you."

"What's the issue? Some kid rambles—"

She leaned in closer than before, reached for his hand, and pulled him toward her. Pauline knew that by touching him in this manner in public she had crossed a forbidden boundary. When he obliged her gesture, she whispered, "Brian, I work for the federal government."

"Wha . . .?" Stunned, his eyes bulged. He yanked his hand back.

She spoke just above a whisper, enough so he could hear her, but low enough that their conversation didn't leave the table. "I work for the Defense Intelligence Agency. My counseling and therapy practice is a cover. I gather intel for Washington on soldiers coming back from the war."

She knew she had blind-sided him but felt she was obligated to let him know. The waiter dropped off her drink and she took a sip right away, hoping it would numb the pain she felt from what she had just told him.

He tried to keep his voice low but failed. "So it *was* you Tancos was talking about!"

"What do you mean?" she asked.

"He told me when we met he knew that the DIA had a covered facility in Tucson run by a female psychologist. I didn't want to believe my ears when I heard him."

Not sure what to say next, she attempted to explain. "I don't know how he would have known that." She began to slur her words. "I never thought this would happen. That you and I would get involved like we have. I never meant for this . . ." Heartbroken, she cried openly. When she stopped, she took one more sip of her drink. "There's more," she sobbed. "The agency records every conversation I have with patients. Brian, my superiors will find all this out when they listen to the recordings."

The last revelation brought a look of shock to Brian's face. "You record patient conversations? What? I thought what I shared was just between you and me. I don't believe you!"

Her eyes beaded again with tears. She tried to keep her voice low and choked back her emotions. The side-effects of the tequila didn't help. "I wish it weren't true . . . "

She stopped to wipe her eyes, hesitating to restart. "Brian . . . I'm not sure . . . but they may have bugged my apartment, too."

Brian slapped his palm to his forehead and gulped a breath. "I don't fucking believe this."

"I swear. I had no control." She pleaded, looking up, his face a blur through her crying eyes.

A veil of concern seized his face. "Are you recording us right now?"

"No!" she cried.

"I don't fucking believe this," he repeated, this time a little louder. He rocked back and forth. He leaned across the table, right into her face. Shaking his head, he spoke through clenched teeth, only loud enough for her to hear. "I *trusted* you." Disgusted, he pulled back, dug into his pants pocket, and tossed a twenty on the table. "I hope you got what you wanted from me."

"Please, Brian," she begged. But he ignored her plea, got up, and headed out the door.

CHAPTER 19

Harley's Italian Bistro
Phoenix
Later That Same Day

Whenever Stan wanted to talk privately about an ongoing investigation, his favorite place to meet was a little Italian restaurant on 7th Avenue north of Indian School Road. The modest establishment was far removed from the noisy, downtown Phoenix eateries lawyers and cops usually frequented. He had called Brian, asking him to meet right away, saying he had news to share with him about their Chandler case.

Stan was feeling antsy, anxious to speak with his partner. As soon as Brian walked in and sat across from him at their favorite table, Stan told him why he had called Brian to meet. He didn't hide the anger in his voice. "Look. I lied. I didn't call you here to talk about the case. My wife dropped a bomb on me last night in bed that Claire told her she thinks you're screwing your therapist." He waited for a reaction from Brian but none came. "I told Maxine that can't be true. That you'd never do something like that." Stan's voice rose, angry. "Maxine even went so far as to accuse me of covering up for you."

Brian still didn't reply. He moved his eyes downward, staring at his water in front of him, playing with the straw in the glass.

Agitated over getting no eye contact, he barked at him. "What the fuck. Aren't you going to say something?"

Brian looked up. "Yeah. It's none of Maxine's goddamn business."

Stan's voice rose, reeking of disbelief. "*So it's true?*"

"Why don't you just tell the whole restaurant?"

"You're playing with me. Right?" Stan wanted to believe this was just Brian being Brian, the constant jokester. "I know. This is one of your lame jokes."

Brian shot him an "I wish it wasn't" look, raising his eyebrows and drooping his shoulders.

Still shocked, Stan tried lowering his voice. "You're *screwing* your therapist?"

"Please wipe the surprised look off your face," Brian said, pointing a finger at him. "You sound like some kind of fucking choir boy for crissake."

Stan pulled himself up straight, enraged. "But I *am* surprised. I mean, I never—"

"Never what? Never looked at another woman? Never wondered if she wanted you as much as you wanted her? Look, I didn't go looking for this if that's what you think. It just happened, that's all."

"But you still love Claire, don't you?"

Brian shrugged in a manner that made Stan think his pal didn't know for sure.

"So now what?" Stan asked.

"Well, I haven't thought that far ahead. As a matter of fact, Claire and I had a big fight right after you and me came back from Red Rock. She's suspected for a long time."

"What did you tell her?"

"I denied it, of course."

"But she *knows*, I mean, at least she thinks she knows. Besides, it's true. And now that she's told Maxine I've got my wife asking me twenty questions. So . . . like I said, now what?"

"Just keep telling Maxine you don't know a thing. If it ever does come out between me and Claire, I'll swear to both of them you never knew."

"No friggin' way! You can't do that to me, Brian. You can't put me in the middle and expect me to lie to Maxine. First, I don't lie to my wife. Second, she's too smart. Anyway, she already believes I know *and* that I'm covering for you. I hate to tell you this, but I think you've only got one choice. End it now and come clean with Claire. Before more people get hurt . . . like your kids."

Brian hung his head, embarrassed. "It's not that easy," he mumbled. "Plus, the situation just got a whole lot worse."

The waiter came and took their order. After he left, Stan prodded Brian.

"What are you talking about? How worse can it be?"

"I just saw her."

"Who? Your therapist? Up here? What's with you?" Stan wanted to slap Brian in the back of the head. "Do you have a death wish."

Brian grabbed his utensils and un-wrapped the napkin, all the while looking like he was trying to avoid Stan's glower. "Look. It was the first time. But . . . it's what she told me that I have yet to figure out all the ramifications."

Stan put his elbows on top of the table and propped his chin on one hand. With the other, he jabbed an index finger toward Brian. "I think you owe it to me to let me know everything."

The server came with their drinks and bread, then left. Brian leaned in toward Stan. "It's about that border agent we met out in the desert, Tancos. Do you remember when he referred to someone working for the Defense Intelligence Agency in Tucson? Well, guess what. It's my therapist he was talking about."

"What? Your therapist? Is DIA?"

"Yes. Evidently, she works undercover for the feds. Keeps track of and gathers intelligence on discharged GIs diagnosed with PTSD."

"You're shitting me." Stan's look of surprise matched the sound of astonishment in his voice.

"This is one time I wish I was." Brian hesitated but went on. "When we were in Tucson, you know . . . waiting for your SUV to get a new windshield . . . well . . . I went to see her."

"*You did?* You told me you were going to the Indian casino."

Brian shrugged off his lie. "I told her about what had happened to us and meeting Tancos out in the Ironwood Forest. I mentioned his name to her. She texted me, asking to see me here in the Valley. She tells me Tancos's name came up during a meeting with a new patient, a recently discharged Army vet. Seems this kid has a full-blown case of PTSD and he started ranting to her about illegals crossing the border."

Their food came. Brian didn't eat but rather continued telling his tale. "The soldier told her he had heard back in theatre that when he gets back to the U.S., if he wants to get involved and do something about the illegals, then Tancos is the guy to see."

"So you're saying Tancos, a high-ranking border patrol agent, working undercover, is also, what—a vigilante?"

"Well, like you told him, there's only one letter separating vigilant from vigilante."

"Yeah, but it's a huge leap to make a decision to get involved in doing harm to illegal border crossers versus protecting the border?"

"I don't fully comprehend it myself. But why would his name get circulated in a war theatre if he wasn't the guy to see back here?"

Stan's shoulders lowered as he listened intently, trying to comprehend everything he had just heard. Was a U.S. Border Patrol Agent involved with criminal activities while performing his sworn duty to protect the border? If true, it would not only be a serious charge but an unprecedented one.

Brian went on. "How about that weird projectile that went through our windshield? Do you think a coyote or a border crosser could have fired something sophisticated like that at us?"

Stan shook his head as Brian went on.

"Let's suppose for a moment it was one of these vigilante nuts who actually shot at us. Tancos admitted he knows those types are roaming around out there in the desert. What if it was one of them who pulled the trigger? And maybe, just, maybe, Tancos let's these guys do whatever they want down there. It certainly would be easy for him to just look the other way and let these kooks help him with his job."

Stan nodded, agreeing with Brian's assessment.

"Plus, remember how anxious Tancos was to take that slug from us?"

"Yeah, I remember," Stan said. "What else did your psychologist tell you?"

"Well, this is where the whole story gets really weird and shitty for me. She told me that now that she's been told this story by the guy she just interviewed, she'll have to give a full report to her superiors in her next briefing. She'll be required to reveal all she's heard. Then, she says, they'll ask if she's ever heard this guy Tancos's name before, anywhere, anytime."

"She can lie about that, right? Her bosses don't need to know you had mentioned it to her."

"Well, that's the problem. The DIA records all of her office sessions."

"What? Christ! What the hell is going on here?"

"But I didn't tell her in her office."

"You told her when you two were—"

"Fucking? Is that what you were gonna say?"

Stan answered Brian's question with another shrug coupled with a raised set of eyebrows.

"Here's where the story really gets shit crazy. Seems her agency not only tapes all of her office sessions but they may have bugged her apartment, too."

"Christ, Brian," Stan gulped. "Her apartment, too? This whole thing is insane."

"Don't I know. I think the saying goes, 'Don't shit where you sleep.' Well, looks like I made my own pillow out of it, too."

CHAPTER 20

Southern Arizona
Thirteen Years Earlier, June 1998

D avis-Monthan Air Force Base boasted having one of the largest and most active A-10 Thunderbolt II fighter wings. The base, just outside Tucson, played host this year to what the Air Force unofficially called their "A-10 Olympics." In preparation for the upcoming competition, teams from A-10, or "Warthog," fighter units from every active U.S. and international base salivated at participating in the hotly contested biennial event. Each wing sent their four best pilots, who affectionately called themselves "hawg drivers." Teams squared off against other teams as well as individually for the chance to win the competition's gold medal and the honor of being called the best A-10 hawg driver in the world—Warthog Top Gun.

As this year's event day drew closer, Chief Master Sergeant Paul Stewart spent an inordinate amount of time as a key member of the ground crew assigned to a rookie pilot by the name of Benjamin Forster. Stewart's six-person team was responsible for loading every single piece of armament on Captain Forster's warthog. This included 1000 rounds of ammunition for the plane's daunting, under-the-nose-mounted, Gatling cannon simply called "The Gun." That was complemented with an under-wing array of eight "Willy Pete" phosphor rockets along with four, similarly-located Mk82, called "Mark eighty-two," five-hundred pound bombs. The only Explosive Ordnance Disposal-trained airman on the ground crew, Stewart's personal responsibility was supervising all the munitions.

The newbie Forster and his A-10 team wouldn't have a chance in hell competing against some of the top hawg drivers in the world without Stewart's ground crew leading the way to victory. The pilot walked into the hangar area while Stewart's unit put their final on the plane. Stewart snapped a salute as the captain approached through the open doors.

Forster returned salute, then addressed Stewart. "We've got two days left before the big show. Do you think we're ready?"

"Oh yeah. We're ready, sir. This is a great crew. Best here in my opinion."

The two men conversed as they walked the circumference of Forster's hawg, giving the A-10 a visual inspection. Stewart hoped his answer reassured the captain, who was about to not only fly in his first Olympics competition, but also concurrently finish his replacement training unit, or RTU, program. Successfully completing the latter would fully earn him his A-10 wings. Not to be overlooked, Forster would also make history and become the first African-American to accomplish either feat.

"I heard from my fellow pilots this isn't your first Olympics, Master Sergeant. Any tips for a nervous rook like me?"

"Yeah. Don't get lost."

Forster forced a chuckle. "I'll make sure not to do that."

"Sorry, just a little ground crew humor."

Forster smiled wide. He'd become accustomed to the extra dose of ball-busting from his veteran crew as he neared completion of his twenty-seven week RTU. The playful jiving was also a big part of the indoctrination for all pilots participating in their first Olympics.

Stewart stopped at the tail of the plane and turned to Forster. He knew the pilot was under an extraordinary amount of pressure due to also having the distinction of breaking the color-barrier in the all-white A-10 community. "But seriously, the folks who run this event are known for trying to throw curveballs at the contestants, especially odd instructions to knock you off balance. Just follow the directives they give you in the event envelope to a T, even if you think the instructions don't make sense. Davis-Monthan lost the last competition because one of our guys tried to think too much up there. Follow your instructions and you'll be fine."

Stewart wiped some dirt off the side of the war bird with a rag he constantly carried in the back pocket of his overalls. "We'll take care of everything down here. The event's Forward Air Controller will be your eyes and ears."

"I hear you don't know who the FAC is until the morning of the event. That'll be tough not being familiar with their voice," Forster said.

"The FAC for this event has to be impartial. That's why they pull them from a base that's not competing. It's the only fair way to do it."

"I also heard scuttlebutt the FACs don't even know the whole game plan until they walk into the control tower."

Stewart ducked under the wing and approached the nose. Forster trailed him.

"That's what I mean. Everyone's on equal ground," Stewart said. "So stay focused because you just don't know what those SOBs who plan this whole shebang will throw at you. Four years ago, they sent one of our guys on a flight path down into Mexico and back again on the segment for the long-range strafing."

"Mexico?" Forster sounded surprised.

"Yep. The event boss caught hell on that one trying to explain why A-10s were flying back and forth between here and the Sierra Madres before they eventually dropped their payload at Goldwater."

"Thank you, Master Sergeant. I appreciate all the background help on this. Being the new guy on the team I want to make a good show of it. Besides, it's my last mission before graduation. I can't afford to screw the pooch. I need to prove to the brass that my skin color's no handicap."

Stewart wiped his hands with his towel and stuck it in his back pocket. He gave Forster a pat under the elbow. "Don't worry, Captain. You're in good hands with me."

* * *

Sabotaging one of the most highly sophisticated military planes in the world would be no easy task. But if anyone could do it Paul Stewart certainly had the knowledge and the freedom of unrestrained access to carry out the sinister plan. This action would be fulfillment of a promise he had made to Jacob Lund. Stewart was at peace with the fact he was about to embark upon a path of no return, a road bordering upon treason.

Stewart's sabotage scheme would not be a quick and easy one. During the upcoming A-10 Olympics, Captain Benjamin Forster and the other thirty-nine participating pilots would each receive a sealed envelope immediately prior to entering their Plexiglas-covered cockpit. This secretive procedure of receiving instructions had been the heart of the competition since its inception.

Included in the plain manila envelope—emblazoned solely with a small white sticky label typed only with the pilot's rank and name—would be heretofore unseen commands detailing where the respective events would happen and in which particular order to complete them. This method of delivery was part of the excitement the extremely competitive hawg drivers thrived upon, relishing the anticipation of a seat-of-the-pants hell ride while they raced against fellow elite airmen.

From his years of planning and carrying out covert operations all over the world, Stewart knew he'd have to devise a careful and non-traceable plan to slip his own forged instructions to the anxious African-American pilot. The only uncertainty the ex-CIA operative had was whether the rookie would follow the altered directives to perfection and not waiver from the intricate course alteration Stewart had plotted. This, Stewart prayed, may require a truly divine intervention from the Lord Melchizedek himself.

*   *   *

On the day of the event, Stewart and Captain Forster finished
the last-minute ground inspection of the Warthog. As they
completed their task, a junior airman approached from the
hangar area. Barely executing a weak salute to the officer, he
had under his left armpit an accordion folder.

"I've got this for you, Captain," the man said.

He whisked the folder from under his arm and unraveled
the cord that bound it. From inside, he pulled out a business-
size, plain white envelope with the typed words:

FORSTER, CAPTAIN BENJAMIN R.

The pilot, in his full flight gear, grabbed the envelope and
tucked it under his armpit. The airman then saluted again.
When Forster returned salute, the airman did an about face
and traipsed off to the next competing pilot to repeat the same
routine.

After the airman was out of earshot, Stewart turned to his
captain and said, "I've got something for you, too." Stewart
held out a pocket Bible. "I give one of these to all my guys
when they take their final flight."

Forster stared with an awkward look at the small, leather-
bound book Stewart held in the palm of his outstretched hand.

"That's . . . very thoughtful of you, Master Sergeant." He
took the book.

"I was thinking it might, you know, sort of help protect
you up there."

"I must say, I am a bit surprised by this gesture," Forster
said softly, a puzzled look on his face.

"Here, give me those while you climb up." Stewart
grabbed the book and envelope, still tucked under Forster's
arm. "I'll put that in here." Stewart pushed the envelope in
between the Bible's pages.

The captain proceeded up the narrow telescopic ladder
leading to his A-10's cockpit. Stewart followed right behind
him. Once inside the cockpit, the crew chief handed him the

Bible again. The envelope extended out over the edges.

"Thanks," Forster said. "What I heard about you since I came, that you hated people of my color, well, I guess that's all been wrong."

"Don't judge a book by its cover," Stewart replied. "You're right. I'm not the man you've heard I am."

"You don't know how much this means to me."

"No need to thank me. Just follow those instructions in that envelope there. And don't forget what I told you—don't over think this and you'll do fine."

Stewart and Forster synchronized watches. After they completed their time hack, the crew chief touched him on the shoulder.

"The Lord Yahweh will protect you. You're one of his fiery angels, you know."

Forster shot him another puzzled look as Stewart retreated down the ladder, jumping down the two feet from the last step to the tarmac. As Forster began to move his hawg out onto the runway, standard operating procedure called for his canopy to stay open. His crew chief snapped him a final salute. Forster returned salute and then gave the standard "thumbs up" signal to Stewart.

The plane then taxied off to the outer runway. Since the prevailing wind was out of the west, he'd take off from the east. In less than a minute, the fully-armed, forty-thousand pound war bird was aloft.

Stewart raised his head to the sky and whispered, "Like a wind from the east, I will scatter them before thine enemies."

CHAPTER 21

Within minutes, Captain Benjamin R. Forster soared upward, steering his Warthog effortlessly through a cloudless Sonoran sky. An unlimited azure ceiling swathed over him, engulfing him and his hawg. Only a few wisps of clouds graced the atmosphere, too thin to be of any concern yet valuable to give him a perspective to the surreal feeling of floating below the endless blue canopy.

He eventually reached an altitude of 10,000 feet AGL—above ground level—the prescribed ceiling limit set in the pre-flight briefing where all competitors had gathered just hours earlier. Cramped like sardines in a tiny classroom, each pilot had clutched their mandatory cup of wake-up coffee. An instructional pilot from the Davis-Monthan replacement training unit school addressed them. On a white board, the IP had drawn a cursory aerial map of the four corners region. Then he proceeded to describe for the contestants the locations of the various bombing ranges the fliers most probably would use during the competition.

The IP went on to tell them that once a team had all four of its planes airborne, they should enter into and maintain a four-man wing formation, until a signal pinged each hawg driver in their helmet radio for notification to open their sealed instructions.

When Forster entered into his prescribed holding pattern along with his other three teammates, they circled the Davis-Monthan airfield within the thirty-mile radius mandated by the IP in the briefing. The team's call sign for the event was "Mesquite." Forster, positioned in the rear as the number four wingman, had the call sign of "Mesquite 4." While he waited for the event to begin, he splayed open the small pocket Bible on his lap. He felt comfort in knowing that Stewart had felt moved enough to give him the special gift in recognition of earning his wings. Not an overtly religious man, Forster still believed in a higher power.

He took a moment and flipped from page-to-page in the Bible. He noticed one was dog-eared. On that page, a section of Psalm 139 Verse 18, highlighted in yellow marker, caught his eye. He read the words aloud, "Were I to count them, they would outnumber the grains of sand. When I awake, I am still with you."

In the margin of the page, handwritten in all capital letters, he noticed the words:

TO MY FIERY ANGEL FROM THE EAST.
GODSPEED.
PAUL

My brothers in the mess hall said Stewart was a stone cracker. They had this man figured out all wrong.

As Forster pondered over the highlighted section and the words in the page margin, the official announcement came through his audio monitor headset:

"All pilots. Open your event envelopes."

He pulled out the event instruction envelope, then squeezed the closed Bible down beside him on his ACES II ejection seat. He ripped open the envelope and read its contents. Pausing, he looked out his canopy window—left then right—looking for a reaction from his teammates who circled in formation with him. He read the instructions again. About to read them a third time, the words of Stewart rang in his head:

"The folks who run this event are known for trying to throw curveballs at the contestants, especially odd instructions to knock you off balance. Just follow the directives they give you in the envelope to a T, even if you think they're nonsense."

Forster looked out his Plexiglas-enclosed cockpit one more time, circling his head in all directions, looking for a visual sign from any of his teammates or movement from their planes.

"I'm not about to screw this pooch," he said to himself.

With that last thought, he full throttled the plane's stick forward. His A-10's General Electric TF34A-GE-100 twin-turbofan engines roared back, screaming their approval. He pulled a hard right-bank on the fifteen-ton Warthog and peeled off formation, turning the dragon-painted nose of his ten-million-dollar warplane north-northeast. Being the number four plane in the back of the formation, he wondered if anyone would notice his bug-out. Within twenty seconds, he reached four hundred knots. Minutes later, he was at the southern edge of the Mogollon Rim.

CHAPTER 22

Remote Northern Arizona

T he sheet Forster had pulled out from the envelope listed eight instruction sets, each consecutively numbered. The first gave him instructions for his opening exercise in the competition, which would be to conduct a PID, or positive identification, of a target on the southern edge of the Mogollon Rim. He didn't second guess the orders, which took him almost four-hundred miles in the opposite direction from the Barry M. Goldwater Bombing Range—the primary range for the event located in an isolated corner of southwestern Arizona. A frequent practice space used by several Air Force bases, it had also been used for competitions hosted by Davis-Monthan. Once more, he recalled Stewart's story of the Davis-Monthan pilot who, in an earlier competition, had been sent all the way down into Mexico.

"They tell me to fly to the Rim, I fly to the Rim. No pooch screwin' for me," Forster muttered under his breath.

Instruction #1 went on to tell him the stationary hard target that had been set up to PID deep inside the Rim's thick Ponderosa pine forest was a lookout tower. A handful of fire lookouts there, abandoned and shuttered by the U.S. Forest Service during the mid-90s federal government shutdown, had never re-opened.

Inside one of these closed lookouts, on one of his numerous camping trips, Stewart had set up a homemade VHF Omni-directional Range locator, or VOR. Only an hour earlier, just prior to Forster sealing himself into his hawg on the tarmac at Davis-Monthan, one of Stewart's fellow Church of the High Country members had triggered on the power to the faux VOR, getting its juice from a bank of dry cell batteries inside the cabin at the top of the structure. The device provided a signal for the A-10's INS, or inertial navigation system. The cockpit's INS device then honed in on the coordinates spit out by Stewart's make-shift, artificial, VOR, luring the unsuspecting Forster into his lair. So far, the ASA soldier's surreptitious plan was working without a hitch.

The closer Forster got to the VOR signal emanating from the abandoned tower, the louder and louder his INS beeped. The pilot finally made visual contact. He was surprised because he thought the structure, rising almost one-hundred-twenty-five feet above the forest floor, seemed easy to PID, sticking out, as it were, like a sore thumb. The tower looked quite distinct to the keen-eyed pilot as he soared over the vast pine forest, the largest in the country.

His first instruction set concluded by calling for him to circle the tower once in a tight two-mile radius before closing in at 200 feet AGL. Then he was to dive at a twelve degree descent for a low-angle strafe. The last line of order #1 then told him that after he zeroed in and put the tower in the firing sight of The Gun, he was to pull off and not fire on the target.

*   *   *

Sitting alone in his quarters, all this time Paul Stewart had listened in on the air chatter from the control tower on headphones. He had tapped into the military frequency on a CIA radio he had kept with him as a souvenir from his Black Ops days. Within minutes of Forster leaving his team's formation with his surprise bug out, the chatter in the control tower at Davis-Monthan had reached fever pitch.

"Mesquite 4. This is Davis-Monthan Air Force Base Event Forward Air Controller. You have left formation too early. Please reply. Over."

No reply came from Forster's Mesquite 4 in response to

the FAC's request.

"Mesquite 4. I repeat. This is the DM EFAC. Do you read me? Over?"

The control room's radio monitor crackled with static.

In his office, Stewart sat up, sweat starting to form on his upper lip.

"This is Mesquite 4 to DM Event FAC. I read you loud and clear."

"Mesquite 4. You have left your team's formation too early and are off course. I repeat. You have left competition airspace. Do you copy, Mesquite 4?"

There was a pause, then static had come across the control room's audio monitor once again.

"This is Mesquite 4. Following event instruction sheet. Over."

"Mesquite 4. Return to your formation. Do you copy?"

A silent pause again and then more static. However, this time no reply came from Forster via his cockpit radio.

Stewart wiped his lip with the back of his hand.

The FAC repeated his orders. "Mesquite 4. Return to your formation. Do you copy? Over."

Nothing. No reply from Forster. At that point, the base's radar operator had called in over the monitor to the Event FAC.

"This is air control radar. We are no longer receiving Mesquite 4's IFF."

Back at his listening station, Stewart slapped his fist down on his desk. "Yes! He did it!" he shouted.

The Event FAC asked the radar operator to repeat what he had just said.

"This is Davis-Monthan Air Force Base air control radar. I repeat. We have lost Identification Friend or Foe Mode C Auto ID signal and his altitude."

"What was his last AGL?" the FAC asked the operator.

"Five-one-zero-zero."

"Five-one-zero-zero? That means he's flying at tree-top level up there. What in the hell is going on here? Radar control, please reconfirm that last reading."

"Last AGL on Mesquite 4 reconfirmed at five-one-zero-zero," the radar operator barked back.

"That'a boy, Forster," Stewart muttered. "You're doing great."

The Event FAC called to the other planes in Forster's formation.

"Mesquite 1, 2 and 3. This is the Event FAC. Are you still seeing Mesquite 4? Over."

Stewart listened intently as one-by-one the other hawg drivers called in a negative, each sounding as if they had realized for the first time their back wingman, Mesquite 4, was no longer on their tail and had no visual on him.

"Perfect!" Stewart cried, jumping up in excitement. "They had no idea he bugged out."

Stewart listened in on the off-air room monitor feed he had also secretly tapped into and heard the FAC ask someone to get the base commander on the phone. When they did, Stewart listened as the FAC spoke.

"Sir, this is the Event FAC. We've got a contestant off course and not responding to our radio calls. We've also lost his IFF. Yes, sir. That's right. His IFF . . . no, I don't know, sir. My guess is he turned it off." There was a long pause. "Yes, sir. I will right now. Stand by, sir."

The FAC called again over the radio headset the call sign of Benjamin Forster's A-10 Thunderbolt, the sound of urgency ramping up in his voice. "Mesquite 4. This is the Davis-Monthan Event Forward Air Controller. *Can - you - read - me? Over.*"

Silence. Then the light sound of static.

The next words from the FAC came matter-of-factly as he spoke back into the phone's receiver. "Commander. Request your permission to scramble two F-16s, sir."

CHAPTER 23

Over Southeastern Colorado

Instruction #1 had confused Captain Benjamin Forster, telling him to fly to the Mogollon Rim, positively identify a lookout tower, but then pull off and not open fire upon his target. An added line to turn off his plane's IFF device had also perplexed him. But, once again, not questioning the odd commands, after he had made his last circle, he honed in on the tower and toggled off his IFF. He had performed this task right after he had told the FAC he was following his instruction sheet.

Instruction #2 had commanded the pilot as follows:

2. Disregard all Event FAC or other instructions and rely solely on this sheet for all subsequent event instructions. Turn off all cockpit radio communications devices.

Following Stewart's words of advice, Forster had complied with the first two written orders exactly as indicated.

After reading Instruction #3, Forster slammed forward on the throttle of his Warthog and headed north-northeast at maximum forward speed to the given the latitude and longitude coordinates. He'd cover the estimated four-hundred miles in less than thirty minutes, all the time being out of radio contact with the Davis-Monthan air control tower.

He surmised the only way he could be tracked now was via conventional radar, but knew he wouldn't paint a consistent signal for the closest military tower—located at Peterson Air Force Base, one-hundred miles north of where he was headed—if he maintained a maximum 1500 feet AGL, as he saw was outlined in Instruction #4.

So far, Forster had performed all of his tasks to perfection. #3's instructions had told him to proceed to coordinates of latitude: N 37° 43' 3.014", longitude: W 103° 4' 33.083". Manually plotting this on his lap map, he realized the heading was toward the Fort Carson Piñon Canyon Maneuver Site in southeastern Colorado. He had participated in several training exercises at Piñon Canyon during his replacement training unit flight classes held in conjunction with Peterson.

Makes sense. Must be a secondary range.

He felt confident he was on course. He then dropped down to 200 feet AGL, as Instruction #5 told him to do, marked his exact lat/long coordinates, then grease-penciled those numbers on his laminated topo map spread across his lap. As per the explanation at the end of this fifth instruction set, this spot was where he would later return to deploy his Willy Pete white phosphor rockets after completing his next two events.

That pair of tasks, outlined in Instructions #6 and #7, would respectively require him to first drop his four Mk82 five-hundred-pound bombs into the farthest northwestern edge of the Great Sand Dunes before heading due north to Crestone Peak for the high altitude strafing event.

Instruction #6's latitude and longitude coordinates—N 37° 49' 33.5"; W 105° 36' 16.7864"—is where he would perform his low-level drop of his Mk82s. For Forster, this is what he'd been waiting for: the thrill of deploying his payload of one ton of bombs via a manual bombing run. The manual bombing event was a highlight for these A-10 pilots, allowing them to call upon their own keen skills versus relying upon technology to do the job.

Forster yearned to perform the drill he had honed to perfection during his long training. Now was his chance to quiet the critics who had fought so hard in trying to keep him from becoming the first African-American to qualify to drive a hawg. He fully knew the smallest mistake would be scrutinized later under a microscope and cast doubt not only on his flying skills but on the cognitive abilities of people from his race.

When he reached the bomb-drop coordinates, he circled over a desolate stretch of land outside the northernmost border of the Great Sand Dunes. The area was identified on his topo map as the Star Dune Complex. The creamy-yellow sand dunes, devoid of any trace of vegetation, stretched for miles back southward, well inside the Monument's northern border.

To the east, the powdery, mustard-colored, wind-swept earth stopped abruptly against the barren western edge of the Sangre de Cristo Mountains. The entire area showed no signs of human habitation for scores of square miles. As he descended to the prescribed 500 feet AGL deployment altitude he was cautious not to scrape the bottom of his hawg's fuselage on the tops of the sandy ridges. At their highest elevation, the dunes reached well over seven hundred feet, the tallest sand dunes in America. His next instruction outlined him to reach his slowest possible forward airspeed before releasing the bombs.

He wondered why he'd been instructed in such a manner but it wasn't unusual at all, as his IP had told him so many times in the classroom and in the air: *"The strength of the A-10 is its ability to fly at extremely low levels and at very slow air speeds in performing its key role: CAS—close air support—for our ground troops."* Flying literally just feet above the dune ridges, this, Forster thought, must be the true meaning of the word "close" in "close air support."

His hawg reached 500 feet AGL and he slowed his airspeed to just over one-hundred knots, all the while watching the lat/long coordinates on his cockpit's heads up display or HUD. When he hit his two points, he pickled his four Mk82s. When they fell, ballutes, a sort of parachute, deployed so the bombs would softly drop to earth. Looking like dark-gray angels, they danced downward, swaying to and fro as their gigantic feathers slowed their descent. Then, one-by-one, the bombs hit, nose first, into the soft sand. As he looked back over his shoulder to see his work, he noticed not one of the bombs had exploded in the pristine yellow earth.

Not sure why the bombs hadn't detonated, he didn't have time to figure out the reason. He grabbed the Warthog's stick and made a hard right bank. Then he pulled back even harder in order to make a rapid ascent to 8000 feet AGL, as Instruction #7 directed, making his lightning-like climb toward the tallest peak of the Sangre de Cristos. There, he'd perform his high altitude strafing event. When done he'd head back east through Medano Pass then south, back toward Piñon, to complete the deployment of his Willy Pete rockets, signifying completion of his last instruction set, #8.

He soared higher, accelerating to the maximum forward air speed. But as he did his primary flight control jammed. The plane stopped responding, causing the pilot to lose control of the Warthog's bank, pitch and yaw. Frantic, he tried pulling back harder on his stick, thinking that if he did he could climb over and avoid crashing straight into the fourteen-thousand foot plus Crestone Peak right at his twelve o'clock.

"Respond, baby, respond!"

Forster yanked as hard as he could. At full throttle, the hawg's jet engines screamed but the A-10 still wouldn't respond to his desperate actions to lift the plane over the jagged peak ahead.

"Our father, who art . . ."

Before he could utter another syllable, he crashed into the Rocky Mountains.

CHAPTER 24

Davis-Monthan Air Force Base
Tucson, Arizona

Within hours of the unofficial news circulating the base that an A-10 airplane and its pilot were missing, Paul Stewart made sure to step forward and volunteer to be part of the search and rescue team when the downed aviator was located. He knew an elite squad would be mustered for such an important mission once verification of Forster's crash site had been confirmed—wherever that turned out to be. Stewart knew they would require an EOD-trained airman for this team. His experience as a trained para-rescue jumper also made him a perfect fit.

After the second day, and after the media's persistent question regarding rumors of a downed pilot, a statement was released by the base's Public Affairs Office of what they called, "An aborted training mission." Public information officials at Davis-Monthan would neither confirm nor deny the plane and its pilot could not be found. They would only say that, "Captain Benjamin R. Forster and A-10 number 80-255 are missing and have presumably crashed somewhere in the wilderness of the southern Rockies in Colorado."

Finding Forster's downed aircraft would be like looking for the proverbial needle in the haystack. In this unprecedented case, however, it would be equally as hard to find the haystack. Contest officials at Davis-Monthan calculated the A-10's fuel at his time of departure and estimated time in the air. Flight experts determined that based upon his last known location at Piñon Canyon in southeastern Colorado, he could be anywhere within a two-hundred square mile radius of that spot. Stewart hoped Forster had crashed exactly where he had wanted him to—in one of the most remote regions of the Colorado wilderness.

Of course, the master sergeant wanted to find the captain and his plane more than anybody could have ever imagined. He needed to get to the wreckage first and find out if the phony instruction letter he had typed and swapped out with the real version had survived the crash. If so, he'd need to find and retrieve the paper, then replace it with the original letter amidst the strewn wreckage. He also needed to plant near Forster's remains a "To Whom It May Concern" suicide note Stewart had penned as the phony last words of the pilot to misdirect the Air Force's investigation.

Probably most in Stewart's favor of being part of the team as its EOD expert was that once at the crash site he would have the sole authority to require all other personnel to remain at a safe distance. Then, he'd approach the craft alone, presumably to render safe any unexploded ordnance. This way, he'd also have time to make sure to cover-up his handiwork of sabotaging the Warthog's controls to fail, ingeniously triggered to occur when Forster released his Mk82 payload. He'd also need time to camouflage his tampering with the ejection seat's firing mechanism for failure.

But all the over-thinking and detailed planning was no more than mental masturbation for Stewart until the Air Force found out exactly where the hawg went down and, hopefully for the saboteur, finding its very dead pilot.

CHAPTER 25

In the Sangre de Cristo Wilderness, Colorado
July, 1998

Days passed, then weeks, without any substantive news coming from the public affairs officer assigned to a special command center the Air Force's Office of Special Investigations had set up near Alamosa, Colorado. Top Air Force brass at Davis-Monthan had tapped the OSI to oversee this first of its kind search for a missing pilot and his plane on U.S. soil. OSI's participation was standard operating procedure, since the office investigated cases involving the theft or loss of critical technologies, like those found on an A-10 warplane.

Major Bill Myers and a small staff had flown in from OSI headquarters in Quantico, Virginia, to coordinate the mission and interface with the news media. Four weeks into the search, Major Myers issued the first significant news release, which read in part:

In the Air Force's ongoing effort to locate the missing pilot, Captain Benjamin R.

Forster, and his A-10 Thunderbolt II aircraft, a special search and rescue team

has been dispatched to an area we believe has indications of wreckage from a

large military plane. The site is in an extremely remote location on the southwestern slopes of the Sangre de Cristo Mountains, northeast of Alamosa. Once this team reaches the crash site, analyzes and assesses the scene and the surrounding area within this wilderness area, we will then update the media with more details.

What Public Affairs Officer Myers had purposely left out of this part and the remainder of the formal communiqué was that Forster's crash site had actually been found two days earlier and Air Force officials were no longer considering the mission a Search and Rescue but rather a Search and Recovery.

* * *

"Keep back five hundred yards," Chief Master Sergeant Stewart ordered the four other members of the recovery crew.

An MH-53J Pave Low III helicopter, flying out of New Mexico's Kirtland Air Force Base, had dropped Stewart's para-rescue team as close as possible to the crash site. The chopper, able to fly at altitudes of up to 16,000 feet, almost two-thousand feet higher than Crestone Peak, also had the ability to withstand gale force winds. Its massive ten-ton lift capacity would be called upon later to handle the demands of the salvage operation that lay ahead.

Stewart went on. "If those Mark eighty-twos, Willy Petes or any other unexploded ordnances are scattered anywhere out there, then I'll need to assess the situation first before I can bring in the rest of the recovery team."

"But what if the pilot's still alive?" The optimistic question came from the team's medic.

It had gotten much colder as the team had climbed toward the crash location near the summit. Although the only snow remaining was on the very peak of the mountain, if Forster did survive the crash, Stewart was certain he'd have succumbed to hyperthermia after being exposed for so long.

"Well, if he is still alive, I can give first aid. But my guess is after all this time, though, he's not. Either way, if I don't render safe any UXOs first, then there's too high a risk of anyone else going near the wreckage to assist."

With that statement, Stewart headed off alone over the

closest ridge. Not being able to carry-in a fully-protective body armor suit, he took along with him his lightweight vest. At the very least, he had to make his other team members believe he was headed off into an unknown and potentially dangerous situation.

This area of the mountain range consisted of a type of rock geologists called Crestone Conglomerate—sedimentary rock formed by a mixture of stones, pebbles, and boulders. The unique combination made climbing easier, since the conglomerate provided climber-friendly, nature-made handholds and footholds. After fifteen minutes of climbing, the tail wing section of an A-10 with its white-painted lettering DM 80-255 on the vertical stabilizer, punctured the backdrop of a picture perfect sky. The smell of aviation fuel permeated Stewart's nostrils.

From his vantage point he couldn't see if the rest of the plane was intact as the spotter plane pilot had indicated when he first located and positively ID'd the Warthog's location. Stewart lowered himself down the other side of the boulder he had stood on and approached the site with caution. He carefully worked his way toward what remained of the fuselage. He had to stay concerned with the potential of unexploded ordnance in the debris field.

After reaching the main debris field, he climbed to the top of another boulder to get a better perspective of the entire crash perimeter. He pushed his wind goggles up on his forehead, craning his neck all around, then rubbed his eyes to make sure he was certain what lay out before him. The rookie pilot had done an outstanding job of flying, somehow managing to find a postage-stamp size alpine meadow and successfully avoided auguring directly into the treacherous rocky cliffs.

I underestimated this guy.

True to its legendary reputation, a good portion of the Air Force's most durable war bird had actually survived the crash. Parts of it, astonishingly, remained almost totally intact. Other sections, though, were nothing more than gnarled pieces of metal strewn across an approximate one-hundred square yard area. The nose of the Warthog up to the missing Plexiglas-covered cockpit, however, had bored into a rock outcropping.

Adrenaline pumping through his veins, Stewart slid down the boulder and two-stepped it over to what was left of the tattered wreckage. He first checked under what was left of the wings.

"No Mk82s! He did it!" he shouted.

Then he saw the Willy Petes, the A-10's white phosphorous under-wing rockets. They were scattered about but he wouldn't have to worry about neutralizing these as he had disarmed them in the hangar the night before the A-10 Olympics kick-off. As for the live, 30mm ammunition from the nose gun, he'd have no problem safely recovering them, presuming he'd be able to locate all the rounds.

After he regained his composure from his euphoria, Stewart's primary focus became finding and retrieving the fictitious instruction sheet he had typed for Forster. He prayed to God he'd also locate the Bible. Stewart thought the book would be an excellent place to plant the suicide note. He hoped both the fake letter and the small book were still inside the relatively intact cockpit.

While looking through the cockpit he would also have to re-engage the ejection seat levers to their original positions. He presumed Forster had pulled up on them to eject and save himself prior to crashing. Feeling little if no remorse for Forster's demise, Stewart figured the captain must have shit his pants when the seat failed due to Stewart jamming all its levers the night before take-off. This was the best workaround, since he knew he couldn't tamper with the two, sealed thermal batteries used to trigger the explosive ordnance that catapulted the ACES II ejection seat. When he put the levers back into their down positions, he hoped it would look to Air Force investigators like Forster had not intended to use the last-minute escape device in his quest to what a final OSI report would later call, "The pilot's successful suicide mission."

Stewart had his work cut out for him and not much time to accomplish it before the team would radio him for the all-clear to follow him in. The cunning saboteur climbed on top of a wing and tip-toed his way to the cockpit. The Plexiglas canopy was nowhere in sight. As he approached the pilot's compartment from the rear, he could see a flight helmet leaning against the metal channel of where the canopy once sat. As he got to the cockpit, Forster's corpse remained strapped in. It looked to Stewart as if parts of the man's arms, torso, and legs had been pecked at, presumably by scavengers. The dead-looking pilot's visor was in the down position, its highly reflective surface thankfully, he thought, not allowing Stewart to see the man's face.

He scanned the interior for the letter and the Bible. The letter was sticking out of the pocket sleeve of Forster's flight suit. Stewart grabbed the paper he had switched on the tarmac the day of the event and swapped it out with the official letter.

"Now where's that goddamn Bible?"

Feeling a bit anxious, he stuck his head further down inside the A-10's cockpit. The smell was nauseating. He held back a gag. His feet dangled behind him as he leaned farther in, fumbling around, looking for the book. He patted the floor around Forster's feet while holding his breath, trying to keep the unpleasant odor of decay from making him vomit. Then his fingers touched something.

"There you are. Gotcha."

As he grasped the small book in his fingers, two hands grabbed him around his neck and began choking him. Then he heard a barely audible voice grovel and repeat, "Why? Why? Why?"

CHAPTER 26

In The Baca Grande, Colorado
August 1998, Late in the Month

The night was moonless when Paul Stewart arrived for his first visit to Tarshish after successfully accomplishing the inaugural part of his mission. On two weeks leave, he pulled up in his car and stopped at the main house. No sooner had he grabbed his suitcase from the trunk, footsteps crackled behind him on the pebble drive. He turned to see Jacob Lund approaching.

"This time of evening I think is the most beautiful part of the day here in the Baca." The old man tilted his head up as he spoke, looking to the east. "In the morning, the Lord Yahweh's light will shine upon us when the sun comes up over the Sangres. There."

Lund pointed to a saddle in the nearby mountains silhouetted by a curtain of stars. He closed his eyes and breathed in the nighttime air, pulling it in through his widened nostrils.

"I feel so serene here. So loved. So thankful the Lord has delivered you unto me, Brother Paul."

The man's words brought an immediate calmness to a fraught Stewart. The elder's deep voice, as dulcet as the soft breeze, made Stewart feel more at ease. This swaddling feeling allowed him to more easily share his next words with Jacob.

"Forster. The A-10 pilot. He was alive when I found him."

Jacob, looking stunned, cocked his head. "Alive?"

Stewart nodded. "I was on the recovery team that went in.

I went in first to the crash site, alone, so I could cover up everything I had done. I had no idea what condition the plane would be in but much of the aircraft was still intact. When I found him, he was still strapped in the cockpit. I assumed he was dead. He wasn't."

"How is that possible? You told me he'd never survive! That if the crash didn't kill him hypothermia, hunger, or thirst would!"

Trying to stay calm and not react, Stewart was rattled, though, by the panic sound of his leader's voice. Stewart went on. "I know . . . it makes no sense . . ."

"What did you do?"

"He surprised me. More like scared the shit out of me. He grabbed me by the throat. Tried to kill me with the last ounce of strength left inside him. As soon as I was able to pull his hands off my throat, he died. That experience rattled me. I feel like it might be an omen."

"Nonsense!" Lund's booming voice shattered the nocturnal tranquility. "Do not let this bother you and jeopardize the mission. He and his military war machine are no friends of ours. He was a casualty of our battle for righteousness. You mustn't let this sway you from your task ahead."

Stewart fell silent in thought. After a few moments he spoke. "But I can't get it out of my mind how he managed to stay alive that long. He had to have figured out that I was the one who had sabotaged his plane."

"What are you talking about?"

"It's what he said to me I can't get out of my mind."

"He spoke to you?"

"Yes. Just one word. He kept repeating, "'Why?' Somehow, he had managed to survive out there, alone. He must have known I'd be the one who'd find him first. He wouldn't allow himself to die until he knew. So he willed himself to live. Waiting. *Waiting for me—*"

"Stop that nonsense talk. Forster was our enemy. He's just one more dead nigger. You have done a wonderful thing for your people. I can't thank you enough for all you've done for our race in our fight to maintain its superiority."

He extended an open hand to Stewart. Grabbing his palm, Jacob pulled him close and wrapped his arms around him. Stewart at first felt awkward from Lund's strong, bear-like hug. The man had never made such a gesture before. He felt obliged to return the embrace. When he squeezed him back, the old man's musky odor wafted up into his nose, reminding him of his own father. Stewart's memory of the way his father had smelled came rushing back. He recalled his father's scent when he had laid his head on his dad's shoulder as he carried him to bed as a child. The reminiscence filled him with sadness. He gulped. His throat swelled recollecting how all those wonderful memories ended the day his dad turned into an angry drunk. A man who yelled and swore at the boy, then beat him for the shortcomings his father constantly saw in him.

Lund's embrace made Stewart feel physically, for the first time in a very long time, the unbending love of a doting, truthful father. He may be many things, Stewart thought, but one thing Jacob Lund was not was a hypocrite. Not like his own father had become when he had married a black woman, a race his father had taught him to hate. Lund was the farthest thing from being a charlatan. At least the Aryan stayed true to his beliefs. Built a whole community around promoting his philosophies. Travelled all across the Four Corners region, proudly preaching his separatist message.

From the time he had first met him in Wilma's secret room, Stewart knew exactly where Lund stood. He made a decision back then that he would follow Jacob like an loving and obedient son. The die had been cast and a deep bond had been formed between the two, sealed during all their time spent together right here at Tarshish. They were now inseparable, both spiritually and in their core belief in the fundamental righteousness of the white race. Stewart would do anything for this man now.

When Lund released him, he reached inside his pocket and pulled out a small card with a picture on one side and writing on the other. Lund placed the card in Stewart's open palm, then closed his hand around it. "The power of the story on this holy card here came to me in a vision last night. I want you to have it as a reminder of your calling."

Stewart smiled his thanks. He put the card in his shirt pocket without looking at it, not wanting to be distracted from relishing the deep feeling of peace and joy he was now feeling. Yet, he couldn't push out of his mind a pressing question he had for Lund—exactly how did the old man plan to use these bombs? Lund had never shared those intentions and Stewart had never prodded him for that information. He figured the fewer people who knew about the absconded military munitions—a federal offense for anyone involved—the better. Although he didn't know what Lund's plans were, Stewart surmised that at some point he'd be involved, since only a trained EOD specialist like him could safely interact with the Mk82s.

For now, Stewart had done all that Jacob had asked of him. But there was more work yet to do. Tomorrow, he would embark upon the last step of his, up to now, flawless plan of bringing the bombs to the sands of Colorado. Tonight, though, he would sleep in peace.

CHAPTER 27

Star Dune Complex
Baca Grande, Colorado

The next morning, Stewart set out well before the sun began its relentless crawl across the barren, arid Baca. Jacob had ordered Micah and Logan to assist him. The two men brought along a third man with blond hair who kept to himself. When Stewart first laid eyes on him, he did a double-take.

I don't fucking believe this! What the fuck is he doing here? He's part of Lund's group?

Upset by his recognition of the blond-haired man, Stewart quickly hopped behind the wheel of one of two, identical 1990 Jeep Cherokee XJ Pioneers Lund had secured for him. Both vehicles had four-wheel drive and were fitted with a Smittybilt twelve-thousand-pound rated, front-end, hydraulic winch, just as Stewart had specified Jacob to provide.

Micah got in the driver's seat of the other Pioneer with Logan at his side. The blond-haired man got behind the wheel of a large flatbed tow-truck. This last vehicle had been retrofitted with outriggers and a small cherry picker on its end, which was connected to a short-armed swivel boom with a hook. The end of the hook was attached to a thousand-foot spool of wire rope cable. Again just as Stewart had instructed Lund to supply.

Stewart led the three-vehicle caravan out on the only road into the Star Dune Complex, the barely navigable old Liberty Stagecoach Trail. When the retrieval team reached the northernmost edge of the dunes, Stewart pulled his Jeep over.

The other two vehicles pulled up behind him. Stewart jumped out of his Cherokee, not wasting any time. From the rear he grabbed a metal detector and donned a protective vest. On his belt he attached an Air Force-issued hand-held GPS device he had appropriated from the base. Then, without saying anything to the other three men, he set out alone across the dunes, leaving them behind.

He spoke out loud to himself when he got out of earshot, "Unbelievable! What are the fucking chances this prick is part of all this? I've got to find out why he's here!"

Although perturbed by the appearance of the blond-haired man, he got back on task and entered into his GPS the same coordinates he had supplied to Forster in his phony instructions for the bomb drop. He prayed Forster had followed the sheet precisely and didn't question why the competition wanted the pilot to drop the bombs all at one time. If Forster did as told, Stewart's retrieval would be much easier if the payload landed within a short distance from one another.

As he walked on the sand he recalled from his Air Force survival school training manual the correct way to navigate dunes: *If you walk in the troughs between the sand hills, it takes less effort versus trying to hike directly up and down the dunes.*

As he traversed the soft mounds he thought of his ingenious idea to jerry-rig the plane's critical arming wire to go down with the bomb versus staying attached to the wing's pylon. This meant that when Forster pickled the Mk82s they would not arm each electronic fuze as it was designed. Stewart couldn't be certain, though, if his trick had worked or that, even if successful, perhaps one—or God forbid all—of the Marks had re-armed themselves upon impact. Either way, he'd have to visually and physically inspect each bomb before trying to move it. Once the inspection was complete and he knew the fuze's detent pin was still flush and not protruding, the ordnance would be safe to move.

Within twenty minutes his metal detector yelped its first discovery, whining and sounding like one of the Baca's wild

coyotes. The machine's piercing siren broke the solitude of the
sublime, high desert morning. He knelt down and began gently
pulling back sand until he saw sheet metal. It was the Mark's
tail fin cowling. He marked the area with a small orange flag
then proceeded to look for the other three ordnances. In a
short time, he had found and tagged them all.

After a cursory inspection of each, he noticed the sheet
metal tail fins on three had harmlessly broken away and lay
stuck in the sand, buried behind the bomb's cast metal casing.
This gave him a direct view to each respective bomb's fuze. He
verified these three bombs were unarmed and safe to move.
Then he approached the last Mk82—the one with its tailfin still
intact. Being intact meant he'd need to gain access through the
tail's side panel in order to actually see the fuze, check its
integrity, and determine if the beast was armed. If the impact
had somehow engaged the fuze—and he didn't know it—then
the slightest movement could detonate the warhead.

The mantra of every EOD technician rang in his ears:
"*Initial success or total failure.*"

He slowly scraped away enough sand to gain access to the
side panel. Then he carefully loosened the three screws
holding the rectangular cover. He took out his long-blade
Bowie knife to pry the panel away from the cowling in front of
the tail fin. If this Mk82 was armed, one wrong move, one
inadvertent thrust, and he'd blow a forty-foot wide, ten-foot
deep crater into the sand and him, in EOD jargon, "into pink
mist."

CHAPTER 28

Stewart could now see the last bomb's electronic tail fuze but was unable to determine its position and identify with one-hundred percent certainty whether its small detent pin had been popped, thus arming the bomb. This left him in the stressful situation of needing to perform what was known in Explosive Ordnance Disposal as a "remote pull." This procedure of jarring the bomb to see if it explodes —albeit from a safe distance—was an EOD technician's most dangerous task.

The remote pull procedure would eliminate his concern as to whether the fuze had armed the ordnance or not. If it didn't explode after he jerked it, then it hadn't armed itself, making it safe to move. But if it did blow, he'd have to be far enough away from the blast zone to stay out of danger from the bomb's concussion. That was one challenge. The other would be explaining the explosion's huge boom to anyone who might hear it within its noise radius.

Successfully executing this risky exercise was a difficult enough job when done with the help of a highly trained EOD team at your side. Doing it solo would present its own set of unique challenges. The hazardous undertaking would require him to rig a hook and line set to the bomb, then attempt to jerk it from its location while he and his three fellow ASA brethren observed from far enough away to keep them out of harm's way.

Stewart's initial step would require him to perform the extremely delicate maneuver of wrapping a rope sling with a slip-knot around the bomb's circumference. Almost all of the warhead's seven-foot plus length was partially buried in the sand. Not having a regulation EOD hook and line set with him, he created a makeshift version using the cable and hook from the Jeep's Smittybilt winch. He hooked the cable rope sling he had successfully slipped over the bomb onto the winch and retreated back to where he had ordered his three-person crew to stay. Now about three hundred yards from the Mk82, he instructed the men to take cover behind a sand berm while he jumped behind the wheel of the waiting Cherokee.

His thoughts turned to the team's blond-haired guy. *Maybe you can stick your head up, asshole, and get it blown off.*

Stewart turned the ignition on the Jeep and, ever so slowly, flipped on the hydraulic system of the Smittybilt. He triggered the powerful winch into slow reverse until he felt slight tension on the cable. Then, with the engine revved to full RPM, he popped the clutch into reverse gear, jerking the Mk82 on the opposite end.

Nothing.

He revved the engine again, trying to get even more RPMs out of the Jeep's whining engine than the last time. He then popped the clutch.

Again, nothing. No blast.

All Stewart heard was the winding down of the engine as he took his foot off the gas. Believing he had completed a successful remote pull and all was safe, he took the tension off the cable by disengaging the winch.

"Let's go!" he yelled to the three men. "All's clear."

Micah, Logan, and the blond-haired man all stood up and followed Stewart who was already tracing his way back to the bomb's location by following the winch's cable. At the other end lay the Mark82, fully exposed on top of the golden sand, which he had jerked about ten feet. When the four of them reached the bomb, Logan spoke first.

"Is it a dud?"

Stewart shook his head. "No. It's still live but not armed."

"Is it safe to move it now?" Micah asked.

Stewart nodded.

The blond-haired guy stood silent.

"We'll winch it all the way back to the Jeep," Stewart instructed, "then pick it up with the cherry picker and put it on the back of the tow truck. We'll have to do that for each one of them."

For the next few hours the three men followed his precise instructions and extricated the bombs. Stewart and the blond-haired man didn't speak during this whole time. Micah stayed silent but his cousin, Logan, ran at the mouth, boasting about what he'd do with the bombs if he had his way.

When they had pulled them all back to where the vehicles were located and fastened them securely to the flatbed, not surprisingly, Logan spoke first.

"You did one heck of a job there, Paul. I knew the first day we met back at Wilma's you were a stand-up guy. I knew you'd come through for us. Now we can really blast a whole shitload of Mexicans from here to eternity with all this firepower."

The blond-haired man spoke his first words in a re-assuring manner, "Let's leave that decision to Jacob."

"Just exactly what does my Uncle Jacob plan to do with these gifts from my good Brother Paul here?" Logan asked. The huge man jumped up onto the back of the tow truck. He stood right next to the strapped down bombs and stared down at the three men below.

"I'm sure my father's answer will come from the Lord Yahweh," Micah said.

"An answer from Yahweh?" Logan shouted. "I don't need no fuckin' answer from Yahweh. We need to blow as many of these fuckin' Mexicans and all those uppity niggers in Phoenix back to where they came from with these here bombs!" He lifted a leg high into the air, then stomped down hard on one of the bomb's casings.

"Logan, you're cursing while using the Lord's name. Control yourself, cousin!" Micah shouted his plea.

"Don't fucking tell me to control myself! How about you and Caleb there go fuck yourselves?" He pointed at his cousin and the blond-haired man. Then he pulled his gun from its holster. Pointing his weapon away from the group, Logan discharged a round into a nearby sand hill.

Stewart couldn't believe the man was stupid enough to fire a weapon standing right next to all that highly explosive Tritonal. He worried if the next shot might hit one of the bomb's metal casings.

Holding up his hands high in the sky, Caleb spoke again. "Hey, Logan, we're all on the same side. So just take it easy now. I don't think it's a very good idea to be shooting that pistol of yours up there. Do you?"

Logan didn't answer.

"Logan, please put down the gun," Micah implored.

Stewart stayed silent but realized Logan's history of possessing a trigger temper and his unpredictable mood swings could pose risk to the whole operation. The man was a loose cannon, unstable at best. Stewart didn't have the skills necessary nor the time to learn how to render safe a human time bomb on the verge of exploding.

"I just don't want anybody telling me who I can and can't shoot. That's all I'm trying to say." Logan re-holstered his gun.

"Logan, I'm sure Jacob has a great plan for the gifts from the fiery angel," Caleb offered.

"Screw the old man!" Logan shouted. "You and Micah don't think I know about his cockamamie plan about blowing up dams and attacking Palo Verde. I heard you three discussing it. But I also know what he'd really like most to do. He'd like nothing better than killing that nigger lawyer in Phoenix. To avenge his poor son!" He pointed right at his cousin. "Isn't that right, Micah?"

Logan's revelation of Jacob's plans for the bombs grabbed Stewart's attention.

"Shut up, you fool!" Micah shouted up at him.

"The best place for all these bombs is down on the border," Logan shouted. "Killing Mexicans and blasting them to bits when they try illegally crossing. That's how I'd use them!"

"You just don't know when to keep your mouth shut. You're insane!" Micah cried.

With his last statement, Micah jumped up on the truck and stood toe-to-toe with his younger cousin. He inched in, close to Logan's face, and whispered to him, "If you interfere with Jacob's plan there will be a price to pay. A very heavy price!"

Out of earshot down on the ground, Stewart struggled to hear what the two men were saying to each other. He waited and watched as the cousins eyeballed each other on the back of the truck, almost a thousand pounds of high explosives at their feet. It looked to Stewart like two cowboys standing in the middle of the town square, waiting for the other to make the first move to draw.

Getting more nervous by the second that the family conflict might jeopardize everything he'd accomplished so far, Stewart pleaded with the men. "Why don't you two come down off the back of that truck before you both do something we'll all regret?"

He prayed the men would listen to him and each keep their cool, knowing an errant shot from any more gunplay could trigger a massive explosion.

Micah's and Logan's fingers were twitching. Each had one hand hovering over their respective side arm. As the tension grew, a car horn blasted in the distance. Surprised, all four men turned and looked to see another Jeep coming down the bumpy road and headed right for them. A cloud of dust swirled behind the fast approaching vehicle.

When the car stopped, Jacob sat behind its wheel. He shouted out to his team through the rolled down window. "Fantastic! You've found all of the gifts from Brother Paul's fiery angel! Alleluia and praise Yahweh!"

Logan muttered to Micah as they both stood smiling at Jacob. "This isn't over. Not by a long shot."

Stewart wondered what the fight between the two men was really all about. More pressing on his mind than this family bickering, though, was the unexpected re-appearance into his life once again of the blond-haired man, Caleb Tancos.

I've got to find out what that son-of-a-bitch is doing here.

CHAPTER 29

Back At Tarshish

Stewart stood alone in an underground bunker Jacob had built solely for storing the bombs. Rather than feeling elated over accomplishing the impossible, Stewart seethed, wondering why Caleb Tancos was at Tarshish and undeniably part of Lund's organization. Jacob entered the bunker, holding his chest out, looking like he was king of the world. He frothed as he asked his question. "How much real damage can I do with these jewels, Brother Paul?"

Besides being angry, Stewart was exhausted and didn't feel like talking. He gave a terse reply. "A lot."

Lund prodded him. "I desire to know specifically."

Stewart forced another reply. "Well . . . it depends . . . upon a lot of factors."

"Such as . . . ?"

He knew Jacob wouldn't give up until he had the answer he wanted. Stewart obliged him. "These types of explosives are meant to be dropped on hard or stationary targets, by plane, from high in the air. Exploding them while they're already on the ground requires a whole different skill set. It's an entirely different animal." Perturbed, Stewart went on. "Maybe it's time you tell me what you want. Then I can tell you how to accomplish that."

"I want to take down the City of Phoenix," Lund said matter-of-factly. "I want a coordinated attack using all four of the Mark eighty-twos at the same time. I want to cripple the almighty Valley of the Sun."

He stared back at Lund, staying silent for a few seconds, then replied. "Phoenix? Why Phoenix?"

"I want the people there to panic, to be afraid for their lives. To not know what hit them. I want them to cry to our Lord for relief from their suffering. I want to hear and see the wailing and gnashing of their teeth."

A four-pronged attack? On multiple ground targets? Did I hear him right? Is this man crazy?

"You'll need a lot of trained people, all working together as a unit, to pull off something so involved as that, let alone needing military-grade remote firing devices." Stewart walked over to the bombs sitting peacefully under a gray tarp. The bunker smelled musty from the recently excavated dirt piled in the corners. He patted the tattered covering. "Plus, you'd need a whole bunch of C-4 to detonate these babies, not to mention a shitload of detonation wire. The list goes on. I'm not really sure something like that could be done."

"Timothy McVeigh and Terry Nichols did it. Why can't I?"

"Because they had one homemade device stuck in the back of a single van with no one suspecting anything at all. And they went after just one target. You're asking me to coordinate a multi-pronged attack, simultaneously, with four, seven-foot-long bombs. That's a little different, sir."

Stewart fidgeted with the tarpaulin, making sure it was pulled tight over the Mk82s, wondering, as he did, if the old man hadn't gone completely mad.

"I remember you doubting you could bring me the fiery angel. You do remember that, don't you?"

Stewart gave a reluctant nod. "Jacob. I can detonate the bombs, no problem. But I'll need help, and lots of it, to get them in just the right place to do the most damage. How do you propose I do that?"

"I know you're about ready to retire from the Air Force. Correct?"

Stewart nodded.

"When you do, I will have a job waiting for you within one of the utility companies in the Valley. It's called SRP. That stands for Salt River Project. I have many connections there. Once inside the organization, you will learn all you can about their infrastructure. I especially want you to learn about the Theodore Roosevelt Dam east of Phoenix. The dam's original walls and foundation were built from thousands of stones, hand cut by masons, each fit tightly together when it went up over a hundred years ago. Just a couple of years ago, SRP added a completely new veneer of concrete, pouring it over the stones. The dam's now higher than before but not much thicker. I want you to breach that dam with our bombs. Do you think you can do that?"

"If I can get one close enough, I should be able to blow a very big hole in it. Though we may need to use more than a single Mark, and add some extra C-4 in each just for good measure. If I don't blow a hole through the dam, I could certainly compromise its integrity and perhaps make it fail."

Lund replied, wringing his hands. "And behold, the veil of the temple was torn in two from top to bottom, and the earth shook and the rocks were split."

"Matthew, chapter twenty-seven, verse fifty-one."

Lund smiled and nodded to his student. "SRP manages the entire Salt River watershed system and its lynchpin is Roosevelt Dam. Once you're hired, I will work on getting you clearance to get inside as a maintenance worker. The rest will be up to you to find out about how each of their other three smaller dams down river from Roosevelt work. You'll need to find out as much as you can about each, especially how to gain access, and the best way to take them all down."

"Why the dams?"

"Why the dams?" Lund laughed at the simple question. "Water and electricity, my dear boy! The two things people can't live without in the desert, especially in the summer when the temperature's one-hundred and ten. Take their lovely air conditioning and sparkling swimming pools away from those naive people living in their beloved desert paradise and they'll be climbing over each other, trying to get out, killing one another, I can only hope. Brother would fight against brother. Son against father. Only those few truly prepared would survive."

Lund stepped over to the covered explosives and pulled the tarp back. He stroked his palm across the cold metal casing of one of the warheads. In a calm voice, he continued telling his attentive disciple his blueprint for disaster. "I also want to strike Palo Verde? Can you just imagine? The great flood coming at them from the east where we've burst their dams, while at the same time instilling in them the fear a radioactive cloud is coming at them from the west." He paused and looked right at Stewart. "When people hear about the explosions, the response would bring about widespread panic. I want people to think it's the end of days."

Lund turned back to the steel cylinders and, using a handkerchief he pulled from his pocket, wiped one of them. In the stillness, he polished the smooth, hardened casing of the drab Mk82. The scene stood in stark contrast to the munitions' formidable power. Then he closed his eyelids and bowed his head.

"In that place there will be weeping and gnashing of teeth, then the righteous will shine forth as the sun in the kingdom of their Father."

Lund opened his eyes and peered up at Stewart with the gaze of a megalomaniac. "I couldn't have thought of a more poignant way to bring about the end of Phoenix."

Jacob answered lots of questions Stewart had in his mind. But not all of them.

"When did Caleb Tancos join your group?"

"Caleb's been an obedient follower for many years."

"He and I have this his—"

"History? I know all about you two and your past time together. That's another life. You have no need to bother yourself with that anymore. All that matters now is the future. To complete the tasks ahead of us. To eliminate the weak and impure. To keep the dream alive of a strong, white, and pure

America. That's why we're all here. To work as one. With one vision. One goal. To manifest our destiny."

Stewart decided, for now, to heed Jacob's words and set aside his anger about the sudden, unexpected reappearance of Tancos in his life. "There is one more thing, Jacob. When we were retrieving the bombs out in the sand dunes today, Micah and Logan were arguing over how you had planned to use them." He nodded toward the munitions on the ground. "Logan spoke about the dams but he also mentioned something about you wanting to kill a nigger lawyer in Phoenix."

"Unfortunately, many times Logan doesn't know when to stop talking. My dear deceased baby sister, bless her soul, spoiled the child. He's been uncontrollable ever since. Nonetheless, he is correct. I was going to tell you when the time was right. Seems that time is now. I have one of your gifts, my son, reserved for a very, very special person indeed. Here. I'll show you."

Lund took the end of his cane and scratched out large capital letters in the dirt: STAN KOBE.

CHAPTER 30

Driving to Davis-Monthan

Recovery mission accomplished, Stewart headed back to southern Arizona. He drove south on Colorado 17 as it turned into U.S. 285, heading down into northern New Mexico. The roads, as usual, were deserted for scores and scores of miles. His only companion was the blue sky and the sweet smell of the high desert juniper pines. The long ride home gave him plenty of time to think about all he had just been part of and witness to at Tarshish.

He replayed in his mind his last conversation with Jacob before he left the Colorado compound.

"I want Stan Kobe dead!" Lund had shouted as the two of them stood on the pebble drive outside Lund's adobe home. The anger in Jacob's voice pierced the quiet stillness of the breaking morn. The sound emanating from his threat was in sharp contrast to another loving, fatherly-like hug the man had just given Stewart.

Stewart had stayed calm the night before in the bunker and showed no emotion when Lund had first expressed his desire to set off one of the Mk82s in downtown Phoenix. Jacob's intent was to kill the only African-American prosecutor in the Maricopa County Attorney's Office—and anyone unlucky enough to be near him when the blast went off.

"You're clear on that, aren't you, son?"

"Yes, I'm clear. But why this vendetta against one man? I don't get it," Stewart had replied.

"That man stole something very precious from my son—

and me. Our pride. No one should get something they're not entitled to merely because of the color of their skin. Besides, what do you care? It's just one more dead nigger. Plus, there's a great deal more money in it for you if you add this target."

Stewart smiled, always liking the sound of more cash. "I can do it, but like I said, I will need help. And lots of it."

"I will get you all the assistance you need. Once you're discharged from the Air Force we can make all the final plans surrounding my plan of attack in detail. You can visit me again, here, at Tarshish. Stay as long as you like." The old man gave him an endearing smile. "In the meantime, think about how to accomplish this task I have set out before you. Think about preparing yourself. Cleanse your body and soul for what lies ahead. Simplify your life. For you are my chosen one, Brother Paul Stewart."

Stewart's thoughts faded of the conversation as he continued his drive southward on two-lane roads, first past Taos, then beyond Santa Fe toward Albuquerque. He turned his attention to formulating a plan to execute Lund's wishes. Lund's promise of getting him a position within the utility company would be critical. He'd need to know as much as he could about the infrastructure of the targets his leader had chosen if he wanted to make sure to destroy the dam or at the very least cripple it and bring about its failure. As for Lund's last target—downtown Phoenix—he didn't sense any stinging concern over being able to remotely detonate the Mk82 wherever Jacob wanted it to go off. The extra money offered was music to his ears, too.

Stewart figured if he could place a bomb in one of Logan's Red Rock police vans it would have a high probability of having unrestricted access to the downtown Phoenix corridor. Knowing Logan's desire to eradicate all non-Aryans, he would chomp at his bigoted bit to supply the transportation. He'd rely upon Logan to concoct a reason for making his out of jurisdiction, official vehicle end up in downtown Phoenix as well as cover-up its disappearance from Red Rock.

By the time Stewart reached the lonely roads of southern

Arizona, his mind drifted back to his days in Explosive Ordnance Disposal School at Eglin Air Force Base. He reminisced about the hundreds of hours spent learning about explosives and how to render them safe. He had always wondered in his training classes about devising a bomb that couldn't be safely disposed of. A bomb whose timing mechanism was so sophisticated no one could figure out how to stop it from exploding—a technician's worst nightmare.

For the last remaining stretch of his eight-hundred mile drive he thought about a fool proof way to carry out Jacob's desires. He glanced at his old Casio G-Shock wristwatch he had bought for himself when he entered EOD training. The timepiece was true to its name, standing up to every type of extreme condition and never failing him through all of his deployments. Simple, yet tough. A first of its kind.

"Wait!" he said aloud. Then he started talking to himself. "The key to making a fail-safe bomb isn't to make it too sophisticated, but to keep everything about its design as simple as possible. The challenge isn't to prevent people from rendering a device safe when they find it, but to make it so no one can actually find it . . . or, at the very least, make the timing mechanism not easily accessible."

As he neared home, driving south on Arizona Highway 60 through Gila County, fatigue set in. His tired mind wandered back to an event in a recurring nightmare he had begun to have shortly after return from his final secret deployment in Bosnia. In the fogginess of the dream he realizes his poorly timed explosive charge goes off too early, while he's swimming away from his target: a bridge over a river. The proximity of the huge blast pushes him down, deep into the swift moving water. Stunned by the blast's concussion, he opens his eyes, trying to see in the turbid river. When he does, he sees his father swimming toward him, hands outstretched in front of him, trying to save his boy. He's not sure if he should swim toward his dad or to shore, which is much closer. He looks back to his father, now struggling against the river's strong current. He reaches for the old man, but the current has pushed him too

far away. Too late to reach him, he watches his father sink
down to the bottom of the river and drown right before his
eyes.

CHAPTER 31

Scottsdale, AZ
Nearly Three Years Later
April 9, 2001

Since his discharge two years ago, Stewart had spent working as much overtime as he could, learning about all the workings of the Salt River corridor dams and Palos Verde Nuclear Power Plant. He had never asked Jacob exactly when he had planned to execute his attack using the high-grade explosives he had delivered to him almost three years earlier, nor was there ever a clear-cut timeframe shared with him as to exactly when Jacob wanted the bombs deployed.

That all changed in April 2001.

When Stewart drove up to his South Scottsdale home in the late afternoon of April 9, returning home from his day shift as a troubleshooter for the Salt River Project, he saw an unfamiliar truck parked in the driveway. Stewart parked his Ford F-150 alongside the other pickup, a late model GMC. The Jimmy, he noticed, had Colorado plates. Stewart's radar went up. Senses heightened, he was thankful his wife and children were away on spring break, visiting her parents, and not due home until later.

Anxious, he jumped from his beater work car and walked toward the house at a brisk pace. His instincts tugged at him to return to the vehicle and retrieve his .45, where he kept it tucked in a holster under the front seat. But it dawned upon him he had left the gun in his footlocker inside the garage, leaving him no choice but to enter his house unarmed. When he walked in through the side door, the same blond-haired man who had helped Stewart retrieve the bombs from the sands of Tarshish sat at his kitchen table.

"Hello, Brother Paul," Caleb Tancos said. He was drinking a beer. Another open bottle sat in front of him.

"I'm not you're brother. How did you get in my house?" Stewart demanded, setting his keys on a narrow kitchen counter. He considered for a moment about reaching for the largest knife from a holder nearby, but decided not to. Caleb wasn't there to kill him. If he had, he would have been dead as soon as he had walked through the door.

"The door was open. Safe neighborhood you got here."

Stewart hesitated, recalling the last time they had seen each other and his loathing of the man. "What do you want?"

"I don't want anything. I'm here as a messenger. Jacob sent me. He told me to tell you that it's time."

"It's *time*?" Stewart's heart started beating faster. Was his three year wait over for Jacob's call to action?

"Do you remember when he spoke to you in the sands of Tarshish about Matthew, chapter twenty-two, verse twelve? He told you the day would come when he would ask you to don your wedding clothes and partake. To call upon you to seize our enemy's servants, mistreat them, and kill them. To go out into this land, gather all the people you can find, the good and the bad, and fill our wedding hall with guests, so that you may destroy the murderers of our country and burn their city to the ground."

Wondering how Tancos knew all of what Jacob had said to him, and based upon his past dealings with him, Stewart was cautious about trusting the intruder. "Yeah. I remember." Stewart fumed that Jacob had chosen Tancos to deliver the message he had waited so long to receive. He thought again about going for the knife, less than two-feet away. He inched toward the counter but his uninvited guest must have read his mind. Caleb pushed his windbreaker back with one hand, exposing a sidearm in a shoulder holster. He put his bottle of beer down on the table, his other hand now free.

The loud ticking of the clock on the wall seemed to mark-off the pulsating tension in the room between the two men. Stewart moved away from the counter. "So, just exactly what is Jacob asking?"

"Sit down. Relax. Have a beer." Caleb pushed another bottle of brew across the table toward Stewart. "Here. I opened one for you, too."

"I would never drink with you."

"I don't get you, Stewart. You still blame me for what happened in Bosnia, don't you?" Caleb took a swig of beer, then continued. "It's time you got over all that. It's in the past. Now it's time for more important things. It's time for you to prove you're fully dedicated to our cause."

His remarks enraged an already agitated Stewart. "Get over it? Fully dedicated? What kind'a bullshit is this? First, don't just think you can sweep what you did to me in Bosnia under the carpet. And second, if Jacob doesn't know I'm dedicated by now, after all I've done—"

Caleb stood up and reached again inside his windbreaker, but this time to the other side. He pulled out a large white envelope and handed it over to Stewart.

"This will tell us if you're really all in. Here's your instructions. Follow them," Caleb said. "Then we'll reach out to you again."

Stewart hesitated, then snatched the envelope. Tancos smiled and walked out the door, then right down to the end of the driveway. There, he got into his truck, backed out into the street, and drove away.

"Drop dead, you prick," Stewart said.

Wondering what lay inside, he fondled the thick envelope for a moment. He grabbed a small knife from the counter holder and slit the seal open. Thick stacks of one-hundred dollar bills, rubber-banded together, filled the inside. Paper-clipped to the top of one stack was a handwritten note. The note had three lines:

This is a third of your payment.
In the next envelope are your instructions.

Remember, many are called, but few are chosen.

He placed the money on the kitchen table and counted it. "A hundred-thousand dollars. Perfect." On the other envelope, this one much smaller, centered and handwritten on the outside, Stewart read the following—

Genesis 22, Samuel 17, John 3:16.

He opened that envelope and pulled out a piece of paper. It was a letter, written in the same handwriting as on the outside.

Brother Paul,

I presume by now Brother Caleb has given you the envelope with the money that's been set aside for you, to help you in your tasks ahead and for the new life I've chosen for you. Caleb, as well, will be heading off on his given assignment, working for our cause against our government enemies on the inside. When you have completed reading this first page, the second page will have further detailed instructions for you and how we will provide safe harbor for you after you've completed your given task.

What I am about to tell you next comes about after a great deal of prayer to our Lord Yahweh. I must know for certain that you are fully committed and ready to deliver our message to the heathens who sin before us, to the weak and spineless leaders of our country, like my prosecutor friend, the shiftless black man, the darkie who intermingles his blood with a white woman. He is an animal like the illegal Mexicans who defile our land with their filthy foreign tongues. These are atrocities our government knowingly and willfully allows and without the desire or the approval of its citizens—the people of this country.

It is time for David to strike down Goliath.

As my chosen one, I now tell you that I, your Lord Melchizedek, have decided that your time has come to fully serve us and without hesitation. To serve us without doubt. You must leave your current life behind forever and devote yourself entirely to our cause. You must commit yourself wholly to the foundation, preservation and growth of the Church of the High Country.

So, as the Lord challenged his early believers, like Abraham, to prove their worthiness and devotion, I now challenge you to prove that same devotion beyond a shadow of a doubt. As God commanded Abraham to kill his only son, Isaac, I now command you to kill your family and leave no sign of them remaining on this earth. Incinerate them in the fires of hell, cleanse them of their sins and extricate yourself completely and totally from your former and present life, now and for all time to come.

Cleanse and prepare yourself to perform the great task that lies ahead for you.

I beseech you, be not worried for your family, for you are giving them everlasting life, martyring them so that they shall precede you into heaven and be waiting for you there beyond the gates of Paradise, sitting at the right hand of the almighty Lord Yahweh himself.

"For God so loved the world, that He gave us his only begotten Son, that whoever believeth in Him should not perish, but have everlasting life."

Your Lord Melchizedek

Stewart was stunned. Had Jacob gone mad? He dropped down on a chair and swigged the entire beer Caleb had left open for him at the kitchen table. Like the letter, the brew left a bittersweet taste in his mouth. Still in shock, he pushed the letter back into the envelope and stuffed it inside his shirt pocket. He grabbed several more beers from the fridge and went into the garage. He walked in circles for a few minutes, downing more beer. His dog walked in step with him, whining for attention.

He swigged on. His dog continued to moan, looking for response from his master. None came. He stopped in front of two footlockers he kept side-by-side in the garage. Inside one were various items, many stenciled with U.S. AIR FORCE. The container held a number of boxes of EOD de-arming slugs, two Mk152 remote firing device transmitters, a handful of Mk152 remote firing device receivers and several Mk Mod 1 .50 caliber de-arming tool kits. The heavy storage box also held some incendiary devices with timers, half-a-dozen mine probe kits and an array of handguns with ammo for each, including several .40 caliber Sig Sauers and another .45.

He opened the second footlocker and visually inventoried its contents: several dozen two-and-one-half pound blocks of C-4 explosives, a roll of detonation cord, and a healthy amount of time fuse packages, each five-hundred minutes to a package. He had absconded with all the various munitions during his time spent at Davis-Monthan.

When he reached down into the locker, he felt woozy. Toward the bottom lay his Bowie knife. He grabbed it and drew the blade out from its leather sheath. The nine-inch length of steel glimmered in the overhead fluorescent lights. He pulled his wallet out from his back pocket and flipped through it until he found the holy card he had carried with him since the day Jacob handed it to him at Tarshish. Emblazoned with the image of a diminutive yet triumphant David standing with one foot on the mammoth chest of the headless giant, he struggled to focus on the image—*am I crying?*—of the boy with a slingshot in one hand and the decapitated head of Goliath in the other.

An intense pain pounded out the words from Jacob's letter inside his head, magnifying their significance and the man's clear message: "*I now command you to kill your family and leave no sign of them remaining on this earth.*"

Head cloudy, he struggled to recall the details of his last conversation he had with the man who called himself Lord Melchizedek—*he never told me I'd have to kill my family!*—but all he could recollect now in his spinning head were memories of images of the bridge over the Miljacka River in Bosnia and children crying for help as they struggled to stay afloat in the frigid water.

Stewart's eyelids felt so droopy. He struggled to keep them open as he forced another swig of beer down. He took his single-edged Bowie knife and, as if in a trance, he honed it awkwardly, stropping the blade back and forth across the face of the holy card, trying to focus on the immensity of his sacrificial task ahead.

Craving sleep, Stewart sat down on a small military cot he kept in the garage. He had received what he understood to be clear-cut instructions from Jacob Lund to eradicate his entire family. Shivering from head to toe, he took one more sip of beer.

Then, the room went black.

CHAPTER 32

April 10, 2001
A little after 7:00 a.m.

"**M**y God! What have I done?"
The words screamed out of Paul Stewart's mouth as a nightmare had awaken him from his fret-filled sleep. He sprang upright on the cot, body shaking out of control. He was drenched in blood. His knife, sticky with the crimson liquid, lay on the garage floor beside him.

Dear Lord! What have I done?

He flew up onto his feet and scanned the garage. Trails of blood from the kitchen door lead back to where he stood.

Oh, my fucking head . . . what did I . . .?

His hangover was monumental. Empties were strewn underneath the small, narrow bed. He couldn't remember ever having such a painful headache from drinking too much. He mumbled to himself, "Oh, dear God. What happened?"

He looked all around his space. Besides all the blood, he thought the room looked exactly like he had remembered prior to passing out. His footlockers remained open. He did a quick cursory scan of each. All seemed to be just as he left it . . . except. He frantically dug through both of his military cases. "Where are my incendiaries?" He placed his palms flat against his temples and cried out in pain. "My goddamn head."

Afraid to go through the door into his house and find out what had transpired inside, rather he tried to conjure up a picture in his blurred memory. He squelched back his gag reflex. He slammed shut the cases and padlocked them. Then he heaved them both into the back of his truck. His dog barked wildly inside the locked cab. He hadn't remembered locking the pet in there, explaining the hound's frenetic behavior.

Panicking, he grabbed everything he thought he would need, including a fresh work jump suit. He quickly put on the new clothes after getting out of his bloodied garments, which he stuffed inside a plastic garbage bag and threw it into the back of his Ford pickup. Making sure all the items were securely stowed, he opened the door and leashed the hysterical dog.

Stewart jumped in the cab, started the engine, and opened the garage door. He carefully backed out, closed the door, drove away, and made himself a ghost.

CHAPTER 33

Somewhere On The Mogollon Rim
Present Day, Ten Years Later
April 12, 2011

Now over ninety, former Maricopa Superior Court Judge Jacob Lund had been mandatorily retired from the state court system for over twelve years. After the demise of Wilma's Red Rock Tap House back in the late 90s as the covert home of the Aryan Sons of Arizona, Lund had needed a new Arizona location to hold his monthly meetings. He had always wanted to distance himself from the northern part of the state, preferring not to hold the gatherings of his Church of the High Country near his ancestral home in Rim Country. His Colorado retreat in the Baca Grande fit the need, giving him separation, but his advanced age made long distance travel to his beloved Tarshish too difficult.

His ASA followers had suggested building a structure to hold their rendezvous in the pine forests east of Payson. After initially balking at the idea, he had agreed to move the secret meetings to a steel-fabricated building members built and surrounded with chain link fence topped off with razor barb. The building, constructed to resemble one of the area's many U.S. Forest Service maintenance sheds, stood alone, hidden deep in the woods off the edge of the Mogollon Rim.

At tonight's meeting, Lund sounded much more somber than usual. His voice was void of hyperbole, subdued in its tone. There was no ranting rhetoric. All night he had paced in front of them, discomfort on his face. He closed his very short talk that night with the words, "Your high priest, your servant, I, your Lord Melchizedek, beseech you to tie him hand and foot, and throw him outside, into the darkness, where there will be weeping and the gnashing of teeth. Help us smite the heathens from the face of the earth."

After these last words, Jacob sat and stayed silent while the assemblage of men standing on the cold, concrete floor, left in subdued silence. As each strode toward the door, one-by-one they retrieved their respective firearm from a footlocker sitting by the door. The last man locked the military-looking container with a large padlock.

Outside in the darkness, each man, wearing their firearm on their hip or in a shoulder holster, jumped inside his vehicle. The majority of them drove the off-road variety or a pickup truck. Rear cab windows boasted gun racks holding one or more rifles.

"Son, please wait up a minute," the silver-haired Jacob said. The old man struggled to catch up, his cane tapping the unlit ground, supporting his slow gait.

Micah Lund turned around.

"Yes, father."

"Everything is ready in the Baca. Caleb texted me just now and told me the last of the equipment arrived and is being wired in. It should all be online by late tonight, tomorrow morning latest. So, it is time to strike. And the timing couldn't be better. The nigger Kobe's wife is speaking in a few days. I will live to see the day that man is dead. It will be sweet revenge for not giving my only son the job he was entitled to."

"I can't wait," snarled Micah.

"Call Stewart down from his sanctuary. I will meet him tomorrow at his place at sunrise. Tell him . . . tell him I'm ill."

"I will contact him," Micah said. "But I should tell you, I am concerned. He's been depressed more than usual. Frankly, he's never really been the same since that day . . . even after all these years. When I was there last time I found him sitting and staring at those pictures he has plastered over the walls of his wife and kids. He had pulled down the newspaper clippings he had pinned up, too, and had them spread all over the floor."

"Do you think he would have doubts after all this time? For ten years we've all waited patiently. Plus, I need to move on our plan *now*. I'm getting pressure from D.C. from the promise I made to the congressman." The father stared at his son. Jacob's eyes glowered. "I've paid Stewart a lot of money. He owes me."

The rumble in the elder man's last words seemed to shake the ground. His booming voice felt like the reverberation of an immense thunderclap delivered by one of the Rim's infamous monsoon storms.

Micah affirmed his father with a few quick nods.

"Stewart needs to prepare the bombs then deliver them to the targets. We will finally turn the table on this government who does nothing to stop this invasion. These fools will come running to us when they have no electricity. We'll have them eating out of our hand."

Micah hugged his father goodbye and jumped in his truck. The diesel engine roared back when he turned the ignition. He grabbed the hand-held microphone from his under-the-dash mounted ham radio and spoke into the mic.

"KF6RIM mobile this is KF7RIM mobile. This is Little Tarshish. Come in, Fiery Angel. Over."

Micah waited for a return call on his ham. None came.

He repeated his CQ. "KF6RIM mobile this is KF7RIM mobile. Fiery Angel. This is Little Tarshish. I repeat. This is Little Tarshish. Come in, Fiery Angel."

A few moments of silence passed before the speaker on Micah's radio crackled a reply.

A military-sounding voice gave a return message, "KF7RIM, this is KF6RIM. I read you, Little Tarshish. This is Fiery Angel. Over."

Micah's voice raised an octave in excitement. "Fiery Angel. Our Lord Melchizedek has told me to tell you, the time has come."

Seconds later, KF6RIM replied. "Roger that, Little Tarshish. I await your orders."

* * *

On The Mogollon Rim
April 13, 2011
Sunrise

Jacob sat in the passenger seat of his son Micah's pickup truck at the base of the abandoned U.S. Forest Service fire lookout. The shuttered tower had been hideout and home to the fugitive Paul Stewart for nearly a decade, since the day he disappeared after the slaying of his family and the torching of his home in Scottsdale. He had hidden on the Rim in relatively plain sight within a few miles from the spot of the discovery of his dead dog and empty pickup truck.

The search posse, largest in Arizona's history, had been supervised by Micah, the sheriff of Gila County and Stewart's fellow Aryan Sons of Arizona brother-in-arms. The shrewd lawman had coached Stewart during the planning stages years earlier, telling him the best place for a fugitive to hide was right under the noses of those who looked for him the hardest. Micah had planned Stewart's disappearing act to perfection. The sheriff's deputy had stocked provisions for Stewart in the hundred-foot-high edifice as well as regularly burying replenishments within a fifty-yard circumference of the hideout. The plan was for Stewart to lie low in the deserted tower for a few months, six tops. Time enough for the excitement surrounding his family's gruesome killing to die down and become another Valley murder story buried in the back section of *The Arizona Republic.*

But what the ASA hadn't envisioned was several days before their planned extrication of Stewart and re-locating him to Tarshish where he could focus on planning and executing Jacob's plans, foreign-born terrorists struck the Twin Towers and the Pentagon, changing the lives of Americans forever. The good news for the ASA was the FBI's search for Paul Stewart was pushed to a backburner. This meant the search for

Stewart went nearly completely cold, along with the nine other domestic criminals at-large posted on the Bureau's famous Ten Most Wanted list. The capture of Osama Bin Laden and other enemies of the government had taken center stage and became a top priority for the most sophisticated law enforcement agency in the world.

The bad news for Jacob Lund, though, was that even the mere thought of moving any type of explosive materials anywhere within the U.S. became impossible. This caused Lund to indefinitely table his domestic terrorism attack using his Mk82s. One year turned into five, then five into ten. So as not to allow him to go stir crazy from the long sequestering, Micah had found a few local odd jobs for the fugitive. Although risky, he got Stewart work that involved little or no interaction with people. The work had barely kept Stewart sane and, although he never complained about his situation, the years of isolation, coupled with the weight on his shoulders of the crime, took its emotional toll.

"My father will tell us when the time is right again to strike," Micah had said to Stewart many times during his years in seclusion.

For the ASA, however, and hate groups like them—as well as for every known terrorist group, both foreign and domestic—the FBI made sure things never cooled off. The pressure from the feds forced Jacob to continuously postpone his attack. But now, Stewart had been told by Micah that Jacob's health was failing, forcing him to move forward.

"You look tired, Brother Jacob. Are you okay?" Stewart stood alongside the truck and spoke through the open window.

"I am dying, my son. I don't know how much longer I'll be of this world. But before I go, I will live to see my plan carried out to strike our enemies. That time has come."

Jacob hoped his unprecedented visit and desire to resurrect their bombing plan would be received well by Stewart.

Although he looked ragged, the lonely man's eyes widened bright. "I have waited a very long time for this visit.

During my separation from society and my past life, rather than diminish, my devotion to the cause is even stronger. While in this exile, I have spent this time in solitude reading the Bible, the Book of Mormon, and the Koran."

"Micah tells me you have an altar, a shrine devoted to your family up there." Jacob looked up the hundreds of steps that inched their way skyward to the small cabin on the top of the tower.

"I pray for my wife and children. Every day. You had told me I would join them one day, beside our Lord. You had said so in your letter to me that day. Do you remember?"

Jacob nodded. "Their loss will not be in vain. You will be reunited with them one day soon."

"Then, so be it."

Jacob gave him an approving look but was overcome with an uncontrollable cough. Micah, sitting next to him behind the wheel, handed him a handkerchief.

"Thank you, son." He gave his only child a smirk.

"You remember Brother Caleb, don't you?" Jacob asked, turning his attention back to Stewart.

Eyes narrowing, Stewart gave Jacob a weak nod. The mention of Caleb Tancos's name after not speaking or hearing it in ten years brought a tense look to his face.

"He helped you all those years ago with the bombs. He was my messenger to you as well. I want you to travel to the Valley and meet him in Chandler. He's been diligently gathering an army there to help you." The old man began coughing again, acting like he was struggling for air. He motioned for Stewart to come closer and whispered in his disciple's ear. "Do not despair. We are calling the wedding guests from the street, to fill our wedding hall. Clothe yourself for their arrival."

Stewart took the old man's withered hand and held it through the open window. "His will be done."

CHAPTER 34

Farmhouse
Chandler, AZ
April 13, 2011

Exactly ten years and three days later, Paul Stewart made his return to The Valley of the Sun. When he had met his ASA leader earlier that morning, Jacob had given him detailed instructions of what lay in store for him in Chandler. An ASA member had obtained a clean car for Stewart for the trip. The plan was for him to meet Caleb, whom he hadn't seen since the day Tancos had surprised him in the kitchen of his home. The very same day Caleb Tancos had left him with Jacob's killing instructions and a stack of money.

He wondered if Caleb would recognize him since Stewart had grown a lengthy beard during his time in hiding. As well, he now wore his hair shoulder length. He looked completely the opposite from his faded photo on FBI posters, which showed him with a shaved head and beardless face.

Jacob's directions led Stewart to a small farmhouse on the rural outskirts of the Phoenix suburb. Stewart barely recognized the area when he pulled up across from a dilapidated house isolated in the 22600 block of South Alma School Road. A faded, rusted metal sign in a white stanchion displayed the words: LAPAGLIA FARMS. Chandler, like most of Maricopa County, had seen a huge building boom during the latter part of the '90s and into the mid-half of the following decade. It was a time when already scarce farmland went under the bulldozer to make way for the next sub-division

of cloned, cookie-cutter homes, threatening to remove every
vestige and memory of farming life in the century-old
community.

Stewart sat in his car on the dirt shoulder. Across the road,
two vehicles stood parked in front of the house. Railroad ties
were lined parallel to the foundation of the diminutive building,
creating the border of a crude-looking parking lot. A rutted
driveway led from the main road to the dirt lot. Although dusk,
he was still able to see that most of the tarpaper had peeled
away from the structure's roof, adding to the place's rundown
appearance. The disconnected electrical feed from the service
pole to the house explained why there were no lights on inside.

He kept his engine running and waited. It was six p.m. and
the sun would fully set in about an hour, the time he had been
told by Jacob to meet Caleb. While he waited, three times an
unmarked panel van had pulled up to the house, then drove
around to the rear of the property. Each time the windowless,
non-descript vehicle remained for only a few minutes before
speeding away.

Five minutes after the third van visit, a Hummer, painted
in camouflage, pulled up to the front of the house. Two men
got out. The driver, a small man, had a dark complexion. The
man who exited from the passenger side, besides being much
taller, was fair-skinned. Blond hair stuck out from under his
cap. Stewart wasn't able to get a more detailed look at their
faces due to the fast approaching darkness. He remained
focused on the two as they entered the structure. He looked at
his watch. Seven o'clock sharp.

That has to be Tancos.

Stewart decided to leave his car where it sat then walked
across the road and approached the house. He carried a
knapsack filled with the items necessary to conduct his task
based upon his final conversation with Jacob. In his tote were
also several handguns, besides the one he wore in a shoulder
holster under his windbreaker. As instructed by Jacob, he
knocked on the door four-times before it opened.

"Come in," the man said. "You must be Brother Paul."

Stewart thought he recognized the face as one of the men he had once seen many years ago at Tarshish. But he couldn't remember his name. Stewart's look must have given his thoughts away to his greeter.

"You may not remember me. I'm Brother Adam. I'm one of the men who helped build the earthen shelter for your bombs."

Stewart lifted his chin in acknowledgement and walked in. A reeking stench collided with his nose and made him gag. He recognized the smell of human waste, both urine and feces, from time spent in a secret CIA prison in Bosnia. He also breathed in the most awful odor in the world—the one you never forget—the redolence of death.

Adam guided him. "Don't worry. It takes a few minutes to get used to all of this Mexican piss and shit. You'll be fine."

Stewart followed him into a large, open space and stopped. In the center of the room sat an empty and heavily worn brown couch. Scattered around were about two dozen men and women of all ages, each looking petrified as they huddled together on the barren floor. Some of the women cried, while others, both women and men, fingered rosary beads in their trembling hands, whispering prayers in Spanish.

"Brother Caleb?" Adam shouted at the blond-haired man standing with his back to them in what looked like the dining room.

The blond-haired man spun around. "Brother Paul! You've arrived. We can start our selection process now."

"Selection process?" Stewart asked.

"Yes," Caleb replied. "My associate Jaime here and I have been gathering the guests from the desert for the wedding feast." Caleb put a hand on the shoulder of a diminutive Mexican man standing beside him. Stewart recognized him as the driver of the Hummer. "These folks, these poor souls, have been wandering in the desert, like Moses and his lost tribes. But now they have been found and we shall ask them to give their services to help us carry out Jacob's plan."

Stewart had no idea what Tancos was talking about. His

look of not understanding the man's words prompted Caleb to continue his explanation. He leaned into Stewart's ear and lowered his voice to a whisper.

"These are the people who will help you plant your bombs. Jaime will ask them questions to see what type of skills they have and how trustworthy they are. Then we'll select the best for you. The others will all be shipped back to Mexico, courtesy of my friends at ICE."

"This is ridiculous." Stewart waved Caleb off. He hadn't waited all this time to be told the "help," as Tancos called it, promised by Jacob would come in the form of illegals, most, he assumed, who spoke no English. "We need trained people with military experience to pull off what I've been asked to do. Are you mad?"

"Military experience? We're looking for American-born recruits all the time but good luck in finding any of those fine men and women. Our enemy—big brother government—has been tracking every ex-military coming back in CONUS. We have a couple of people who passed through their screenings and are under the radar, but, as you know, the old man's time is near, so these illegals will have to do. They will act as our foot soldiers."

"And, *Señor*, they can be very good as—" Jaime turned to Tancos, asking him for help to complete his statement, "—*como se dice in ingles, señuelos, amigo?*"

"Decoys," Caleb replied.

"But they don't speak English!" Stewart's anger grew. "How will we get them to understand, or even cooperate?"

"Oh, they 'sah-bay in-glaze.' Don't you worry about that." Caleb beamed a menacing grin. "We will get them to understand and cooperate. No worries there." He looked at Jaime. "Let's show him how. Okay, *amigo?*"

Caleb got up and grabbed one of the starved-looking illegals, pulling him over by the scruff of his neck. He stood him right in front of Stewart. The boy, probably no more than fifteen, looked like he hadn't eaten in a week. His foul odor brought Stewart's gag reflex rushing back.

"Tell our friend here, Jaime, what we need him to do."

Jaime rattled off words so fast in Spanish Stewart wondered if the boy could understand what he was saying. When Jaime finished, the kid's eyes bugged out. He whipped his head back and forth, saying, *"No, Señor! Por favor! No!"* His skin became even more pallid than it was before Jaime's rant.

"Explain to him one more time," Caleb scowled. Jaime repeated his words. The boy shook his head even harder, this time not speaking.

"Sit him down on the couch!" Caleb ordered.

He grabbed another illegal by the front of his shirt. This man, a bit older, smelled even worse than the first. Several of the women started praying a little louder, pressing their rosaries to their chests. Questions were asked again in Spanish to this man, who pleaded with his captors even more than the first, shaking his head left and right half-a-dozen times.

"Sit down next to your pal!" Tancos screamed as he pushed the man down onto the couch.

Stewart watched and listened as Caleb and his Mexican sidekick repeated this same act with a third man, quite a bit older, getting the same results. When the last man stopped shaking his head, Caleb, standing behind him, pushed the man down on the couch. Tancos looked over at Jaime and nodded his head. Jaime then repeated his speech in Spanish to all three of them. Same reply: all three men shook their heads back and forth.

Caleb snatched the first one, the boy. He forced him to kneel down in front of him with his back to him. He drew his knife from its sheath on the side of his boot. Then with his free hand he grabbed the teenager by his scalp, jerked his head back, and slit his throat. Blood gushed like a raging river from the open wound. Using the serrated-edge side of his military knife, Tancos then sawed back and forth until he decapitated his victim.

CHAPTER 35

Stewart stood dumbstruck as his ASA comrade finished the decapitation of the illegal Mexican National. The wailing and screaming coming from the mouths of the women in the room, some too frozen with fear to even turn their heads away, sounded like they had all just seen the face of *el diablo* himself.

Eyes glazed over, Caleb spoke. He emphasized his words to his Hispanic comrade by pointing with the tip of his blood-drenched knife toward the two men left on the couch. "Ask that son-of-bitch there one more time if he's ready to serve his new master and help us carry out our tasks."

Sounding to Stewart as if Jaime's own life would be at stake if he failed to obey Caleb's order, Jaime shouted in Spanish to the second man, who sniffed back tears. Eyes bulging, Jaime shrieked his words louder. The illegal, uncontrollably crying now, gulped air between tearful jags. He swallowed for a breath and looked like he was about to pass out in the squalid room. The older man next to him remained silent, frozen in panic.

"A cry baby's no good to us," Caleb said. "I can tell right now he won't follow through with anything we tell him to do." He crept up behind the young man and in the blink of an eye cut his throat ear-to-ear with his razor sharp blade. When he slit the man's taut skin blood spewed everywhere. His gurgling scream died as quickly as he did. The walls echoed with the cries from the wailing women, some emitting spiritual ejaculations from their lips, asking *Jesu Cristo* to please save them.

Caleb then sawed off the second victim's head, again with

the serrated edge of his blood-soaked knife. When he was finished, he tossed the dome to the living room floor where it rolled to a stop. The man's bloody *cabeza*, with its eyes still frozen wide open, looked as if it was taking the entire macabre scene all in, wondering what had just happened.

Then Caleb flung his leg over the back of the couch and kicked the now headless man square in the back. As the body slumped to the floor, a still energized nervous system caused the corpse to writhe and convulse.

Screeching yelps from the remaining illegal men and women filled the large room. Caleb clenched his teeth and covered his ears with the palms of his hand. Blood fell down his wrist and forearm as he held high the dripping knife.

"*Callarse!*" Caleb shouted, hoping to silence them and still their hysteria. "*Callarse*, I said! *Silencio!*"

Nobody in the room listened to Tancos. As the group continued to scream and cry, a few vomited. Stewart thought they must have believed their own beheading was only moments away.

Caleb came around the couch and stood in front of the remaining older man, who stayed seated. Except for the sounds of regurgitation and whimpering, the room fell silent in shared terror. The man wouldn't look at Tancos but rather stared past him at Stewart. The Mexican man's blank gaze felt to Stewart like it seared right through him. He was in awe that the man hadn't flinched once as the sordid executions had unfolded right in front of him.

Caleb turned back to Stewart. "Did you bring your supplies as instructed?" He spoke calmly as if the bloodbath at his feet from his own hand hadn't even happened.

Tancos's question snapped Stewart to attention. He jerked his thumb back toward the knapsack wrapped around his shoulder.

"Pull out one of your remote firing device receivers. I need to show *mi amigo* here what one looks like and tell him what we want him to do. He looks like he *sabes* now what's in store for him if he doesn't cooperate. Isn't that right, *mi amigo?*" Caleb snarled his words. The killer was covered in blood, literally from head to toe. His face, splattered with human muck, truly looked diabolic. He wiped his eyes with the back of his sleeve but it did little to diminish his sanguine death mask.

Stewart pulled his knapsack off his back and brought it in front of him. He dug down and pulled out a plastic, electronic-looking device. He handed the small, olive-drab box to Caleb, who then looked at Jaime.

"Please explain to our *amigo* here what this is and what we need him to do for us," Caleb said calmly.

This time, Jaime spoke slowly and very deliberately in Spanish to the man on the couch. Caleb's cohort sounded as if he wanted to be perfectly clear what he desired the captive illegal immigrant to understand. Jaime turned the receiver he had been handed from Caleb a few times in his hand, then gave it to the seated man. The man took it and stared at it. He showed no emotion as Jaime continued with his speech. Jaime finished, saying, "*Es verdad? Tu comprendes ahora que queremos tu que hacer?*"

The man on the couch nodded several times, looking like he had succumbed to the questioning, averting the imminent threat to his life after watching two of his fellow border crossers have their heads lopped off right before his eyes. Those men lay dead now on the floor in front of him. Their heads sat awkwardly beside their torsos, blood still oozing from where necks once connected heads to shoulders.

The man on the couch continued his inspection of the remote firing device, turning the strange-looking box in his hands. His look went from the box to the beheaded men on the floor and back again. Then he set the plastic box on the floor between his feet and proceeded to stomp it with his boot, shattering it into pieces.

CHAPTER 36

South Phoenix

Stewart sat in the passenger seat of Tancos's van in the parking lot of a Denny's along the interstate while Jaime had gone inside to use the restroom. A still agitated Stewart wondered why Tancos had decided to execute—Sinaloan cartel-style—three Mexican illegals he'd held hostage.

"What purpose did it serve killing them that way?" Stewart asked.

"I was testing those men to see if they'd obey orders. You and I have been instructed to carry out Jacob's task. To deliver the gifts from your fiery angel," Tancos said.

"I'm not questioning our mission. What I am questioning is the beheading—"

"Like your family?"

Tancos's statement rattled Stewart. He was not only stunned by Tancos's words but angered. "Beheadings? That was never reported in the papers."

Tancos squirmed in the drivers' seat, looking uncomfortable. He stumbled with his answer. "You forget . . . the power and the reach of Jacob . . . he has many friends in high places in Arizona's government—"

"What are you fucking talking about? I want to know what you know about the deaths of my family!"

"Look. I know what I know. The police may have kept that detail from the media but Jacob's instructions to you were clear."

Stewart thought of reaching inside his jacket and pulling

out his .45. "Jacob gave me very little time to pull off this mission. If I didn't need you, I'd kill you myself, right here and now."

Stewart turned his head and looked out the passenger window at the flickering neon lights of the Ahwatukee neighborhood shopping center. The glittering colors hypnotized him as he tried to remember the details of the night of the slaying of his family. None came. All he could remember from that night before passing out was looking at the holy card of David . . . the one where the boy carried Goliath's head after severing it from the giant's body. He remembered thinking Jacob had sent him a message. One from the Lord himself.

He never stopped thinking of his wife and two boys, picturing them in his mind every day for the last ten years. Yet he still had no recollection of that dreadful night. All he had been left with was the sordid memory of his clothes and the cot he laid upon, both drenched in blood.

"I did it to mislead the authorities," Tancos said, changing the subject back to Stewart's original question. "Chopping off *cabezas* is the trademark of the Sinaloan cartel. They've been dumping headless corpses all over the border towns of Mexico, sending a message to their enemies. I thought this would make the police think the drug cartel was somehow involved, leading them in that direction versus ours."

Stewart refused to even give him the courtesy of a nod. He didn't think it was possible but the chasm between the two white supremacists had gotten deeper. He thought back to the day Caleb Tancos showed up in the Baca, sent by Jacob, Stewart presumed, to help him retrieve the bombs. It was the first time he had seen Tancos since the debacle at the Miljacka River in Bosnia. He had wondered how the ex-Army Ranger had ended up in Jacob's camp, a member of Lund's inner circle, no less. Coincidence? Perhaps. But, if so, one he'd decided not to dwell upon. Caleb had not brought up back then the fact the two men knew each other at that surprise Colorado meeting, so Stewart went along. Years later, when the blond-haired man showed up at his house, it had crossed his mind that perhaps Jacob had sent Tancos there to kill him, or that Tancos had come to settle, once and for all, who was at fault for the Pale tragedy.

Sitting in the van only inches away from his nemesis, he refused to look at Tancos and converse with him any longer about the past. "Let's get to the task at hand. I need to get these bombs prepped."

"That's already underway. Micah has them in route here," Tancos said. "In fact, he sent me a text not long ago that the truck should already be in Phoenix. We're supposed to rendezvous with the shipment at a warehouse on the west side."

"Let's get over there then. I've got a lot of work to do to get those Mark eighty-twos ready."

Still angered, Stewart put his head against the passenger window and closed his eyes, wishing he were somewhere else. Emotionally drained after being called to action after so long in hiding, he drifted off. When he did, he revisited the nightmare that had haunted him for so many years.

CHAPTER 37

West Phoenix

The van's swerving motion jolted Stewart awake as Tancos exited the northbound lanes of the I-17 freeway at Thomas Road. "Where are we?"

"Near west side. Maryvale," Tancos said.

Tancos turned the unmarked panel truck westbound onto Thomas, pointing it toward 35th Avenue. Once there, he made a hard right, leading him into one of Phoenix's manufacturing districts.

"Right down this street is an old printing company that belongs to a friend of Lund's." Tancos pointed out the window. "He's contracted with him to store what he thinks are some of Jacob's farm equipment he's getting ready to sell. He's even left him a forklift inside to move them around."

The seedy industrial park was located in a high crime district, a place where people didn't work late at night. Their nondescript vehicle pulling into the back of the building on North 35th Avenue wouldn't be noticed. Tancos wheeled the panel truck into the alley behind one of the buildings and pulled-up beside a semi-truck, which stood idling, running lights on. When he stopped alongside the truck, Stewart noticed the drab tarpaulin side panels on the attached trailer. They had no markings on them but the door of the red cab was stenciled in white letters: SDCI&DC -- MOFFAT, COLORADO.

Tancos put the van in park, got out, and walked up to the truck. Stewart watched him as he exchanged words with the driver who remained in the big cab. When the two finished speaking, Tancos walked over to the building, unlocked the overhead door, and heaved it open. Stewart hopped out of the van. Jaime followed him and climbed onboard a small forklift inside the building and started it up. He wheeled the Hyster-brand utility vehicle into the alley. When the driver of the truck pulled down the canvas sidewalls from one side of the truck, he exposed four large wooden crates and one smaller crate. The larger crates were each about ten feet long and two feet wide and were stacked side-by-side. Stenciled on each crate were the words: FRAGILE—HANDLE WITH CARE—FORK FROM LONG SIDE ONLY.

Following Stewart's hand signals, Jaime pointed the Hyster toward the first crate and forked it off the truck bed. He placed it inside the empty printing warehouse. He did the same with the other two but as he moved the last crate into position alongside the others, a hydraulic hose broke on the lift, causing the Hyster's two forks to drop unexpectedly.

"Mother fuck!" Stewart screamed as the crate crashed to the floor. "Take cover!"

The EOD expert remained motionless, not a muscle moved. The wooden box had slipped from the fork lift's short steel tongs and hit hard against the concrete floor and smashed open, shattering into half-a-dozen pieces. Stewart's face went ashen. He knew too well the instability and the devastating power of the two-hundred and eighty-five pounds of high explosives contained within the monster ordnance.

As soon as Stewart screamed, Jaime jumped from the Hyster, leaving it running. Hydraulic oil sprayed across the room, covering the floor, the broken pieces of wood, and the bomb's casing with the engine's viscous fluid. Stewart worried if jolting the bomb from the unexpected three-foot drop might have compromised its electrical fuze and inadvertently armed the beast.

The truck driver had run out of the building while Tancos and Jaime took cover behind two steel pillars on the other side of the forklift. They crouched there, looking as if their feet were frozen to the concrete floor. Eyes bulging, they stared at Stewart, waiting for the bomb guy to let them know whether everything was okay or if the place was about to blow up.

As if reading their worried minds, Stewart spoke. "Help me get these broken pieces of wood out of here so I can take a look at this thing."

"Is it safe, *amigo*?"

Stewart gave Jaime a disdainful look, thinking what a stupid question the man had asked. "We're working with bombs! It's never safe! Especially when you drop one!"

Sheepishly, Jaime tiptoed around the Hyster and helped Stewart remove all of the busted crate material. With help from Tancos, they gingerly set the pieces aside, except for the wood that remained under the bomb's belly.

"You better see if you and the truck driver can fix that oil line before we float out of here," Tancos instructed his partner.

"*Sí*," Jaime said, then took off.

Stewart took out a Swiss army knife and removed the bomb's side access panel. He breathed a sigh of relief when he saw the tail fuze was still intact.

"We dodged a very big bullet," he told Tancos. "Once those two repair the forklift, have them get that last crate down off the semi—carefully. That one should have all of my bang inside."

"Bang?" Tancos asked.

"The C-4 explosives."

"By the way, I'll be moving all the warm bodies you'll need over here," Tancos said. "The illegals will help you with whatever you need. After those beheadings, they'll do whatever we tell them."

"For your sake you better hope that's true," Stewart snipped.

"They will," Tancos replied. "I also have that side-load dump truck you told Jacob you needed. It's been re-painted with the SRP logo, like you asked. I also have the white van. The Arizona Public Service logo has been painted on it. Both vehicles look one-hundred percent authentic."

"And the police van?"

"It's here. I had Logan bring it up earlier from Red Rock. He had to meet some people but he should be back here any time now."

"Let me see all the vehicles. I want to give them a final check."

The two walked to the far side of the huge warehouse. There, the three vehicles sat alone, each painted and detailed as Tancos had just described.

"I'm going to need a two-person team for both the dump truck and the APS vehicle. Get me someone who speaks at least *some* English."

"I've got that covered," Tancos said.

"Then we're all set to put my plan in place. I presume you and Jaime will be assigning ASA people to tail the SRP truck and the APS van to make sure they get where they need to go."

"Yes. They should be here any minute. But you should know, I've got other plans for Jaime."

"Whad'ya mean?"

"Jacob said no loose ends. Jaime's almost done with fulfilling his role for us. When that's over, I'll be digging a hole in the desert for him."

CHAPTER 38

Stewart couldn't allow himself to continue to be distracted by his seething hatred of Tancos and the additional news the ex-Army Ranger had planned to kill his own sidekick. Why should he start questioning Jacob's orders now? This was no time to develop a conscience. Killing people was what this mission was all about. It had all started with the murder—because that's what it really was—of Captain Benjamin Forster. It continued with the massacre of his family. Then more bloodshed with the beheading of the Mexican Nationals.

The smell of death, wafting through his mind, wouldn't drift away anytime soon. Leaving no loose ends was a given. Besides, more deaths would occur when his bombs struck their intended targets. No one, not even he, knew what the toll from the outcome of those strikes might be. Hundreds? Thousands? Tens of thousands of innocent people?

Let the blood-letting continue, he thought. He had no time to dwell upon the directive Tancos had been given by their leader to leave no trail. Stewart needed to concentrate his waning energy on prepping the four Mk82s for detonation on their intended targets.

Stewart was drained, but not just physically. Mentally, he was exhausted and had aged before his time. The lost memory of murdering his wife and two children hadn't ceased haunting him, never leaving his mind. He had spent the last ten years of his life in hiding, most all of that time inside a twenty-by-twenty-foot room on the top of an abandoned fire tower. He had remained isolated from society, an unwilling prisoner, sitting alone in a cell high above the Mogollon Rim.

Frankly, he was surprised he had evaded capture so long. Obviously, the breadth and scope of the power of Sheriff Micah Lund on his Rim stood above reproach as the felon hid right under the noses of local, state, and federal law authorities.

Nonetheless, for ten excruciating years, Stewart had suffered. To stay sharp, he worked on his meticulous plan over and over again, figuring and refiguring every detail of how, where, and when to strike the targets Lund had prescribed. Stewart knew he had to be ready for the call since he was the anointed one, the chosen one, to put Jacob's plan in place. A plan Jacob had given him little time now to pull off. He had no time to be tired.

In hours, he would deliver and detonate the gifts he had diverted from the fiery angel of Captain Benjamin Forster. He would do as Jacob had demanded and "smite the heathens from the earth."

Stewart began disassembling the crates surrounding the three still encased bombs. Unwittingly, Jaime had helped save him time when he dropped the load and split open the crate of the fourth Mk82. Once all of the bombs were exposed, Stewart used a small crowbar to pry open the fifth wooden box retrieved from the flatbed. Just as he thought, the crate was filled with sticks of his M112 C-4 explosive. This was no standard bang either. This M112 version of the malleable plastic held a much more powerful knockout punch—a bigger "bang" than standard issue C-4, hence its affectionate EOD nickname.

He had made sure to steal as much of the M112 military-grade C-4 as he possibly could, sneaking it off the Davis-Monthan base during the final months prior to his retirement twelve years ago. He would stuff this special explosive into each Mk82's fuze-well. This assured him a high-degree of certainty in detonating the 285 pounds of the high explosive Tritonal housed inside each bomb's metal casing.

He plan was to detonate the bombs remotely, in essence turning each one into a very large improvised explosive device, the inglorious IED. Three of them, earmarked for Theodore

Roosevelt Dam, he would put on a delayed timer powered by a 9-volt battery connected to his modified Casio watch. These IEDs he planned to sink on the water side of the huge dam. The fourth, targeted for downtown Phoenix, he would set off using an Mk152 remote firing device, assuring him a high degree of confidence for detonation.

As a seasoned EOD tech, he knew using the improvised timer for detonating the bombs at the dam carried a much higher risk of failure versus using the classified military Mk152 firing device. He had one Mk152 transmitter left in his cache of stolen military parts, saved for what he was beginning to believe was Jacob's most important target. Using that device would require him to hardwire the remote firing device to the bomb, meaning he'd have to be as close to it as physically possible in order to guarantee detonation. He needed this degree of certainty since Jacob had told him the Maricopa County Attorney Stan Kobe was the one he most wanted assurance of being hit and killed.

"Kill that son of a bitch," Lund had told Stewart when he gave his disciple his farewell up on the Rim. *"Send that uppity nigger Kobe straight to hell."*

CHAPTER 39

MCAO Building
Phoenix, Arizona
Days Later

A s Stan Kobe entered the beginning of his twenty-third year in the Maricopa County Attorney's Office, he remained the lone African-American prosecutor in one of the busiest legal jurisdictions in the country. The office handled thirty-thousand cases per year so he had seen his share of extreme and deprived behavior during his tenure. What troubled him today was the explosive growth, since 9/11, of paramilitary and hate groups in his state, especially those promoting either the violent overthrow of the United States, white supremacy, or, most frightening to him, both.

"We got an interesting report on that separatist group the feds have been monitoring. They've been holding their gatherings up north on the Rim in Navajo County. They call themselves the Church of the High Country."

"What's your source?"

The question came from Stan's current boss at the MCAO, Bill Montgomery. Elected in 2010, Montgomery had become the fourth County Attorney Stan had the distinction to serve. The two sat in the boss's corner office.

"A covert, multi-agency, domestic terrorism task force has been tracking the group for quite some time. My guy at the U.S. Attorney's Office shared with me they were able to get one of their men inside. This person has been to several meetings where they've preached extreme white supremacist rhetoric."

"Is the task force up there planning on sending the State Attorney General's office or the Navajo County Attorney anything either can use to bring charges?"

Stan shook his head. "My guy says his office will most likely be handling the charges when they're ready. He said their infiltrator overheard the group discussing plans to disrupt the pro-immigration rally coming up downtown here on the nineteenth. Previously, they were taped discussing plans to form a militia group and send it down to the border. The latter has been their MO lately, going to the border under the guise of helping to watch for crossers in distress. But we're certain they're not Good Samaritans."

Stan opened a manila folder and flipped his index finger through the papers inside. "We believe this so called 'church' is just a front. They're no different than any number of recent nativist groups doing the very same thing, like this J.T. Ready guy and his U.S. Border Guard that just came on our radar. These whackos all make it sound very official, but they're vigilantes, plain and simple, luring extremists."

Montgomery made some notes on a legal pad on his desk. He spoke as he wrote. "Where are you culling all this background info from?"

Stan looked up from the open file on his lap. "Primarily the feds and their reports. Like these that they've pushed over to me from the task force findings. I've read all the FBI bulletins, too. And, I've reached out on my own to a few think-tank groups in academia for insight. There's one at Cal State San Bernardino that specializes in the study of hate and extremist factions. They also keep track of all the right wing Web sites and attend their public demonstrations. They keep tabs on what they're up to and what makes them tick. They've been extremely helpful."

"Good. What have they shared?" Montgomery asked.

"When I spoke to their director, a guy named Nigel Ballantyne, he told me there could be as many as two dozen formally organized groups in Arizona at the present time, all preaching some form of white supremacy or at the very least, promoting a very aggressive nativism stance. Some of these groups also fall under what Ballantyne refers to as "sovereign citizen" movements. I also haven't discounted what was portrayed in a recent investigative piece in *The New Times.* The article's writer went underground and claims to have traced one of these fringe groups as being started by some radical members of the Tea Party."

Stan continued as Montgomery now pecked on his computer's keyboard.

"Our local KPHO-TV is working on an expo piece, too. Their lead reporter contacted me for a comment. She shared with me her sources have corroborated that this Church of the High Country is headed by Jacob Jeffrey Lund."

"The media has been trying to tie Lund to neo-Nazi groups for decades and they've never been able to get anything to stick," Montgomery countered. "Plus, my understanding is no one's actually seen him since he retired. That's been almost twelve years. Is there anything new from this task force anyone can actually use?"

"Yes. I was told by my U.S. Attorney's Office connection that the group's informant has not only seen Lund at these meetings of his church but has observed him leading the proceedings. The insider said Lund actually headed a service very recently in their meeting place up near Show Low. The place is hidden deep in the woods. It's fortified and heavily protected by armed men. They've done a good job, too, of making it look like a forest service building."

"If they're operating as an official religious group then there's no law against congregating for worship. We need it on tape at one of their gatherings that he or someone in his group is planning to do something illegal. Or perhaps acknowledge that they've already done something against the law. Something solid. A right-wing gathering of fanatics doesn't count."

Stan nodded in agreement.

"So why are you so involved in this anyway? This isn't even in our county. How does our office fit into all this?"

Montgomery asked.

"I'm still working that out."

Stan got up from his chair and walked to the wall of windows on one-side of the room. He looked out, staring across the distance. The view provided a wide vista of the city and surrounding desert. He wondered how much longer he could keep secret from the chief county attorney his desire to resurrect the ten-year-old Paul Stewart cold case investigation. Montgomery's next question confirmed his suspicions.

"Scuttlebutt going around the office says you've pulled out your Paul Stewart case files again."

Stan turned to him and gave a weak shrug of his shoulders.

"I also heard about what happened to you and Hanley the other day down in Pinal County. I found out when I got a call from their sheriff. He wasn't too happy you two were back in his jurisdiction again . . . and without his knowledge."

When Stan didn't reply to Montgomery's statement, his boss pressed the topic. "So? Why were you down there talking to Police Chief Athem?"

"Word is you're looking at starting a cold case unit here in the office."

"I'm all ears," Montgomery said.

Stan hit a responsive chord with his boss. There had been rumors flying around 301 West Washington since Montgomery's arrival after winning a special election last year that one of the new guy's pet projects was to create a cold case unit, something never done before at the MCAO.

"What better way than to start with the Stewart family murders?"

"And the tie-in with Lund is . . . ?" Montgomery said.

"Logan Athem is a nephew of Jacob Lund. His cousin is Micah Lund, Jacob's son. I had a run-in with Micah ten years ago over the pursuit of Stewart after they found his truck abandoned up on the Rim. Some of his comments back then never sat well with me. Still don't. They've always made me wonder about him. Since that time, I've been holding on to this theory I have, but I still haven't been able to piece it together."

"Are you ready to let the office in on it?"

"Like I said, it's still just a theory."

"And like I said, I'm all ears."

"Okay. Well. Then try this on for size." Stan sat back down and leaned on the boss's desk. "Doesn't it seem strange to you that two law enforcement people, related to each other, both with alleged ties to white supremacists, have each crossed paths with Paul Stewart?"

"It's circumstantial . . . at best."

Stan couldn't disagree with his chief's assessment of the opening crumbs to a weak theory. Although five years his junior, he had come to admire Bill Montgomery in the short time he had worked under him. The West Point graduate's victory brought a new order and direction to the highest law enforcement position in Maricopa County, one welcomed by Stan since the unexpected departure of Montgomery's beleaguered predecessor, Andrew Thomas.

"There's more," Stan said. "When Detective Hanley and I were down in Pinal County the car I was driving was hit by a foreign object, smashing the windshield, forcing us off the road. We were lucky we weren't killed."

"Where did this happen exactly?"

"About ten miles west of Red Rock, out in the Ironwood Forest National Monument."

"That's not very far from where Border Patrol Agent Terry was gunned down."

"That's right. Thankfully, we were helped out by another Border Patrol agent and a Mexican CISEN agent, both working UC down there."

"Our Border Patrol hooking up with Mexico's CISEN?"

"Yep. Hanley was surprised too. So he checked with the Mexican Consulate and they told him they have no knowledge of any of their deep cover agents in our state. Officially, that is."

"Intriguing," Montgomery said. "Go on."

"As for our smashed window, we found a metal projectile in my car we're pretty certain caused it. Hanley turned the piece over to his Chandler crime lab. He just emailed me the report on what the object is. I printed it out before coming in here."

Stan pulled out two sheets from his folder and shoved them across the desk.

"And . . . what is it?" Montgomery asked.

"A de-arming slug."

"A what?" Montgomery looked at the report and a black and white 8x10 blow-up of the slug.

"I did some research since meeting an Explosive Ordnance Disposal tech at our Chandler crime scene. Technically, this slug is placed inside a .50 caliber firing device," Stan explained. "EOD units use the firing device to de-arm unexploded bombs. To render them safe."

"Why on earth would anyone fire one of those things at you?"

"My question exactly. The BP agent who helped us explained how they've been running into clear signs of vigilante activity down there, all under the guise of protecting the area from crossers. He told me these wackos have been known to shoot at anything that moves out there, friend or foe."

"Like our guy Ready and his U.S. Border Guard Militia."

"Exactly. And maybe like Lund's so-called church group."

"You *were* lucky then you weren't killed," Montgomery said. "So, where would someone get their hands on these types of military items?"

"That's what I'm trying to work out and wrap my head around now. The local Alcohol, Tobacco, Firearms and Explosives office told me illegal explosives of all kinds have been found whenever they make a raid on a supremacist, nativist, or sovereign soldier compound. Like the huge cache they discovered up in New River. They find stuff none of these idiots should ever be able to possess or have access to. Yet somehow they do. Hanley's crime scene unit's tech, the one who's an EOD technician for the National Guard, said the only people who should or would have access to the slugs or to the firing device are police or military EOD teams."

"EOD units were lifesavers for us tank guys when I served

in Iraq. So I'm still waiting to hear the connection."

"Well, this is where it gets interesting. How about with the triple decapitation case in Chandler? That same tech also discovered a small, plastic fragment of what she believed was a receiver for a Mark one-fifty-two firing device receiver. A device used for remotely detonating all types of explosives."

"Mark eighty-twos? Those are only carried on war birds. A-10s mostly." Montgomery sounded skeptical. "Are you sure?"

"We sent the fragment to a lab at Eglin Air Force Base in Florida. EOD techs for all the service branches train there. Their experts verified her guess."

"That's not good." Montgomery shifted in his chair, rubbing his chin. "How and the heck does a fragment of a Mark one-fifty-two firing device receiver end up at your crime scene?"

"I thought you'd never ask."

Stan flipped through the pages inside the manila folder he had protected ever since entering Montgomery's office. He pulled out several sheets of paper and flattened them out on his boss's desk. He then pointed to a section on the top paper. He took a deep breath before proceeding.

"Look. This is part of Paul Stewart's secret military record."

Montgomery's eyes widened. His eyebrows nearly touched the top of his hairline as he glared at his top prosecutor.

"Right. Don't ask where I got it." Stan pointed back down at a place on the sheet. "Just read this right here."

"This?" Montgomery placed his finger below a series of numbers. It was one of the few bits of type left untouched in the highly redacted sheet.

"Yep."

"It says, 3E851. What does that signify?" Montgomery asked, looking up.

"It signifies Stewart was an Air Force EOD technician."

Montgomery widened his eyes again.

"Right. I'm intrigued as well. But, look here. He also had

top-secret clearance." Stan repeated himself to make his point. "Stewart is EOD with top-secret clearance. For years, his military whereabouts and his service record are dark." Stan pointed again to an area on the paper in front of Montgomery. "See these redacted sections here? I've been able to decipher that he comes back on the radar, here, and then ends up in our state down at Davis-Monthan, here. When he arrives in Tucson, he's still active EOD but is reduced in rank and ends up as an A-10 ground crew member. I found out from my friends at the Department of Defense that the Air Force would never let an enlisted EOD guy just voluntarily transfer to become a munitions loader on an A-10."

Montgomery scanned the document. "So, how did that happen?"

"That same guy said something had to go wrong with Stewart. Most likely some sort of punishment to deserve the demotion. My guy's guess is he must have done something criminal. But it had to be something almost certainly committed on base since I can't find any criminal complaint filed against him in his public record. Whatever happened was probably kept compartmentalized by the military because it doesn't seem it was serious enough for him to get kicked out. Or for him to permanently lose his top-secret clearance, which, by this notation here, he maintained until he was separated."

Stan went on from memory, describing Stewart's life and movements, all indelibly etched in his mind.

"Stewart married while stationed at the airbase. Two kids soon followed. He's discharged in April 1999 but not before he works his way up to become ground crew leader for an A-10 wing. He lived for a very short time near Red Rock, off I-10 on Mogollon Rim Drive. Then he moves up to the Valley. Up here in Phoenix he lands a job as a troubleshooter with SRP. Everyone at the utility company he works with tells us he's a loner. Keeps strictly to himself."

Stan stood up and paced Montgomery's office, continuing his presentation as if he were in front of a jury, ramping up the intensity of his voice.

"Then, one day late in the fall of 2000, he goes up north, we think to the Payson area, camping somewhere up there for almost three weeks. His entire vacation. Just him and his dog."

Stan stopped and looked right at his boss.

"We verified this during our first investigation from an interview we had with a guy who worked with him the most. This co-worker said Stewart had slipped once and told him what those vacation plans were. Seems Stewart left the wife and kids behind for this trip. Actually, we can't confirm they *ever* travelled there with him. When he comes back to work from that trip, this same guy says Stewart's a changed man. If he wasn't talkative before now he's mute. Plus his workmanship falls off. He begins arguing with fellow employees, even his boss. One day he never returns to work. His last day at SRP is April 9, 2001. The next time anyone hears the name Paul Stewart is the following day when it's spread all over the news that his home has blown up with his wife and kids inside and he's nowhere to be found."

Montgomery nodded. "Okay, I'm getting the picture. But we need a warm body here, Stan. Do you really think Stewart's still alive?"

Stan knew he was on the spot. If he flinched at all in answering his boss's question, Montgomery was sure to question his entire theory. He cracked his knuckles, then answered.

"My gut tells me he is."

"Stan, you're my best guy and you know I trust your intuition, but can you give me a little more this office can sink its teeth into here other than your gut feeling? I mean, where's the smoking gun and the person who fired it?"

"There's more. As part of their covert operation inside Jacob Lund's group up on the Rim, the feds have been eavesdropping in on phone calls, monitoring IMs and emails, even listening to ham chatter."

"Ham?"

"Yep. Ham radio. The task force's inside guy has reported most of the members are ham radio operators. It's old school but a very efficient means of communicating up there. The fed's listening station heard someone calling out to another mobile after a meeting. They traced the call signs and one is registered under the acronym SDCI&DC, which is tied to a PO Box in Moffat, Colorado. While they listened in on the exchange the feds heard one ham asking another's location."

"And?" Montgomery prodded.

"The thing is all of the known members who have call signs were supposedly at the meeting. These guys have all had their call signs for fifteen, twenty, some even thirty years. The license for the person who initiated the call was granted to Micah Lund almost twenty-five years ago. The license to the person he called, the one registered in Colorado, was applied for on February twenty-sixth 2004."

"And that date is significant?"

"On its own, it has no significance until you hear what name was used on the FCC application when the license was applied for. The applicant's last name was Buford."

"Buford? The same name as the guy awaiting trial for the Scottsdale office bombing?"

Stan nodded.

"I don't get it," Montgomery said. He sat up straight in his chair, giving Stan his full attention. "You think there's some sort of connection to Stewart with that bombing?"

"Not sure." Stan replied. "But, consider this. The guy awaiting trial is an avowed white supremacist. According to all the research I've done on these types of groups *and* by talking to the experts who track them, like Nigel Ballantyne, these nuts all seem to somehow know each other in one way or another. Many of them have crossed paths at some time or some point in their lives. They've even been guests together on the same right-wing radio and TV shows, becoming familiar with each other's activities, their movements, and ideologies. I think this is some sort of sick salute to Buford and what he did. Some weird way of paying homage to the nut . . . and . . ."

Stan paused, knowing he had gone out on very long limbs before with the previous men sitting in the chair across from him. But this time, he wasn't so sure if the branch he was on was about to snap. He wasn't convinced his theory had enough evidence behind it. Maybe he was just grasping for straws, knowing that what he wanted most was to get the gnawing feeling out of his stomach that he could never explain Paul Stewart's motive and then his inexplicable disappearance. The one case he had never closed.

"And what?" Montgomery asked.

"And . . . a message."

"A message? A message to who?"

"A message to who might be the target for their next bomb."

"And you think you know who that might be?" Montgomery asked.

"I've got a *very* strong suspicion from seeing the first and middle name on that ham license application."

He pulled out a copy of the FCC Form 605 from his manila folder and laid it in front of Montgomery. He pointed with the tip of his pen so his boss knew right where to look.

Stan read aloud as he underlined the first and middle name, "Stanford Phoenix."

Montgomery looked up at him, wide-eyed. "*You?* You think you might be their next target?"

CHAPTER 40

After Stan Kobe shared his intricate theory with his boss, Montgomery gave him the go ahead to dig deeper with the caveat to make sure he crossed all his t's and dotted all his i's. Boosted by his boss's blessing, Stan quick-stepped back to his office and flipped through a stack of 3x5 index cards on his desk. Each contained notes about key pieces of evidence, both hard and circumstantial, he had gathered to date on the Stewart family and Chandler murders.

He separated the cards from his current triple decapitation case and spread them out. He did the same with the cold case. Then he color-coded all the cards, based upon similarities tying both cases together. One particular bit of data stood out as he worked on arranging the cards. After the feds had intercepted the cryptic chatter on the Mogollon Rim, they traced the call sign through Federal Communications Commission registrations. Call sign KF7RIM was licensed to Micah Lund. FBI voice-recording comparisons also verified Micah's voice in the exchange. Like he had just told his boss, the other mobile call sign—KF6RIM—was registered under the name Stanford Phoenix Buford. But, that name didn't appear anywhere on the roster of known members of the Church of the High Country.

Especially curious to Stan was the first name used on the license, Stanford, his formal first name and one he rarely used.

Interrupting his thoughts, a clerk walked into his office.

"Mister Kobe, here are those records on the Buford case you asked to have sent over from the U.S. Attorney's Office."

Zacharias Buford was currently in custody at Maricopa County's 4th Avenue Jail awaiting trial. He had been charged with sending a targeted delivery of an explosive device to an African-American office worker in Scottsdale, a federal offense. Stan took the files, thanked the worker, and skimmed through the contents of the folder. He was looking for any names or locations that might look familiar or have any commonality with the Chandler decapitations or the Stewart family cold case. He read the bios of everyone involved in Buford's case, even looking at relatives and friends of the accused mail bomber.

These skinheads all seem to know one another . . . ahh . . . here we go . . . bingo!

A known associate of Buford had once listed a mailing address in Moffat, Colorado. Stan added this tidbit to one of his index cards. The detail became another piece to his complex puzzle. As he looked at all the cards and moved them around, an idea popped into his head. He called his friend in Washington, D.C.

"Yeah, Clayton, it's me. I gotta question for you. Do you remember the letter bomb that brother here in Scottsdale got sent to him a few years ago? Yes. That's the one. I need your help with something."

CHAPTER 41

Later That Same Day

Stan continued to work on his note cards while waiting for the information he had asked his Washington, D.C. pal, Clayton Thomas, to send over. After getting green-lighted by his boss to pursue the evidence, Stan was determined to tie the two cases together. Within a short time, he received an encrypted email from Clayton. Stan unzipped the file and opened it. The top page of the .pdf attachment read:

SECRET
AIR FORCE OFFICE OF SPECIAL INVESTIGATIONS
RE: FORSTER, CAPT. BENJAMIN R.

He pored over the report, reading the secure document twice. Then he made a phone call. After that, he phoned Brian Hanley and asked him to meet out at the house where the triple decapitations had occurred—a location Stan's gut never stopped telling him Stewart was once at.

* * *

When he pulled up to the farmhouse, a lone Chandler Police Department squad car stood idling out front. Stan had agreed with Brian's earlier decision to station a beat cop 24/7 there due to the nature of the crime, versus only sealing the house with crime tape. Ever since the *Arizona Republic* splashed their headline **MYSTERIOUS BEHEADINGS STUN**

CHANDLER on the day after the crime, drive-bys from curious gawkers who desired to see the ghoulish scene had been non-stop.

Right before Stan stepped from his vehicle, his phone chirped with an email notice. He finished reading the message as Brian pulled up in his unmarked Crown Victoria.

"Whatcha got, Stan?" he said, closing his car door behind him, keeping it all business.

Stan's tone was direct as well. "Let's go inside. I want to walk this scene with you again."

After peeling back the tape sealing the front door, the two men entered the house. The malodorous smell of blood and human waste still hung strong in the house's stale air, causing them to gag. Each grabbed their handkerchief and in unison covered their mouth and nose. It took Stan about thirty-seconds for his stomach to settle down.

"I can't let go of this Stewart connection." Stan waited for Brian's reply. None came. He wondered if the pallid look on Brian's face was more an outcome of revisiting the sordid crime scene or the result of his just ended affair.

"You've got something new you want to tell me?" Brian spoke matter-of-factly.

"I just got a fresh report from the feds. They've got a man on the inside of an ASA group up on the Rim. It's one they've been watching for some time. These white supremacists had a meeting in their new hideout up there where both Jacob and Micah Lund were in attendance."

"Your old pal, Micah, huh? You're still not pissed at his deputy for calling you names all those years ago, are you?" Brian's voice drooled with sarcasm.

Stan was thankful Brian broke the unspoken tension between them with his wisecrack. "Very funny. The report also said that after this particular assembly they intercepted a ham radio transmission from someone using Micah's call sign. The caller asked for the location of another ham. They ran both call signs through the FCC's database and, here's the interesting part, the second ham's license was applied for the same day that bomb went off a few years back at the City of Scottsdale offices. And, the license was registered in the same last name as the guy who is going on trial for sending the bomb."

"Buford?"

"Exactly."

Brian looked puzzled. "I don't get it."

"I believe it's either a sick joke or a clue someone didn't think we'd find." Stan shrugged his next words. "Then again, maybe it's both." He rubbed the top of his head, thinking. "There's something else. You know that A-10 pilot, Forster, I was telling you about on the way down to Red Rock?"

"Yeah. The guy who went off the rez and committed suicide."

"I was able to get a copy of the Air Force's Office of Special Investigations report on that case. After I read it . . . well . . . what he did just doesn't make any sense at all. Why would this guy commit suicide? There were no indications in his psych profile. No mention of it anywhere in his family or medical history."

Stan continued his re-look of the days-old crime scene while talking with Brian about all of his unanswered questions and nagging thoughts. He also discussed the reports from the cops who performed a canvas within one square mile of the home, first conducted the evening of the murders, then repeated over the next several days after the discovery of the bodies. During that time, nothing of significance—meaning no eyewitnesses or anonymous tips—had turned up. Stan knew Brian felt the same pressure he did, brought on by the caveat with murder investigations that the longer they went past the critical forty-eight hour timeframe the odds dropped significantly of finding the killer or killers. For them, the clock was ticking on the downward side.

Brian brought up the results of his search of Maricopa county tax rolls for this particular parcel of land. Records showed the property held in a REIT under the name of the Sangre de Cristo Land and Development Company, a Delaware Corporation, but with a mailing address linked to a

P.O. Box located in Moffat, Colorado.

"After you gave me that county tax info," Stan said, "I looked up that town on MapQuest. Seems like that story I told you about the A-10 pilot keeps popping back into the picture. Moffat's not far from where Captain Forster's plane was found. No more than ten miles as the crow flies."

Brian raised his eyebrows but didn't reply. Instead, he also re-concentrated on the crime scene in front of him. In detective school, seasoned instructors had always emphasized to students the importance of re-walking your crime scene as many times as necessary. Brian did that now, circling the living room—always in one direction as his teachers had trained him—taking special care to step over the spot where two torsos had bled out on the floor. A bloodstain from each created a wide splotch on the ratty carpeting.

Stan spoke to him as he watched Brian loop the room. "That piece of that firing device your forensic tech found here still intrigues me—a lot. Why would it be at a scene like this? Her estimation we have a rogue explosive ordnance disposal guy on our hands troubles me."

Brian nodded while he continued circling, eyeing everything around him. His habit was to walk in a counter-clockwise pattern.

Stan went on. "So . . . what do we have? Stewart's a top EOD guy, Black Ops, no less, who ends up on the ground crew—meaning he and his team are responsible for every single component—of an Air Force warplane that goes off course loaded with four bombs that are never found. On top of that, he's the one who goes in first to check the wreckage *and* the first to find the dead pilot. At a crash site, I might add, which we come to discover is only ten miles from where this house's owner gets their tax bill mailed."

Brian stopped and made a comment. "And let's not forget that little detail of almost being killed when that EOD detonation slug slammed through our windshield."

Stan affirmed Brian's point with a quick nod. His eyes narrowed and an uneasy frown came over his face. "Ten years later and I still can't get the thought out of my mind of why we were never able to find Stewart during our manhunt. Not even one hint of his trail. My gut still tells me he *never* walked off that Rim and that peckerwood Micah was somehow involved."

"Why's that?" Brian spoke, barely moving his mouth or moving his eyes from the bloodbath site at his feet.

"One of the places Stewart frequented during his days down at Davis-Monthan was a known hangout for members of the Aryan Sons of Arizona. In Red Rock. The stronghold of none other than Micah's cousin, Logan Athem. I have reports given to me by the FBI documenting Athem's attendance at these meetings during the same time frame Stewart was there. That place was so small those two must have crossed paths at one time or another."

Brian concurred. "It makes sense that if they were fellow white supremacists and went to the same bar then they must have bumped into each other."

"Right. Exactly. And what if they did? What if Athem and Stewart befriended each other? A guy like Athem with white supremacist ties and nativist leanings would have loved nothing more than to have someone like Stewart as a friend, especially with his military connection. He would have fit that bill perfectly."

"Yep, just like those guys buying and selling explosives out the back door of the arsenal up in Flagstaff all those years ago," Brian added.

"And so . . . if these two did connect, then there's a high probability Stewart gets introduced to the Lunds, both father and son."

The two men took their conversation outside, getting some fresh air while walking around the perimeter of the building. They continued their search there, looking for any clues, hashing out possible theories, going back-and-forth with each other.

"So, here's what we have," Stan said. "Stewart's EOD, he's trained in everything there is to know about bombs and how to explode or to not explode them. He frequents a known hangout of a white supremacist group, who—"

"—who would love nothing better than to get their hands on some military-grade high explosives. Look at what more damage they could have done when they derailed that Amtrak train back in ninety-five," Brian added. "Can you imagine if they would have gotten their hands on a significant quantity of high explosives versus just a couple of sticks of C-4? They might have knocked every car off the tracks instead of only two. I'm certain many more people would have died besides just the one."

"You worked that case with my office partner at the time, Gabe Lowen, didn't you, Bri? I was on vacation, I think."

"Yeah, it crashed down near Palo Verde. It was an Aryan group who took credit for it. Called themselves 'The Sons of the Gestapo.' They claimed they did it because of what our government did at Waco."

"Waco. That's right. I've been in regular communication with a domestic terrorist think-tank group at a college in California. They told me Waco and Oklahoma City are both triggers or flash points for these para-military and supremacist groups, catalysts for them to justify the perpetration of further acts of extreme violence."

"And don't forget Ruby Ridge," Brian reminded him.

"Yes," Stan said. "That stand-off in Idaho has been acknowledged by everyone who studies right-wing extremism in the U.S. as the seminal incident for the increase in the popularity of anti-government groups." Stan circled the conversation back to the EOD fragment. "So why is a smashed part to a remote firing device found at our crime scene?"

"Uhh . . . to fire something remotely," Brian wisecracked.

"Right. But what?"

"Let me get Mary Ann, my CSRU tech who was at the scene, on the phone and see if she can offer any more help."

* * *

Later That Same Day

Brian set up a meeting with Mary Ann Burnett and the two men made the short drive to Chandler Police Headquarters. They met the forensic technician inside her Crime Scene Response Unit lab.

"Hey, Mary Ann, you're not still mad at me for calling you a bomb girl, are you?"

"Hanley, you're too ugly to stay mad at."

"I deserved that," Brian replied. "Let me buy you lunch sometime to make it up to you."

"You're on, detective."

"Me and my pal, Stan here, are up shit creek with our decapitations case. We're looking for a canoe and paddle."

"I gave a lot of thought to your questions on the phone and I think I may have something for you to use. As you already know, that plastic piece I found has been positively ID'd by the folks at Eglin Air Force Base as part of Mark one-fifty-two firing device receiver. Every EOD tech carries one in their bomb kit in case they need to detonate an unexploded ordnance remotely."

"What a kind of explosive is it used with and where is it used?" Stan asked.

"Good questions. To the best of my knowledge it's used on all types of ordnances. As for exactly where it's used, in EOD class we were told it was designed only for use by special operations forces in an active theatre outside CONUS."

"CONUS. That's continental United States. Right?" Brian said.

She confirmed his statement with a nod.

"So, if they're not meant to be used *inside* the U.S., then there's no reason for them to be here at all, especially not at our crime scene," Stan added.

"Correct," Mary Ann said, "hence my comment on scene that night that I thought you might have a rogue or possibly an ex-EOD guy—"

"Or girl," Brian chided.

Mary Ann smiled. "Or . . . *girl* . . . somehow involved with your murders, or at the very least, being at the scene prior to, during, or after the killings."

Looking over at Stan with a concerned look about a possible rogue EOD technician, Brian scribbled in his notebook as he struggled to connect his own set of dots. She went on.

"Before we sent the piece to Eglin for the rush ID, I ran several lab tests here. I swabbed the piece for blood, of which I didn't find any. However, I did find traces of three things. Expectedly, fibers from the carpet. I also found specs of dirt on it as well as drywall dust. The dirt and dust I expected to see but not how I found it and not the type of dirt it was. You had requested that night that I scrape all the vics' shoes. I did and then attempted to match that dirt with the dirt I found on the plastic part. Not surprisingly, it matched, but it only matched the one vic's shoes. The one who remained on the couch. It didn't match the dirt from the other two vics' shoes."

The two men hung on every word of her scientific findings and clinical assessments.

"And, in addition, the dirt wasn't lying on the *surface* of the plastic part. It was actually slightly embedded *into* the plastic, meaning the vic on the couch would have had to have ground the piece with his shoe, maybe even stomp on it or possibly smash it with his foot."

"That's odd," Stan interjected.

"Yes, I'd agree. And here's another oddity I discovered. As I expected, all the victims' shoes had dirt on them from the property outside the crime scene. But all three also had traces of rhyolite on their shoes, a substance only found in a region in the Avra Valley, not far from the Picacho Peak area, out in the Ironwood Forest National Monument."

Brian turned to Stan, who raised his eyebrows, acknowledging the tech's intriguing comment about a possible Ironwood Forest connection.

"So, my guess is the victim we found on the couch stomped or smashed the Mark one-fifty-two with his foot first," she said, "then grabbed what remained of it and perhaps threw the device against the wall. Hence, the trace of gypsum powder—which is a component in drywall—I found on the part."

"Great work, Mary Ann." Brian turned to Stan, voice rising. "That all makes sense. If this victim was the last of the three, it probably explains the stab wound. The killer might have gotten pissed at him for stomping on the device."

"Maybe the vic lunges at him. Maybe that's when the killer stabs him. Huh?" Stan added, looking to Brian for agreement.

"But, it still doesn't explain the beheadings or why a Mark one-fifty-two firing device is there in the first place," Brian said.

Stan shot up from the table where the three had sat. "Let's go, partner. I got a hunch and it means we need to take another little road trip."

Brian got nervous. "I gotta' think about that first. Our last ride I ended up in a ditch with you way out in the desert."

As they all stood there, Stan asked Mary Ann two more questions. "I want to find out a little more about this unique dirt you found. Can you send me a link to tell me a little more about it?"

She made a note while nodding.

"And before we leave, can we get you to scrape some dirt from the bottom of *our* shoes?"

CHAPTER 42

On The Road To Payson
The Next Day

It would take Stan two hours to wind his way up the Beeline Highway, the only direct route from Phoenix to Payson. The pavement meandered past the sides of the lush rocky ledges of the Mazatzal Mountains, bordering both sides of the road. The Sonoran desert looked magnificent in its colorful splendor and smelled just as beautiful with the mid-Spring air. The long ride gave Stan time to work again on his theory in solving the drop house murder case. He'd test it on Brian, sitting beside him.

"Hadn't heard of rhyolite before yesterday."

"Me neither," Brian replied. "It was quite interesting Mary Ann found the traces of the rock on the shoes of all the victims, too."

"That's an understatement. She said she was certain these three had to have recently walked through the Ironwood Forest National Monument, the only place rhyolite's found in significant quantities in Arizona. At least enough to be picked up on the soles of their shoes. So, my assumption is, after she runs her tests she'll find traces of rhyolite in the dirt she scraped from ours shoes, too."

"If that's the case, then that means these victims had to have come through the area Agent Tancos and his Mexican sidekick patrol."

"You're so bright they call you, Sonny," Stan teased. "I've already made a call to my D.C. buddy and asked him to get me the dossier for Tancos and the scoop on his pal, Ramos."

"I knew when we first met them you didn't buy into that whole undercover border patrol-Mexican secret agent bullshit."

"No, and I know you didn't either," Stan shot back. "Plus when Tancos told us he was a Cubs fan . . . never trust a Cubs fan."

Brian chuckled then paused a beat. His face changed to a serious look. "What my therapist shared with me about this Tancos guy is still kicking around in my head."

"Speaking of your therapist."

"Yeah. What?" There was no missing the defensive sound in Brian's voice.

"How do you do it?"

"Do what?" Brian replied.

"You know what. Screw another woman and still make love to your wife."

"For your information, Claire doesn't sleep with me anymore."

Stan couldn't hold back the sound of surprise in his voice. "You're kidding."

"I wish I was. We haven't screwed in over a year now."

Stan felt bad after Brian exposed his secret. Revealing the intimate detail he and his wife weren't having sex any longer had to have been extremely hard for Brian to admit. He could feel Brian's pain and embarrassment in what he had just shared. The look on Stan's face must have given away his emotion.

"I'm not happy about what I just told you. Besides, this all happened between me and Claire long before my decision to get involved with Pauline."

"If you're marriage is broken, Bri, you gotta try and fix it. I mean, don't you want that? You two have been together a long time to throw it all away over one mistake."

"Well, tell that to Claire. It's a two-way street, ya' know."

"I know . . . but what about the kids?"

"You think the thought of how they'll be affected isn't killing me? Knowing I'll end-up hurting them makes it even more painful."

"Hey, I'm not trying to make you feel any worse. I just want you to know I'm here for you. Whatever you need. Just say the word."

"All I want is what's best for everyone, but I really don't know how to fix it . . . I can't even . . ." His voice trailed off as he turned his attention out his side window. "Let's change the subject. Okay?"

Stan obliged and put his focus back on the case.

"So, about this Tancos character. Maybe you're right with your earlier theory that he's possibly working both sides of the fence. If he's somehow involved with the *coyotes,* what would be the advantage to him? Extortion? Getting cut-in on a piece of the drug action? Slave trading? Gun running? What?"

"They're all possibilities. But which path do we follow?" Brian replied.

"Maybe when I get his federal file it will all become a bit clearer."

* * *

Stan was back on the Mogollon Rim to have his long overdue face-to-face meeting with Gila County Sheriff Micah Lund. As soon as he and Brian had left the Chandler lab he had phoned his old nemesis to announce his planned visit. When Lund had asked the nature of his visit, Stan had simply replied he was working on a cold case.

Stan had requested Micah meet them at the site where they had found Stewart's abandoned pickup truck ten years ago. That place was just off a fire road not far from State Route 260 near Christopher Creek. When they got there, Lund had already arrived. He paced outside his police SUV.

"Thanks for meeting us, Sheriff." Stan held out his hand. Lund didn't oblige the handshake request. Rather, the sheriff dipped his fingers into his pouch of Redman, pulled out a pinch of chaw, and stuffed it in his lower lip.

"So, what brings you all the way back up to my Rim, Kobe? You two don't look like you got your fishin' gear on"

"Like I told you on the phone, it's about a cold case."

"You workin' cold cases now, huh? Not enough to keep you busy with just arrestin' and tryin' all the regular, everyday vermin you catch down there?"

"It's a case we think you'd be fairly interested in," Stan said. "The Stewart case."

"Is that why you called me here?" Lund fumed. "Why in the hell would you two wanna spend anyone's valuable time, especially mine, on *that* case? Not enough senseless killings going on in your county that you got time to go chasin' Stewart's ghost?" He spit a glob of tobacco down at Stan's feet, barely missing his shoes.

Too focused to get sidetracked by Lund's uncivilized gesture, he restrained his contemptuous feelings for the high country lawman. Rather than punching him in the face, Stan gave him a sarcastic reply. "Not resurrecting. More like still working on solving it is the way we idiots in the Valley like to look at it."

"Make a note that was your choice of words, not mine." Micah adjusted his Colt holster, then patted its worn leather. "Look, I'm a busy man, Kobe. Gotta' big county to take care of here, one with my own set of problems. I got illegals running all over my county like rats. You weren't quite on my agenda today. So, cut the crap and get to the point of your visit."

Stan wanted so badly to pummel the redneck with both fists but instead relieved his tension by cracking a knuckle.

"Okay, Sheriff, I will. Something's been sticking in my craw ever since you officially called off the search for Paul Stewart up here all those years ago."

"And what is that, pray tell?"

"Let me refresh your memory. One of the reasons you had told me you had made the decision to call off the search was because you thought maybe I was right about the theory I had back then. The theory you ridiculed me about in front of the entire posse regarding my belief a man could survive out on your Rim and walk his way out."

"Just what in the hell are you babbling about? I think that

heat may have gotten to you after all those years down in that inferno where you live, boy."

Stan clenched a fist, wanting to clock the bigoted bastard, but didn't bite the bait dished out to him by Micah's slur. "I've come up here to tell you, Lund, that I agree with you after all. That a man couldn't survive up here alone. As a matter of fact, I'm sure you were right. You remember your reference to 'the Lord Yahweh's creatures,' don't you? Maybe they did get to him, just like you prophesized."

"I hear your sarcasm, Kobe." Lund spit another glob of wet chaw to the ground, again barely missing Stan. "You may think your irreverence invoking the Lord's name is cute, but I don't need to apologize to you or any of your ilk."

Stan put a combative foot forward, but held his composure. "Don't misread me, Sheriff. Actually, I was thinking just the opposite. Maybe it was *you* who was right after all and Stewart wasn't capable of surviving out here in your Rim country. Maybe he couldn't have done it alone. Just like you said."

"What the hell are you inferring?"

"You know I've done a lot of research on our man Stewart. Become a sort of expert on him. Seems one little interesting tidbit is that back in the nineties he was actively involved in white supremacist activity while he was stationed down at Davis-Monthan Air Force Base. At the time, he lived near Red Rock. I think you have family down there in that region if I'm not mistaken. Don't you?"

"Yeah. So?"

"Well that's just it. I've also made note of how a lot of your family has ended up in law enforcement in one form or another, like your cousin, Logan Athem. He's Police Chief down there in Red Rock, right?"

"That's public record, Kobe. I'm still trying to connect all these dots you seem to be trying to string together here and, I have to tell you, boy, I don't see any lines coming together."

Staying calm, Stan went on. "Well then, try this. Like Stewart, your family has also had a history of alleged connections to white nationalist groups. We have on record that one of these groups, the Aryan Sons of Arizona, used to have regular meetings at one of Logan's favorite watering holes right in his own backyard—Wilma's Red Rock Tap House. We also have reports that show Stewart and Logan attended those meetings at the same time."

"I'd be careful where you tread here, boy."

Stan didn't hesitate from the implied threat. "You made a very clear point the first day we met, Lund. You said unequivocally that you believed no man could survive on the Rim for more than a few days, let alone walk out, without any help. So I'm thinking maybe, just maybe, these 'creatures' that got to Stewart weren't four-legged but two-legged. Maybe those animals were the Aryan Sons of Arizona, the group your father Jacob Lund is currently connected with up here on *your* Rim."

"Are you accusing my father of aiding a felon-on-the-run, Kobe? I'll throw your black ass in my jail with a slanderous statement like that."

"Oh, no. I wasn't accusing your father. But my investigation has taken me in the direction of pointing my finger at you."

"Go fuck yourself, you black bastard!" With his last words, Lund stomped off toward his truck. Right before opening the door he stopped and pivoted, looking back at Stan. "You better watch your nigger ass up here," he yelled.

"Are you threatening me, Sheriff?" Stan yelled back.

"It's not a threat, Kobe. If I was threatening you, you'd know. Just some friendly advice." He got into his vehicle, gunned the engine and peeled away, spitting rocks and pine cones as Stan and Brian stood motionless on the gravel road.

Stan turned to Brian and deadpanned, "Looks like this here *negro* got that old peckerwood to take *my* bait. Hook, line, and sinker. Now I've got that smug sonofabitch right where I want him."

CHAPTER 43

Stan looked at Brian, whose ear-to-ear grin shone as bright as the northern Arizona sun.

"That guy isn't going to be winning a diversity award anytime soon," Brian snickered.

Stan sneered as he looked down the road on which Micah Lund had just sped away. He wasn't sure how he had kept himself from beating the shit out of the overt bigot. But he knew he had to take the higher ground and not risk jeopardizing building his case. "Would you say that man there's hiding something?"

"Oh, yeah. Big time. He's wound up like a spring. A very, very tight spring. I wouldn't want to be anywhere near him the day he pops from whatever he's got bottled up inside."

Stan looked around, scanning the area. They stood near the very spot where both men had stood ten years ago as part of a huge posse about to embark on the historic manhunt for Paul Stewart.

"Something was never right with me about that search," Stan said.

"How so?"

"Lund was so sure of himself that day. So overconfident. I didn't realize it then but by the way he just reacted to my accusation, I know now, in my gut, he knew where Stewart was."

"But if he and his group were hiding him, where would they have kept him?"

"K-I-S-S."

Brian pondered Stan's statement. "Keep it simple, stupid.

Hmm. Well then, how about hiding him in a cave? Stewart could have hunkered down in one of those for days, maybe even weeks."

"That posse searched every known cavern in the area. Plus, too risky for him to use a place like that for shelter. Long term, anyhow. If I'm on the run and I know how to survive in the wilderness like Stewart did, I avoid staying where bears could be waking up any moment from their winter hibernation."

"Good point," Brian said.

"After they did the aerial sweeps, I talked later to the copter pilot myself. All he saw was nothing but Ponderosas for hundreds of miles," Stan said.

"There's literally no place to go. No place to hide."

Stan agreed with Brian's simple summation but he believed they were missing something very obvious. He wasn't leaving without figuring out what that was. As he worked on a theory in his mind, his phone rang.

"Hey there . . . Oh, that's great. I knew you'd come through for me," Stan said into his cell. "Uh-huh . . . yes . . . e-mailed? Oh. Okay . . . right. I'll download it as soon as I can. Thanks, man. Talk later."

"That the call back from your old pal up on The Hill?" Brian asked.

Stan nodded.

"What'd he say?"

"He let me know I've been sent Tancos's encrypted personnel file."

"*Encrypted?* That says tons. So, did he recognize the name?"

"Didn't say, which tells me he knows more than he's letting on."

"Border Patrol is under Department of Homeland Security. He's still on that Senate committee, right?"

"Yes, he's now majority chairman on DHS's Permanent Subcommittee on Investigations."

"That probably explains why he'd send the file encrypted."

Stan nodded. "Let's get to a Wi-Fi hotspot. I have my laptop in the car and I made sure to bring the special USB drive he sent me a while back for downloading and extracting secure files."

The men jumped into Stan's vehicle and drove back out the forest road toward the main highway. As they did, a vehicle approached them. Stan recognized the light green pickup with brown and white lettering. It was a truck from the U.S. Forest Service. The driver of the government vehicle slowed down, flagging his arm through his open window. The two vehicles stopped side-by-side. Stan rolled his window down.

"Howdy," the forestry worker said. "You fella's lost?"

"No." Stan read the man's first initial and last name emblazoned above his left breast pocket: D. PERRY. Stan flashed his credentials. Brian stretched his arm over the steering wheel. He had his badge exposed in his open wallet so the truck's driver could see it.

"We're from Maricopa County on a follow up investigation," Brian added.

"Phoenix, huh? Long way from home."

"We're working on a cold case from the Valley. Just doing some back-tracking, that's all." Stan didn't want to divulge too much, meeting the man for the first time, knowing Lund's cronies were everywhere. "We're allowed up in this area here, aren't we?"

"Oh sure. We chain this road off at dusk. You got plenty of time. Mind if I ask what you're lookin' for? Maybe I can help."

Stan shook him off.

"Let me guess," said Perry. "This is where they found that guy's truck and dog. The one who killed his family all them years ago. You still lookin' for him, are you?"

Stan gave the smallest of nods, barely acknowledging his question.

"I was in high school back then. Sure never made sense to me why they never found that guy. I mean nothin' out there for hundreds of miles 'cept pine trees and scrub. Unless, of course, you don't count the fire lookouts."

"Fire lookouts?" Stan asked.

"Yep. Only a couple left now, though, that is if you don't count the inactive ones. I guess back-in-the-day there used to be a whole bunch of fire towers up here. Quite a few were shuttered up in the mid-nineties, though, when the government went belly-up. Democrats never could manage money."

"Where are these boarded up towers?"

"East and south of here, mostly, although there is one not far from this road here, I'm told. I'm kinda' new to this particular area but I heard the place hasn't been used in almost twenty years. I guess at one time it was one of our tallest ones. It's called Anasazi Lookout."

"Anasazi! Of course! It makes perfect sense!"

CHAPTER 44

Stan couldn't hold back the exhilarating feeling from the somersault his stomach had just turned hearing the formal name of the abandoned U.S. Forest Service lookout.

"Huh?" Ranger Perry asked.

Stan didn't do a good job of holding back his enthusiasm. "This Anasazi tower. Can you take us there, Mister Perry? Now?"

"Dave's the name." The government worker smiled. He then paused, a moment of doubt on his face. "I guess . . . don't see why I can't, since you're investigating and all. But I haven't been up the primitive road that leads up to the trailhead all spring. So I'm not sure if it's even passable, especially with the last snow melt. Don't see no harm in trying, though. I need to tell you, after you get to the trailhead, you'll have to hike in quite a ways." He peeked over his door frame and shook his head. "My guess is you won't do too well in those city clothes."

Brian piped in. "He's got a point."

"We can run back to town and get some gear." Stan pressed him, "Can we meet you back here as soon as we do that?"

The ranger looked at his watch. "Yeah. I can make that happen. I'll need to let my supervisor know. He may even want to come along. He's been in the forest service over thirty years. He knows this area way better than me."

"What's your supervisor's name?"

"Marshall Brauer," Dave replied.

"Great, Dave. Here's my card. Call my cell if you have any issues. Otherwise, we'll meet you back here in forty-five minutes. Hour tops."

Elated, Stan stepped on the gas and pulled away. He turned back out onto Highway 260 heading east toward Payson. As soon as he picked up a cell signal, he dialed Jake Zadnik at the U.S. Attorney's Office.

"Yeah, Jake, it's Stan. Look at your list of names your inside guy has gathered on that group on the Rim. Let me know if a Dave Perry or Marshall Brauer are on that list." Stan spelled the names for him. "Just text me the info . . . Yep . . . Thanks . . . I owe you one."

*   *   *

When he got back to Payson, Stan dropped Brian off at a sporting goods store, instructing what size pants and hiking boots to buy for him. Then he drove to a McDonald's a few blocks away. It only took him a couple of minutes to login on his laptop and grab the email his friend Senator Clayton Thomas had sent to him. Clayton and Stan had reconnected half a dozen years earlier after a three-decade long separation. Since the reunion, the two had stayed in regular touch with each other, Clayton helping Stan several times from his position of power in Washington.

Stan opened the email and read it. He skimmed the pages of several .pdf attachments all related to the career of Caleb Eugene Tancos, the U.S. Border Patrol agent Stan and Brian had met in the Ironwood Forest National Monument. Tancos's dossier read like a movie script, decorated innumerable times while in the military as an elite Army Ranger. He had served in multiple overseas operations, including a deployment in Bosnia, as well as in Iraq.

Hmmm. Same places Paul Stewart served.

From there, his record became foggy with a ton of redacted content. This was an overt sign indicating that at least part of Tancos's government life had been spent doing covert operations too sensitive to be released, even in his classified profile. His record ended with an honorable discharge from the Army, after which he hired on with U.S. Customs and Border Protection, assigned to the Nogales, Arizona crossing station.

As he read the pages, Stan made notes, both written and mental. Then, he shut down the computer and headed back to pick up his partner. They made a quick change in the men's room and drove to their meeting point. While they did, he shared with Brian what he had learned about Tancos.

Stan's cellphone chimed. It was the incoming text from Jake. He read the display: NEGATIVE.

*   *   *

When Stan and Brian returned to the forest road rendezvous point, there waiting for them was Dave Perry and another uniformed man.

Dave made the introduction. "This is my supervisor, Marshall Brauer," The men shook hands all around.

"My man Dave here says you two men are interested in finding out more about one of our abandoned fire lookouts."

"That's correct, Marshall," Stan said. "My name's Stan Kobe. I'm with the Maricopa County Attorney's Office. This is Brian Hanley, Chandler PD."

"Yes, Dave told me you're working again on that case where that fella disappeared up here all those years ago. Stewart, right?"

Stan and Brian nodded their heads in unison.

"To me that whole thing smelled fishy the way he just disappeared."

Stan and Brian stayed mum. Stan knew the value of learning more from just listening to what people had to offer versus pushing them with probing questions looking for quick answers.

"Leave your car here and let's all ride up in my four-wheel vehicle. We'll need it where we're going."

The four men piled into the supervisor's truck. Stan looked at his watch and then made notes on a small pad.

Brauer drove at no more than ten miles an hour for about fifteen minutes on a long, narrow unmarked road. Except for their restricted passageway, the area looked untouched by humans. After another ten minutes, they came to a dead end. Walking backward in his mind, Stan struggled to recall any memory of being at this same location ten years prior as part of the search posse. None came.

"Does this look familiar to you?" he whispered over to Brian, sitting next to Stan in the back seat. Brian shook his head.

Brauer parked the vehicle and turned off the engine. As they stepped out Stan recalled a vivid memory of how he felt the first time he had been on the Mogollon Rim as a child, when his parents had taken the whole family on a trip there after first moving to Arizona. The sweet scent of tree sap stung his nose and the absolute stillness felt as eerie today as it did back then. The only thing he could hear was the wind rushing through the pine needles, sounding like a whisper, then fading away to silence as quickly as it came. That, along with the crunch of dried needles under their boots, was the only other discernible sound. He loved the feeling of peace it gave him.

"We have about a mile or so hike from here to get to Anasazi Lookout," Brauer said. He headed off toward a hidden opening to what turned out to be an overgrown path.

"I don't remember you or the Forest Service being part of the search for Stewart," Stan commented as they followed Brauer in single file. "You must have been working here at the time then, right?"

"Oh yeah. I'm one of the last of the old-timers left in the bureau. Been up here thirty-two years. All the thirty-plus year guys are all gone now, 'cept me. I'll be next. I'm looking forward to retirement, though. Next year as a matter of fact. I'll be glad to be away from all the politics and cronyism that goes on around these parts."

"Whadya mean?" Brian asked.

"Well, for example. The reason why you didn't see me or any of my men on that big search all those years ago was because we aren't part of the Sheriff's clique. That's why we never got invited to the party."

Add a point on the side of the power of learning from listening, Stan said to himself.

The hike in, almost all uphill, took the group a little less than an hour. As the trail ended, it opened to an alpine clearing. In front of them, piercing the cloudless sky stood an ancient looking wooden tower, rising over one hundred feet in the air. It literally rose above the treetops. It was, Stan thought, as if it had appeared out of nowhere. How something so big could remain so hidden amazed him. After what Brauer had told him, it dawned on him that the helicopter pilot Stan had spoken to after the posse's search ended must have been one of Lund's inside men, since the man never mentioned spotting the tower in his aerial sweeps.

"I haven't been back in here for a very long time," Brauer pointed out. "Must be ten years, maybe more. Once we stopped using her for a lookout and started relying more on real-time satellite imagery to spot fires, there didn't seem to be a need for having a paid lookout up here during fire season anymore. We boarded her all up and then fenced it in. That was almost twenty years ago, when the government shutdown. Towers up on the Rim are becoming a thing of the past."

"Can we take a look inside?" Brian asked.

"Don't see why not," Brauer said. He fumbled with the set of keys on his belt. He tried several to open the large padlock securing the only gate. A chain-link fence, topped all around with barbed-wire, encircled the entire perimeter. Brauer tried all the keys on his ring but none worked. He tried them all again but still had no luck opening the padlock. He looked frustrated. "Hmm. I know it's got to be one of these."

"You sure you've got the right set of keys?" Dave asked.

"I may be old, son, but I'm not senile."

Stan and Brian chuckled.

Brauer turned the padlock upward toward him and leaned in to get a closer look. He pulled out his eyeglasses and plopped them on his nose. A puzzled look came over his face.

"This padlock . . ." He frowned as he inspected it further. "This isn't one of our Forest Service locks."

"What do you mean?" Stan asked.

"All of our locks around the time we shut this unit down were bought under a GSA contract we had with a lock company out of Chicago. I know that because I was the guy who made out the purchase requisition. What's unique about the locks we bought was that they were all stamped with the company's very odd name, Junkunc Brothers. That's one way to know for sure. This lock here doesn't have that name on it anywhere."

Stan took a close look and saw no markings of any kind on the padlock.

"No wonder these keys wouldn't fit." Brauer said. He turned to his helper. "Dave, can you go back and get me the bolt cutters from my tool box in the rear of the truck."

"Gotta pair right here, boss. Grabbed 'em just before we left. Figured we might be taking down some fence."

Brauer smiled his approval at his well-prepared underling. "Taking down and putting up fence in the remote areas we work in is as common here as folks down in the Valley using valet parking."

Brauer laughed at his lame joke then proceeded to cut the chain attached to the lock. He pulled the gate open. The rusted hinges squeaked loudly, disturbing the silence and stirring some birds from the trees. The four men walked through the opening. A stairway wrapping around the outside of the structure, snaking its way up to the top, greeted them.

"Holy shit." Stan's face turned pale as he looked skyward. "Exactly how high is this thing?"

"Almost one-hundred-thirty feet," Brauer stated.

Brian stepped to the front of the group. "If someone unauthorized has been here, then better let me go first." He re-arranged his Glock, holstered on his side, and began walking up the steel-girder steps. Brauer followed.

"You go next, Stan. Don't worry. I'll be right behind you."

The encouraging words from Ranger Dave helped Stan

muster enough fortitude to make the heart-arresting ascent. He loathed heights and the tower swaying in the stiff Mogollon wind didn't help calm him. As he climbed, the structure creaked with the weight of the men, adding to Stan's apprehension.

"Don't look down," Dave called up to him as the young ranger brought up the rear.

"Does it show that I'm that nervous?" Stan shouted down at him.

"The shaking knees and your vice grip on the hand rails do give it away just a bit."

It took the group several minutes to reach the trap door under the deck surrounding the lookout room. Brian pushed the door upward. It made a loud thumping sound as he flopped it open onto the landing above. He pushed his head through the small opening and looked around for any sign of life, all the while resting his hand on the butt of his gun.

A three-foot wide, wooden-planked deck encircled the top of the lookout whose windows were all boarded up. The weathered plywood had the words U.S. FOREST SERVICE stenciled in black paint, followed by even larger letters in red that read:

NO TRESPASSING!
VIOLATERS WILL BE PROSECUTED
TO THE FULL EXTENT OF THE LAW!

Brian climbed onto the deck. The three other men followed him. They stood behind him as he walked up to the entry door to the lookout room. The window over the top half of the door was shuttered as well. Another locked padlock, secured to a rusted hasp, prevented entry. Once again, Brauer tried to open the lock using the set of keys dangling from his belt but with no success. His assistant stepped forward and snapped the padlock off with a quick snap of his tool.

"Stay back," Brian said, his hand now gripping his drawn weapon. He entered the room everyone waited on the deck, the ever-present wind swirling around them. Stan, heart still pounding out of control, clung as tight as he could to the steel handrail encircling the tower deck.

Brian was only in there for a few moments when he reappeared. "Stan, I think you better see this."

CHAPTER 45

Downtown Phoenix
Later That Same Day

Stan drove as fast as he could back to the offices of the Maricopa County Attorney. When he got there, he rushed into Bill Montgomery's office to report what he had discovered in the long ago shuttered Anasazi Lookout Tower.

"Boss, I just came back from the location where Stewart's truck and dead dog were found. You've got to see this." Stan closed the door behind him. Waving a small camera in his hand, he walked up to Montgomery's desk.

"You went back up to the Rim? What on earth for?"

"The theory I told you about. The one I've been following. What I discovered today may prove me right."

"How so?"

"That Paul Stewart's not dead and that he's been in hiding all this time with the help of a white supremacist group."

"You're sure about this?"

"Take a look." Like an excited kid showing off a new present, Stan handed him the camera. Montgomery looked at the image displayed on the tiny screen while Stan rattled on. "We found what we think is—or perhaps was—Stewart's hideout. He's been right under our noses all this time, for an entire decade, holed-up in an abandoned fire tower!"

Stan came behind the desk and stood over his boss's shoulder as Montgomery scrolled through the pictures. "That one there, we think, is some sort of homemade transponder. I've already emailed these jpegs to the Public Affairs Office down at Davis-Monthan."

Montgomery clicked through more captures, eyes popping at each new picture.

"Stop there," Stan said pointing to the screen. "Those are bricks of C-4 explosive. I believe Stewart may be planning on using these to detonate some sort of improvised weapon."

Stan took the camera back from his boss. Still bursting with excitement, he flipped through the remaining pictures, showing them to Montgomery and describing each in detail.

"Hanley and I went through the place with the blessing of the U.S. Forest Service who manages the property. Besides those sticks of C-4, we also found some other military-grade bomb-making paraphernalia. But what were most intriguing were all the newspaper clippings we found of the Stewart family murders. The eeriest part was that the walls were covered with them. We even found some small, framed pictures of Stewart's wife and kids. They were displayed on a table surrounded by votive candles."

"Maybe some sort of sacrificial altar?" Montgomery offered.

"No, no. I don't think so," Stan said. "It looked much more like a place of honor or devotion. A memorial, perhaps. I've emailed those pics to Nigel Ballantyne at Cal State San Bernardino. The expert I mentioned to you earlier. I want his evaluation. The FBI is also doing an analysis of the entire scene."

Montgomery nodded. "Good."

Stan continued. "I surmise Stewart has been living up there since the murders of his wife and kids. My gut tells me that's been with the help of the Church of the High Country. The group I told you about headed up by Jacob Lund and his son, Micah."

Montgomery leaned back. "I hope you have proof of that."

Stan looked up from the camera and stared at his boss. "I had a very revealing chat with Micah a short time prior to discovering the hideout. When I point blank asked him if he'd been hiding Stewart all these years, he refused to discuss it with me."

"You accused a highly-decorated, career lawman of aiding and abetting a felon-at-large?"

"You bet I did. And when I did, he threatened me. Right in front of Hanley. We also found this."

Stan unraveled a map of the four corners region of New Mexico, Arizona, Utah and Colorado and laid it out on Montgomery's desk. Various points had been circled on the map, including Phoenix, Chandler, two locations on the Mogollon Rim, another point west of Phoenix and several points east along the Salt River corridor. As well, several large circles had been put around Red Rock, Arizona and Colorado's Baca Grande region.

"I'll need some time to go over all of these markings," Stan said as he pointed to each. "When I do, I think I'll literally connect all the dots together to support my theory."

"I'll make a call to the Gila County Attorney's Office and ask them if we can share jurisdiction on this."

"It might be too late for that. I phoned the FBI as soon as we found what we did because Stewart's still on their Ten Most Wanted List. They're taking over the investigation. Their advance team hopefully is already up there. I had the Forest Service seal off the tower and the whole area back to the main road. I instructed them to let no one in except fully-credentialed federal law enforcement personnel."

"Good work. But what about Sheriff Lund? Has he found out what you know?"

"I can't be sure. If the FBI finds any prints in the tower of him or any of his deputies, or gets a hit in the agency's Integrated Automated Fingerprint Identification System, our office will be notified right away."

"I don't need to tell you that you need to tread very carefully here, Stan" Montgomery cautioned. "Accusing a veteran lawman like Lund is a very serious charge. I don't want this blowing up in your face. Let's wait and see what happens once the FBI does their sweep of the tower and gets the results from their IAFIS search."

One of Stan's law clerks knocked on Montgomery's closed office door, interrupting the conversation.

"Come in," Montgomery called out.

"Excuse me," the clerk said. "This just came in for you, Mister Kobe."

The clerk held a single sheet of paper and handed it to Stan. As the clerk walked out, Stan read it and smiled.

"What is it?" Montgomery asked.

"The FBI lab's already got a multi-point match on two sets of the prints they found up there."

"Lund's?" a concerned Montgomery questioned.

"Almost as good," Stan said. "One matches Lund's top deputy, Kirby Ferrin."

"And the other?"

Stan smiled wide, like the cat that ate the canary. "Paul Henry Stewart's."

CHAPTER 46

West Phoenix
Abandoned Print Warehouse
April 19
12:05 a.m.

Paul Stewart's final mission—for he knew full well this one would be his swan song—was in high gear. Adrenalin surged through his veins. The feeling brought back a stark reminder of his many CIA demo ops assignments in a past life. Only he knew in his heart there'd be no coming back after he set in motion the calamity Phoenix was about to experience.

Holed-up in the abandoned warehouse, the domestic terrorist team of white supremacists had been prepping for the attacks for days. He waited patiently while Tancos explained—using Jaime as his interpreter—to a now docile and cooperative group of illegals, what each of their tasks would be to carry out their plan. The executioner, Tancos, explained to them that if they reneged or refused not only would he slit their throats like their *tres compañeros* at the drop house, but their families in Mexico would face certain death.

After eliciting a coerced agreement from each of the illegals, Tancos motioned to Stewart to take the floor. As he did, he referred to maps pinned to the walls for the drivers—selected because Jaime said they understood the most English—showing them where to drive their respective vehicles and how to place each in position for their part of the mission. Stewart's knowledge gained from working that time at SRP would now pay off.

As Stewart spoke, Jaime interpreted. "Listen up. Follow my instructions precisely and all will go smoothly. There's no room for error with any part of what I am about to tell you." Stewart pulled out the SRP and APS-logoed ID cards obtained through Jacob's network of corrupt government workers. "Here. Take these. There's one for each driver and his helper."

Jaime had earlier snapped Polaroid pictures of the chosen illegals and affixed them to the phony badges. Stewart made sure each ID looked as authentic as possible. He knew this was a critical detail that couldn't be taken lightly and was key in pulling off his gambit.

Another way Lund's secret group of surreptitious sympathizers helped was by providing the terrorist team the most current Arizona Department of Transportation information on the roads to, from, and around the intended targets. Except for some minor changes, the ingress and egress had remained as unchanged as Stewart remembered when he had worked as a utility company troubleshooter. The job which he had so abruptly left a decade earlier.

Tancos stepped in and instructed Jaime to tell the illegals that five-thousand-dollars awaited each when he returned here, mission complete.

Stewart was surprised by this announcement and highly doubted the reward would ever get doled out. Instead, he believed Tancos had plans to kill all the illegal alien teams, slaughtering them and anyone else left in the print warehouse; or perhaps whack them while out in the desert where he'd have Jacob's henchmen dig a hole for each of them as their final resting place.

Suddenly, loud pounding came from the outside of the overhead door to the back alley.

"That must be Jacob's men," Tancos shouted.

When the door was raised, members of the Church of the High Country walked in. Stewart scanned the group. He thought they were an odd-looking bunch—part-cowboy, part-outlaw biker. Each man expressed disdainful looks as they passed the Mexicans standing before them.

Tancos whispered to Stewart, "These guys are here to make sure these wetbacks don't chicken out at the last minute. They'll follow the vehicles to their targets."

So these are Tancos's henchmen. I was right. I knew he'd never let the poor slobs come back alive.

Stewart shook off his fleeting feeling of pity for the illegals. This was war. And in war, the enemy dies. He approached Jaime and explained to Tancos's Mexican sidekick he wanted to give a final set of instructions to each team. Stewart grabbed the ID hanging around one of the illegal's neck and read the man's name.

"Guill . . ."

"*Guillermo, jefe,*" the young man said, his lower lip trembling.

"Right. Guillermo. You're the driver to Theodore Roosevelt Dam. Access to Theodore Roosevelt Dam is going to be tricky. But we have a big advantage because Highway 88 runs right alongside the dam's infrastructure for several miles." Stewart pointed to the winding, two-lane switchback roadway on the map. "When you and your helper reach the dam at this spot I've marked for you on your map, you'll need to look off to the shoulder for the access road. You'll use this point for your entrance."

Fortunately, the main road to the dam, commonly known as "The Apache Trail," still remained as desolate at night as it did when it was first carved out of sheer bedrock over one-hundred years ago, literally by the hands of Apache Indians. Driving the bogus SRP side-dump truck down the highway with explosives inside would be the easy part. But Stewart's plan of sliding the bombs out from a load of sand inside the truck over the edge of Theodore Roosevelt Dam would require precise execution—and a lot of luck. For this critical step, he wondered if he should do the task himself.

Guillermo nodded at Stewart's words spoken through Jaime, affirming he understood the instructions on how and where to drive the dump truck once he was on the access road running alongside the dam. This abandoned and little known causeway still had a direct connection that went right over the top of the century-plus old structure. Stewart pointed to the exact area on the map where the hidden turn-off from the highway was located. "It should be marked with a tall metal stake and orange barrel pylon. You'll need to make a very sharp turn there to get onto this dirt road."

The driver blinked his eyes and gave quick nods in confirmation as he listened to Jaime.

Stewart went on. "Drive your dump truck on that road until you come to a gate. It will be locked. Bust through it. Follow it for about two hundred yards and you'll end up right on top of the dam. Then, drive very carefully until you see a large, white stripe painted across the concrete at the center of the dam. That's your drop spot where you'll side-dump the load of sand over the edge of the dam. When you're done, you and your helper double-back on foot to the tail car sitting on the shoulder of AZ-88. Your job will be done."

Stewart hoped the men would follow his directions precisely. At most, they'd have five to ten minutes maximum to complete their mission before SRP security was aware of their presence. The most recent satellite imagery Jacob provided had verified for Stewart data he already knew: that the long-forgotten dirt road to the original dam was still as accessible and unmonitored as it was ten years prior.

Stewart turned and looked at the others. "Now, who is the driver to Palo Verde?"

"This one." Jaime pushed a small-framed man in the back toward Stewart. The man looked to be in his late thirty's or early forty's. "This is Ricardo. He's been to the U.S. many times, *Señor*, but they keep sending this *mujado* home. Wetbacks never learn. But his English *es muy bien*."

"Okay, Ricardo. That's good you *sabe ingles*. There will be at least two checkpoints you'll have to talk your way through."

The Mexican remained stone-faced, showing no emotion.

"If—more like, when—the guards at the first gate ask you

where you're headed, tell them you're delivering gasoline for the tools of the crew working on the waste berms. They're always running out of gas out there and everything is brought in for them. They'll verify that when they check the back of the truck and see your barrels. When you get to the berm, wait there until we call you."

Tancos stepped over and handed the man a throwaway cellphone.

Stewart could only hope that this attack on the nuclear power plant would act as intended—a diversion for the bigger plans later at Roosevelt and downtown Phoenix. Although he hoped for success, he had always felt Palo Verde was the wrong location for creating such a distraction. From the first time he had heard this was one of Jacob's targets, he had pleaded with the old man numerous times to avoid the nuclear plant and pursue a less highly secure target. He thought he had proved this point to Jacob when he had done a test with the small pipe bomb he had his men place at the unprotected rubber dam on Tempe Town Lake.

But the curmudgeon would not bend, demanding an attack on the world's largest nuclear power plant. Each time Stewart had challenged Jacob's idea, the leader steadfastly defended choosing the site. Even now, Stewart couldn't get the megalomaniac's voice out of his mind, echoing inside his head after all these years:

"I want people to panic, to be afraid for their lives. To not know what's hit them. I want to take down the City of Phoenix. I want to cripple it."

"Brother Paul? Are you finished?"

Tancos calling him "brother" pulled Stewart from his thoughts. He didn't believe for a moment this man was his brother, other than perhaps for this mission as a brother-in-arms. Stewart's extreme loathing of the border agent had come rushing back seeing him again after all these years. He especially despised the fact he had been thrust unknowingly into being part of the man's slaughter spree at the farmhouse. Stewart took a deep breath and worked at pushing his anger aside.

I'll deal with this motherfucker later.

He returned his attention to the Palo Verde team. Like the dam, Stewart believed the only way certain to assure success at Palo Verde would be for someone like him, an Anglo, highly skilled and fully dependable, to do it himself. Instead, illegal immigrants—of all people—would be used to carry out the risky task. Stewart laughed to himself at the irony of the whole scheme, a warped version of indentured servitude concocted and carried out under the direction of his old nemesis Caleb Tancos, an immoral U.S. Border Agent, and his equally corrupt Mexican pal. All under the blessing of none other than Jacob Lund.

Fucking incredible.

Ricardo, one of these unfortunate "guests" invited to Jacob's "wedding" after he was abducted in the desert by Tancos and Jaime, had just been instructed he would drive a van into the Palo Verde Nuclear Power Plant. What he was not told, however, was that the six, 55-gallon drums of gasoline sitting behind his seat each had multiple packs of C-4 plastic explosives deftly placed under them, all connected to an improvised, cellphone-activated remote firing device.

The perfect end result: Ricardo and his helper would get the vehicle close enough to the outgoing main transmission lines right next to the waste berms so that when the van blew—with the men still in it, most likely—the blast would destroy the lines, compromising the delivery of power to a huge portion of the power grid for the southwestern United States.

Poor dumb shits. Hey! No time to be sentimental, Paul.

All instructions delivered, Stewart refocused. He put his energy back on finishing his final preparation of the Mk-82 IEDs.

"Jaime, they're all yours. Take them to their vehicles and give them another once-over to make sure they know exactly what to do and how to operate everything."

Jaime followed Stewart's order and shuffled the men off. Tancos and Stewart stood alone at the wall with the maps pinned to it. He hated the fact he'd have to interact with Tancos but he had no choice if the downtown portion of the attack were to go off flawlessly.

"Let's go over to the police van. I'll show you how to operate the firing device." Stewart didn't hide the sound of resentment in his voice.

They walked over to the stripped-out Red Rock police van. Sitting in the back was a single Mk82. Right next to the ignoble monster was an Mk152 transmitter along with its paired receiver.

"When do me and Logan detonate the bomb for downtown?" Tancos asked.

"Jacob wants it to go off at exactly o-nine-o-two in honor of McVeigh's attack on Oklahoma City. This is a perfect time since the nigger lawyer's wife is the rally's first speaker. She's scheduled for nine a.m. and sure to be on the dais by that time with him, we're certain, right nearby. Let's synchronize our watches."

The two men looked down at their timepieces. The tension had subsided between them just enough to get back on track to the task at hand.

"O-one-hundred," Tancos said.

"Mark," Stewart replied. He looked up. "By the way, when is Logan due back?"

"He should have been here by now."

"When you two get to the target, all Logan needs to do is leave this police van anywhere within one-hundred yards from the stage. Then get back to the triggering site. Keep this firing unit stable, flat on the seat between you. You'll need to have line-of-sight to the van after you're in place. All you'll have to do is push this button here at our prescribed time." He pointed to the largest button on the top section of the Mk152 remote firing device transmitter.

"Perfect. Understood," Tancos confirmed. "I just hope I can keep that hothead under control long enough to get the job done. I'm sure you remember how he lost his cool out in the dunes when we retrieved the bombs."

Stewart dismissed Tancos's comment and reached into the side pocket of his satchel. "Here's the throwaway cell for blowing the Palo Verde van. Make sure your men in the tail car give the Mexicans plenty of time once they're past their first checkpoint."

"So how will my guys know when to call the number to blow this thing up?"

"The van driver has a phone. Have Jaime explain to Ricardo, the van driver, to call your tail car's cell when he's cleared the last checkpoint. That should be about ten minutes after they reach the main gate. If he doesn't make contact within fifteen minutes, call this phone number. It's the number for the cell in the back of the van."

Stewart pulled a folded piece of paper from his shirt pocket and handed it to Tancos. He had written down the number for the cellphone that would trigger the C-4 blasting caps under the gasoline drums in the back of the APS van.

"When will this van here be ready for Logan?" Tancos asked.

"I just need to wire the fuze up to the receiver then add my finishing touches to connect everything together."

"Right. When will that be?"

Stewart didn't like Tancos's persistent tone. He looked him square in the eye. "I'll do that when I finish re-checking the bombs for Roosevelt."

"Do you really have faith this whole thing you dreamed up at the dam is going to work?"

Stewart jerked at the sound of Tancos's question. It sounded like the prick doubted his skills. "Once they go in the water the only people capable of getting at the devices and have any chance in hell of rendering them safe will be a Navy EOD team. And the closest unit is in San Diego. By the time they find out, get there, and figure out what I've done, it'll be too late." He smirked at Tancos. "Don't forget, I'm the one who graduated top in my EOD class. From what I recall, you washed out the first week."

"Is that supposed to make me feel bad?" Tancos's voice

filled with sarcasm. "You seem real edgy, Brother Paul. You sure you're up to this?"

Stewarts eyes lit up, blazing hot, like a white phosphor rocket. "First, stop calling me 'brother.' I'm not your fucking brother. Second, when this is all over, you and I will settle our score." He turned away from Tancos and grabbed a wiring tool.

Tancos seemed to dismiss the threat when he changed the subject. "I plan to have my men trigger the Palo Verde explosives while the two Mexicans are still inside the van," Tancos whispered.

Stewart, hesitant about having his back to the cold-hearted executioner, stopped wiring the connections and turned around, staring his nemesis in the eye. He didn't speak.

"Did you hear what I just said?" Tancos asked.

The two stood face-to-face, inches apart. Caleb Tancos was a ruthless killer who would have neither hesitation—nor remorse—in completing the task he had just shared. Stewart was sure now Jacob had instructed his top soldier to leave no one alive connected to what they were doing in Phoenix. Stewart wondered if that meant him, too. He finally answered Tancos's question. "Don't you think I know that?"

"Just wanted to make sure you were onboard with that. I wasn't so sure if you would be after seeing the look on your face at the drop house." Tancos paused. His voice changed. "I did enjoy seeing the look on those Mexicans' faces when I slit that first guy's throat."

Stewart felt like gagging when he re-pictured the bloodbath at the Chandler farmhouse. But he refused to give Tancos the satisfaction of seeing him wince. Stewart had committed his fair share of atrocities, all under his role as a soldier in war. But Tancos's actions had been inhuman.

Tancos changed the subject. "I just hope those two wetbacks Jaime chose can get off the top of Roosevelt Dam in time to get back to the tail car. Once they do, our brothers will take care of them from there."

Stewart turned away and finished attaching his final wire to the blasting cap. He pulled his satchel close to him. He spoke without looking at Tancos. "Just worry about your own job and make sure you and Logan get your van exactly where you're supposed to. Once that's taken care of, I don't give a fuck what you and your men do."

"Brothers!" bellowed Logan Athem as he barged through the service door in the back of the warehouse. The shout from the burly man brought the tense confrontation between Stewart and Tancos to an abrupt halt. "This place smells like a taco factory!" Athem urged his massive frame past the doorway.

Stewart turned and greeted him with a smile. "Brother Logan. You always had a way with words."

The two men embraced, patting each other on the back. "It's good to have you back with us," Logan replied. "Ten years is a long time."

"Yes. Much too long. But I am here now, ready to finally put Jacob's plan in place."

"Yes," Logan said, close to Stewart's ear. "We finally get to use your bombs. And one of them is for our old friend, the miscegenist, Kobe."

Stewart nodded, smiling in agreement. "Look here. I'll show you the details of what we've got planned for the gifts I brought Jacob."

Stewart guided the rotund man toward the wall pinned with the various maps and pictures and explained the downtown plan in detail to him.

"Great," Logan said. "I smell some grub." The big man lifted his nose in the air like a hungry dog, sniffing away.

"There's some food in the other room," Stewart laughed. "Better chow down. And get some coffee, too."

Logan made a beeline for the eats. When he was out of earshot, Tancos approached Stewart and picked up their earlier conversation. "Listen, I know you're still hanging on to that thing in Bosnia. You don't have to like me. I get it. I just don't want the past to get in the way of jeopardizing this mission. I know how much Jacob's counting on you to come through for him and our cause. I know how much this means to him, especially hitting the downtown Phoenix target. Let's just both make sure we make this nigger dead. So, are we on the same page with—"

Livid, Stewart's eyes glazed over. "—Don't worry about me. Just make sure your blast goes off when scheduled and we blow this guy Kobe to kingdom come."

CHAPTER 47

1:15 a.m.

Stewart shouldered past Tancos who then left the room. When he was gone, Stewart crawled inside the back of the Red Rock police van to finish wiring the bomb. The cold metal ceiling and sidewalls seemed to close in on him and a strange feeling came over him. The unreflective steel of the bomb's casing didn't help his discomfort level as he knelt in the eerie silence.

He thought about the mission, an indirect outcome of the anger harboring deep within him from his father's betrayal. The anger had consumed every part of his being, first showing itself when he took a punch at an African-American Air Force major at Eglin upon return from his final off-the-grid deployment. That episode had landed Stewart in the brig and being busted down two ranks. He had decided to start over, begin a new life, away from all the bad memories Florida held for him. That's why, given the courtesy due to his exemplary and up until then flawless record, he had requested the transfer to Davis-Monthan so he could be three-thousand miles away from all his pain.

His life changed forever when he arrived in Arizona and met Jacob Jeffrey Lund, a man who showed him fatherly love and honesty and not the hypocrisy his real father had ultimately shown. Stewart's hurt from his own father's actions justified his decision to join Lund's cause of hating all people of color. Lund had eventually led him down a road to where he was told to strike down his own family to prove his loyalty.

If Stacey just wouldn't have taken our children to meet that nigger wife!

Stewart's thoughts rattled on, non-stop, as he sat in the back of the van, leaning against the bomb. He rubbed his temples with his palms, feeling the onslaught of another one of his migraines. The headaches had started and never left him since the slaughtering of his wife and children. Pain hammered at him from the sordid memory of their blood splattered all over his body. An incredulous void inside his brain of the recollection of slitting their throats and setting off the incendiary devices to cover up the hideous crime left him numb. Their lost faces haunted him, burned forever into his memory.

Stewart pushed aside his painful feelings over the loss of his wife, children, father and his deceased mother. After the chilling remembrances had passed, he thought about how, very soon, this vehicle and all of its parts would be blown into a thousand pieces by the military bomb's formidable power, throwing shrapnel everywhere, wreaking havoc in all directions. Just like the aftermath of all those bloody IEDs he had witnessed kill overseas. To explode without notice and without regard to the victims' wealth or status, age or sex, in the streets of Sarajevo and Baghdad. No warning. No time to defuze. No chance to render safe.

He struggled to get back on track for executing the pre-planned schedule he and Jacob had mapped out for detonating each of the bombs. But another nagging thought re-entered his mind. He wondered again why Jacob had never discussed how he would claim responsibility for the acts about to unfold. *Would he take credit for the attack as a member of the ASA or refer to his Church of the High Country? Or, would he stay silent?* Once more, Stewart let the pestering thoughts pass.

He clutched his camouflage-colored satchel across his chest. Inside the bag were his precious blasting caps. He carefully pulled one out and inserted it into a fist-sized wad of M112 C-4. Then he stuffed the plastic explosive deep into the bomb's fuze-well. Last step: he connected wires from the cap to the Mk152 receiver. "There. All ready to go," he whispered, patting the bomb. "Thy will be done."

CHAPTER 48

1:30 a.m.

Stewart had instructed Jacob to have a special side-dump truck and eight tons of construction grade sand waiting in the printing warehouse. When Stewart first laid eyes on the vehicle intended to carry the bombs to Theodore Roosevelt Dam, two feet of sand already sat in the back. To prep its bombs, earlier Stewart had unscrewed the shipping plug of the first Mk, exposing its fuze well, and stuffed the well with his special M112 C-4. Into the C-4 he inserted an electric blasting cap. He then had done the same for the other two bombs. From the blasting caps he ran wires from each to the TPU, or time power unit, which he had placed inside a small metal pipe to protect its vital components from water damage and tampering. Also into this pipe he inserted an evidence destruction charge made up of more C-4, a sly trick used by bomb makers to destroy their signature.

The wires for all three bombs ran to his simple yet inventive TPU, which consisted of using a modified wristwatch—his own tried and true Casio—piggybacked on a 9-volt battery. To this, he connected the electric blasting caps, all primed-in and wired in parallel. He made this firing mechanism water-tight and tamper-proof by placing it inside a four-inch diameter metal pipe. Then he welded a lift ring to each bomb. To these rings, he had attached one-hundred-feet of industrial grade chain, securing all three bombs in a daisy-chain fashion, one to another. Lastly, to the chain closest to the top bomb, he had secured his TPU.

To get the device to suspend exactly as he needed for the desired effect in the deep-water reservoir, Stewart rigged a special flotation device to the ring of the top Mk82. In order to destroy the dam, he'd have to submerge the bombs as close as possible to the concrete wall of the century-old structure. He connected the float so it allowed the chained bombs to hover just below the surface of the water, keeping them not only out of sight but lined-up in an upright position.

His design assured when the timer went off all the blasting caps would ignite the C-4, triggering the high explosives inside each bomb simultaneously. The resulting concussion would push against the water side of the dam with so much dynamic force the energy would have no place to go except against the concrete.

After Stewart had finished prepping these three bombs, with Jaime's help, they had fork lifted the Mk82s and placed them gingerly on top of the sand. Stewart had then instructed Jaime to have the Mexican hostages shovel buckets of the golden-colored powder into five gallon plastic pails. They formed a fire brigade, passing the buckets off one to the other, finally reaching an ASA man at the top of a ladder. They continued this until the truck was piled high, covering Stewart's weapons of mass destruction.

Fully-loaded, the short, ten-ton, SRP-decaled, Versalift side dump truck looked like a miniature pyramid on four wheels. In reality, Stewart had created an unassuming, yet deadly, Trojan horse. An ingenious and devastating multi-device IED. He believed it was a brilliant contrivance, one even the finest Navy EOD team would be challenged to render safe. When it blew, he estimated the explosion would crack and compromise the dam, ideally making the structure fail from the pressure of the 17,000-acre expanse of water behind it. The ensuing flood from the rush of over one-and-one-half-million acre-feet of water held back in the lake would smash and overrun the remaining smaller dams in its path all the way down the Salt River corridor westward toward Phoenix.

When that deluge of water joined the nearly half-million

acre-feet of water stored in reservoirs behind those smaller dams, the torrent would convulse in a never-seen-before ferocity. The rumbling confluence would create a raging river, obliterating an area ten miles wide down the ever-dry Salt River, creating a flood of historical proportions through Phoenix and its neighboring cities. The torrential rush of water would destroy a huge portion of the Valley of the Sun. The sheer devastation to life and property in the area affected would be catastrophic. Last, but not least, the largest supply of fresh water for the most densely populated area of the state would be wiped out.

*   *   *

1:50 a.m.

The SRP dump truck for Roosevelt Dam and the van for Palo Verde were scheduled to depart in forty minutes. Both locations would be reached easily within an hour at this time of night, arriving at their targets ideally at three-fifteen a.m. With his vast experience of traveling so many times in the remote desert, he knew this period of the night would provide the least amount of notice. "The calm before our coming storm," Stewart mused.

Anxious yet thorough, he had checked and re-checked the electronic timer he had devised a decade earlier for the three daisy-chained bombs headed to the Theodore Roosevelt Dam. He tested and re-tested the battery and its back-up and verified the mechanism for functionality. Even though he had successfully deployed a prototype on the small, rubber dam at Tempe Town Lake, concern niggled at him as to whether his device would work deep underwater as he needed to have happen at Roosevelt.

He set the trigger date for tomorrow: Wednesday, the twentieth of April. Jacob had told him he wanted the detonation on Adolph Hitler's birthday. Since history had failed to record the actual time of Hitler's birth, Jacob had chosen three in the afternoon for the blast to occur. He had explained to Stewart the significance: the time coincided with the hour the Bible said Yahweh expired on the cross. The moment when the temple curtain was torn in two from top to bottom.

Next, for the van departing out to Palo Verde, Stewart also re-checked his wiring. He made sure the throwaway cell he had hard-wired to the IED's blasting cap was fully charged. This phone would act as an RC, or remote control. When its number was dialed, the cell's ring tone would send a low-voltage signal, triggering the blasting cap and detonating the C-4 under the gasoline barrels.

As for the single warhead IED, that device would be headed to its target in seven more hours. Its destination: a morning demonstration in Wesley Bolin Memorial Park, next to the state capitol. Pro-immigration activists had planned a full day of speeches, decrying the current county sheriff Joe Arpaio's controversial tactics in rounding up and incarcerating illegals. To get the bomb there, Logan Athem would drive his Red Rock police van with the Mk82 in back. Trailing him would be Caleb Tancos in Logan's police cruiser, the Mk152 remote firing transmitter on the seat beside him.

When Stewart was all done, he looked at all three vehicles, lined up next to each other in the staging area. Alone now, he spoke to himself out loud. "For you, Jacob, dear father. I am sending David out to meet Goliath. To bring the City of Phoenix to its knees and then chop off its head."

CHAPTER 49

Tonto National Forest
3:00 a.m.

With The Apache Trail illuminated by a full moon, the dump truck driver, Guillermo, along with his helper, reached the Roosevelt Dam. They looked along the shoulder for the markers Stewart had mentioned, signaling the hidden entrance for the dam's long lost road.

"*Pilón di naranja!*" the helper cried out.

As Guillermo reached the orange barrel-shaped pylon, he made a sharp turn onto a dirt road. Decades ago, after the resurfacing of the dam, the old causeway had been closed-off but remained intact. Known only to a handful of SRP employees with special clearance, the utility company had kept the road for back-up access to the top of the dam in case of emergency. As instructed, Guillermo turned off his headlights and let the moonlight guide his way. A locked chain-link gate soon came into view and the truck rolled to a stop.

"*Vaya! Vaya!*" his helper shouted.

Guillermo throttled the ten-ton truck's Jasper diesel engine, shifting into low gear. He popped his foot off the clutch. The truck roared forward, plowing through the fence with ease, leaving mangled metal and wire strewn along the shoulder. He slowly navigated his way until they came to a ribbon of pavement. He followed the asphalt as it curved ever so gently, taking them directly over the structure. They wouldn't have much time as they had been warned that security cameras were almost certain to pick up their presence from this point forward. Hopefully, as Stewart remembered from his times of visiting the dam during the wee hours of the morning, the night crew security staff would either be asleep at their stations or watching DVDs and not the CCTV monitors.

The Mexican men turned to each other, a wild look in their eyes, as moonlight shimmered off the dark water a mere forty-feet below. On the other side of the truck, the ground opened up into a black abyss. They were riding right on the top of the Theodore Roosevelt Dam.

Guillermo yelled out, pointing ahead, "*La linea blanca!*"

The wide, white stripe Stewart had told them about came into view. They had reached the center of the dam. As Guillermo came to a stop, his helper jumped out. He then motioned for Guillermo to pull forward, guiding him so as to get the side of truck as close as possible to the edge of the water-side of the dam. He held up his hand, palm open to the driver. "*Alto!*" the helper cried.

Guillermo stepped hard on the air brakes, bringing the truck to a sudden stop. His partner gestured a thumbs up signal. Guillermo then flipped the switch on the dashboard, labeled DUMP, into the up position. The Versa-lift's hydraulic arm creaked into motion and the back-end of the truck began its slow rise. As the bed lifted skyward, tipping toward the water below, the hinges attached to the steel side panel screeched and the side door swung open. Gravity took its full effect and sent sand spilling downward, pouring out from the side of the truck into the black water. Along with the nearly eight-tons of sand also went a ton of bombs, chain-linked together, topped off by the flotation device. Their job was done.

All they needed to do now was as instructed: leave the truck and run back to the tail car waiting for them at the entrance to the frontage road back off AZ 88; scamper back to their freedom and to Tancos's phantom five-thousand-dollar prize. They ran as fast as they could until headlights blinded them from a vehicle coming straight toward them. Trapped, their exit was blocked, and the two men stopped dead in their tracks.

CHAPTER 50

Scottsdale, Arizona
5:00 a.m.

Stan had worked much later than usual in the study of his home located in a neighborhood called The Sweetwater Corridor. He had moved his family to the North Scottsdale area not long after the explosion and killings inside his neighbor Paul Stewart's house.

By the time he had gone to bed it was well past midnight. He had finally decided his brain had suffered enough battering going over and over his index cards he had brought home with him. Cards containing clues he hoped would tie together the recent Chandler triple decapitation to the Stewart family cold case murders. When his cellphone rang a few hours after his head hit the pillow, he fumbled for the chirping device on the nightstand before answering and pressing it to his ear.

"Stan, it's Jake. I'm really sorry to call you at this hour."

Stan sat up on the edge of the bed, whispering, trying not to wake Maxine. "Jake?" Concerned why the U.S. Attorney Jake Zadnik would be calling him at this hour, he knew it couldn't be good news. He left the room and headed for his study on the other side of the house. He talked as he walked. "Yeah, Jake . . . what is it?"

"Salt River Project security stopped a couple of guys a short time ago out at Roosevelt Dam. Their officer in charge couldn't get anything from them but his guards who stopped them think the two may have dropped something into the reservoir."

"Wha? . . . how did they do that?"

"They used a dump truck and got access to the top of the dam from an abandoned service road."

As he rubbed his eyes, Jake's explanation shocked Stan to attention. "Did you say Roosevelt?"

"Yes. SRP security checked out the truck but it was empty. All they could find was some sand on the ground next to it, right at the edge of the dam."

"Sand? Were there signs of anything else?"

"So far, nothing. But they're driving out an array of portable, high-intensity lights up there now to do a better search. If they did dump something, though, no telling what could have been in the back of that truck. It's pretty big. In the meantime, the area around the dump truck and the road they were on have both been cordoned off. SRP also has their hazmat and dive teams headed out there now."

"Shit, Jake." Stan paused while he rubbed his eyes again, still not fully awake. "But why are you calling me?"

"Well, based upon what I was told, I think they may have been caught on your side of the dam?"

"*My side* of the dam?"

"Yeah, a surprise to me, too. I just learned that tidbit when I got called. Seems half of the dam's in Maricopa County and the other half's in Gila County. Same with the reservoir, that is, at least from the dam up to the Theodore Roosevelt Bridge. From what I've been told these guys were caught on your side of the dam. So that would be in your jurisdiction."

"But the dam's federal property, right? Wouldn't you guys handle this?"

"Well, yes and no. The Bureau of Reclamation technically oversees the dam, Salt River Project runs it, and the U.S. Forest Service maintains the area around it. Since there are two federal entities involved, our office got a call. Plus there's a chance this could be a terrorist act, so every federal agency's being notified."

"FBI?" Stan asked.

"Of course. But to my knowledge there's been no threat

phoned in to any agency about this. SRP security said they didn't find any explosives in the truck nor guns on the two men, both of whom refused to answer any questions when they were caught. So, at least as of right now, I see it as a county thing."

"Then I need to talk to those two men."

"That may be a little problem. Gila County sheriff already has them in his custody."

"Gila County? I thought you said they were caught in Maricopa County?"

"That's why I'm calling you. Somehow, Micah Lund got wind of this, showed up out there on the scene before anyone else, made the arrest, and took off with the two subjects."

"Come again?"

"Just what I said. The SRP guys said Micah Lund wanted these two guys real bad, couldn't wait to get his hands on them. Claimed he had the right to make the arrest. They didn't argue with him. It's sort of a clusterfuck right now, especially since I know you two aren't love birds. I feel a pissing match coming on."

"That's an understatement."

"See, I'm your friend, Stan. I look out for you. Plus you know how much I think of that fabulous wife of yours. It's the least I could do to help her husband."

"You Navy guys . . . do you ever stop?"

"Hey, I'm just sayin' how lucky you are, that's all. Anyway, better get a hold of your old pal Micah and see what charges he's going to level against those two. Or maybe you can convince the Maricopa County sheriff to talk to him and he can go get them out of Gila County lockup. Then you can charge them in Maricopa County. But you better hurry because I'm sure at some point the FBI is going to send out a special agent. Plus, from what I was told, these guys are Mexican Nationals with no papers. So ICE will be on the case faster than flies on shit to ship 'em back to Mexico."

"I owe you, Jake."

"No problem. But better move quickly. I'm sure the

federal public D.A. will get a call when they walk in the office in a few hours, telling them to get over to the Gila County jail and talk to the two men who were caught."

"Can you do anything on your end to delay that a bit?"

"Hey, for you, whatever you need."

"Thanks again, Jake."

"Listen, don't thank me. I got no love for that peckerwood Sheriff Lund. His old man's no boy scout neither. You know that from the task force info I was told to share with you, Mister 'I got connections in Washington.'"

Stan chuckled. "You're just jealous. Listen, Jake, next time I talk to my buddy on The Hill, I'll mention how much you've done for me. Of course, that may mean you'll get bumped up to D.C. and you won't be able to ogle my wife anymore. So long, Jake."

Stan hung up and pondered the situation. His jaw clenched. What could illegals have been doing at Roosevelt in the middle of the night, presumably dumping something into Roosevelt Lake? His recent conversation with Kelli Begay at the Arizona Department of Emergency Management came rushing back in his head. Her words rang in his ears:

". . . if these dams were breached, the flooding caused along the Salt River would reach five miles north and south of the shoreline."

"Who would be motivated to attack the dam?" Stan muttered aloud as he remained seated in his study, spinning his cellphone on top of the desk. "And why was Micah so dead set about arresting these guys? If I didn't know better I'd say—"

Suddenly, his phone chimed, signaling an incoming text. He picked up the cell. The small screen read: MEET ME...LA GRANDE ORANGE...2 HRS

CHAPTER 51

Inside a Phoenix Restaurant
6:55 a.m.

When Stan walked into La Grande Orange, as usual the busy Arcadia neighborhood eatery was packed with breakfast patrons. A Beatles tune played through the speakers, fighting to be heard above the din of the hungry crowd. He spotted Brian sitting in a booth in the back, waving him over. An attractive woman, wearing chic glasses and sporting long black hair tucked behind her ears, sat across from him.

"Good morning," Stan said, reaching his hand out to his buddy.

"Hey, there." Brian shook his hand. "Sorry to roust you so early, buddy. I hope Maxine's not mad at me."

"Nope," Stan frowned. "I was already up." He stayed standing, waiting for Brian to introduce him to the woman.

Brian motioned toward her with an outstretched hand across the table. "Stan. This is Doctor Pauline Dorrey."

"Doctor Dorrey." They shook hands. "It's so nice to meet you. Brian's mentioned your name many times. He's told me how much you've helped him."

"The pleasure's mine, Mister Kobe. And, thank you."

He could see why Brian might have fallen for the psychologist. Her piercing blue eyes were mesmerizing. "Please. Call me Stan."

Dorrey gave him a nod. "Only if you promise to call me Pauline."

He smiled and sat down next to Brian. Thinking he

already knew the answer to an obvious question, Stan asked it anyway. "So, Pauline, what brings you all the way up to Phoenix so early in the morning?"

She turned her head over toward Brian then back at Stan. "It's not what you think. Brian told me he's told you all about me, or I should say, about us. That is, our past relationship."

Stan flashed a look at Brian. The color of embarrassment reddened the cop's face.

She reached over and gave Brian's hand a pat as he nervously fumbled with his silverware. "We're all adults here. I just want you to know I meant no harm to anyone, especially Brian."

Stan raised an eyebrow, wondering where the conversation was leading. Brian hadn't told him in his text message his ex-mistress—if that's what she really was—would be joining them this morning, so the awkwardness he felt was difficult to hide. "Look—"

Brian jumped in. "Stan. Pauline came here to share something with us about our friend, Border Agent Tancos. I wanted you to hear this directly from her."

"Tancos? What?"

Pauline jumped in. "Brian's told me he already told you that I have this new patient, a soldier who just returned from the war in Afghanistan."

"The vet suffering from the severe case of PTSD," Stan said.

She gave a nod. "This guy, my patient, that is, just called me."

Stan raised an eyebrow.

Pauline explained. "I give patients my cellphone number in case they need to reach me in a crisis situation. So, like I said, he called me and told me he wanted to tell me something to do with national security. Of course, when he said those words, I told him to go on. After a bit of dancing around, he shared with me that one of his military buddies—he wouldn't give me a name—had just heard a rumor that this guy Tancos is rounding up illegals in the desert and holding them hostage for ransom."

Stan's eyebrows rose to the top of his forehead. "Yes . . . go on."

Pauline took a sip of water and then continued with her story. "When I asked him how he knew this at first he evaded answering the question but after more prompting he told me a bunch of the guys from his old Army unit living here in Arizona are white supremacists. One of the sick things these guys have been doing—they call it "fun"—is hunting down illegals in the middle of the desert, shooting them down like dogs—as he described it—and then burying them, leaving no trace. I asked him if this guy Tancos was involved in this and he said yes."

"Do you believe him?" Stan asked.

"I really have no reason not to. Like I've already said, although he's off the scale on the paranoia meter, he's not delusional. He's a decorated hero, both in Iraq and Afghanistan. He served four tours." She took a long pause, looking to Stan as if what she was about to say next she was going to regret. "You already know from Brian that I work undercover for the DIA. If someone tells me he thinks a government employee is doing something illegal, I've got to listen. Then, if I think it's credible, I've got to report it in to my superiors in D.C."

"Okay, I've got that, but why are you telling me?"

"Brian told me you two are working that high profile homicide case in Chandler. The one where you suspect the victims were illegals."

Stan glared at Brian, this time not hiding his disapproval, wondering what else he might have shared with his part-time lover.

"Don't be angry with him for sharing that with me. I saw the story on the news, too. Actually, you should thank him because when my patient spoke to me he told me he also heard Tancos was moving a big group of illegals up to a drop house in the Phoenix area and that he might need more help from some of his 'brothers.'"

"Tell him exactly what your patient called them," Brian coaxed her.

"He referred to them as 'his ASA brothers'"

"ASA? He actually used that acronym?" Stan asked.

"Yes, he did. I know who they are since our DIA people have eyes and ears on them, too."

"What else did this patient say?"

"He rambled on a bit about some of the other things he'd already talked to me about, like the importance of protecting our borders . . . about Afghan militants coming into our country disguised as Mexicans . . . the typical vigilante rant."

"Anything else?"

"Yes. I didn't think anything of it at first but when I mentioned it to Brian he thought you really needed to hear it. What the soldier said didn't make any sense. He quoted something from Scripture. I found it odd because he hadn't spoken in that manner before. I made sure to write it down."

She opened her purse, pulled out her spiral notepad, and flipped to a page.

"Here it is." She read from her notes. "He said, '*Tie him hand and foot, and throw him outside, into the darkness, where there will be the weeping and gnashing of teeth.*' When I asked him what this was, he said it was Matthew twenty-two-twelve and that *they*, whoever *they* are, were being called to action. I prodded him and asked him *who* is calling them into action. All he said was, 'The Lord Melchizedek.'"

CHAPTER 52

Stan thanked Dr. Dorrey for sharing her story. Then she said her goodbyes and headed for the exit. He took the seat in the booth where she had sat across from him and Brian. "I thought you told me this was over."

"It is. And, she's been called back to Washington. She also suggested that I come clean with Claire and be honest with her, since she knows I still love my wife."

Stan reached for his cup of coffee. "That's good advice."

"I know it is . . . so I'd really like to just leave it at that."

Stan acknowledged his request by changing the subject. "I have to admit, her last bit of information *was* very interesting."

"Yeah. Seems our thoughts about Tancos may have been right after all. That perhaps he's working for the other side and may even be an ASA member himself, like the Lunds."

"If you think that then you'll love to hear this. Before you got here, I got an email from Zadnik over at the USAO's office. The message contained a transcript of the audio recorded at an assembly of the Church of the High Country by a man the feds have inside the group. Jacob and Micah Lund were both present." Stan took the cellphone and made a few swipes until he saw what he was looking for. "Here it is. I bookmarked the section where Jacob is speaking."

Stan read aloud the words on his screen:

Your high priest, your servant, I, your Lord Melchizedek, beseeches you to tie

him hand and foot, and throw him outside, into the darkness, where there will be

weeping and the gnashing of teeth. Help us smite the

heathens from the face of the earth.

Brian raised his eyebrows, then asked, "So you think this Lord Melchizedek Lund refers to himself as here is the same one Pauline's patient spoke about?"

Stan gave him the look they had both learned from a puppet character they had grown up watching on TV as kids, Lambchops. The handler used to scrunch the puppet's face and push its upper lip over the bottom when asked a dumb question.

"I'd bet my job on it. With her statement and this transcript, I believe it gives us probable cause to search Tancos's residence and Lund's gathering place up on the Rim. I'm going to call my office and have them contact Zadnik to execute federal warrants. By the way, speaking of Jake, I want to tell you why I was up so early this morning."

CHAPTER 53

Caleb Tancos drove in an unmarked police cruiser. He followed Logan Athem, ahead of him driving his police van with the quarter-ton bomb securely fastened down in the back. The two-vehicle convoy headed toward downtown Phoenix, less than ten miles from the shuttered warehouse they'd left minutes ago.

The downtown Phoenix streets were relatively quiet, considering the magnitude of the approaching event. Most of the city's police were already at their assigned posts, directing traffic or involved with prepping for crowd control. All local law enforcement had been put on high alert after two "incidents," as they had been referred to in a Department of Homeland Security bulletin, had been reported last night. Specific details were not revealed by DHS officials, but the brief asked supervisors to tell their officers near today's event to keep an eye out for any suspicious vehicles or persons.

Tancos tailed Athem down Grand Avenue, staying a few car lengths behind his ASA pal. The remote detonation transmitter Tancos would use to wirelessly trigger the bomb sat beside him on his car's front seat. One wrong move, one inadvertent slip, and Tancos could accidentally ignite the armament well before its intended destination.

At Grand Avenue, Athem made the turn south down 19th Avenue. Tancos followed, knowing they only had a few quick miles left until they reached their target. They drove on 19th

Avenue until they reached West Jefferson Street. There, they made a hard left. Two and one-half blocks away was the southern entrance to the Wesley Bolin parking lot.

Logan wheeled the van onto the semi-circular drive where a young, White, Phoenix police officer, standing behind an eight-foot-wide sawhorse, held a hand up for him to halt. While Tancos waited behind, he could see Athem, wearing his Red Rock Police uniform, chatting with the cop through the rolled down window. After what seemed like an eternity, the officer waved them both through.

Athem pulled his vehicle into a parking space nearest the podium. The bomb was now no more than twenty yards from the speakers' platform. He rolled up the tinted driver's window, turned off the ignition, got out, locked the van and walked back to Tancos, waiting in the unmarked Crown Vic.

"What did you tell the cop?" Tancos asked.

Logan grinned. "I told him I couldn't find any parking at the Starbucks at the corner. I promised to bring him back a latte if he let me park there while I ran in to get a drink.

Tancos chuckled. "These kids are hooked on that shit. Nice job."

What the police officer didn't realize was that he unwittingly allowed Tancos and Athem to put in place their WMD. When they triggered the weapon of mass destruction within milliseconds the explosion would generate seven-hundred-tons-per-inch of pressure and temperatures of up to forty-five hundred degrees Fahrenheit. Its explosion would blast a hole at least ten-feet-deep by twenty-feet-wide. Most everything and everyone within three-thousand-feet from where they had left Stewart's color-blind and unforgiving gift to Jacob would be adversely affected in some manner.

Now all Tancos could hope for was that Stanford James Kobe would be as close to ground zero as possible or at the very least somewhere within a death zone ten-times the size of a football field.

CHAPTER 54

Downtown Phoenix
8:10 a.m.

When Stan arrived at the MCAO's office after meeting Brian and Dr. Dorrey, phones were ringing non-stop. He worked his way through the bustle of law clerks to get inside his office. As soon as he did, Maricopa County Prosecutor Bill Montgomery walked in behind him and closed the door.

"Did you hear about—"

"The incident at Roosevelt?" Stan said, interrupting him. "Yep. Jake Zadnik woke me up with that good news."

"So you're probably also aware that Micah Lund has taken into custody—"

"Two illegal Mexican Nationals?"

"Is there anything you don't know?"

"I don't know the next time the Cubs will win another World Series," Stan joked.

"Very funny. How about the explosion inside Palo Verde?"

"That one I hadn't heard."

"Two occupants in a van were killed. Burned beyond recognition. They had passed two checkpoints and were driving out on the interior perimeter road, near the outgoing 500Kv transformer lines. Thankfully, the on-site fire department was able to douse the fire with no significant damage to the lines."

"Whose van was it?" Stan asked.

"According to the logs at one of the checkpoints, it was an

APS van. It all looked normal but the feds are investigating as we speak."

"Does the press have it yet?"

"No. DHS has clamped down on leaking anything to the media about incidents that happen in or around nuclear power plants for fear of causing a panic. They're especially tight-lipped about this and the dam incident, as you can imagine."

"Makes sense. But how will they keep a lid on it?"

"No idea. That's their problem. In the meantime, we've got our own issues out at Roosevelt, as you already know."

"Yes, Zadnik told me the Gila County Sheriff's Office took into custody the two trespassers at the dam last night. But he wasn't sure why they grabbed them since he told me they were caught on our side of the dam."

"Our side?"

"Yes. Seems the dam is half in our county, half in Gila. First I've heard of it, too. Zadnik said SRP security told his office these two guys were stopped as they were retreating back toward Highway 88. That's definitely on the Maricopa side."

"So then why does Lund have them is his jail?"

"That's what I'd like to know."

"I'll look into this Lund thing to find out what's going on there. Maybe I'll give our county sheriff a call. He might know why Gila apprehended them versus his guys."

"No, don't call him just yet. He'll find out soon enough, especially since these guys, from what I've been briefed, are illegals. If he grabs them, he'd get in my way. Here. Call this number." Stan scribbled a number from memory on a notepad sitting on his desk. "I've got a connection inside the U.S. Marshal's Office. Have them contact Micah's office. Or better yet, get them to send some agents down there unannounced and spring the two from his jail. Tell my guy I need him to get them down into one of our jail's isolation interrogation rooms so we can have our people have a run at them."

"I'd like to find out how Gila County knew about these guys getting caught by SRP and out to the dam so fast to pick them up." Montgomery sounded pissed. "Find out who called them in."

Stan nodded. "I'll need to put an associate on it. I have to get down to Wesley Bolin Park. Maxine is scheduled to speak in just a little while and I promised her I'd be there for her big speech. Okay?"

Montgomery nodded his blessing. "Then you better get down there. Wish I could be there. Tell her to break a leg."

CHAPTER 55

Phoenix Print Warehouse
8:12 a.m.

After waiting for over six hours for any type of news, Paul Stewart's cellphone rang.

"Yes."

"There's been a change in plans." On the other end, Jacob Lund's voice sounded ominous.

"What's happened?" Stewart asked.

"Our men in one of the tail cars had called me much earlier and said the two you sent out to the dam were caught. I called Micah and he was able to pick them up. They're in his control now."

"Did they complete their assignment?"

"Yes."

"Good. What will Micah do with them?"

"He has his instructions. As well, the Palo Verde van has been detonated. I'm waiting for more details but my people have been slow to respond."

"What about Caleb and Logan."

"I expect our brothers will be calling me very soon to confirm delivery once they're at the detonation spot. Then we should soon be seeing on the local news the fruits of their labor."

"What do you want me to do?"

"Just tell me that you're certain your gifts for the dam will detonate at the prescribed hour tomorrow."

"They will."

"Good. Your final payment awaits you when that happens."

Stewart gave no reply.

"Lord Melchizedek is praying for you, my son."

CHAPTER 56

Downtown Phoenix
Near Wesley Bolin Memorial Park
8:15 a.m.

"**S**o much for Phoenix's finest being on their toes, huh?" Athem belly laughed from the passenger seat of his Crown Vic.

Tancos nodded his head in agreement. "Sometimes I wonder if these kids they're hiring can tie their own shoes. These little jag-offs wouldn't last a fucking minute out in the desert with me, chasing down coyotes and mules." He looked over at Athem. "You get behind the wheel."

Tancos pulled over to the curb. The two men exchanged spots and buckled themselves back in. Stewart had given them precise instructions to stay within line of sight of the bomb. This assured avoiding any interference with the FM transmission signal between transmitter and receiver. At this moment they sat at the corner of 17th Avenue and Madison, far enough from the blast effect zone but close enough to see the van in the plaza parking lot and the rapidly growing crowd.

"This looks like a good spot," Tancos said. "I can spot the van from here." He had his forearms wrapped around the sides of the Mk152 transmitter, gripping it tight on his lap. He cuddled the box like a baby.

Logan was antsy, chomping at the bit. He couldn't wait for the clock to strike 9:02. "You're one lucky son-of-a-bitch. You get to push the button to kill that nigger Kobe and his half-breed wife."

Tancos paid no attention to Athem's babble, keeping his eyes focused on the van and the plaza. He checked his wristwatch waiting for it to tick down to the prescribed detonation time.

"I didn't wait all this time and come all this way to just sit here and watch while you get to push the button that blows this bomb. I'll give you a thousand dollars, right now, if you let me do it."

Tancos's jaw clenched. His nostrils flared.

Logan taunted him. "Why should you have all the fun? You're not even family. This was my cousin's and my uncle's plan. They made this whole thing happen."

"You heard Stewart," Tancos replied. "He assigned me to the transmitter."

Logan wouldn't give up. He squirmed in his seat, grasping the steering wheel so tight it looked like he'd twist it off the column with his massive arms. "Really. C'mon. A thousand bucks. If you don't believe me, look." Athem struggled to get his immense paw down inside his pants pocket. When he succeeded, he yanked out a wad of hundred dollar bills and began peeling them off, one at a time, holding them in front of Tancos's face. "One-hundred, two-hundred, three-hundred . . . ." He kept going until he reached one-thousand dollars. Then he scrunched up all the bills and held them up in the air with his fat hand. "There. A thousand-dollars. All yours. All you gotta do is just let me blow that spook to kingdom come."

Tancos looked at the bills but said nothing.

"You albino prick," Athem said. "Playing hardball, huh? Okay. Two-thousand!"

As he went down to dig back into his pocket for more cash someone tapped on his driver's side window. He jerked his head to see who it was. At the same time, he moved his right hand down toward his Glock, next to him on the seat. An African-American Maricopa County Sheriff's Office deputy stood outside the vehicle. Athem rolled down the window.

"Restricted parking here, even for police vehicles," the deputy said. "You'll need to move it along now. Okay?"

Logan was not going to take orders from a black man, uniformed or not. "We're on special assignment, Barack," he replied. A chuckle escaped.

Stiffening to attention, the deputy replied, "I beg your pardon?"

Athem carefully moved his right hand over his Glock, grasping the handle. "You heard me, Obama," he barked at the deputy. He tugged at his beard with his left hand as his right hand remained over the gun.

"Logan. Let's just move the car." Tancos spoke calmly as he squeezed his arms harder around the firing device. As he tensed, the deputy looked in his direction.

"What's that, sir?"

Tancos didn't look at the officer but Athem shot him a sneer. "You couldn't just let us be, could you, Reverend Al?"

The deputy reached for his microphone clipped on the shoulder of his uniform.

Athem pulled his Glock from the seat and aimed it at the deputy. "I wouldn't do that if I were you, LeBron."

"No!" Tancos shouted. "It's not time. They're not there yet!"

The deputy jumped back toward the rear of the vehicle but not before Athem was able to fire a shot. He hit the officer in the shoulder. The force of the shot spun him and slammed him against the side of the Crown Vic. He drew his weapon and returned fire into the car through the driver's side rear window. Then he shouted into his shoulder radio as he got off two more shots. "Shots fired! Officer down! Officer down!"

CHAPTER 57

8:25 a.m.

Screams erupted from the street as bystanders ran for shelter between the buildings near the shootout. Some people fell to the ground, taking cover in the grassy area just to the south of where an MCSO deputy and two men in a parked car engaged in a gun battle. Others bystanders stood frozen, watching in horror, as the wounded officer took a kneeling stance and unloaded his weapon. He fired into the vehicle multiple times through the car's back windshield before falling unconscious to the pavement.

When the shooting stopped, the sheriff's deputy lay ten-yards behind the Crown Victoria, its two occupants still inside. Besides the first round fired by the person sitting on the driver's side, witnesses saw the same occupant get off several more rounds, all aimed back at the crouched deputy through the destroyed back window. Not one of those shots hit their intended target.

When the gunfire had started, other nearby law enforcement personnel scrambled to the scene but by the time they arrived the shooting was over. Another sheriff's deputy rushed to the aid of his wounded comrade, while two Phoenix police officers—each approaching from opposite sides of the bullet-riddled car—cautiously advanced, guns drawn. When they reached the vehicle, both men inside looked dead. Behind the wheel was a very large, bearded man. He wore a Red Rock, Arizona police uniform. Soaked in blood, he was slumped over the steering wheel with what appeared to be a mortal head wound. The man in the passenger side, dressed in military fatigues, looked fatally wounded, too, blood oozing from his head and neck. Hundred dollar bills were scattered across the front seat, some drenched in blood, others as crisp as if they had just been minted.

The Phoenix officer on the driver's side felt for a pulse on his victim's neck. He shook his head, then stated matter-of-factly, "He's dead." He looked over to his partner at the passenger side window. "How's your guy?"

"Faint pulse."

"What's that on his lap?" the first cop asked.

Splattered with blood, the device that lay across the passenger's legs had an array of switches, one of which—a large red button under a clear plastic enclosure—the wounded man's right hand half-covered. On the top of the device, a blood-smattered sticky note had written on it: 9:02.

The second cop's hand started shaking. "I don't know but it doesn't look like no Gameboy." He nervously stepped back from the side of the vehicle. Then he turned and shouted to the crowd that had gathered and inched closer, straining necks to see inside the car. "Step back! Step back! There could be a bomb here!"

Screams and moans sprang forth from the people as they turned and ran for cover. He looked over at his partner, still standing at the driver's side window. "Moore, I'll evacuate the area. You call the bomb squad."

CHAPTER 58

8:30 a.m.

A crisp blue sky greeted Stan on his walk to Wesley Bolin Memorial Park, less than one mile west of his office. Still high with emotion with his breakthrough discovery at the Mogollon Rim fire lookout, he was now weighed down with the last night's unexplained activities at both Palo Verde Nuclear Power Station and Roosevelt Dam.

He felt pressed now to spend every waking minute working on wrapping his arms around everything that had transpired. These last two events had him especially perplexed and worried over the prospect for what dire consequences they could bring forth. Kelli Begay's stern warning about a failure of the grid's infrastructure interdependencies popped into his mind.

What if someone compromised Palo Verde on one end and Roosevelt on another? There'd be widespread panic.

How would he keep his family safe? Where would they go if there was no power or water? What would he do to survive? He didn't even own a tent or camping stove. Talk about not being a survivalist. That was him.

He pushed these despairing thoughts from his mind and concentrated on the excitement he felt for Maxine and her upcoming speech. Filled with pride, his wife would be the inaugural speaker at today's immigration rally. She had become active in the cause when she had discovered a direct paternal ancestor was a member of the San Patricio Battalion. Some of the long-forgotten group of Irish-born U.S. soldiers were tried

and executed as traitors for defecting to fight for and defend
Mexico during the Mexican-American War.

As he walked down Jefferson Street he hoped the fifteen-
minute stroll would give him a chance to clear his mind. That
desire came to an abrupt end when he neared the park and the
wailing sound of sirens pierced the air. The alarming noise
seemed to come from all directions, bouncing off the virtual
wall of downtown office buildings dotting either side of the
street. As the sirens grew in volume and number, he stepped
up his pace. By the time he reached 15th Avenue and Jefferson,
the area was closed to pedestrians and vehicles. He flashed his
MCAO badge and was let past a set of barricades. Within one
more block he reached another barricade line. This time, even
with his credentials, the police would not let him pass.

"What is it?"

A Phoenix police officer answered him. "Bomb squad's
orders. Can't let you past here, sir."

"Where is it?"

"Somewhere in Bolin Park, near the rally, from what I've
heard."

"You're positive?"

The cop nodded.

Frantic, Stan pulled out his cellphone and dialed Maxine.
No answer. He hung up and tried again. When she answered,
he blew out a relieved breath. "Sweetheart, where are you? Are
you in the park yet? . . . No? Good! Don't go anywhere near
there! Then you know. Yes, yes. Go to my office. I'll meet you
there."

Stan grabbed a ride in a city police car. By the time he got
back to his office building, Maxine had beat him there and
stood waiting outside his building. When he got out of the car,
she ran to him.

"What's going on?" she asked, trembling.

He held her, squeezing her as tight as he could. "I don't
know for sure. Something about a bomb in the park."

His phone vibrated on his belt. Brian.

"Hey, I just got a call from my CSRU technician, Mary

Ann," the detective said. "She thought we'd like to know her EOD team just got called to downtown Phoenix. I think they found one of your bombs."

CHAPTER 59

9:15 a.m.

After Stan was sure Maxine was okay, he went into his office and arranged for an intern to drive her back to her ASU office. Then he immediately ran down the hall to share the news with Bill Montgomery that a team from the National Guard's 363rd EOD Company had been sent to Wesley Bolin Memorial Park to render safe a bomb.

"Five'll get you ten it's one of the missing Mark eighty-twos from Captain Benjamin Forster's A-10 Thunderbolt," Stan told Montgomery. "There's a unique identifier on every ordnance. Presuming the detonation team safely immobilizes it, we'll see if I'm right."

In turn, Montgomery informed Stan about the details their office had at the moment regarding the shootout not far from the same park.

"We're waiting for positive identification but it looks like one of the men killed in the vehicle was Red Rock Chief of Police Logan Athem."

"Athem, huh? Hanley will enjoy hearing that."

"According to witnesses, seems an MCSO deputy approached Athem's unmarked police vehicle. Words were exchanged and Athem shot the deputy. The deputy returned fire, killing Athem and gravely wounding the passenger in the car."

"Who was the passenger?"

"A Border Patrol agent."

"My guess is his last name is Tancos."

Montgomery's mouth dropped open. "How did you know that?"

"He's the BP agent I met in the desert with his Mexican sidekick."

"Did his partner look like this guy?" Montgomery pulled a snapshot out from a manila file he had on his desk. In the photo, a Hispanic-looking male lay sideways on a dirt surface. He had a bullet hole in the back of his head. Montgomery handed the crime scene evidence photo to Stan.

Stan recognized the sweat-stained Dbacks baseball cap lying on the ground next to the victim. "Yep. That looks like him. When did this happen?"

"He was found in an alley about five this morning in west Phoenix. In Maryvale, near Fifty-Fifth Avenue and Verde Lane."

"Looks like the Lunds are tying up loose ends."

"You're still convinced the Lunds are behind all this?"

Stan nodded. "Athem's a nephew to old man Jacob. I'd bet my job he and his son Micah are involved."

"Get down to the morgue. Ask Hanley to meet you there. See if you two can positively ID these two."

"What about Tancos?" Stan asked.

"He's at Good Samaritan in surgery. If he makes it, yes, talk to him. And find out how our deputy is doing. He's over there too."

*   *   *

Stan headed to meet Brian at the county morgue. After they signed in, the technician took them to see the corpses of Athem and Ramos, both of whom he and Brian positively ID'd.

"I wonder what prompted Athem to shoot the deputy," Brian said.

"I understand he was black."

"Well that explains it." Brian said as his cell rang. He had a short conversation with the caller, hung up and turned to

Stan.

"What's up?" Stan asked.

"That was Mary Ann. Good news is her Explosive Ordnance Disposal detail rendered safe the bomb. It was definitely a Mark eighty-two. It was wired for detonation and in the back of a Red Rock police van parked at Wesley Bolin. They've already contacted Davis-Monthan. They traced the lot number from the bomb's fuze. It's definitely one of Forster's four missing bombs."

"And the bad news?"

"It looks like the bomb was wired to the other end of the military-issued remote detonation device found in Logan Athem's car. So, it looks like her theory a rogue EOD guy has come true."

CHAPTER 60

Inside The Warehouse
11:00 a.m.

An edgy Paul Stewart sat on top of a pile of wooden crates. Across from him an ancient refrigerator stood silent. An encrusted microwave sat dormant on a stained Formica counter. Mustiness hung in the air of the unkempt room. All night and through the morning he had stayed glued to a vintage, black-and-white TV, watching the twenty-four-hour local news station.

If a bomb had gone off in Phoenix, this television station wasn't reporting the event. Nor were they reporting any incidents at Palo Verde. Hours earlier, Jacob had told him the improvised explosive device in the back of the APS van sent to the nuclear plant had indeed been detonated.

Why no news of this? And why no news of the bomb downtown?

As those thoughts crossed his mind, the local TV news station broke in with story of a police shootout near the planned downtown immigration rally.

His cell rang. He answered. "Yes. Have you heard any more?"

"Brother Paul, we have failed."

Stewart could barely hear Jacob's dejected voice. He struggled to understand Jacob's next words.

"My people on the inside have told me the Palo Verde van caused only minor damage. Not only that but my beloved nephew, Logan, is dead. Killed by a cursed black man, no less."

The vein on the side of Stewart's neck pulsed with anxiety hearing the news. "Were he or Tancos able to detonate their bomb?"

"No. They were stopped before they could trigger it. I've been told by another one of my people that it seems this fucking nigger deputy approached him and my nephew in his car as they waited for the agreed upon time to detonate my gift. Something obviously went wrong. The border agent survived the shootout. They transported him to Good Samaritan. I presume he's under guard."

Stewart noticed Lund's unusual use of profanity and that he now referred to their heretofore brother-in-arms, Caleb Tancos, in the third person.

Sounding detached and emotionless, Jacob went on. "I can't take a risk of this goddamn fool talking. He needs to be fucking silenced."

CHAPTER 61

After their trip to the morgue, Stan sat in Brian's unmarked car in the county medical examiner's parking lot. While Stan leafed through confidential file folders, he spoke without looking up.

"Stewart's here. In Phoenix. I can feel it. I know it as sure as I'm sitting next to you."

"And you know this because . . ."

He looked over at Brian. "Because my gut tells me. My gut also tells me he put the bomb in Athem's van. A bomb I believe was intended for me."

"Whoa. What are you talking about? You never shared that theory with me."

"I wasn't sure, until now. They had to know I'd be at the rally with Maxine speaking." Stan tapped on a folder across his lap. "After reading what I have here, I don't have to second-guess what my intuition's been screaming at me. That Jacob Lund is behind the whole thing."

Brian turned down his car's police radio, silencing the chatter from dispatch. He eyed Stan's folder. "That from Clayton?"

Stan gave him a wry smile. "I've been doing some digging in a whole new direction, drilling deeper into Lund's past. We already know he formed a shell company called The Sangre de Cristo Land and Development Company. They own a large tract of land in southeastern Colorado. In a place called the

Baca Grande. This land just so happens to be extremely close to where Forster's plane crashed. This land company is also the same group that applied for the ham radio license in the name of someone called Stanford Phoenix Buford. That's no coincidence."

"I'd agree."

"Moffat, Colorado. That's the little dust patch of a town whose name keeps popping up in our case. Besides the ham call sign registration listing a Moffat Post Office box as its mailing address, you discovered Moffat was also where the owner of the Chandler drop house was having their tax record mailed. Then, Jake Zadnik shared files with me on the City of Scottsdale bombing, linking a white supremacist to yet another PO box in Moffat."

Brian stretched his arms out ahead of him and put his hands on the steering wheel. "Lot of dots there. How about some lines between them?"

Stan heard his doubt. "Not convinced? How about this little tidbit I just read from what Clayton sent me." He pulled out a page from the folder and read from it. "Seems Jacob Lund is chairman of the board of this land development company I mentioned. It only has four executives according to the corporation's Delaware filing papers." He looked over at Brian. "Guess who the other three people are? Micah Lund, Logan Athem, Caleb Tancos."

Brian raised a brow. "That's pretty interesting."

"According to this, the company has been buying large amounts of stock in a closely held water and utility company in southeastern Colorado."

"Why would they do that?" Brian asked, sounding even more intrigued.

"My thoughts exactly. From these aerial images Clayton sent me, they've also built several very large buildings on this land. No one's sure exactly what's inside them but they seem to be powered by solar panels and wind turbines located there. Lots of them."

"So, what do you think is inside those buildings?"

"I have an idea but it's only a hunch. My gut tells me they're Internet server farms."

"Server farms. For who?"

"Don't know that yet. There's nothing in these papers Clayton sent me showing this group has had any publicized transactions with clients."

"Not one?"

Stan shook his head.

"Server farms in the middle of nowhere, yet no customers? I smell fish."

"That's what makes you such a good cop, Hanley." Stan smiled. "You see past all the smoke and mirrors. But I didn't say they didn't have any customers. I said these records don't *show* any. My guess is they've built it for just one. For a client that will be required to come to them when they have no place else to go to store their critical data—and pay any price. Someone like the federal government."

"Or China."

"That's a distinct possibility, too. Both are the two biggest data users in the world. But I'm leaning more toward a domestic buyer. Think about where this server farm is located. Our federal government will have to go somewhere when there's no water or power supplying one of their critical locations. Phoenix."

"Phoenix? What? What are you saying?" Brian sounded hooked.

"What I'm getting at is I think Lund, with the help of Paul Stewart, is planning a catastrophe of monumental proportions. And, if I'm right, I think those two illegal Mexicans caught on top of Roosevelt Dam may be key in helping me answer all of my questions."

CHAPTER 62

Paul Stewart got the word from Jacob Lund that Caleb Tancos had survived his surgery and been transferred to an intensive care unit. He jumped into the van the border agent had left behind at the warehouse and headed to Good Samaritan Hospital.

Without difficulty, he got past the first obstacle by asking the elderly volunteer sitting behind the information desk what floor Mr. Tancos was on. When Stewart found out he was in Room 1220 of the Surgical Intensive Care Unit, he then asked her where he could by a gift for his "only brother, Caleb." After the sweet gray-haired woman smiled her directions to the gift shop, he purchased a potted cactus and made a bee-line for the unguarded elevators.

The doors opened and he stepped off into the hallway of the twelfth floor, twenty-feet from the SICU nurses' station. He glanced as medical staff fielded questions from anxious-looking family members. Stewart painted his face with a look of both confusion and concern and walked right by them. Cactus held out in front of him, no one paid attention to him as he scanned the walls, looking for the sign to Room 1220. After circling the U-shaped corridor, he came to Tancos's room. The door was closed and there was no guard.

Perfect.

He reached inside his jacket and felt for his nine-inch Bowie knife tucked tightly in its shoulder sheath. He grabbed the door handle, slowly pressed it downward, and pushed open the heavy wooden door. A privacy curtain circled a patient in bed. High-pitched electronic beeps pierced the darkened room lit only by dim LEDs emanating light from various devices.

Stewart set his gift on a counter and ever so gently pulled the drape aside, allowing him to positively identify his target. The patient's head was wrapped almost in its entirety with bandages but blond hair straggled out from under the gauze.

That fucking blond hair.

Tancos's eyes were closed, his breathing shallow. Tubes and wires ran everywhere from his body. They all snaked to either an IV drip stand or to an equipment rack above his bed holding a bank of medical machines displaying his vitals.

Stewart squeezed the handle of his knife, the warm leather grip nestling in the palm of his hand.

Finally, you get what's coming to you.

A rustle behind the curtain on the other side of the bed caused him to look below the edge of the drapery. He saw a pair of men's shoes and froze.

The curtain flung open. A man standing behind the drapery said, "You know, I never did think you walked off that Rim."

CHAPTER 63

Downtown Phoenix
4th Avenue Jail
9:00 p.m.

When Stan arrived at the jail around nine, now nearly six hours after Stewart's capture, Maricopa County Sheriff's detectives had already been grilling the two Mexican illegals caught at the dam. Stan's friends at the U.S. Marshal's Office had removed them from Micah Lund's custody, telling Stan the Gila County Sheriff had put up quite a fight over relinquishing his prisoners.

Earlier, Stan had kept his word by calling Karl Stewart and telling him of the arrest of the man's only son.

"Where have you taken him?" Karl had asked. The elder Stewart's voice crackled through Stan's cell.

"He's in lock-up at 4th Avenue Jail. I requested he be isolated from the general population. For his own protection."

"Thank you for that. Has he asked for a lawyer?"

"No. As a matter of fact, from what I've been told, he hasn't spoken a word to anyone."

"How is he, Mister Kobe?"

"Actually, he looked relieved when the police cuffed him. He didn't put up a struggle."

"I want to see him."

"Sir, that's impossible right now. He's still being processed through the system. But in due time we can arrange a family visit."

"You misunderstood me, Mister Kobe. I'm requesting to

see my client. I told you when we met I planned on representing my son."

Stan felt the uneasy feeling come back like he had the first time Karl had made the unusual request to represent his son. "Are you sure you want to do that, Mister Stewart?"

"Yes, I'm sure. I want to hear the full-story, directly from him, before he speaks to anyone else. So, I am officially notifying you that as of this moment I am formally his attorney of record."

"I'll alert the Sheriff's authorities and make note of your request."

"Thank you, Mister Kobe. I appreciate what you've done in keeping your word. There aren't many left out there like you. Goodbye, sir."

When Stan had ended the call he questioned himself as to whether he had done the right thing in calling the father. He hated second-guessing himself but a promise was a promise. He didn't need any distractions or grand-standing right now, knowing he needed to prep for what was sure to be a barrage of questions directed at him and the Maricopa County Attorney's Office. Once the news hit the wire of Stewart's arrest and incarceration, there would be a media frenzy. All hell was sure to break loose from the capture of one of the FBI's most wanted fugitives.

As for his high-profile prisoner, Stan wanted to get to him before his father arrived. He wanted to speak to the former man-on-the-run who had dominated Stan's thoughts for the last decade.

Walking into the corridor outside the main interrogation room, Stan recognized one of two people already standing there. "I was hoping they'd send you!" Stan greeted FBI Agent Malori Schwartz with a hug. "Who's your friend?"

"This is Alcohol, Tobacco, Firearms and Explosives Officer Ron D'Antonio," Agent Schwartz replied. "First, here's that report you asked to have rushed from our forensics team up on the Rim. As soon as they finished working the tower, they followed your instructions and went back to the spot where the truck was originally found. After sweeping the area with hand-held sonar devices and metal detectors they found the dog's grave and skeleton, just as you suspected."

"What's this about the dog?" Brian Hanley asked as he walked in on the conversation.

"Hey, partner. This is Agent Schwartz, FBI, and Officer D'Antonio, ATF," Stan said to Brian, making the introductions. The trio shook hands all around as Stan continued with answering Brian's question. "It never sat well with the FBI profilers—or with me—that Stewart shot his dog. Their guess was that, based upon how the house fire victims were killed, the killer would have slit the dog's throat, not shoot it. Plus a gunshot would have risked drawing too much attention and I don't think attention is what a man on the run would have wanted. When you and I discovered later Stewart was holed up not far from the spot where they found his truck and the dog, my gut told me someone else killed his dog."

"Someone else?" Brian asked. "Who?"

Stan looked at the report then over at Schwartz. "You tell him."

"The bullet came from a revolver," she said. A Colt .38 Special."

"That's an old-school police revolver," D'Antonio chimed in.

"You son-of-a-bitch." Brian gave Stan a wide grin. "Micah shot the dog! When did you figure that one out?"

"Kind of all started when he fed me that line of bullshit about 'Yahweh's magnificent creatures.'"

"Huh?" Brian's face echoed his voice's sound of confusion.

"Never mind. Let's just see when I share this fact with Stewart, if I get the same rise out of him I just got out of you." He turned to the group. "We've got a solid arrest on him. He was Mirandized at capture. He didn't resist. But he hasn't spoken a syllable, even throughout his booking."

"What about Scottsdale PD?" Brian asked. "The original crime was in their jurisdiction."

"Detective Kemp has been notified and is on his way," Schwartz said. "He was on a late spring ski trip up in Whistler so it'll take some time for him to get back. Their chief understands the high-profile nature of this case. So, he cleared it for our team here to take the lead and get the show on the road."

D'Antonio spoke. "The clothes Stewart was wearing when he was picked up have been sent to our lab to swab for explosives residue and other trace evidence."

"Good. Can you rush the results?" Stan asked.

"Copy that," D'Antonio said. "Also, we've got personnel and equipment headed to the dam."

"Good," Stan said. "Keep me up-to-speed on the clothes analysis as well as any news about what exactly got dumped in the water out there."

D'Antonio opened his cell and dialed a number, walking away from the group to converse.

"Has he asked for a lawyer?" Schwartz asked.

Stan shook his head. "No, but there's one who should be here any minute. His father."

She raised her eyebrows. "His *father* is going to represent him?"

Stan nodded. "Turns out his dad is an attorney."

Schwartz shook her head, a concerned look on her face. "That muddies the water."

"We have no control over it. It's perfectly legal," Stan said. "But I am surprised he's not here by now."

"Jake Zadnik called me on my way over here and said there are other federal agencies, not to mention the military, who all want a piece of Stewart," Schwartz said. "I'm with you, Stan. Why don't we take a run at him before the place is full of uniforms and bureaucrats?"

The three of them nodded, then Stan spoke. "Let me and Hanley take the first round. You and D'Antonio watch and take notes from the monitor room."

Stan entered the county jail's interrogation room, Brian at his side. The space had been recently updated with full electronic monitoring. Paul Stewart sat alone at a brushed aluminum table, shackled to the top by his wrists as well as by both feet to the floor. Brian, standing to the side of Stan, reread the prisoner his rights. Stewart didn't respond, looking like he was in a catatonic state.

"I know you didn't shoot your dog," Stan said as he sat down across from Stewart.

He hoped opening with the non-accusatory statement versus an expected question asking him to admit his guilt would jar Stewart to attention. It worked. The prisoner raised his head, seeming to awake from his lost look.

"I also don't think you killed your wife and kids."

Stewart's eyes widened when Stan completed his second sentence—as did Brian's. Stewart stared straight back at him. In less than twenty seconds he had broken through to a man who for the last decade had eluded every law enforcement officer in the country.

"What did you just say?" Stewart asked.

"You do remember me, don't you?" Stan asked. "I used to live on your block, only a few doors away. We never met but my guess is you'd remember a neighbor who looked like me."

"Yeah. I remember you. The spook married to that pretty little white professor."

Stan's jaw tightened. "I'm the only friend you've got right now, Paul, so my recommendation would be for you to work harder on getting on my good side."

"Why would someone like *you* want to help *me*?"

"Because, like I said, I know you didn't kill your dog and I don't believe you slit the throats of your wife and children."

Stewart's gaze went blank again, confusion on his face.

"Do you remember the man who lived across the street from us? That guy with all the antennas in his backyard and on top of his house?"

Stewart shrugged, nodding a small acknowledgement.

"Well, his name was Carter Coffel. He was a geek's geek. Had all the latest techno- gadgets. First one in the neighborhood to have closed-circuit video cameras monitoring his house. Even back then. I asked him one day why he had installed all the electronic surveillance stuff and he told me someone was stealing the fruit from his orange trees. He was determined to catch whoever was doing it. He told me he even put up some night vision cameras. First of their kind. He was obsessed with catching whoever was taking the oranges from the overflowing trees in his front yard. Can you imagine the time and effort he must have put into catching the thief?"

"What do I care about that guy?" a frustrated sounding Stewart asked. "What the hell is your point?" He pounded his fists on the table, his hand shackles clanging loudly on the metal top.

Stan kept his composure from Stewart's outburst. He stayed calm and continued his line of questioning. "My point is, he never got any pictures of his orange bandits but he did capture a picture of the man I believe murdered your wife and children and set your house on fire."

Stan reached inside a folder he had carried in and took a black and white photo out. He laid it on the table. It showed a man in what looked like Army fatigues walking down Stewart's driveway. Long, light colored hair came out from underneath his baseball cap. The snapshot, taken in daylight, was remarkably clear. Stan slid the photograph across the table to Stewart.

"I think you know this man. Don't you?"

Stewart stayed quiet, but his eye twitched. Then he growled under his breath. "Tancos."

CHAPTER 64

9:30 p.m.

Paul Stewart refused to speak any further to Stan after he had showed him the photo of Caleb Tancos approaching Stewart's Scottsdale residence. Stan had him transferred back to his isolated cell in a remote section of the jail. The antiquated cells were rarely used any longer, except when the veteran prosecutor requested sequestering of a high-profile prisoner.

Stewart paced back and forth inside his cell, muttering to himself under his breath. He seethed with anger. He kept asking himself if what that nigger lawyer had just said was true or just a ploy to get him to talk.

Is it possible it was Tancos who killed my family and not me?

The prospect of that even remotely being true made Stewart gag. He was about to vomit in the nearby toilet when a voice yelled at him.

"Paul!"

Startled, Stewart held back his regurgitation and looked up. He was shocked to see his father standing there with a guard next to him on the other side of the iron bars.

"I need a few minutes alone with my client," the elder Stewart said to the guard.

The officer opened the cell door. Once Karl Stewart was inside, the jail keeper locked the gate and walked away. Karl waited until he was sure they were alone before he spoke to his son.

"Are you sick? You look pale? They didn't hurt you, did they?"

"What the fuck do you care?" Paul took a paper towel and wiped his mouth. "What in the hell are you doing here anyway?"

"I'm your lawyer."

"*You?* I don't want *you* as my lawyer."

Karl stood holding his briefcase in one hand, cane supporting him in the other. "I knew you'd be alive. I told myself you would survive, that you couldn't have done to your family what they said you did. I vowed to make it up to you if I ever saw you again. This is how I'm keeping that promise. By being your legal counsel. I'm here to help you. Someone you can trust."

Paul crumpled his paper towel and threw it into the toilet. "*Trust?* Trust *you?* You're kidding, right? You've got a lot of nerve!" He paced in the small space.

Karl set his briefcase on the cot and leaned both hands on the cane propped out in front of him. "You have a right to be angry. I know that more than you'll ever believe. But you have to let go of your hate."

Paul stopped and stared at his father. "Like you did? You really think that just because you started a whole new life with that black bitch that everything you ever did to me and Mom is gone? Magically forgotten? Everything you taught me about not trusting niggers is just swept aside? Do you really have the balls to come in here and try to make me believe all the pain you caused can just be swept under the carpet, like it never happened? Why? Because of your guilt?"

"Son, please. You don't mean—"

"I mean every word of it!" Paul stepped toward his father. He wanted to punch him in the face then beat him to a pulp. "I am *not* your son any longer! I never want to hear that word coming from your mouth ever again!"

Karl inched back, pleading with him. "Paul, I can't go back and reverse the wrongs I've done. But I can move forward. Like I believe you should right now."

Paul turned his back and stepped away but Karl followed, prodding him. "Please, Paul, please."

Paul didn't answer. He put his hands on the back of his head, interlocking his fingers. His head throbbed. He wasn't sure at this point what made him sicker—the thought that Tancos may have wiped out his family or his father standing behind him right now.

"Paul, I know you're in pain. But please . . . don't hurt innocent people just because of your hate for me. Tell them where the bombs are."

Paul dropped his hands and spun around. He grabbed his father by the shoulders, making the old man wince. "What do you know about the bombs?"

"Kobe. The prosecutor. He told me everything before I came in here. He told me he believes Jacob Lund, Tancos and the others duped you into thinking you were serving their cause."

"How does he know Jacob Lund?"

Karl shook his head back and forth. "I don't know. I don't even know who this Jacob is. But Kobe says this man tricked you into helping him strike back at the government for everything it's not doing to stop illegals from coming into the country. But it's a sham. Lund's a liar."

He shook his father hard. "What are you talking about? What does that uppity-nigger prosecutor think he knows, telling you all his lies? The only one I know is a liar is you!"

He pushed his father away. The old man fell back on the bed.

"Paul, I don't care if you hate me. But this guy, Lund, Kobe says he's used you like a pawn. He took advantage of you, knowing how you were filled with so much hate after what I had done to you. He convinced you to use that misdirected anger for his own benefit!"

Paul stood over him, screaming. "I don't believe you! You're lying! My Lord Melchizedek would not misuse me. He will not forsake me." Like a child throwing a temper tantrum, he banged his fists on top of his own head several times, then ran to the gate of his cell. He cried out loud, "Guard! Guard! Get this man out of here!"

CHAPTER 65

9:55 p.m.

"**B**y the look on your face my guess is your visit didn't go too well," Stan said to Karl as he shuffled back into the hallway beyond the prisoner's cell area. Brian stood alongside Stan.

Karl shook his head. "All he wanted to do was hold on to his anger. To pay me back for all that pain I inflicted upon him. My son wanted to beat me. I wouldn't have blamed him if he did." He straightened his rumpled sport coat and skewed neck tie. "He blames me for all his pain, for everything. Maybe he's right. Maybe I am to blame."

Brian jumped in. "Your son's a grown man. He has to take responsibility for his own actions." He looked over at Stan. "Trust me on that."

Stan nodded to his partner. "My friend here is right, Karl."

"Maybe you were correct," the dejected sounding father replied. "Maybe it wasn't such a good idea to be his counsel. I thought I'd be able to reach him, have him tell me everything. All he wanted was for me to get out of his sight."

"Let the two of us have another talk with him," Stan said.

"I should be in the room with you."

Stan gave Karl an affirming look. "You're welcome to join us as long as Paul allows it."

The three men walked back to the interrogation room. Karl took a seat on the far side of the table. Stan and Brian were across from him. When the deputies brought Paul Stewart back into the room, Stan motioned with his head to have them seat him next to his father.

The deputies started to chain the prisoner in place as they had before.

"Is that really necessary?" Karl asked.

Brian looked at Stan, who shook his head, giving the okay.

"Paul, if you remain calm we won't shackle you to the table and floor," Brian said.

Paul didn't speak.

"Thank you," Karl said.

As soon as the deputies left the room Stan immediately began his questioning, hoping to preempt any anticipated protest from the prisoner. "We're working on getting you a public defender. But at this time of night it can take quite a while for someone to get over here after they've received the call and been assigned the case. By law, we can't speak to you alone now that you have legal counsel. So I trust this will do until another lawyer arrives."

Stan realized he was treading on shaky legal ground and worried for a moment that he might perhaps later regret his actions at trial. But he didn't care. He knew Stewart knew where Forster's remaining three bombs were and finding that out was the only thing that mattered. He didn't wait for a response from the prisoner.

"The two illegal Mexican nationals we caught on top of Roosevelt Dam haven't told us anything—yet. You and your crew have them pretty scared. My guess is you've threatened to hurt their families back in Mexico if they talk. Or maybe even threatened to cut off their heads."

Stan hoped to get a rise out of Stewart with his last statement, but the CIA-trained operative remained silent.

Stan went on. "That's not your style, is it, to frighten people and their families? I'm sure that was the idea of your pal, Tancos—"

"He's not my pal," a defiant Paul said, breaking his silence.

"Well then, maybe it was his Mexican 'secret agent' sidekick here." Stan pulled out a photo from a manila folder he had placed on the table. He pushed the picture over to Paul, face up. The glossy, color snapshot showed Jaime Ramos's ashen-colored corpse lying on a chrome autopsy table.

Paul didn't flinch.

Brian jumped in. "He was shot once in the back of the head at close range. We positively ID'd him down at the morgue. My guess is he became a liability. A bit like you are now or anyone else left alive after the failed downtown bombing."

Stan resumed the questioning. "Your friend, Jacob Lund. He's known for leaving no trace of his trail; he's been a ghost for years, that is, up until the last few months when he made the mistake of coming back on radar with his so called 'church' up on the Rim."

Paul made no movements or offered any reply.

Stan forged on. "We found your pet's grave, exhumed the remains and pulled a bullet from the skull. It was from a Colt thirty-eight special. Same gun, coincidentally, used by Sheriff Micah Lund. I believe he shot your dog. We're getting a warrant now to retrieve his gun for a ballistics match. Once we have that match, which I'm betting we will, we'll charge him as an accessory."

Stewart remained silent but couldn't hide his anger as he heard details about how and by whom his dog was killed. More importantly, Stan wondered what the man's thoughts were over hearing Stan's bombshell statement earlier believing Stewart innocent of his family's massacre.

"I never did think you could kill your own dog, just like I've never believed you killed your family. I knew both for sure when I was sent your records from your dark time in Bosnia, spent as part of a secret Air Force EOD advance team sent in by the CIA. Seems you were just one of a few, very select, demo ops and combat control technician units sent over there with Special Access Program clearance. Kept completely off the radar."

Stan's last statement drew raised eyebrows now from both father and son. Stan pulled a sheet of paper from his folder.

He read from the page.

"Says here your last assignment was when you were sent to blow up a bridge across the Miljacka River. A bridge that was being used during the night to secretly transport munitions to Serbian Muslim resistance fighters in Pale. Unfortunately, you blew it up while a school bus filled with Croatian children was coming back from a field trip. Seems their bus had broken down and they were many hours overdue. No one anticipated they'd be travelling across the bridge that late at night, hours after curfew. Especially not you. All forty children on board plus the driver perished."

Stan checked for Stewart's reaction. This time his face roiled with anger. His eyes glazed over. Stan went on with his chilling reading. "Your Army Ranger lookout, according to what you say here, seems to have missed the school bus coming past his checkpoint. Unfortunately, this report never saw the light of day as pro-Croatian forces used the event to spread the word that their children were killed by Muslim sympathizers."

Stan waited for a reaction. When none came, he went on. "I learned an awful lot more about you after I read the Air Force psychiatrist's debriefing interview he had with you where you had shared your recurring nightmare about the bus incident." He picked up a piece of paper and read from it. "The one in which 'the faces of my own unborn children appeared as riders on the bus.' Those are your exact words from the therapist's session notes."

"How did you get that information?" Karl demanded.

Stan slid the sheet back into the folder. "Does that really matter right now? I think what does matter is that these pages and your own belief in your son's innocence convinced me Paul didn't have it in him to do what he allegedly did to his family." Stan turned his attention directly back to Paul. "And I based it upon that shrine you put up to your family in the lookout tower. I'll bet you never believed yourself you had done what they said you did. Isn't that so?"

The prisoner didn't respond but just stared straight ahead.

Stan waited a beat, then pulled another sheet from his folder. He scanned it as he spoke. "I read here where you punched your therapist. A high-ranking officer. Why? Because he was black?"

"Where did you get this information?" Karl demanded an answer again.

"Oh, you'd be surprised what stuff my pardner here can get his hands on," Brian said.

Karl turned to his son. "Is all this true?"

"None of it matters now," Paul said. "I sent the bomb to the plaza. Charge me if you want."

"As your lawyer, I advise you to not make any more statements like that."

Paul Stewart gave no reply.

"I can make this go real easy for you if you cooperate," Stan interjected. "We've ID'd the Mark eighty-two bomb rendered safe in the plaza. The Air Force has told us they're certain this ordnance came from an A-10 Warthog that crashed in Colorado about a dozen years ago. There are some irrefutable facts about that odd case. One, the plane's four, live bombs were never found. Two, you worked on the ground crew as chief weapons officer on that war bird's last flight. Three, the plane was found no more than a few miles as the crow flies from Jacob Lund's compound in the Baca Grande region of Colorado. Four, you were also part of the Air Force para-jumper team that dropped into the crash site. As a matter of fact, according to the Air Force's Office of Special Investigations' classified report, you were the very first airman to go in, prior to anyone else on the team. Are you following where I'm going with this?"

Karl leaned toward his son. "Paul, is this all true?" he asked again.

His son lifted his head upward and stared at the ceiling. "From the book of the Apostle Mark. Chapter ten. Verse eleven."

Stan thought for a moment, then replied. "What God hath joined together, let no man pull asunder."

Stewart pulled his gaze down and stared at Stan.

Karl jumped in. "Please, son. Whatever you've done, please tell them. If not for me, then do it for the sake of all the innocent people out there who would be hurt. Just like your family."

Stan looked at the beleaguered father. He thought Karl's plea for his son to think about the martyred lives of his wife and children might trigger Paul to confess. But the prisoner didn't respond.

"My guess is, Mister Stewart, sir, is that your son doesn't care if he has the blood of innocent people on his hands, and that he knows all about the other three heretofore missing bombs. I also believe their whereabouts may somehow be connected to whatever those two men dumped into Roosevelt Lake last night." Stan waited for something from Paul other than a verse from the Bible. He got his wish.

"It's too late for you to be a hero and save the world, Mister Kobe."

As Paul Stewart spoke, someone knocked on the door, interrupting the session.

CHAPTER 66

April 20
1:05 a.m.

Before Stan got up and left the interrogation room, Paul Stewart referenced another Bible verse, this time quoting Matthew 27:51. Once back in the observation area behind an array of wall-to-wall monitors, D'Antonio spoke first to Stan.

"It took a while to slow down the operation of the dam to make it safe enough for a dive team to go in the water. We just got their preliminary report. Salt River Project stated their divers couldn't see much in the darkness but there's definitely something suspended below the surface."

"And?" Stan prodded him, urgency in his voice.

"They're not sure what it is. They only have handheld lights and the reservoir is extremely murky. But, they believe they saw what looks like some type of flotation device suspended about twenty-feet below the water line, and—"

Still irritated for being called out of the room, Stan got impatient with the deliberate-speaking ATF specialist. "And? And what?"

"And to that device they've reported seeing a length of chain attached, presumably to something below."

"Is that all?" Stan asked.

"For now. It's just too dark to see any more. They're working with minimal light in about thirty-feet of water. Portable lights from above haven't helped since the water is so churned up, a residual from the dam's operation. They'll keep looking, but as soon as daylight breaks we should be able to see and know more."

"When is that?" Brian asked.

The ATF officer pulled out his cell, then swiped and poked the screen a few times. "Sunrise should be a little after five-thirty. First light maybe thirty minutes before that."

Brian looked at his watch. "That's about four, four-and-a-half hours away."

"That could be too late," Stan interjected. He paced, rubbing his head. "We've got to find out what's attached to that chain dangling from the flotation device," he implored. "If it's the other bombs then we need to know that STAT."

"Roger that," D'Antonio said.

Stan continued pacing in front of his three person team. He was deep in thought. He cracked one knuckle, then another. Abruptly, he stopped and squared his look upon the ATF explosives specialist. "D'Antonio, could the force of three, Mark eighty-twos actually blow up Roosevelt Dam?"

"Theoretically . . . I guess . . . I mean . . ."

"*Is it possible?*" Stan's voice raised two levels.

Ron snapped to attention. "There are certainly enough high explosives in each one of those bombs to do an awful lot of damage. But blowing up a structure like that would not be an easy feat. There would be multiple challenges in fact. First, there would need to be some type of reliable underwater timing device to detonate all of the bombs. And the bombs would presumably all have to go off simultaneously. Plus, the bombs would need to be set as close as possible to the water-side of the dam, almost leaning against the dam's submerged concrete wall, for its entire height."

"So, it *is* possible."

He nodded. "Possible . . . but highly improbable."

"It was improbable anyone would fly jets into the twin towers and bring them down too," Stan countered. "Now, explain to me what you meant by 'for its entire height'."

"When a bomb explodes, there's a physics principal that takes place called reflective energy. This reflective energy—or pressure—gets dispersed into the air around where the explosion occurs. As well as, of course, against its intended target. If a Mark eighty-two were to explode underwater versus on the ground, then its reflective energy would act differently."

"I understand. Go on."

"Well, if these bombs were to explode underwater right next to the dam, then they would disperse their energy not only against the concrete but also against the water. But water, since it's denser than air, would in essence deflect . . ." D'Antonio slapped an open palm against his forehead. ". . . Oh my God."

"What?" Stan asked.

"If these bombs were somehow placed in a vertical line for the entire height of the dam, then the water would not only deflect the percussion against the dam but *magnify* this deflection."

Stan coaxed him. "In layman's terms, please?"

"Imagine for a moment the opposite scenario, say, if these bombs were placed against the dam's concrete wall on the *dry* side of the dam. If they detonated there, then the damage they'd cause would be minimal, since most of reflective energy from the blast would push outward, un-resisted against the open air. Underwater, though, the opposite would happen. The water would deflect back all of the energy against the dam's wall. Not only that but the reflection from the water, with its higher density, could actually double or even triple the effectiveness of each bomb."

"Stewart would be aware of this principal, too?"

D'Antonio glumly nodded.

Stan knew the answer in his gut but asked his next question anyhow. "Do you think that's something he may have done?"

"He's certainly capable. If he did, it's brilliant."

Stan's nervous twitch took hold of him and he cracked a knuckle. "I need you to get your bomb team out there now."

"Hold on," said D'Antonio. "If these bombs are really in the water, then there's no bomb team in the state who could handle this type of an assignment. I know because I used to be an EOD diver before a ruptured ear drum ended that part of my career. The only unit qualified to approach a potential unexploded ordnance operation like this would be a highly-specialized Navy EOD dive team and the closest one is in San Diego."

"Then get *them* out there!" Stan barked. "If he's able to compromise or, God forbid, destroy the dam the valley wouldn't recover from a catastrophe like this for months, maybe years. And I don't even want to speculate on the potential loss of life."

"Mister Kobe," D'Antonio said. "In all due respect, sir, as an explosives expert *and* a former diver, I have, I believe, a keen insight into this potential situation. But, I must tell you, sir, if there are three, five-hundred pound, Mark eighty-two warheads in that water, then we can't just dive in with a screwdriver and a pair of wire-cutters between our teeth and try to disengage whatever timing mechanism he may have created and connected to the bombs' electronic fuzes. We would need to know exactly how Stewart armed them and, most importantly, when they're set to detonate. Without those details, any team going into that water is going in completely blind."

Stan didn't want to be short with the highly experienced ATF expert. But right now, not bruising an ego was the last thing on his mind.

"It's been almost fifteen hours since those men were caught on top of the dam. I don't care where you get them, Ron, but put someone qualified in the water. Now. If they've dumped bombs then get me a confirmation. And make it fast before we're picking up bodies floating down the Salt River."

CHAPTER 67

1:45 a.m.

Stan turned to Brian and FBI Agent Malori Schwartz while ATF Explosives Specialist Ron D'Antonio stepped away and made a call on his cell.

"I've got to get this guy Stewart to talk to me," Stan told them. He nodded toward the door of the interrogation room. "I'm going back in there. Alone this time. But first, I need a Bible."

"This is no time to pray, pardner," Brian quipped.

"I have one in my briefcase," Malori said. She pulled the book out and handed it to Stan. He looked at her, eyebrows raised in curiosity. "The boss had me join a 'Jews for Jesus' bible study class in Paradise Valley," she smiled. "Doing some research for an upcoming assignment."

Stan took her book, grabbed all of his folders, and went back inside the small room. Both Stewart men remained silent, neither looking at the other. Karl glanced at Stan as he sat down across the table. Stan looked up to the ceiling and yelled, "Shut everything off. Video, audio, everything. This isn't going to be on the record."

Agent Schwartz turned to Brian as they sat next to each other in the monitor-filled observation room. "He knows that's not possible. Right, Hanley?"

"Yeah, he knows it. My guess is he's hoping they don't."

Back inside the interrogation room, Stan continued. "This is just going to be between the three of us for right now. No one else can see or hear."

Stan locked his gaze onto Paul Stewart. Neither spoke.

"I want you to know something about me." Stan placed the Bible on the table, laying his left palm on top. "When I was just a boy, living in Chicago, I witnessed the murder of a man who was my mentor. He was brutally beaten. I watched it all happen, hiding nearby, scared to death. I froze and did nothing to help my friend while evil people took their toll, snuffing him out of my life. Afterward, I couldn't live with myself and all the guilt bottled up inside. I decided, much against the advice of most of my family, to come forward as a witness. Everyone told me I was a fool. Everyone . . . except my father."

Stan picked up the Bible, opened it, and fanned the pages. He set the open book on the table in front of them.

"From the time I stepped up as an eyewitness, doing what I thought was the right thing, my life changed forever. And because of that decision, my actions led to the ruination of my family. Within a very short period of time in my still young and impressionable life, I lost everything in the world that mattered to me. My father wasn't able to live with the guilt he carried from the advice he had given me. In time, he'd walk out on our family. Not long after, my mother died from a broken heart. To make matters worse, to this day, my siblings don't even speak to me."

Stan paused. He smoothed the open pages of the book. He took a deep breath, wondering if he was getting through to Stewart with his personal testament. He wondered how much more it would take to make the man open up. "I tell you all this, Paul, because I know how easy it is, especially for a heart that's hurting, to have your father go from being your hero one day to despising everything about him the next. Like the way I felt about my own father when he abandoned our family, literally killing my mother. I hated him for what he had done. But when I became a man I realized my father was human, just like me."

Stan waited for a reaction from Paul. None came verbally but Stan believed by the sallow look on the prisoner's face he may have chipped away a tiny bit at the ex-CIA operative's steel-like façade.

Stan flipped to a page near the front of the Bible then read aloud. "Exodus. Chapter twenty-three, verse four. *You must not bow down to their gods or worship them. Do not imitate their practices. Instead, demolish them and smash their sacred pillars to pieces.*"

"It would have been easy for me when my father turned his back on his flesh and blood to follow the wrong crowd, to listen to others who might falsely take his place. It happened to many of us youngsters when we lived in the projects on the south side of Chicago."

Karl looked at Stan with a confused look. Paul remained stone-faced.

Stan continued. "Jacob Lund has fooled you. He is a false god. He, his son, his nephew, and Tancos, all conspired to deceive you."

Stan waited again for even the smallest sign from Stewart that he might be getting through to him. None came.

"Paul, from what I read in those papers my friend in Washington sent me is the Army Ranger in charge of the team who missed their assignment on that bridge you blew up was none other than Caleb Tancos."

"What?" Karl cried.

"That's right. Isn't it Paul?" Stan replied. "The very same Caleb Tancos who flunked-out of Navy EOD school in the same class in which you finished at the top. I'd say based upon what I read in his psych profile that couldn't have made Tancos very pleased. Who knows? This situation might even have been the start of the bad blood between you two. Maybe the embarrassment over failing made him jealous, pissed him off so much he wanted a little revenge over the hotshot, know-it-all, fighter-pilot's son and set you up on that bridge in Bosnia. Doesn't matter, though, because your anger toward him—and later at your psychologist, an officer, no less—got you thrown in the brig and demoted two levels when you knocked the poor major out with one punch."

Stewart made a slight fidget in his seat. Stan also noticed

Paul's father turn his eyes downward, as if embarrassed by his son's altercation with his non-white superior officer.

Stan went on. "And that's how a top-level, Special Access Program, EOD technician ends up loading bombs on an A-10 Warthog crew down in this hell-hole they call the Sonoran Desert. On the one-hundred-and-fifty-degree tarmac at Davis-Monthan Air Force Base. So, you must have been really surprised—and really fucking angry—the day you found out Tancos was one of Jacob Lund's foot soldiers."

Paul didn't blink.

Keeping his patience, Stan forged on. He got more deliberate, though, with each sentence, leaning forward in his chair. "My guess is Logan Athem is the one who probably met you first. I'm sure it was during one of your frequent visits to Wilma's Tap in Red Rock. Once Logan found out how you felt about people my color, he certainly introduced you to his uncle, Jacob Lund, and the rest of their Aryan family. Lund no doubt shared with his number one man, Tancos, about Logan's new found recruit—Paul Stewart from Davis-Monthan, the guy who had access to explosives."

Stan paused a moment, waiting for Stewart to react. He didn't, so he continued on. "Shit. Tancos must have been floored when Jacob mentioned your name. Tancos, of course, knew who you were. I'm sure he shared with Jacob all he knew about you. That you were one of the few men he knew who had all the skills and expertise to help them pull off the remarkable scheme Jacob was planning."

Stan stopped his story and paused to take a drink of water. He did so slowly and deliberately. He pursed his lips after his last sip. "Thirsty?" he asked Stewart. When the prisoner didn't reply, Stan leaned back in his chair and lowered his voice. "Tancos was certain to share with Jacob how you blew up that busload of kids. Don't you think? He knew Lund was a great one for capitalizing on the weaknesses of others and using it for his own good. Unfortunately for you, by the time you found out your enemy Tancos was linked to Lund it was too late. Jacob had already snagged you and pulled you into his web of hate and violence."

"Tancos is a scumbag!" Paul Stewart screamed. Then he lowered his voice. "But Jacob is my Lord Melchizedek. A true father."

Even though he knew those words must have pained Karl to hear, Stan nonetheless felt encouraged by Stewart's outburst. Stan was certain everything about Tancos was Kryptonite to Stewart's superman persona. He didn't waste time jumping on the opportunity to break through to his prisoner. "I agree on the first part. Tancos is a piece of shit. Pure scum. He'll spend a lot of time in jail, if he survives from his wounds *and* if Jacob Lund doesn't get to him first. That's the real reason you went to the hospital. Isn't it? It wasn't due to your devotion to Lund. No, no. We both know you should have skipped town right after you sent those bombs on their way. But no. You had unfinished business—killing Tancos."

"Paul, is this true?" Karl pleaded with him. "If it is, it's over, son. Please tell him what you know."

Son didn't answer but rather glowered at his father.

Stan intervened. "Like I said earlier, Paul, your father is not your enemy."

Stan opened one of his manila folders. He shuffled and flipped through the contents inside. He spoke in a nonchalant manner, not looking up. "I believe you've dumped Captain Benjamin Forster's three remaining Mark eighty-twos into Roosevelt Dam's reservoir. I believe you have them rigged in such a way that when they explode their reflective energy will be magnified by the water they're suspended in and double or perhaps even triple their destructive power." He pulled his head up from the papers he had pretended were of importance to him and looked straight at Stewart. "It's ingenious. I commend you."

Stan reinforced his compliment with a dip of the chin to his prisoner.

"But . . ." Stan took a deep pause. "Consider this. You have set in motion a calamity the likes of which Arizona and the whole southwest of the United States has never seen before

. . . and only you can stop it."

Stan waited for a reaction. When nothing came, he went on.

"You know what the irony is here? If what you've planned actually takes place, in the end, only Jacob Lund will profit from what's about to happen. You know why?" Stan lunged forward, looking as if he was going to jump across the table. His voice rose to a shout. "Because he's not your Lord! And he's not your father! You don't see him sitting next to you right now, do you? No! That's because he doesn't care about you! He only cares about himself! He's a money-grubbing, self-serving traitor who uses his bigotry as a disguise!"

Stan pulled himself back into the chair and straightened his tie. He regained his composure. "While you've been in hiding all this time he's been building huge server farms in the Baca Grande in Colorado. My sources tell me Lund may have a secret contract in place for renting those servers, most likely with our own government, the group he supposedly hates so much. He now has the ability and the capacity to store big data at this remote site, conveniently set up off-the-grid in case of a disaster, just like the one he's had you so unwittingly set in motion. And when that happens, he'll stand to gain over a hundred fold. Maybe more. Is that what you really want? For that two-faced liar to use you and get away with it? To have your family killed and to profit from all this while you take the fall?"

A knock on the door interrupted Stan. D'Antonio stuck his head into the room. "Mister Kobe. We need you out here, sir."

CHAPTER 68

2:25 a.m.

B elieving he had Stewart right where he wanted him and ready to break, Stan was pissed at having to again stop his interrogation. Nonetheless, he stepped outside into the hallway and joined D'Antonio and Schwartz as well as Brian. "This better be *very* important," Stan chided them.

Schwartz spoke first. "It is. Phoenix PD just called. Tancos is dead. Someone gave him a lethal dose of a narcotic through his IV line."

Stan now fumed. "How in the hell did that happen?"

"They don't know yet," Schwartz replied. "Our people are already there, looking at hospital security surveillance footage of the entire facility, inside and out. The only people on the floor to the room where they had moved him were cops and medical personnel. We've put the hospital on lockdown."

"Do they know what he was given?" Stan asked.

"Yes. They pulled the drip bag and sent it to the hospital's lab. They positively ID'd it—Propofol."

"Propofol? They're sure it was Propofol?"

She nodded. "The bag had markings on it from their own hospital pharmacy. Why?"

Stan hastily flipped through papers in one of his folders. He stopped at one to read it. He didn't look up from his reading.

"Now what?" Brian asked.

Stan remained calm, not letting this bad news of Tancos's death sidetrack him. He was too close to getting Stewart to tell him what he had done with the remaining bombs. "I've got one more card up my sleeve." He pushed the paper back inside the folder and then took out a photograph. "Let's see who flinches first."

Stan marched back into the room and didn't bother to sit down. "Okay, sorry about that but my team was just triple-checking something for me. Okay now. Where were we? Oh, yes. I want you to see something."

Stan pulled out a plastic sleeve from one of his folders. Inside was a copy of the small thermal image he had pinned to his wall for years. He placed it on the table, looking right at Paul.

"This is a picture of you taking money from a bank's ATM five-minutes away from your house. It's time-stamped seven-forty in the morning, April tenth, 2001." Standing over the table, Stan pulled out another photo. "This is a picture of Caleb Tancos snapped by the neighbor, our security aficionado, Mister Coffel. This image was taken from one of his high-quality, low-light cameras. Coffel kept all of his surveillance devices connected to his home time-synchronized to an atomic clock. His photo of Tancos is time stamped the same day, April 10, at precisely one-forty-one . . . in the morning."

Stewart stared at both pictures, eyes moving rapidly between them. His frustrated look turned his face ruby red. A blood vessel in his forehead swelled. "That's impossible," he cried. "There must be some mistake. Something's wrong with that guy's camera. That must be a picture of Tancos from when he visited me the day before."

"You mean this one?"

Stan pulled out a third photo, which showed Tancos walking up Stewart's driveway. The very clear snapshot had a date and time stamped in the margin of 04-09-2001/16:45.

"This is the first photo. The one I showed you earlier. It's from when you said Tancos had paid you that surprise visit when you came home from work. That's about right since it's time stamp is four-forty-five in the afternoon. My guess is that during this meeting Tancos probably slipped you a narcotic. Maybe he placed something in one of the beers that you drank. There were several empty bottles found in your burnt down garage. The FBI's lab found traces inside one of them of what could have been Propofol. But the heat was so intense they couldn't make a one-hundred percent positive analysis. Propofol also happens to be the same drug someone just injected into Caleb Tancos at the hospital. He's dead."

"Dead? No. You're lying."

"If you like, I'll get a photo emailed over here of his dead body to prove it."

Paul dropped his head, looking deflated.

Karl turned to his son. "What's going on here?"

Paul pulled his head up and stared at all three pictures on the table, each with a different date and time clearly stamped on them. He looked befuddled.

Stan pulled out a chair and sat down. "The guy I shared an office with when I joined the County Attorney's Office told me a story once that might help explain a lot," Stan said. "Jacob Lund's name had come up in my first staff meeting. I asked my associate who the man was. He told me about the time Lund had spent there as a prosecuting attorney and his extraordinary record of winning cases. But he also told me about Lund's open bigotry, especially his bitterness toward my hiring. My new office mate told me Lund was extremely pissed because the HR department for the county chose, in Lund's words, "a goddamn nigger over his own son."

Stan carefully chose his next words. "I became enraged when I heard that story, considering all of the hard work I had done and the battles I had faced to get where I had gotten to. But I set my anger aside and decided to brush off Lund's racism—from a man who didn't even know me—since I had run into that type of blind ignorance my whole life. But my rage all came rushing back when I met his son up on the Rim years later when you supposedly disappeared all those years ago. I had never met Micah before, yet he treated me like some kind of fucking dog. Since we had no history together, I figured his outright hatred toward me must have been an outcome of his father's prejudice, transferred over to him. Seems like those types of biases being passed on from father to son are more common than we'd like to think—or even admit."

Karl winced and hung his head.

"So, Paul," Stan said. "Tell me what you remember when you woke up that morning in your garage."

Stewart shook his head back and forth. "I . . . I don't . . . I can't . . ."

"Try, son. Please. Try to remember," his father pleaded.

Paul Stewart focused his gaze on the photos before him. "I do remember Tancos coming to my house. You know. The day before. When I saw him, I had this notion he may have come to kill me. But the bastard was just sitting there, all calm and cool. Sitting at *my* kitchen table. The prick was actually drinking a beer he had taken from *my* refrigerator. One was sitting opened for me too. He had the gall to ask me to have a drink with him. In *my* home! I should have killed him right then and there."

"What happened next?" Stan asked.

"He gave me an envelope. Said it was from Jacob. Then he left. After he was gone, I opened it. There was money inside. Stacks of bills. A hundred-thousand dollars. Jacob knew I had gambling debts. He knew I was desperate. Also inside the package was a letter from Jacob. It was long and rambling. He went on and on, but I remember him writing about the proverb of many being called but few being chosen. He also referred to David and Goliath. After I had read it, I believed he was sending me a message . . . a message to kill my family."

Stewart touched each of the photos with his fingertips, continuing his stark stare.

"Go on," Stan said. "What else?"

"I was shocked. Didn't know what to think. I wanted to obey Lund but I wasn't sure I could do what he was asking me to do. But I had already taken some money he had given me earlier and lost all of that. I was in too deep with him. I wondered how I could ever get out from under him. If I ran, I knew he'd find me. Plus, what about my family? Tancos had already gotten into my house once. He could easily do it again. I'd never be able to protect them. I was desperate."

Stewart paused and stared at the wall across the room. Stan saw the look of desperation flooding back into the man's eyes.

"Go on," Stan said.

"I grabbed that beer Tancos had opened for me and went into the garage. I downed it in a few gulps. Then I had another and another and drank myself into a stupor. When I woke up, I was on my cot, still in the garage, soaked in blood. It was all over me. There were also bloody footsteps from the door going into my house to where I had passed out. My knife was lying next to me. It was all covered in blood. I also remember my dog, barking like mad, inside my truck. I didn't even remember putting him in there. My head was so groggy."

Stewart paused again, looking as if he was trying to recall all the details. Stan nodded for him to continue.

"I remember opening my two footlockers when I first went into the garage after reading Jacob's letter. Silly, but I do recall leaving them both open. But when I woke up their lids were closed. I looked inside both and everything was still there except . . . except for—"

Stan urged him on. "Except for what?"

"My incendiary devices. What had I done with my incendiary devices? Where were they? I tried to force myself to go into the house but I couldn't bear to think what I might find. To see what I could have done. My head felt like it was going to explode. Then, I thought for a moment that maybe I was dreaming. I couldn't push all the thoughts out of my mind about what Jacob had said in the letter. Could I possibly have done this monstrous act he had commanded me to do?"

Stewart hunched over, folding into himself. He began to shiver. Karl put a hand on his back, a loving gesture of compassion.

Stan recollected the elder Stewart's stories from when they

had first met in the trailer park. Stan couldn't help but think the roles had come full circle as father now consoled his son.

CHAPTER 69

3:15 am

Stan stepped out of the interrogation room, responding to another knock on the door. Ron D'Antonio met him first.

"Stewart was about to break. This better be awfully goddam important, Ron," Stan scowled.

"It is and it's not good news. The SRP dive team is out of the water. They can't go any deeper due to not only the lack of light but not being on mixed air."

D'Antonio's words drew a snap reaction from Stan. "I understand the lack of light but what in the hell is mixed air?"

"Divers can only go down to about forty meters without needing to decompress before surfacing. That's about one-hundred-and-thirty feet. If we need to dive any deeper, it will require what's called a technical dive, meaning the divers will only be able to stay underwater for a very limited time and need to use a special mix of gases so they can decompress safely when they surface. The SRP team's not trained or equipped for a mission like that. The reservoir is nearly three-hundred feet deep. More people have been to the moon than have dived to that depth. And even if they could go deeper, they'd eventually be faced with total darkness."

"We need whoever is out there on the scene now to get us more answers until a deep water team arrives then," Stan snapped back.

"Stan, even if the SRP dive crew had discovered a Mark eighty-two down there they're not trained in any way, shape or form to handle a situation like that. Getting an inexperienced diver near that type of ordnance would be much too dangerous. There is some good news, though."

"Well it's about damn time."

"I was just informed the National Guard's Explosive Ordnance Disposal unit from the Coolidge Armory has someone on their staff with diving experience. They're the same team that rendered safe the Mark eighty-two downtown. Their unit is on standby, prepped and ready to go in the water at first light."

D'Antonio went on, not holding back in expressing his irritation with the situation. "But, we really need to find out as soon as possible exactly what Stewart's done so we know specifically how to respond. Until you can get something solid out of Stewart we can use, then we can't even assign a proper threat level to this incident. Before my agency can order an official render safe procedure, we need to know the risk level for the local EOD personnel prior to sending them into harm's way. And, we really need to know that info *now*."

Although he wanted to spew a few more of his favorite expletives, Stan controlled himself in his reply to the testy-sounding ATF expert. "I presume the Navy can do this technical dive thing?"

"Of course, but like I explained earlier, they're in San Diego. It will take time to prep them and have them on site with all the gear they'd need to execute a deep water exercise."

Stan didn't like D'Antonio's answer and shook his head in disbelief.

D'Antonio went on, prodding Stan. "Stan, you've got to find out if he has actually placed a bomb or bombs in the water and, if so, how he's rigged them."

Stan looked down, shaking his head again. He clearly felt D'Antonio's urgent desire to get answers to the same exact questions he had. He turned to Agent Schwartz. "Malori, grab that evidence box and bring it back in the room with us, would you please?" He looked over toward D'Antonio and gave him a sinister smile. "I'm not quite done with Paul Stewart yet."

CHAPTER 70

4:05 a.m.

When Stan walked back into the interrogation room, Paul Stewart stared blankly, looking straight ahead. Before he or Schwartz had even sat down across from Stewart and his father, Stan spoke.

"What kind of knife?"

Paul turned his look toward Stan. "Huh?"

"Your knife. The one you mentioned that was covered in blood. What kind was it?"

"The same kind I was going to kill that motherfucker Tancos with at the hospital today. My Bowie."

"The one we have in our possession now?" Stan opened the top of the evidence box Agent Schwartz had carried in. He pulled out a sealed plastic bag. "This one? The one with no serrated edge. Correct?"

Paul nodded.

"What are you getting at?" his father asked.

"You see, Karl, Paul's wife and children were decapitated. The killer used a knife with a serrated edge. Just like the kind taken off Caleb Tancos when he arrived at the hospital ER. And just like the one I saw him cut up an apple with the first time I met him. My guess is when we analyze Tancos's knife the blade's serrations will match the marks left on the three decapitated victims we found recently in a Chandler drop house. But, more importantly, I believe the knife will also match the results from the autopsies on Paul's family."

Karl cringed hearing the gruesome details as Stan crossed his fingers, hoping neither father nor son would call his bluff regarding his last statement. He could only hope his speculative guess would turn out to be true.

"Paul, they kept you convinced you had committed the crime. They needed you to believe that. Most importantly, they also needed you to fear they'd leak the truth if you didn't cooperate with their plans. How else do you explain a man agreeing to stay in hiding for a decade?" Stan pulled the photos off the table and stuffed them back into his folder, patting it closed. "Hate and fear will make a man do things he never thought he'd be able to or agree to do."

Paul Stewart scoffed. "I . . . I don't believe you."

"The evidence doesn't lie," Agent Schwartz said, speaking for the first time.

"I can't believe I could . . ." Stewart stumbled over his next words. "How could I . . . how could I have been so stupid. So gullible." Paul turned to his father. "Dad?"

Karl put his hand on his son's shoulder. After an awkward moment, the father wrapped his arms around his son and the two embraced.

"I knew you couldn't have done such a thing," Karl said. "*I knew it.*"

"Paul, now that you know the truth, you've got to stop this madness you've put in motion," Stan said. "Otherwise, only Jacob Lund wins. And, trust me, nobody but Jacob Lund benefits from that."

CHAPTER 71

Roosevelt Dam
5:45 a.m.

Detective Brian Hanley arrived at the boat ramp to Roosevelt Lake just as the sun was peeking over the mountains to the east. A yellow glow glimmered across the murky water's surface. The reservoir, created by the dam of the same name, was absent of boat traffic and eerily empty after having been sealed off from all public access. High above, the winding Apache Trail was equally silent. Roadblocks set-up by county sheriff's deputies and Department of Public Safety officers had accomplished their task, detouring motor vehicle traffic for twenty miles in each direction.

Mary Ann Burnett, a member of the Arizona National Guard's 363rd Explosive Ordnance Disposal detail and her five-person unit, had already arrived. The only female on the team, she spent her free time as a recreational diver when she wasn't working her day job as a Crime Scene Response Unit technician for the Chandler Police Department.

"Seems you're a lady of many talents," Brian said as the two stood on the pier, soft waves lapping below.

"If you only knew." Not looking up, she checked a piece of her gear, and then tossed it up to her partner inside a twenty-two-foot Cobalt dive boat.

"What's the latest?" Brian asked.

"The SRP divers reported seeing an approximately foot-long, cylindrical-shaped object attached to a piece of chain about twenty feet below that flotation device. ATF's issued a

Category A incident, speculating the observed device might perhaps contain a timing mechanism to detonate explosives."

At that moment, D'Antonio joined them on the pier with another ATF team member. "Burnett, this guy Stewart is a mastermind with explosives. There's no telling what he's done. If the time power unit is inside that cylinder, there will have to be at least one pair of wires coming out of the container. Those must be disabled. My guess is the only way you'll be able to do that is by cutting one of the wires and you know the risk in that. But that's the only hope we have right now."

"Roger that, sir." Her response was firm.

"You be safe down there," Brian said.

"You're not worried the 'bomb girl' might screw up, are you Hanley?"

* * *

Burnett hopped inside the red Cobalt, joining her dive partner. As soon as she sat down, the boat's captain throttled forward and took them out to the location where the SRP divers had left a yellow marker buoy. The lake's water moved in endless motion toward the massive concrete wall of the dam. Below the surface, monster-sized intakes sucked in hundreds of thousands of gallons of water, feeding the dam's ever-churning century-old hydro-electric motors. Power generating operations had been reduced to a minimum but not halted. SRP couldn't shut down the dam entirely since the electricity it generated supplied millions of Phoenix residents forty miles away.

The relative calm of the water did allow the dive boat's captain to maneuver right next to the dam's wall where the marker buoy innocently bobbed to and fro. A Maricopa County Sheriff's Office Lakes Patrol dive team member acted as Mary Ann's buddy for the treacherous dive. Although her partner had no explosives expertise, he had performed hundreds of dives in dam reservoirs as part of his job as a recovery diver, albeit he normally searched for dead bodies. She felt confident his first-hand experience diving Roosevelt would be invaluable.

They each wore dual tanks filled with regular air. Her partner had ruled out the option of running surface air to them through rubber hoses, which would have allowed a longer dive. He had made the recommendation in the pre-dive briefing, warning the threat of debris in constant motion toward the intakes posed far too much risk of getting entangled in their supply lines.

The SRP dive team had left a rope anchored from the silt-filled bottom to their marker buoy. Burnett and her partner entered the water and headed into the unknown. Her dive buddy followed the guide-rope downward, she right behind. They stayed close to each other, fighting the pull of the steady current created by the intakes, a constant tug at them, wanting to suck them against the steel grates that covered their massive openings.

Within a few minutes, they reached the gray cylinder.

CHAPTER 72

Downtown Phoenix
4ᵗʰ Avenue Jail
6:00 a.m.

Stan stood with FBI Special Agent Schwartz outside the interrogation room. After taking a break to get updated on the situation at the dam—and to freshen up—they were ready to restart the questioning of Paul Stewart.

"I got a text from Detective Hanley. He and D'Antonio are at the dam. They both spoke to the EOD diver and her partner before they hit the water."

"*Her* partner?" Stan asked.

"Yes, seems the EOD diver is active National Guard. Hanley says you know her. She also works as a crime scene technician for the Chandler PD."

"I'll be damned. Mary Ann. What doesn't she do?"

"Huh?" Schwartz asked.

"Oh nothing. Any word yet on when a Navy EOD dive team will get here?"

"According to my office, last update was they were still waiting for official orders to clear."

"Fucking bureaucrats," Stan lamented. He changed the subject. "I still can't get out of my mind those Bible verses Stewart referred to earlier. I wonder what significance they have."

Neither of the interrogators had slept, except for five-minute power naps followed by splashes of cold-water to their faces while Stewart had been escorted to the bathroom several times throughout the interrogation.

"Stan, do you think he's just toying with us?"

"I don't know. Right now, all I know for sure is that two lives depend upon me getting Stewart to tell us more—our divers in the water."

CHAPTER 73

Roosevelt Lake
6:05 a.m.

Brian Hanley kept looking at his wristwatch. His co-worker, Mary Ann Burnett, had been in the water nearly fifteen minutes with her dive partner. Next to Brian stood ATF's Ron D'Antonio. The two stood inside one of several tents set up as a forward operating command center in the boat launch parking lot manned by D'Antonio, now in charge of the dive operation, and his ATF ground team.

On site now were all manner of official vehicles from the various departments of the joint operation. Notable were a slew of National Guard trucks, some equipped with satellite dishes pointed skyward. An ATF guy running the console had established a two-way radio link between the divers and the command center via their acoustic microphones installed inside their full face masks. That link, in turn, was shared real-time with each involved agency's communications center plus the Navy's EOD School at Eglin Air Force Base in Destin, Florida. From a small video camera mounted on top of their dive masks, the divers also fed a live video signal back to the surface.

Mary Ann's voice crackled through a pair of portable speakers sitting next to a video monitor displaying her video feed from an experimental camera D'Antonio had provided each diver. "I've got eyes on the cylinder."

The voice of the ATF guy at the con was calm as he replied. "What we're looking for first, Burnett, is a close-up on that cylinder. Over."

"Roger that," she said.

Each diver's camera fed two, side-by-side monitors. The output from their hand-held flashlights barely illuminated the murky water.

Brian watched the monitor as Mary Ann stretched the light ahead of her, wondering when the burgeoning daylight would reach down to them through the churned-up water. He leaned toward Ron and spoke. "Do you think this cylinder has the timing device inside?"

"If there are bombs down there, Stewart had to devise a way to detonate them while underwater. The only way he could have done that was by creating some type of sealed timer. If Burnett sees wires coming from the cylinder then most likely there's a timer inside connected to whatever's below."

Both monitors showed the dark, blurry images being sent up by each of the heretofore untested cameras. As Mary Ann approached the gray metal body, she directed her hand-held beam directly on it. "The object looks to be about ten-to-fourteen inches in length. Approximately four-to-six inches in diameter."

As she got in closer, she reported more. "There are wires extruding from the bottom end of the object."

"How many?" asked the ATF tech at the con.

"Not certain. Going in closer."

"One wrong move . . ." D'Antonio whispered to Brian.

Burnett's calm voice broke the tense silence. "I see six wires. They lead out of the cylinder, which is attached to a heavy chain, then wind downward through the chain." Her helmet camera's video filled one screen with images of what she described. "They all look the same. Can't tell exactly what color they are but if I had to guess I'd say they're brown."

Brian heard sighs from a couple members of Burnett's EOD team on shore as they too watched the scene unfold. Brian asked Ron if there was any significance of the wires all being brown in color.

"It means it's highly likely they're military issue,"

D'Antonio told him, "which would mean it's a very sophisticated device. Unfortunately, there's no way of knowing unless we trace the wires to the bombs."

Brian's phone buzzed, announcing an incoming text message. He read it, then turned his mobile over to D'Antonio to read. "You may have gotten your wish," Brian said.

After D'Antonio read the message, he gave an order to the guy at the console. "Instruct the divers to follow the chain down sixty feet from where they are now."

With Burnett now in the lead, her video monitor displayed the image of the iron chain with the wires, twisted into three pairs, snaking through its links. For the next few minutes, Brian's heart pounded as the divers descended into the unknown, silent except for the sound of their breathing.

Minutes passed. Then Burnett's voice crackled over the speakers, startling him. "I've got a rather large unidentified object ahead," she reported.

The divers clung tight to their guide rope, going hand-over-hand alongside the heavy steel chain, deeper into the abyss. As they got closer to the body, Brian kept his eyes glued to the large screens. Moments later it became obvious to him that what he was seeing was much bigger than the small cylinder sixty-feet above. This metal object, although the same drab gray, looked ten-times bigger.

"Scratch that last comment," Burnett said. "I've got a positive ID. It's definitely a Mark eighty-two. I'm going in tight to see if it's another one of the Air Force's missing cache."

There was radio silence for the next few moments. Brian sensed the rest of the observers—especially Burnett's fellow EOD team members—felt as anxious as he did while they waited for a reply from the underwater team. The tension in the tent was palpable. He looked over at D'Antonio and noticed beads of sweat forming on the man's upper lip.

"PID complete. Numeric markings match the bomb from downtown Phoenix. It's another one of Forster's missing bombs." Mary Ann's voice remained clear and calm.

Thrilled at finding another of Forster's bombs, Brian was

also in awe of Stan's skills in discovering another piece to the complex puzzle. Brian turned to D'Antonio and said, "I'd better call Stan. That son-of-a-gun pardner of mine was right again."

CHAPTER 74

Downtown Phoenix
4ᵗʰ Avenue Jail
6:30 a.m.

Stan sat silent in the hallway outside the interrogation room, massaging a temple with one hand, cellphone to his ear in the other. Brian updated him from the incident command center at the dam.

"So, it's definitely one of Forster's bombs," Stan said.

"Yep. Our friend Mary Ann made the positive ID. I'm proud of you, pardner. How'd you know there'd be one another sixty-feet deeper?"

"I'll explain later. So D'Antonio said disabling these bombs may not be as easy as I had hoped, huh?"

Brian replied. "Nope. Looks like Stewart has run military-grade wire in pairs to each of the bombs. The expert from Eglin confirmed that detail after he heard Mary Ann's precise description of what she saw."

"So what does that mean exactly?" Stan asked.

"According to this instructor from the Navy's EOD School, Stewart was one of the smartest guys to ever go through the program. This Eglin guy says it's highly likely Stewart may have rigged-up something called a collapsing circuit."

"*Collapsing* what?"

"Here. I'll put us on speaker phone. Specialist D'Antonio can do a better job of explaining it."

"This is D'Antonio, sir. Each pair of wires carries a command signal to a blasting cap on its respective bomb. If

Stewart created what we call a 'collapsing circuit,' then cutting any of those wires would likely trigger a charged capacitor to dump, initiating an immediate detonation of all the bombs."

"So, how do you tell if it's this collapsing circuit?"

"You can't. Only the maker would know that."

"So there's literally no way of determining if it's wired this way?" Stan continued.

"Correct. Not without Stewart telling us. The only other way would be to open the cylinder and look inside. But before we'd attempt to do anything like that we'd typically x-ray it. That way we could see the circuit he's created as well as determine if he's put in place an evidence destruction charge inside the cylinder. But being that the device is underwater makes x-raying impossible."

"*Evidence destruction charge?* What's that?" Stan asked.

"It means he might have piggy-backed an explosive charge, most likely using some C-4, inside the cylinder so that if we try to open it, it blows."

Stan rubbed his temple harder while he listened intently to the news coming from his explosives expert—news that had gone from bad to worse. The pounding headache hadn't left him since he'd started his interrogation and the pain had gotten worse. He wanted an end to the desperate situation, no matter how it came about. And he wanted it now.

"Thanks, Ron. I'll get back to you. In the meantime, tell those two divers great job and to stay safe." Stan ended the call and turned to Malori. "It's now or never. Let's do this."

They re-entered the interrogation room where Paul Stewart sat silent. Karl was still by his side. Stan knew both men had to be as tired and exhausted—both physically and mentally—as much as he and Agent Schwartz.

"How'd you do it?" Stan asked Paul. "How'd you get Forster's bombs?"

Paul stayed silent for a long time before he replied. "I sabotaged his plane."

"As your lawyer, Paul, I advise you not to speak about that," Karl said.

"No. I want to talk. I want it all to be over."

"So do I," Stan said. "Our divers have positively identified another one of Captain Forster's Mark eighty-twos with wires leading to it from a cylinder above. Inside that cylinder is your timing device, right?"

Paul nodded.

"Did you run a collapsing circuit?"

Paul didn't answer.

"Forty cubits," Stan said. The first bomb was exactly sixty-feet below the timing device. Lund is trying to recreate the tearing of the temple curtain in Jerusalem. Isn't he?"

Paul smiled. "You're a smart man, Mister Kobe. I underestimated you."

"The Bible tells us the temple was torn in two when Christ expired on the cross. History tells us that was about three in the afternoon." Stan looked at his wristwatch. "That's less than nine hours from now. Is that when you set the bombs to explode?"

Paul Stewart's only reply was a blank stare. Stan was puzzled by the prisoner's sudden disconnect, but he forged on.

"We might be able to get a Navy EOD team out before then, but you know, don't you, the chances of that are getting very slim. Tell us how to disable the timing device. You don't want to be part of any more killing. Do you want to be remembered like Tancos? You hated him and all he stood for. Our divers in the water out there are both married with children."

Karl jumped in, unhesitant. "Paul. As your lawyer—"

"It can't be stopped," Paul said. "If they cut the wrong wire, they'll all blow."

Stan pounded his fist to the table. He was ready to explode himself. He had come too far, worked too hard, had too many sleepless nights, to hear Stewart's nonchalant-sounding comment, telling him that what had been put in motion couldn't be stopped. Stan's mind recalled a picture he had on his desk of Maxine and the twins at a baseball game. The snapshot was his favorite. The thought of losing them

PASCAL MARCO

made him snap. "I won't let that happen! And I don't believe you really want that to happen! Do you?"

Stan looked deep into Stewart's eyes, believing that, although he had done many evil things, in the man's heart he cared.

Stewart looked back at him, then looked at his father, whose distraught look was clear. "It can only . . ." Stewart paused, swallowing.

Stan leaned forward toward Stewart. "Only what," he asked.

C'mon, Paul. Do the right thing. I know you want to.

". . . only if they don't cut the right wire and they'll never know which one, since I kept them all the same color."

"But you know which one is the right one. Don't you?"

Stewart gave a small nod. "Yes. I rigged it so that if the correct wire is cut it will render safe the bombs."

"I knew it," Stan beamed.

Stewart interrupted Stan's small moment of satisfaction. "But . . ."

"But what?"

"But I put an evidence destruction charge inside the cylinder. The divers wouldn't have time to escape that blast. I packed almost two pounds of C-4 inside that pipe."

Stan was too close to getting a solution to allow anything to stand in his way now. He leaned back and sat upright in his chair. He was all business now with the bomber. "Paul, deaths resulting from a planned explosion are subject to the death penalty. If you did sabotage Forster's A-10 you're already accountable for that death. The feds have the death penalty. Is that something you'd like to face without my statement you did everything you could to help us now?"

"What are you offering, Mister Kobe?" Karl asked.

"If he cooperates, I will do all I can with my connections in the federal government to keep him from facing the death penalty."

A long pause filled the interrogation room. The only discernible sound was the crack of one of Stan's knuckles. He had run out of options. If the timer had indeed been set for three in the afternoon, then that was only a little more than seven hours from now. He would get Stewart's cooperation, whatever it took. He prayed his offer to speak on his behalf to a federal prosecutor would be the tipping point, even though he knew a promise like the one he'd just made would be nearly impossible to keep.

"Is that a promise?"

Stan nodded at Paul's question.

"Then I'll cooperate. But . . . in order for me to help, I'll need to render safe the bombs myself."

CHAPTER 75

Roosevelt Dam
9:00 a.m.

As Stan stood outside the row of tents alongside Theodore Roosevelt Dam, he couldn't stop looking in awe at the immense structure before him. Since 9/11, few people outside of Salt River Project utility company employees and Federal Bureau of Reclamation workers had been allowed this close to the mammoth dam, built over a hundred years earlier as the first in President Teddy Roosevelt's landmark Water Reclamation Act.

But the tired prosecutor had no time to admire the magnificence before his eyes as he fought to explain to Brian and D'Antonio why he'd agreed to Paul Stewart's request to make the dive to render safe the bombs.

"I believe what Stewart told me and Agent Schwartz. That he's the only person who can successfully disable what he's created and that he should be the only one put in harm's way and make this dive," Stan said matter-of-factly.

"You're sure about this?" There was no denying the sound of Brian's voice questioning his partner's sanity.

"We have no other choice," Stan replied. "Otherwise, I wouldn't agree to it."

"It's against every protocol I've ever known," D'Antonio said. "It's just damn crazy!"

"Yes, I realize it's unprecedented, Ron, but so is this whole situation."

"But what if he doesn't do what he says he's going to do

and makes an attempt to escape?" D'Antonio countered.

"Where's he gonna go, Ron?" Stan rebutted. "There's only one way in and one way out. I believe, and I know you do too, that what Stewart says is true. He's the one person who has the highest chance to successfully accomplish this. He's the only person who knows exactly which wire to cut."

"Why can't Stewart just explain to our divers while he's watching their video feed?" D'Antonio asked.

"You've seen that video feed yourself, Ron," Brian jumped in. "That technology is new and was breaking up half the time. Plus, it's barely visible through all that silt and debris floating in the water."

"But I just don't see how you can trust him," D'Antonio countered.

"What choice do we have? He's already told us that if the wrong wire is cut his evidence destruction charge blows and kills whoever is next to it," Stan said. "It's a potential suicide mission for any diver who goes down there."

D'Antonio shook his head while he marched back and forth. Stewart, bound in wrist shackles and leg irons and guarded by Maricopa County Sheriff's Deputies along with U.S. Marshals, had been brought down to the incident site and sat inside a nearby utility tent.

"Are you going to take responsibility then for what is, in essence, the prospect of sending an untried man to his own execution?"

He knew D'Antonio's point had ethical merit but Stan didn't care. At this point, he was willing to roll the dice on that factor and deal with it later. "Ron, think about this. What if we send our own divers down there and the wrong wire gets cut? Do you want to be the one to call their next of kin?" Stan had painted him into a corner and hoped his last words would finally sway the ATF veteran who was supervising the entire operation at the dam.

Stan didn't wait for him to think any longer about his decision. "We're six hours from the time I believe Stewart set the devices to detonate. The Navy EOD team out of San Diego still hasn't received final orders. We're running out of time, Ron, *and* options." Stan waited a moment for the visibly perturbed man's reply. "Ron, we need your blessing on this. I'm convinced Stewart's the best choice for achieving the highest probability of rendering safe those bombs. I don't think that after all he's been through, knowing as he does now he's been used and someone else killed his family, that he'd have any motive to continue to help them and not help us. I believe that as sure as I'm standing here."

D'Antonio fumed. "Okay, okay! He can make the dive! But you better pray your gut is right on this one."

"If I were a betting man," Brian piped in, "I'd put my money on my pardner's belly."

CHAPTER 76

11:00 a.m.

Inside the utility tent, Paul Stewart sat and spoke with Mary Ann Burnett and her Maricopa County dive partner about what the two had seen below. Stan, Brian, D'Antonio and Schwartz all sat around the large, rectangular table, listening to the conversation. Karl Stewart was there, too, observing but silent. Hours earlier, when a federal public defender had showed up to represent Paul, the prisoner had declined his services, telling him he had his legal representation—his father.

"We didn't have any women in EOD back in the day," Stewart told Mary Ann. An armed Maricopa County Sheriff's deputy and a U.S. Marshal stood behind Stewart, eyes glued to the prisoner.

Mary Ann nodded. "I love my work. I'd love it even more if these folks would let me dive down with you." She looked around the table.

Stewart disagreed. "There's no need to send anyone else but me into harm's way. I need to do this solo."

D'Antonio spoke up, looking directly at Stewart. "You know my position on this. I'm totally against it. But Attorney Kobe believes you're the only hope. My prayer is that he's right and you won't screw us down there."

"I want an end to this just as much as the rest of you," Stewart replied.

D'Antonio had his own reply for Stewart. "How do we know the 'end' you want is the same one we want. How can we trust you that you'll cut the correct wire and not purposely set off the Mark eighty-twos?"

Stewart bristled at the ATF explosive specialist's accusation, scowling at D'Antonio. "My wife and children are dead. No thanks to me and the path I was led down, yet agreed to follow. Plus, I'm directly responsible for an innocent Air Force pilot losing his life. All of these outcomes were due to my arrogance and my blind hatred." His tone softened. "The last thing I want right now is for anyone else to be injured or killed, especially a fellow EOD soldier." He nodded toward Burnett.

D'Antonio admonished him. "You've got one hour to accomplish the task . . . *One hour.*"

His phone chimed an incoming message. He read it then looked up and spoke to everybody in the room. "Looks like Navy brass finally gave formal permission to dispatch their team out of San Diego. They're mustering now."

*   *   *

Stan, Brian and FBI Agent Schwartz stood side-by-side next to D'Antonio. His ATF team, along with Burnett and her EOD detail, plus the Maricopa County dive unit, all encircled the command console. Even though a Navy team was assembling, the Chief Petty Officer coordinating their dispatch said they were at the very least four hours out from arriving at the dam. Maybe more. With that knowledge, the decision was made to allow Stewart his wish and dive down to render safe his own weapon of mass destruction.

With D'Antonio's words still ringing in his ear, Stan was anxious, wondering whether he had made the correct decision in trusting Stewart. He kept nervously looking and re-looking at his wristwatch. Stewart had been in the water ten minutes. The captain of the dive boat had pulled away after dropping him next to the SRP marker buoy. Stewart had recommended the boat and its crew maintain at least a five-hundred yard distance so that if his evidence destruction charge detonated they'd be out of the blast zone.

"I've reached the cylinder." Stewart's voice came over loud and clear on the command center's speakers. "Do you have my video feed?"

"Negative," replied the ATF technician at the console. "No visual feed yet."

"How about now?"

"Still negative."

"Damn camera," D'Antonio murmured.

Stan heard Ron's words and turned and looked at him. Both men gave each other a blank stare.

"Not sure why video isn't feeding back to you," Stewart said. "All good down here."

"Can we do a system reboot?" D'Antonio asked his man running the con.

"I can but it will take a bit for everything to come back online."

"We need to have eyes on him and what he's doing down there," D'Antonio shouted. "Reboot it now."

"Roger that." The ATF tech told Stewart he'd be offline for a few moments while he re-started the system. He then punched a series of buttons and flipped some switches. Equipment lights flickered off and on before him. "Standby," he said.

As the various electronic monitoring gear came back up, each went through its own sequence to reconnect to the remote command station's main server. The momentary action seemed to drag on for minutes to Stan.

"We're back up," the tech at the con said. "All systems are green. Video should be back now." The screen popped back up with an image of the murky water. Stewart's gray timing cylinder sat squarely in front of the camera's lens and filled the screen. Then, everything went blank.

"What happened?" D'Antonio asked.

His technician shrugged his shoulders. In rapid succession, he switched some levers up and down and pressed various buttons.

"Hail Stewart," D'Antonio instructed his tech.

"Stewart. This is the command center. Come in, please. Over."

No reply.

"Call him again," D'Antonio barked.

The man repeated his call. No reply. Heads began turning around, looking at each other with wide eyes.

"I don't like this," said D'Antonio.

Stan's eyes and D'Antonio's locked. All Stan could say was, "Fuck."

*   *   *

With the tips of gentle fingers, Paul Stewart parted the six wires coming out of the timing cylinder. Each was identical. One, though, he had wrapped around a nut he had welded to the cap on the end of the cylinder. He grabbed his wire cutter from his belt.

"I love you, Stacey. Daddy loves you, too, boys."

*   *   *

The explosion from the nearly two-pounds of military grade M-112 C-4 Paul Stewart had stuffed into the steel timing cylinder acted like a Navy destroyer's depth charge. The surface of Roosevelt Lake erupted in a huge cannon ball, splashing water nearly one-hundred feet in the air. Dead and stunned fish immediately began floating to the top of the water. The captain of the Cobalt dive boat made a beeline for the point of the explosion. When he got to the spot, all that was left were remnants of the marker buoy and pieces of the flotation device, all bobbing innocently on the water.

Stan waited on shore along with the entire team for a report from any of the other authorized boats launched into the water immediately after the explosion. As they scoured the lake and its shoreline, Stan waited for a signal from any craft that Stewart's corpse, or what was left of it, had been found.

But the body of his prisoner never came to the surface.

* * *

The proximity of the huge blast pushes Paul Stewart down, down, deep into the water. Stunned by the explosion's massive concussion and mask-less, he opens his eyes in the murky, silt-filled water. He isn't sure if he is dead or alive but after a few seconds the water becomes crystal clear. He spots someone swimming in his direction. It's his father.

He's trying to save me. He's trying to save his boy.

He struggles to stay afloat as Karl Stewart, arms open, urges his son toward him. Not sure if he should swim toward his dad or make an attempt to try and reach shore, Paul fights the relentless current pulling him toward the water intakes of the dam. He looks again to his father, who now battles himself against the swift current created by the massive suction chutes. Paul sees the frail old man's futile attempt to get to him. He races to his father. As he gets closer, he realizes his father is not only being held back by the strong current but by a grasp from behind. It's none other than Jacob Lund. Paul screams at Lund to let his father go, but his words just come out as gurgles. He increases the speed of his swim stroke to reach the two, elderly men. But the current is relentless. He's helpless.

Too far away to reach his father's outstretched hands, Paul Henry Stewart disappears into the darkened water below.

CHAPTER 77

Weeks Later

S tan sat at the bistro table on his Saltillo tile backyard patio, eyes scanning the pages of *The Arizona Republic*. Smooth jazz music spilled softly from outdoor speakers disguised as strategically placed garden rocks. Maxine came out through the sliding doors to the kitchen.

"Tea's ready," she chirped, holding a pot in one hand.

The two rarely missed their Sunday morning ritual sitting under the mesquite tree, its enormous canopy shading them from the burgeoning late spring sun.

Stan didn't look up but just pushed his cup and saucer toward her.

"Any more details in today's paper?" she inquired.

He shook his head. Weeks' earlier headlines of the failed bombing attempt in downtown Phoenix and the police shootout, where the top cop of Red Rock, Arizona had died in a blaze of gun fire, had been relegated to small, one or two column stories in the back pages of the front section. To date, no one had publicly stepped forward to take credit for the bomb left in the back of the deceased chief's police van.

"There is another story about Logan, though."

Following the incident, investigative reporters had delved into the clandestine life of Police Chief Logan Athem, revealing his ties to neo-Nazi hate groups. Tenacious reporters in today's story had uncovered a direct connection to the dead man and the derailment bombing of an Amtrak train south of Phoenix years earlier.

"Any news about the other bombs?" Maxine asked.

Stan shook his head, happy to see that there still were no stories being reported about the incident at Roosevelt Lake or the explosion at Palo Verde Nuclear Power Plant. Release of news of either event had been quashed by the Department of Homeland Security. As he continued to read the follow-up story about Athem, he couldn't push out of his mind the feeling of deep frustration over the inexplicable disappearance, once again, of Paul Henry Stewart. Maricopa County recovery divers had never found any remains of the ex-EOD technician and eventually gave up their search. Nonetheless, the county attorney's office had taken an internal beating after discovering Stan's approval of allowing the captured Stewart to attempt to disarm an evidence destruction device he admitted having placed in Roosevelt Lake.

"You keep reading that stuff and you'll need a mimosa instead of the tea."

He looked up from the paper. "You're not kidding. Were you reading my mind?"

"I can tell by the look on your face," she replied, pausing for a long moment before continuing. "It's not your fault, you know. No matter what anyone says."

His dour look intensified as he dropped the paper to the table. "But it was my idea to send him down there. Losing him took away any hope of bringing and winning a case against Jacob Lund. I'm still convinced he was the mastermind behind everything."

"But his son, the sheriff, the one who shot the dog. At least he's going down. That's a start."

In the days after the incident, Stan had shared with Maxine most of the details of the case, something he had always done. But with Caleb Tancos dead, as well as presumably Paul Stewart, the ability to bring Jacob Lund to trial vanished, leaving Micah, Jacob's son, the only one to take a fall.

"Even if I am able to positively tie Micah's gun to the dog, it in no way implicates Jacob. And I'm quite sure son won't roll on the father."

PASCAL MARCO

"Something else is bothering you, though. Isn't it?"

Stan pulled the paper back up in front of him, ignoring her question but not denying her intuition.

"Don't shut me out, Stan. Tell me what's gnawing at you."

He paused for a long time, knowing she wouldn't relent until she got a satisfactory answer. He had promised long ago not to lie to her or keep secrets anymore. He came out from behind the paper, folded it and placed it on the table. He looked her in the eye.

"I didn't think I needed to be concerned anymore about protecting you, protecting the kids, you know, after Chicago and all . . . but now, I worry . . ." His voice trailed off as he looked out at their blossoming flowers.

"What are you talking about?"

He paused for a long while, grappling with his emotions—some still a carryover from his youth—before giving her an answer. "All those years I lived in hiding, wondering if Pick and his gang would come looking for me. Then, after we married and had children, I had the added worry for my family's safety. When that all went away, I felt free for the first time since I was a boy. Finally, I thought, I would never have to be consumed ever again about the possibility of anyone hurting us. But when I discovered what Jacob Lund was about to do, about his plan to take away our water and electricity, to tear Phoenix apart . . . well . . . I could never protect us from something like that."

"Stan, you can't dwell upon the 'what ifs.' You *will* get him. Someday, he'll make a mistake. You've told me time and again, every criminal does. They all make that one big miscalculation."

He nodded, feeling some slight comfort in her reminder of one of the key tenets of his business: the bad guys at some point always trip up, leaving them open to discovery and capture.

How would Jacob Lund make his fatal mistake?

Stan heard a pop come from the electrical panel on the outside of the house, not far from where they sat.

Maxine looked up at him, frowning. "There goes that breaker for the dishwasher again. When are you going to call an electrician and get that thing fixed?"

Stan frowned at her chastisement but pushed himself up and walked over to the circuit-breaker box. He opened up the panel and noticed that all the breakers were in the ON position.

"Problem's not here." He walked back to the table and paused, turning his head around. "The music's stopped."

Maxine gave him an odd look. "Yeah, you're right."

They both walked inside into the kitchen. The dishwasher stood silent and no hum was coming from the refrigerator. Stan flipped the toggle switch on the wall for the ceiling light. Nothing happened. He tried it several more times, flicking it up and down. Same result.

"We've lost power." He turned to Maxine. "Call the Smiths. See if they have too."

Maxine picked up the phone on the wall and dialed the neighbors. "You don't have power either?" she said, shaking her head at Stan as he listened to her side of the conversation. "Oh? He is? Oh. Okay. Thanks, Melissa. Call us when your power comes back on. Yes, we will, too." Maxine hung up the phone. "She said Jeff is on the other line with SRP. They're telling him all of north Scottsdale is out. Customer service is saying they aren't sure what the problem is, but it might be a blown transformer."

Along with the appliances and the rest of the house, Stan stood silent. A deep crevice furled in his brow. Although the warm glow of daylight through the windows washed over the space, the room's stillness emanated an uncomfortable eeriness. He hated having that feeling of uncertainty, of not knowing what to do. Of not knowing the answers. Of things around him being out of his control. Yet, Stan knew all too well that there were things—and people—out there in the world he couldn't control or stop before they hurt someone.

Just then, the power popped back on. The refrigerator's compressor jumping back into action jolted Stan from his depressing thoughts—pushing them out his mind for yet another day.

The End

EPILOGUE

Even though this book is a work of fiction, two events occurred in Arizona that played a key part in helping me develop the main story. The first was the crash of an Air Force A-10 Thunderbolt II plane in 1997. In that event, the pilot of the plane, Captain Craig Button, inexplicably left his formation on his final training flight out of Davis-Monthan Air Force Base near Tucson. Button flew all over the central and northern half of the state of Arizona and as well as parts of southeastern Colorado before mysteriously crashing his plane into the Rocky Mountains. The four, live Mk-82 bombs he was carrying on the flight have never been found and the Air Force still has not made an official ruling on what caused Button's actions.

The second event revolves around the mysterious disappearance in 2001 of a man by the name of Robert Fisher. The very religious Fisher, who worked as a medical technician, was last seen withdrawing money from a Scottsdale bank ATM just after his nearby house exploded with his wife and two small children inside. An avid outdoorsman and hunter, Fisher's abandoned truck was found ten days later on the Mogollon Rim. No one has seen him since and he still remains on the FBI's Ten Most Wanted List.

Pascal Marco
June 30, 2016

ACKNOWLEDGEMENTS

Once again there are too many people to thank for supporting me to allow me to mention here. I especially want to thank my fellow authors Deborah Ledford, Virginia Nosky and Arthur Kerns. Your faithful and pointed feedback as we gathered every other week in our intimate Scottsdale Writers Group was invaluable.

I must say "Thank You" to all of the fans who bought, borrowed, stole, and promoted my first book, *Identity: Lost*, and your never ending encouragement to continue writing. Thank you for your unending patience in waiting for book two. Your attendance at book signings, your emails and your social media interaction, has simply been remarkable and quite frankly overwhelming. You all know who you are. To each and every one of you, I thank you from the bottom of my heart.

A very special thanks goes to my wife, Karen, whose love and support as I have chased my dream has stayed unwavering. Saying "thank you" will never be enough to tell you how much this has meant to me. I love you.

To my children, Regina, Dominic, Della and Anna, and my grandchildren, Jordan, Emilia, Madeline, Anthony, Sofia, and Mila: I hope I have been and will continue to be an inspiration to you. To my siblings—Mickey, Eddie and Mary Ann—your love of and pride in your brother will never be forgotten. And to my mom, my biggest fan, who faithfully attended every book signing in Chicago even as she was days away from turning 90. I know you're very proud of your son and I love you very much, too.

To Dan Waltenbaugh of the ATF: your never-ending enthusiasm, help, and guidance were not only contagious but key in developing my story. Eric White, A-10 pilot (and fellow Chicago White Sox fan) was another invaluable resource. Sean Kemp, Gary Peterson, Dave Ryon, Waya Schiller, and Ken Sebahar all shared their expertise in their own specialized areas within military and law enforcement. Thanks to Mary Palomino and Dan

Killloren of the Salt River Project (SRP) as well as to Patrick Myers and Danielle York of the National Park Service for their input and support. An important shout out goes to Terri Rossi, Mary Beth Hendron Lubert, and Joe Simanski who acted as "first readers." Your feedback throughout the manuscript development process was a godsend. Very special thanks goes to Augie Aleksy, Pinna Joseph, and Barbara Peters as well as to Rich Siegle, Beth Lichty, Robin Thomas, Rees Candee, Andy Abbott, the gang at IMP, Steve Wargo, Jim O'Hara, Mike D'Antonio, Rick Kogan, Mike Deacon, Della Kemp, Terry & Mike Cipolletti, Brenda Boychuck, Sue Shidler, Teresa Burrell, Doug Preston, Brad Thor. To those I may have inadvertently overlooked, or wasn't able to mention due to space constraints, know I still deeply thank you too.

Lastly, I must thank librarians from Chicago to New Zealand who checked out my first book to their patrons. Please support your local library in any way you can.

Pascal

Also by

PASCAL MARCO

Identity: Lost

PRAISE FOR *RENDER SAFE*

"In a sprawling tale of the Southwest, *Render Safe* by Pascal Marco hurls Phoenix prosecutor Stan Kobe into a cauldron of violence, lies, and prejudices that tie cold cases and old hatreds with modern greed. A colorful palette of unforgettable characters brings to life all the complexities of a great city and an untamed frontier. Toss in international black ops, love affairs, and family loyalties for a page-turning entertainment that enlightens. Truly enjoyable. A wonderful book from a new author who addresses a lot of complicated issues important to our world and whose writing I admire a lot."

—Gayle Lynds, *New York Times* best-selling author of *The Assassins*

"Stan Kobe is back, and he's better than ever! *Render Safe* takes readers on a spine-tingling tour of Arizona: from the remote wilds of the Mogollon Rim to the courtrooms of Maricopa County, from the terrifying vulnerability of our nation's utilities to the twisted psychology of white supremacist groups. This is a suspenseful and thought-provoking novel about racial tensions baking in the heat of the desert. I couldn't put it down."

—Allison Leotta, best-selling author of *The Last Good Girl* and *A Good Killing*, named a Best of the Best books by *O, The Oprah Magazine*

"*Render Safe* delves into the twisted minds of white supremacists from Arizona, whose bigotry and hatred fuel maniacal plans bent on death and destruction. Pascal Marco weaves a chilling tale of domestic terrorism in a charged thriller that cuts a disturbingly fine line between fact and fiction."

—Anne A. Wilson, author of *Hover* and *Clear to Lift*

"*Render Safe* opens the door to real world concerns in this timely thriller. Engaging and thought provoking, author Pascal Marco presents a wealth of compelling possibilities, certain to engage readers."

—Deborah J Ledford, award winning author of the Inola Walela Suspense Series *Snare, Causing Chaos* and *Crescendo*; Anthony Award Nominee for Best Audiobook 2014 - *Crescendo*; Hillerman Sky Award Finalist - *Snare*

"A highly suspenseful novel of twists and turns with accurate military rhetoric and well-studied A-10 references, all leading to a fantastic ending. A brilliantly written piece sharing Stan Kobe's struggle through classic government deception, burgeoning white supremacists, and crooked politicians to solve the mystery of ex-soldier Paul Stewart. A must read for suspense enthusiasts. An absolutely fantastic book."

—Ryan "Jinks" Mestelle, Major, United States Air Force, A-10 Thunderbolt II Instructor Pilot, Mission Commander, Forward Air Controller, 163rd Fighter Squadron, Fort Wayne, IN. Recipient of four Air Medals and flown over 100 combat sorties in Iraq and Afghanistan.

"As a current consultant on security and explosives, I was thoroughly impressed with the level of accuracy I found in Pascal Marco's novel, *Render Safe*. It's a fascinating read with action coming at you nonstop. Marco does an excellent job on attention to detail involving the technical matters of both investigative techniques and the lucid technical world of EOD. I was completely impressed in the way he used real life events that occurred over a decade in time and wound them together into this fictional tale of an ex-EOD soldier seduced by a right wing radical group to use his knowledge and access to explosives for their grand plans to bring the city of Phoenix to its knees. He's written an all too real story of a powder keg ready to explode."

—Anthony L. May, President, ALM Security and Explosives Consulting, LLC.; United States Army EOD Explosive Ordnance Disposal (Ret.); ATF Explosives Enforcement Officer (Ret.); CNN Expert Spokesperson

PRAISE FOR *IDENTITY: LOST*

"... a story that melds a powerful sense of an impoverished and violent place, cops who are decent and cops who are not, and rich baseball lore will find a large audience. Here's hoping Marco has more such tales to offer."

—*BOOKLIST* Magazine, May 1, 2011

"Pascal Marco's electrifying debut puts him firmly in the hunt to succeed John Grisham. Fresh, compelling and incredibly intricate, **Identity: Lost** is 'Exhibit A' on the docket of this year's hottest legal thrillers."

—Brad Thor, *NY TIMES* #1 best-selling author of *The Athena Project*

"Identity: Lost, by Pascal Marco, is a grand slam of a novel, swift and sure and true to life, with spot-on characters, an evocative setting, and a relentless plot swirling around the brutal killing of the last surviving member of the Chicago Black Sox team. Imbued with a deep love and understanding of the South Side of Chicago, homicide cops, and the history of baseball, this novel is as true as it is gripping. Don't miss it!"

—Douglas Preston, *NY TIMES* best-selling co-author of *The Monster of Florence* and *Fever Dream*

"History and homicide collide in Pascal Marco's fascinating novel."

—Lisa Black, *NY TIMES* best-selling author of *Takeover*

"Identity: Lost is a thriller with heart and passion. Its intriguing plot takes us from the bad side of Chicago to Arizona and back again as the story's hero searches for himself and finally finds justice and truth. I recommend it."

—Karl Alexander, author of *Jaclyn the Ripper* and *Time After Time*

"Pascal Marco's debut novel is a corker, a well-told tale of race, murder, injustice, and redemption. This is the real deal-- *Identity: Lost* confidently heralds a strong new talent."

—Raymond Benson, author of the James Bond anthologies *Choice of Weapons* and *The Union Trilogy*

"*Identity: Lost* is a riveting mystery novel involving the murder of the last surviving member of the infamous Chicago Black Sox team. Marco cleverly blends elements of a true crime, weaving it into an extraordinarily believable tale of intrigue, suspicion, and in the end, retribution. The writing seamlessly fuses the worlds of baseball, Chicago in the '70s, and the legal system with such finesse you can do nothing but keep reading until the very last page."

—Deborah J. Ledford, author of *Staccato*

"If you love Chicago, the White Sox, and a thumping murder mystery, you'll love this story.

—Virginia Nosky, award-winning author of *Blue Turquoise, White Shell*

"Marco's *Identity: Lost* is a realistic portrayal of what it was like to be a homicide cop on the South Side of Chicago in the 1970s. Reading it made me miss the job. That's how good the writing and how true the action is."

—Andrew Abbott, Homicide Detective (Ret.), Chicago Police Department

"*Identity: Lost* is a nail-biting story based upon real life. Marco's raw, from-the-gut writing style gives readers a seminal insight into the way the South Side of Chicago has worked on the street level for the last 35 years."

—Jim Nasella, veteran Hollywood Writer/Producer and Attorney

"Surprise is the word that best describes Pascal Marco's novel *Identity: Lost*. Surprised by the debut author's impressive writing, capturing so well the spirit of big city detectives and keeping my interest from the first chapter to the surprising ending. And, I'll be surprised if it's not a best seller."

—Philip J. Cline, Former Superintendent, Chicago Police Department

35092539R00223

Made in the USA
Middletown, DE
19 September 2016